ARTHUR [illegible]OME

Missee Lee

(Based on information supplied by the Swallows and Amazons)

RED FOX

A Red Fox Book

Published by Random House Children's Books
20 Vauxhall Bridge Road, London SW1V 2SA

A division of The Random House Group Ltd
London Melbourne Sydney Auckland
Johannesburg and agencies throughout the world

First published by Jonathan Cape 1940
Puffin edition 1970

Red Fox edition 1993

This Red Fox edition 2001

1 3 5 7 9 10 8 6 4 2

Printed and bound in Great Britain by
Bookmarque Ltd, Croydon, Surrey

Papers used by The Random House Group Ltd are natural, recyclable products made from wood grown in sustainable forests. The manufacturing processes conform to the environmental regulations of the country of origin.

THE RANDOM HOUSE GROUP Limited Reg. No. 954009

ISBN 0 09 942725 7

www.randomhouse.co.uk

To
HERBERT J. HANSON, O.B.E.,
SCHOLAR AND SEAMAN

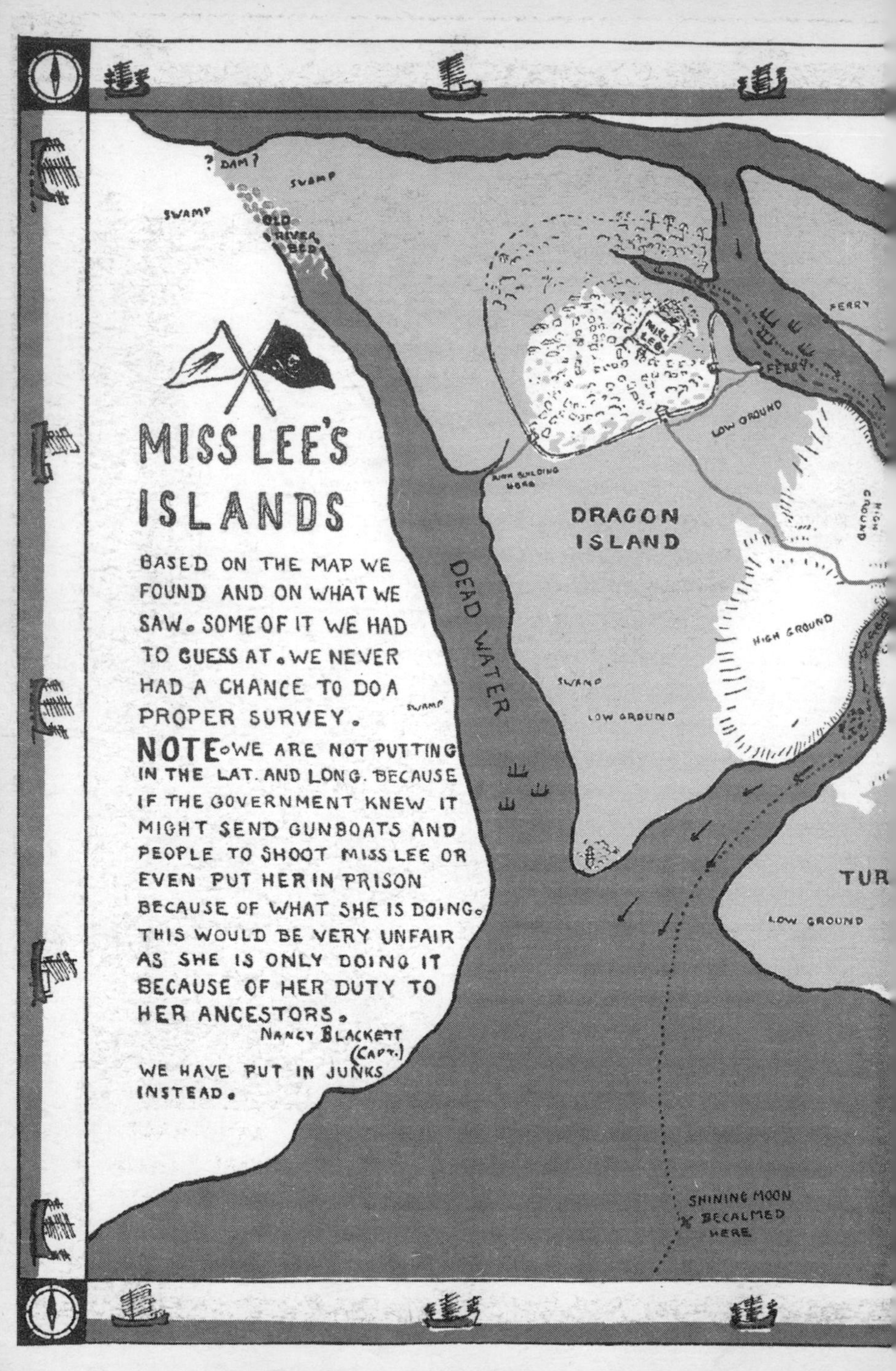

? DAM ?
SWAMP
SWAMP
OLD RIVER BED
MISS LEE'S ISLANDS
BASED ON THE MAP WE FOUND AND ON WHAT WE SAW. SOME OF IT WE HAD TO GUESS AT. WE NEVER HAD A CHANCE TO DO A PROPER SURVEY.
NOTE. WE ARE NOT PUTTING IN THE LAT. AND LONG. BECAUSE IF THE GOVERNMENT KNEW IT MIGHT SEND GUNBOATS AND PEOPLE TO SHOOT MISS LEE OR EVEN PUT HER IN PRISON BECAUSE OF WHAT SHE IS DOING. THIS WOULD BE VERY UNFAIR AS SHE IS ONLY DOING IT BECAUSE OF HER DUTY TO HER ANCESTORS.
NANCY BLACKETT (CAPT.)
WE HAVE PUT IN JUNKS INSTEAD.
SWAMP
DEAD WATER
MISS LEE'S
FERRY
FERRY
LOW GROUND
HIGH GROUND
DRAGON ISLAND
HIGH GROUND
SWAMP
LOW GROUND
LOW GROUND
SHINING MOON BECALMED HERE

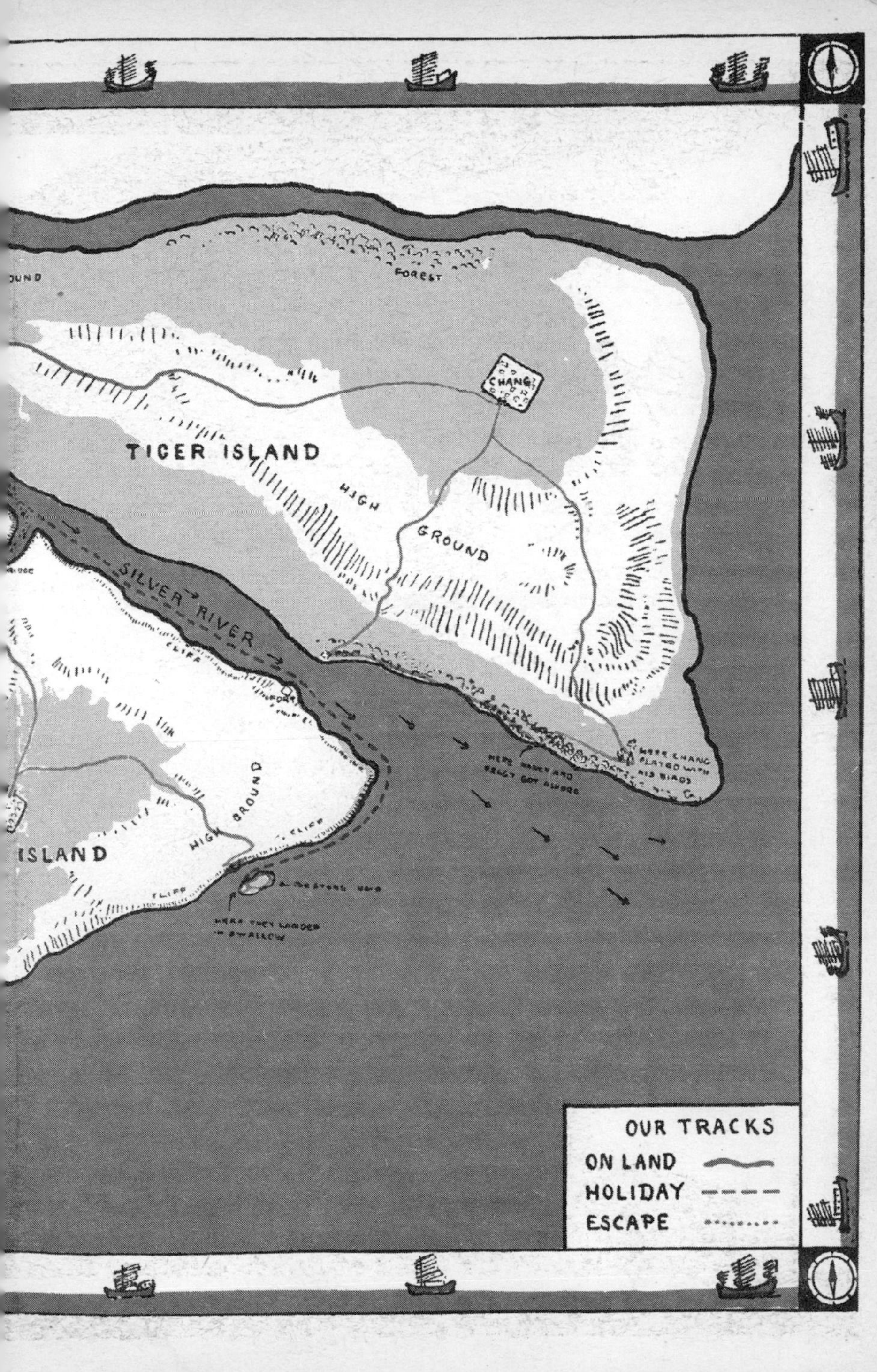
FOREST
CHANG
TIGER ISLAND
HIGH
GROUND
SILVER RIVER
CLIFF
FORT
HIGH
GROUND
CLIFF
ISLAND
CLIFF
OUR TRACKS
ON LAND
HOLIDAY
ESCAPE

CONTENTS

ILLUSTRATIONS

LANDING ON THE ISLAND

CHAPTER 1

THE HUNDREDTH PORT

"SAILING in half an hour," said Captain Flint.

The thin, brown harbourmaster, who had been having a farewell supper in the cabin of the *Wild Cat*, nodded, and glanced up at the cabin clock. "You'll have the lights to help you out."

"Much easier steering from light to light than trying to pick up the landmarks by day," said Nancy. "We always go out by night if we can."

"You've had plenty of practice," said the harbourmaster, flicking a crumb off his white shirt, flicking it again when it dropped on his white duck trousers.

"Our hundredth port," said Nancy.

"On this voyage," said Roger.

"Glad to leave it?"

They looked at each other and smiled doubtfully.

"Not much sleep," said Nancy.

"We've loved coming to your house," said Titty, "and seeing all those butterflies. But it's not a very quiet harbour."

"No, I suppose it isn't," said the harbourmaster. "I've been fixed here so long I've come not to notice it. But I suppose it must seem noisy to you."

"Well, just listen!" said Nancy.

In the whole harbour perhaps the quietest place was the cabin of the *Wild Cat*, but even there the noise was deafening. The little green schooner was moored to the quay. Just ahead of her lay a Japanese merchant steamship, and Japanese seamen slung on planks were chipping rust with the noise of a boiler factory. A hundred yards away a steam dredger was at work. A piledriver could be heard further along the quay, rumble, rumble, rumble as it wound up the weight and then CRASH! as the heavy lump of iron dropped on the head of the teak pile. Another steamship seemed to be changing its mind about blowing off steam. There was the rattle of derricks taking cargo out of a third. Trolleys were running to and fro on loosely fastened rails. Stevedores, sailors and dockhands, Chinese, Japanese, Dutchmen, Malays, were yelling orders at each other trying to make themselves heard above the din. Somewhere close by people were hauling on a warp. You could hear the shouts . . . "Hey . . . la. . . . Hey . . . la. . . ." Coolies were staggering along under heavy burdens. . . . "Hi . . . ya . . . hee . . . yo. . . . Hi . . . ya . . . hee . . . yo. . . ."

"They always seem to think that shouting makes things easier," said Captain Flint.

"*You* oughtn't to mind the noise," said the harbourmaster. "You've had enough of it before."

"Good long time ago," said Captain Flint. "Didn't I tell you I've been living in a houseboat on a lake where there's no noise at all . . . bar ducks . . . unless Cap'n Nancy here starts fooling about with fireworks."

"You'll hear plenty of fireworks if you're going across to the China coast," said the harbourmaster. "They let 'em off whenever a ship comes in."

"Good," said Roger.

"Can't think why you don't make straight for Singapore."

"Oh, look here," said Nancy. "When we're so near. We can't go round the world without just having a look at China. . . ."

"It's a rum place," said the harbourmaster. "And rum people. I'd be sorry if the next I hear of you is a finger in a matchbox and a hint of more to follow."

"Swatow's all right," said Captain Flint. "Treaty port . . . and I've got another old friend there."

"Go by steamship and get the visit over," said the harbourmaster.

"Jibbooms and bobstays," exclaimed Nancy. "But what's the fun of that?"

"Well, make a good landfall. Don't go and fall foul of Missee Lee."

"Missee Lee?" Everybody looked up with a question.

"Who's Miss Lee?" asked Roger.

"Thought everybody had heard of her," said the harbourmaster. "She's the bogy the Chinese women here frighten their babies with . . . just as our great grandfathers' nannies used to keep our respected ancestors quiet by telling them Bony would come for them."

"Where does she hang out?"

"I don't know. And the Chinese say they don't know. On that coast somewhere. It used to be Olo Lee when I first came here thirty years ago. It's Missee Lee now. Pirate of some sort. You know these Chinese. Can't get a word out of them. We'd have had gunboats after her long ago if we knew where she was. But they won't say. Not they. They pay her to leave them alone and not a word to us, of course. Rum people, the Chinese."

"We'll steer clear of her," said Captain Flint, glancing at a sketch chart of the harbour entrance which he had brought with him down into the cabin. "Now look here. Which do you call the best of those two channels?"

The harbourmaster ran the tip of his finger along a dotted line. "That's the best," he said. "Leave the red flash to starboard . . . make for the white occulting. . . . Get the two white fixed lights in line . . . and carry right on into clear water. . . . I suppose you're wanting to speed the parting guest? . . ."

"Well," said Captain Flint, "it's been jolly to see you, old chap . . . but . . . time's up."

"Good-bye, Polly," said the harbourmaster to Titty's green parrot sitting in his cage. "Where's that monkey of yours?"

"Keeping watch," said Roger.

One by one they went up the companion ladder out of the little cabin to meet the full shindy of the harbour as they came on deck. It was already dark. Arc-lights were sputtering overhead. There were lights in the little town beside the quay, lights in the houses dotted about the woods on the hill, lights on the ships anchored off shore, flashing lights of buoys marking the entrance, and far away out at sea the lights of lighthouses on distant rocks and islands.

Under the light of an arc-lamp they saw Gibber, sitting on the rail of the *Wild Cat*, chattering angrily at a couple of Japanese sailors on the quay above him. Perhaps glad to have allies, he came hopping along to meet the ship's company.

"Sing out when you're ready," said the harbour-master. "I'll have your ropes cast off for you."

"We're ready now," said Captain Flint. "Not enough wind in here. Going out under power. The engine's all ready, eh, engineer?"

"Aye-aye, sir," said Roger.

"Good-bye then," said the harbourmaster. "Look in on me when you go round the world again."

"Good-bye . . . Good-bye . . ." He shook hands with each one of them, including Gibber, and ran up a ladder to the top of the quay. He blew a whistle. Men came running and went to the bollards where the *Wild Cat's* mooring-ropes had been made fast. Aboard the little schooner people had gone to their places. Each one of them knew exactly what he or she had to do. Captain Flint was at the wheel. Roger had disappeared, to start the engine. Already it was throbbing away down below. John and Nancy were on the foredeck. Titty, Peggy and Susan were on the after-deck, Titty with a dangling fender, the others ready to haul in on warp or spring.

"Let go forrard," sang out Captain Flint. "Let go aft. . . . Haul on the spring. . . . Cast off. . . . Slow ahead. . . ." The *Wild Cat* was moving from the quay.

"So long," called the harbourmaster. "Don't run into Missee Lee!"

"Banzai!" shouted the Japanese sailors, stopping their rust-chipping for a moment to watch the little schooner move slowly out from under the lights of the quayside.

"So long!" shouted the hurrying coolies.

Then the deafening noise of rust-chipping started again. The pile-driver and the dredger and the derricks had never stopped. The little schooner moved slowly out towards the dark and quiet of the sea.

*

Ropes were being carefully coiled down on deck. Sidelights had, of course, been lit. Captain Flint glanced at the compass card, swinging slowly in the glow of the binnacle lamp, and glanced far ahead at the flashing light buoy and at another beyond it.

"Come on, Peggy," said Susan. "You, too, Titty. Let's get the supper things cleared off before we're out at sea. It won't take five minutes."

John came aft. "All coiled down forrard," he said. "Nancy on look-out."

"Good," said Captain Flint. "You take the wheel, and leave me free to check the buoys as we go out. Keep her as she is. We leave that buoy to starboard. . . ."

He slipped into the deckhouse, half closing the door so that the light should not bother John's eyes, while he ticked off the buoy on the chart. A moment later he was out again, standing by the steersman's side.

Roger climbed up from the engine-room and slipped quickly out of the deckhouse.

"She's running beautifully," he said.

"Good. . . . You'd better put that monkey to bed. . . . We'll be making sail later."

Half an hour passed, an hour. . . . The last

of the flashing buoys was left astern. . . . Far, far ahead, a light on a rock, miles away, was blinking below the horizon. There was a gentle breeze.

"We'll have that mainsail up," said Captain Flint. "You take the wheel for a minute, Titty." With John and Susan to help him, he hauled on the halyards and set the mainsail to help the engine. Nancy hoisted the staysail. Peggy was waiting at the foot of the foremast with the halyards ready for Captain Flint and Susan to help in sending up the foresail. The jibs were already hoisted, in stops, bundled up and tied with wisps of rope yarn, ready to break out the moment there was a pull on the sheets.

"Break out the jibs," called Captain Flint.

"Aye-aye, sir."

Captain Flint went from rope to rope, here easing up a little, here hardening in. The *Wild Cat*, hardly heeling in the gentle wind, was moving faster. Everybody knew it and rejoiced to be under sail once more.

"What about stopping the little donkey?" asked Titty, when Captain Flint came aft to take the wheel again. "So that we can have it really quiet. . . ."

"We'll keep it running till we pass that light," said Captain Flint. "I'd like to get clear of everything as soon as we can."

"Isn't it lovely to be at sea again," said Titty, "and out of all that noise! I wish we could just sail on and on for ever. . . ."

"Oh, look here," said Nancy. "You have to go into harbours sometimes."

"How soon is the next one?" asked Susan.

"Depends on the wind," said Captain Flint. "But, with luck, we'll have someone at the masthead in four days' time, looking for the coast of China."

"Giminy," said Nancy. "I'm jolly glad you decided not to miss it."

"Look here," said Captain Flint. "We're back at sea. Watches to keep. No good everybody staying up. I'll carry on till we're clear. John and Nancy'll take over at eight bells. They'd better be getting some sleep now. Susan and Peggy stand by till we pass that light. No need for anybody else on deck. . . ."

"I'm not sleepy," said Roger.

"It's the first night at sea," said Titty.

"Right-o," said Captain Flint. "You two can keep a look out forrard until the first yawn. Mind that. The first yawn and off you go. That all right, Susan?"

"So long as they get their eight hours' sleep," said Susan.

*

"Roger, you've yawned," said Titty half an hour later.

"Did I?" said Roger.

"Go on. You've done it again."

Roger, in spite of himself, yawned a third time and went off aft to say "Good night" to Captain Flint.

Titty, alone on the foredeck, felt its regular lift and fall beneath her feet, as the *Wild Cat* moved through the dark sea under a starlit sky. The noises of the harbour and the land had died away. A glimmer in the sky far astern showed where was the hundredth harbour they had left. The lighthouse they had to pass was blinking now high and clear. Beyond it was open sea. And beyond that? The next land they sighted would be the coast of China. Titty thought of willow-pattern plates. Would it be like that? she wondered. Would it be a noisy, crowded port like the harbour they had just left? Would it be like Papeete, with palms and houses on the very edge of the quay? She hoped it would be like Papeete. And she hoped they would be a long time getting there. This wind was just right. . . . They were moving quite fast enough. . . . The longer they stayed at sea the better. . . . And it would be better still as soon as Captain Flint shut off the chug-chugging of the engine.

The blinking light came nearer and nearer. Its flashes lit up the deck every time the light swung round. It was abeam. Somebody in the lighthouse was signalling with a flash-lamp. She looked aft. Yes. Captain Flint was answering, flash, flash . . . flash. The flashing stopped. She heard low voices talking by the deckhouse. The *Wild Cat* changed course. There was nothing ahead now, nothing . . . only dark sea and starry sky. Titty yawned, caught herself at it, and went aft.

Peggy was at the wheel with Captain Flint.

"You off?" said Captain Flint. "No need for anyone to stay up now. I'll carry on till John's watch. I'm sending Peggy below in a minute. Susan's gone."

"What about the engine?" said Titty.

"Let's get well away from land," said Captain Flint. "This is a paltry wind."

Titty went below, down the companion, through the saloon where the hurricane lantern hanging from the ceiling was hardly swinging, so easy was the motion of the ship. She found that Susan had left the lamp alight in their cabin. Susan was asleep. Titty undressed and slipped into the lower berth after blowing out the lamp and laying her torch beside her pillow in case of a call for hands on deck during the night.

She could hear the quiet sliding noise of water past the side of the ship. Bother that chugging engine. She lay awake. After all this voyaging, after a hundred passages, she still enjoyed the first night of being at sea. She lay there, thinking back, remembering the noise of the port, the harbourmaster, sitting in his shirt-sleeves at the table in the saloon, his talk of Missee Lee. "Quite possibly no such person," he had said. "Missee Lee . . . And Chinese mothers telling their children to be good or Missee Lee . . ." Titty fell asleep. She waked much later with the stopping of the engine. . . . Now there was nothing to listen to but the gentle slap of a rope and the noise of water outside. She fell happily to sleep again.

CHAPTER II

LOSS OF THE *WILD CAT*

FOUR days later the small green schooner lay motionless on a glassy sea. No land was in sight nor any other vessel. It was close on noon. Captain Flint was standing by the deckhouse with his sextant at his eye. John was beside him with a stopwatch. At any moment now the sun would be at its highest, Captain Flint and John would work out latitude and longitude and presently a new red-inked circle on the chart would show exactly where they were. Titty and Roger were watching the navigators, Susan was sewing, sitting on the skylight, and Nancy was up at the foremast cross-trees looking hopefully out through a telescope.

"Now," called Captain Flint.

John pressed the button of the stopwatch to get the exact second, and the two of them went into the deckhouse to work out their position.

"Look at Gibber," said Roger with a grin.

"Navigating," said Titty, looking at the monkey who was standing with feet wide apart, as Captain Flint had stood, and something very like a sextant to his eye.

"Gibber, you little beast," cried Susan. "He's got my scissors."

"Come here, Gibber," said Roger. "No, don't touch him, Susan. He'll go and spike his eye."

"Belay there! What are you shouting about?" They looked up at Nancy, high on the foremast.

"Gibber's using Susan's scissors for a sextant," called Roger. "It's all right now. He's dropped them. Good! Well done, Peggy! Peggy's got them."

Peggy had come quietly out of the galley door and had snatched the scissors from the deck. The monkey chattered at her, jumped on the rail, ran along it and up into the mainmast rigging. Here he stopped, looked down on deck and chattered again and then, catching sight of Nancy who was again looking through the telescope, forgot about sextants and began to mimic her, peering out through his fingers.

From inside the deckhouse came the murmur of the navigators, words like zenith, meridian, versine, logarithm, words that Susan, Titty, Roger and Peggy did not even pretend to understand. Nancy knew what some of them meant but could never remember which word meant what. But the whole crew of the *Wild Cat* knew that somehow or other out of that murmur of strange words, and out of a lot of sums worked out again and again by Captain Flint and John until they both got the same result twice running, came, by a sort of miracle, the knowledge of where the *Wild Cat* was. It always seemed a miracle when they had seen nothing but water for a long time, and, after marking their position on the chart, Captain Flint would send John or Nancy up aloft and tell them to look out for three palm trees, or a high rock, or a lighthouse that could not be seen from the deck. Whatever the thing was that he expected them to see, it was always there. But now even from the masthead there was no land in sight. For four days they had seen none. They had seen nothing

THE NAVIGATORS

at all but a burning sun by day and blazing stars by night, and water stretching to the horizon. And for the last twenty-four hours there had been no wind.

"They've done," said Roger, as the voices in the deckhouse stopped, and he heard the noise of books being put back in a shelf and the click of the lid as Captain Flint put his sextant away in its case.

"No change," said Captain Flint through the deckhouse window.

"Can we have a look?" said Roger.

"Practically where we were yesterday," said Captain Flint as they crowded into the little deckhouse to look at the chart on the table. The new mark showing their position was almost on the top of the mark made at noon the day before.

"Day's run . . . Nil," said Captain Flint.

"We've just drifted a bit," said John, "and drifted back again."

"Good thing we're still out of sight of land," said Captain Flint.

"Why?" asked Titty.

"Nobody likely to come along in the dark to have a look-see. Our friend the harbourmaster's quite right. You never know what sort of people you may meet along the China coast. No, don't you worry, Susan. We're all right out here. And anyway they've got no engines in their junks. We can always start up the little donkey. . . ."

"No, we can't," said Roger. "You never filled up the working tank after running it dry on the first night out."

"No more I did," said Captain Flint. "But the

main tanks are full. We'll shift some later when it isn't quite so hot. Now then, out of here, everybody. Who's cook today?"

"Peggy," said Roger.

"What's become of her?"

"Gone back to the galley."

"Good girl," said her uncle.

"Curried eggs," said Roger. "I saw her getting the shells off. And then oranges to cool our burnt tongues."

"Trust you to know," said Captain Flint coming out from the stuffy deckhouse into the scorching sunshine. "Ahoy there, Nancy, you'll get sunstroke if you stay up there. Come on down and lend a hand. We'll swing the gaff off and make it fast to the rigging and use the sail for an awning."

Nancy came slowly down the ratlines and joined the others.

"Somebody might have shouted to say what we've done. How far have we moved since yesterday?"

"No far," said Roger. "We haven't moved at all. But we're going to fill up the tank and get the engine going."

"We don't want the engine," said Titty. "It's much better here than in harbour."

"It'll be very hot below with the engine running," said Susan.

"Hot, anyway," said Peggy through the galley door. "Look here! Grub's ready. Where are we going to have it?"

Captain Flint was already turning the lowered mainsail into a sort of tent. "Take that rope to the shrouds, John. Haul in and make fast. Here you are, Nancy. Make this one fast aft. That'll give us a few square feet of shade."

"If we had the engine going we'd be moving and there'd be a bit of a draught," said Roger.

"Bother the engine," said John.

"I didn't say I was going to use it," said Captain Flint.

"Beastly, sitting still," said Roger.

"We'll shift petrol, anyway," said Captain Flint, "but not till evening. What about those curried eggs?" He glanced in through the deckhouse window to see the clock. "One o'clock."

John said nothing but struck the ship's bell, one . . . two . . .

Titty looked up as the clear tone of the bell rang in the still air.

"It sounds quite happy," she said.

Captain Flint laughed. "Got more sense than we have," he said. "What's the use of us all getting edgy just because we aren't reeling off the knots. This isn't the first calm we've had to put up with."

"It's the hottest," said Nancy. "Barbecued billy-goats are nothing to it. Look out, Peggy, you can't sit there. The pitch is bubbling up out of the decks."

"If those eggs are hot enough we'll feel cooler," said Captain Flint. "Nothing like a good Malay curry when salamanders are fainting from the heat.

*

In the shadow of the sail stretched between gaff and boom above their heads they ate their hot curry and sucked their oranges. They felt better.

They had a long afternoon sleep, one after another of them waking for a moment and, with half-closed eyes, looking round the horizon for the first sign of a ripple. The parrot watched with one eye. The monkey began by copying Roger and ended by falling asleep in good earnest. Hour after hour went by and still the little green schooner lay motionless like a toy ship on a looking-glass.

It was already late in the afternoon (and night comes early in the tropics) when the smell of tobacco smoke woke Titty. She opened her eyes to see that Captain Flint was smoking one of the cigars he had bought in Papeete instead of his usual pipe.

"Hullo," she said.

"Hullo, yourself," said Captain Flint.

"No wind yet?" said Titty.

"Not enough to stir a feather," said Captain Flint. "And whatever you say, I don't like it. Roger's right. We'll wear a hole in the chart if we keep on marking noon positions all in the same place. As soon as the engineer's awake, we'll shift some petrol from the main tanks and let the little donkey push her along."

"I'm awake," said Roger. "Do let's get her moving."

"Come on, then," said Captain Flint, taking a puff at his cigar. "Anybody else like to lend a hand?"

"Look at Gibber," said Roger.

Everybody was awake by now, and laughed to see the little monkey, so thin, so narrow-waisted, so unlike Captain Flint, copying his every motion, the pull at the cigar, the slow, happy blowing out of the smoke, the little flourish of the cigar when

Captain Flint had said "Come on, then. . . . Anybody else like to lend a hand?"

"Gibber would love to," said Roger.

"If it's got to be done," said Nancy, stretching.

"Much better," said Captain Flint. "We'll make Swatow tomorrow and then Hey for Hongkong and Singapore. Come on everybody. We want eight two-gallon tins filling from the main tank . . . sixteen gallons. . . . Bother. I wish I hadn't lit that cigar." He stood up and was going to throw it overboard.

"Don't waste it," said Titty.

"It's a good cigar," said Captain Flint, and reached into the deckhouse and put the cigar on an ashtray on the chart-table. "It'll be all right there, till we've done."

Two minutes later he was passing full petrol tins up through the forehatch.

"Eight," he said, as he came up with the last. "What are you doing, Roger?"

"Only sniffing it," said Roger. "Gosh! Sorry! I haven't spilt much."

"Only about a gallon," said John.

"Less than a quarter of a pint," said Roger. "And I wouldn't have spilt any if people hadn't asked questions just when I had the thing unscrewed to sniff."

"No need to sniff now," said Nancy. "It fairly reeks."

"Oh, never mind," said Captain Flint. "It won't be there long. Drying up already."

The tins were carried aft. Captain Flint unscrewed the round brass bung in the deck to pour the petrol into the working tank. Roger held the funnel and Captain Flint tipped in the first can of petrol. Susan handed him the second and that went in too. John gave him the third. Titty gave him the fourth. Nancy was herself pouring in the fifth when she heard Captain Flint shout "Grab him!"

"You've made me slosh," said Nancy, and then saw what had made Captain Flint's shout. "Grab him!" she shouted herself. "It's still alight."

Gibber was in the deckhouse doorway and in his hand was Captain Flint's half-smoked cigar. A thin wisp of smoke trailed from it.

Captain Flint reached for the monkey and missed him. Gibber dodged round the deckhouse and was nearly caught by Roger who had slipped round to meet him. John all but got him as he swung himself up on the boom and ran chattering over the sail that had been serving for an awning. Captain Flint missed him again by a few inches as he hopped down by the mainmast.

"Chase him up the rigging," he shouted. "Then we'll get him. Keep him forrard, anyway, and off the deck. Got you!"

But again he was too late. Gibber, cornered in the bows, chattering with anger, dodged under Captain Flint's reaching arm, shot between Roger and Susan, swung up the mainmast shrouds, down again by the halyards, raced along the boom and over the deckhouse roof, using his legs, his tail and one arm, but never for a moment letting go of the cigar. The whole ship's company closed in towards the after-deck.

"You take the port side, John," said Captain

Flint. "I'll take the starboard. We'll get him one way or other."

And then, as they charged round the deckhouse, the thing happened. Gibber, looking for a hiding place for his cigar, saw the round opening in the deck.

There was a horrified gasp from the whole ship's company.

BANG!

A sheet of flame shot upward. A screaming monkey was gone, over the deckhouse roof, and up to the top of the mainmast. Peggy, without a word, got the fire-extinguisher from behind the galley door and gave it to Captain Flint, who had already thrown the three full cans of petrol overboard and was trying, with John and Nancy, to put the flames out with the bucketfuls of sand that were kept under the bulwarks. Susan was rubbing out a smouldering bit of Titty's skirt. "Where's Roger?" she asked.

Roger came up the companion way.

"It's no good," he said. "I can't get them. The engine-room's full of flames."

"What?" cried Captain Flint throwing himself down the companion.

"What were you trying to do?" asked John.

"Get the fire-extinguishers, of course," said Roger, who, as engineer, knew where they were kept in the engine-room.

Captain Flint was gone only for a moment. He was back on deck.

"Roger's right," he said. "There's not a hope of putting this out. We've got about four minutes to save what we can from the cabins. You see to that,

Susan. You'll know what to take. Don't take a single thing you can do without. Peggy, Roger and Titty, help Susan. The moment the flames come through the after bulkhead go forward and out by the forehatch. You've got only about a minute to deal with the after-cabins. Do them first. John and Nancy, come and help me. We have to get the boats out. The ship and everything in her's as dry as tinder. . . ."

There was time to save very little. They got their sleeping-bags, a few towels, Susan's first-aid box, John's box with his compass and barometer. Titty saved the parrot and a bag of parrot food and the pocket telescope. Roger saved nothing but Gibber's lead before the flames, bursting through from the engine-room, drove them all hurriedly forrard. Within the first few seconds flames were pouring up the engine-room hatch into the deckhouse. Captain Flint, with people's lives to think of, forgot all else, even the ship's papers, and nothing would have been saved from the deckhouse at all if John had not dashed in, snatched the sextant and the nautical almanac (which seemed to him the things that mattered most in the ship) and got out again with a scorched arm and a burning sleeve. Luckily the two dinghies, *Swallow* and *Amazon*, had been treated as lifeboats throughout the voyage, so that they were all ready for their work, each with a small sea-anchor, a beaker of fresh water, a watertight box of iron rations and a hurricane lantern. Susan and Peggy were packing the other things in even while Captain Flint, Nancy and John were heaving on the davit tackles, swinging the boats out and lowering them over the side.

Swallow was lowered first and lay there waiting, while Captain Flint fixed a rope ladder.

"You four had better be in the boat you know. Nancy and Peggy in *Amazon* and I'll be with them to even things out. No good overcrowding and there isn't room for us all in one boat. What are you doing, Titty? Fishing?"

"Lowering Polly," said Titty. "He's all right now."

"But what about Gibber?" said Roger. "I've got his collar and lead, but look where he is!" He pointed up at the top of the mainmast.

"I'll see what we can do," said Captain Flint. "Now for *Amazon*. Lower away, John. Easy now. . . ."

Amazon went down to the water.

"Hurry up," said Captain Flint. "Everybody aboard. The fire'll be at the main tanks any minute."

"Peggy, you go down that ladder," shouted Nancy. "Go on. Shiver my timbers. This is going to be a lark."

"Lark!" exclaimed Captain Flint, but said no more. Like Roger, he was looking up at the monkey perched on the top of the mainmast. Flames were already dancing along the bulwarks. Flames were already licking up from ratline to ratline, and the short lengths of thin tarred rope stretched between the shrouds flared, broke in the middle and dropped like fiery tassels. Already the heavy tarred lanyards at the foot of the shrouds were burning.

"Get aboard," said Captain Flint, "and get

the boats clear of the ship. That mast's going in a minute."

"But, Gibber!" wailed Roger.

"It's the best chance he's got," said Captain Flint. "He'll be thrown clear whichever way it falls. Get aboard, everybody." He took off his sun-helmet and sent it spinning down into *Amazon*. "Well caught, Peggy!"

"Do what you're told, Roger, and get aboard," said John. "You can't do anything to help. Look out. Here it comes."

There was an explosion in the bows of the ship. Deck planks were forced up. Flames poured through.

"John," called Susan from *Swallow*. "Don't wait."

"Come on, Uncle Jim," shouted Nancy from *Amazon* at the other.

"Get the boats clear," shouted Captain Flint.

"Come along," cried Nancy.

"Pull clear," shouted Captain Flint angrily.

John was already in *Swallow*, hauling in what was left of the painter, burnt through on the rail. "Go on, Susan," he cried. "Pull, Susan. Pull."

"But, Gibber!" wailed Roger. . . . "And Captain Flint!"

"Look out! It's coming."

Deckhouse and galley were gone. The mainmast rose out of a mass of flames, its shrouds hanging loose, their lanyards burned through. There was a loud crack and then another. The mast swayed. . . .

"Oh, Gibber!" cried Roger in despair.

Slowly the mast began to fall. . . . Slowly . . .

then faster. . . . It did not fall straight. The wire-stay that joined the mainmast head to the head of the foremast pulled it sideways. It swung in towards the ship. Something small was shot away from the masthead. No one saw the splash it made as it hit the water, but everyone in *Swallow* saw the much larger splash that was made by Captain Flint. A minute later and they saw him swimming towards them.

"He's got him," shouted Roger. "Well done, Gibber!"

"Well done, Captain Flint!" said Susan.

"Thanks, most awfully," said Roger as the dripping monkey scrambled aboard the moment Captain Flint had laid hold of *Swallow's* transom.

"Aren't you coming too?" asked Titty.

"You tow me round," said Captain Flint, "and I'll go aboard *Amazon*. They've got my sun-helmet."

"Gosh!" said Roger. "How did you know what was going to happen?"

"I didn't," said Captain Flint, blowing cheerfully as they towed him along. "I only thought there was a chance of it, and I'd better stand by. I couldn't be sure which way the thing would fall."

Amazon came into sight from behind the burning schooner.

"Ahoy!"

"Uncle Jim's still aboard!" screamed Nancy.

"No, he isn't," shouted Roger. "We've got him. Gibber too."

"Keep well away," puffed Captain Flint. "That foremast'll be coming any minute now."

"Aye-aye, sir," said John, who had taken the

THE BURNING OF THE *WILD CAT*

oars from Susan. Captain Flint let go of the transom, swam across and was presently climbing in over the stern of the *Amazon*. Fifty or sixty yards from the blazing vessel the two dinghies floated side by side.

Crrrr . . . ash!

Down came the foremast and the *Wild Cat*, crackling and roaring, lay a flaming, mastless wreck, reflected on the mirror of that oily sea.

"Better get well clear of her," said Captain Flint. "I'm not sure both the big tanks have gone."

"Can't we do anything to save her?" said Nancy.

"Not a thing," said her Uncle. "She'll burn to the waterline and that'll be the end of her. Poor old girl. She'll go to the bottom or break up. Well, we've had some fun with her. Pity we couldn't have taken her right round the world and let her end her days at home."

"There are towels with the sleeping-bags," called Susan.

"Drying fast," said Captain Flint. "Salt water, anyhow. And warm. I'll be all right. Thank you, Susan, all the same."

"What do we do now?" asked Nancy, and the whole crew of the *Swallow* strained their ears to hear what he would say.

"Sit tight if we can," said Captain Flint. "We know exactly where we are and that is plumb in the track of steamers. We've only got to sit tight and we'll be picked up before this time tomorrow. Land's not so very far away, but the China coast's a queer one. No good landing just anywhere. It's got to be a treaty port or nowhere. Much better wait here to be picked up. We've got a week's water in each boat, more if we go slow on it. We've got grub. And best of all, we've got a calm. The only thing we haven't got is a barometer. . . ."

"I've got one," called John. "Susan saved it."

"Good for you," said Captain Flint. "Dig it out. It'll give us plenty of warning if we have to change our plans."

"Get it out of the box, Titty," said John.

"When did you set it last?" asked Titty as she handed it over.

"This morning," said John. "Gosh! It must have had a bump or something. I say, Captain Flint, I've got the barometer, but something's happened to it. It's gone down half an inch since breakfast. . . ."

"Are you sure? Give it a gentle tap."

"Still going down," said John.

Captain Flint looked round the horizon. "All right, so long as we keep together," he said at last. "Dash it, I wish we had one big boat instead of two little ones."

"More fun with a fleet," said Nancy.

"John," called Captain Flint. "Have a look at your sea-anchor. Make sure it's all ready to put over the bows. And don't spare chafing gear where the rope works over the stem. Use anything you've got rather than let it chafe through."

"Aye-aye, sir," said John seriously.

"May be a dirty night," said Captain Flint.

"There's a hurricane lantern in each boat," called Susan. "I trimmed the wicks the day before we left port."

"Good for you, Susan. We'll put the sea-anchors over if there's a breeze, and, with the lanterns burning, we ought to be able to keep in touch. . . ."

"What do we do if we get separated?" asked John.

"Best we can," said Captain Flint. "Best of all if we can stay here till we get picked up."

*

Side by side the little boats floated, while the crew of the *Wild Cat* watched and listened to the burning of the old schooner. Three parts round the world they had sailed in her. She had become almost part of themselves. At the beginning Captain Flint had had a paid hand to help him, but for a long time he had found that with the six of them he needed no one else. And now she was going. And there they were afloat in the two dinghies watching her burn.

They had had no time to be frightened. There had been too much to do. Even now, when they could do no more and lay there with the crackling roar of the burning vessel in their ears, their minds were more on the new life that was beginning than on the old that had come to so melancholy an end. If she had caught fire in an English harbour, it would have seemed the end of everything. But here it was not the end. They had still to get home and home was many thousand miles away. This was not the end and they were thinking not of days gone by or of days to come but of what they had to do that very night. "If you've got a burn on your hand, don't lick it, Roger," said Susan. "I've got some tannic jelly in the first-aid box."

"Gibber's scorched too," said Roger, "and John,"

and for a minute or two Susan was busy with the cooling jelly.

"Anybody burnt in your boat?" she sang out.

"Nothing to matter," Peggy answered. "Only clothes, not skin."

Captain Flint looked up from *Amazon*'s bows, where he was overhauling the sea-anchor, and saw Susan holding Gibber's hand and putting jelly on his arm. He laughed.

"Don't laugh at him," said Roger. "He's had a lot of hair burnt off."

"He's a good, clever monkey," said Captain Flint consolingly.

"Almost too clever," said Nancy, looking at the burning schooner.

"There's the beginning of a swell," said John suddenly.

"From the south-east," said Captain Flint. "Wind coming. Better than a westerly, anyhow."

For a moment there was silence, except for the crackling of burning wood. Then the crew of the *Swallow* heard Peggy say, "You do think we're all right, don't you, Uncle Jim?" They heard Captain Flint reply, "Right as rain, of course. Right as rain."

"Not quite," said Roger quietly. "Rain might have put the fire out and saved the *Wild Cat*."

They were all looking at her. The sun was dipping now below the sea in the west and the sudden dark of the tropics was sweeping up out of the east. The *Wild Cat* flamed against the dusk like a row of torches.

"Two sunsets at once," said Titty.

"The real sun's gone now," said Roger.

"Here comes the wind," said John.

They all felt it, a faint breath out of the south-east. Already they were lifting and falling on a smooth swell. A line of ripples swept towards the sunset. There was a new noise of hissing from the burning ship.

"Water on the fire," said Captain Flint gravely. "Burnt to the waterline, and now this bit of swell. . . ."

And suddenly, as he spoke, the burning stern of the *Wild Cat* lifted from the sea. Her bowsprit quenched its flames as it plunged. There was a long drawn hiss as the sea swept through her and the last flame went out as the little schooner disappeared for ever.

John, Susan and Roger heard Titty's gasping sob and hoped it had not been noticed by the others.

Captain Flint spoke.

"She was a good ship," he said . . . and then, in an altogether different voice, "more wind coming. Put the sea-anchor out while it's light enough to be sure the rope's not chafing. Get your lantern lit. Have something to eat now. Go very easy on the water. If it blows really hard, keep right down in the bottom of the boat. . . ."

CHAPTER III

WHAT HAPPENED TO *SWALLOW*

"I'M opening the grub-box," said Susan.

"Good," said Roger.

"Right," said John.

Looking across to the *Amazon*, they could see, as she lifted and fell, that Nancy and Peggy were busy in the stern, while Captain Flint, paddling gently, like John in *Swallow*, was keeping her head to wind.

"Digging out their grub too," said Roger. "I say, Susan. We've got plenty of biscuits, anyway. Are those 'Thin Captains'?"

"Yes," said Susan. "Two tins of them. . . . Four of condensed milk. . . . One tin of butter. . . . Eight tins of pemmican. . . . And a lot of dates. Chocolate. . . ."

"*Amazon*, ahoy!" shouted Roger.

"*Swallow*, ahoy!"

"What's your cook got in her box? 'Thin Captains,' we've got, and butter, lots of pemmican, dates, chocolate . . ."

"Sardines," said Susan.

"Sardines," shouted Roger.

"We've got just the same," called Peggy.

"Hullo, Roger," called Nancy. "Captain Flint says we may have to make things spin out. So you're not to start hogging everything just to see what it's like."

"As if I wanted to," said Roger. "I only wanted

to make sure we'd all got plenty of everything."

"Half a mug of water's the ration tonight," Captain Flint called out.

"Aye-aye, sir," called Susan.

"When do you think we'll get home now?" asked Titty.

"If we get picked up by a liner going the right way," said John, "we'll be home much sooner than if we were sailing in the *Wild Cat*."

"We don't want to do that," said Roger.

"When do you think there'll be a steamer?" said Titty. "We ought to let Mother know we're all right. . . ."

"Four biscuits each," said Susan. . . . "Two sardines . . . eight dates . . . and half a mug of water. We'll take turns with the mug. And we'd better put off drinking till we really want it."

Dark in the tropics comes down like the fall of a curtain. There was already much more wind.

"Putting our sea-anchor over now," shouted Captain Flint. "There's enough wind to keep us clear of it. . . . You'd better do the same."

"Aye-aye, sir."

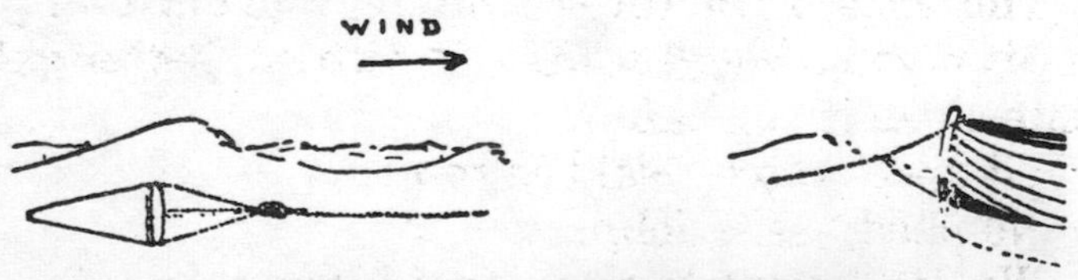

HOW A SEA-ANCHOR WORKS

John dropped his sea-anchor over the bows and paid out its long warp. It was a conical bag of canvas with a hole at the pointed end. A bag of that shape, pulled wide end first through the water, keeps a boat from drifting too fast. Paid out over *Swallow's* bows it kept her head to wind. There was no need now to use the oars. John stowed them, wrapped the rope in a towel where it crossed the gunwale (Susan had to agree that it was better to use a towel than a sleeping-bag) and settled down with the others to their first shipwrecked supper.

A light flickered over the waves.

"They've lit their lantern," said John.

"Ours is all ready," said Susan, lighting it as she spoke.

"It's blowing a lot harder," said John half an hour later.

"Ahoy, there! How's your anchor warp streaming?"

John peered over the bows and pulled at the warp while Susan held up the lantern behind him.

"Straight ahead and pulling hard. I can't get it in an inch."

"That's all right. How's the barometer?"

There was a pause.

"Gone down another two-tenths, sir. But it jerked up a bit when I tapped it."

"That means whatever's coming won't last long. But it may be tough while it's with us. Better get some sleep if you can."

"I'll keep watch," said Susan.

"No need," said John.

"We don't want to sleep," said Roger.

"Good night. . . . GOOD NIGHT." A shout came through the darkness.

"Listen. They're going to sleep in *Amazon*."

"GOOD NIGHT!" the Swallows shouted back.

"Let's have that lantern, Susan," said John. "They must have fixed theirs on the middle thwart in case of splashes. I'll do the same. Bother the mast and sail. . . ."

"They won't matter when we're down on the bottomboards," said Susan. "All right, Roger. Gibber'll go in his sleeping-bag. You push him in. Lie right down, Titty. . . ."

"It's Polly's cage in the way," said Titty.

"Put it bang in the middle," said John. "Susan and I'll manage all right."

"Go to sleep."

And, after what they had gone through that day, go to sleep they did, Roger and Gibber, Titty and Polly, Susan and, at last, John himself, who had made up his mind to stay awake to watch that flickering lantern in the other boat.

*

John was waked by a splash of warm water on his face and the taste of brine in his mouth. For one second he was puzzled. Then he felt for the hurricane lantern, which had been blown or shaken out. He looked round in the darkness to find *Amazon's* lantern, but could see nothing at all. There was a fierce wind in his face when he lifted his head above the gunwale. There was a sea running too. *Swallow* was pitching and tossing as each wave lifted her up, passed under her and dropped her. There was another splash. She could not be heading as straight to windward as she had been. John reached forward and felt the warp over the bows. Yes, it was still there, wrapped in the towel. He reached further forward, took a grip of the rope and pulled, never thinking for a moment that he would not find it bar-taut. He gave it a hard tug and felt it yield to him. Yet the wind was much stronger than it had been. He pulled again and found that inch by inch he was able to haul in. Better have a look at that sea-anchor. Presently the rope began to come in more and more easily and then, as if to warn John that he was doing wrong, a wave hit *Swallow* broadside on, splashed over the gunwale, woke everybody and set the parrot screaming in the dark.

"John!" called Roger.

"What's happening?" said Susan.

"My fault," said John. "The sea-anchor's gone. There's only the rope holding her to windward, and I've been hauling in without thinking. I'm letting it out again. She'll be all right in a minute. The rope must have gone at the sea-anchor. This end's all right."

He paid out the rope he had hauled in. There was enough pull on it to keep *Swallow* heading up to windward and there were no more serious splashes.

"She's probably moving," said John. "She may be moving pretty fast. The rope by itself'll stop her a bit but not much."

"Is it all right?" asked Roger.

"All right as long as people keep still."

"Polly must have got wet," said Titty.

"Where's *Amazon*?" asked Susan.

"Lantern's gone out like ours," said John. "And with that anchor going we aren't anywhere near her."

"Can't we row back?"

"Couldn't row against this," said John. "And we might miss them if we could." John was shouting to make himself heard. "Look for them when it's light. It won't blow like this for long. We'll be all right if we keep down in the boat. . . . Down in the boat. . . . Captain Flint SAID SO."

"There's a lot of water in her," said Titty.

"WHAT?"

"SHE WANTS BALING."

"BALE BUT DON'T GET UP. BETTER WET THAN DROWNED." That was what Daddy would have said, and John, having said it, felt better himself. It was almost like having Daddy in the boat.

"Warm water, anyhow," said Susan.

John thought hard. Was there a single other thing he could do? There was not. He thought for a moment of putting the sail and spars overboard and tying them at the end of a rope. He decided against that. If the rope broke again, the sail would be lost, and they might come to need it badly. If only he had had any idea how fast they were moving and how long it was since the sea-anchor went. Titty and Roger could bale a bit to keep them quiet. He would start baling himself if much more water came in. Gosh! What about *Amazon* with her leaky centreboard case? They would be doing some baling there. Saying nothing to the others he kept on looking round for the glimmer of her lantern, though he was pretty certain now that she was many miles away. He tried to light the lantern, but it blew out again at once. He gave it up and flashed his torch on the barometer. It was going up. That was something.

He flashed his torch on his compass. They were heading south-east. That meant, as they were driving stern first, that they were going north-west. But of course there might be a current of some sort.

"Which way are we going?" shouted Titty. "She isn't very wet now. Only a little slosh about my ankles."

"North-west," said John. "China. We'll hit the coast somewhere if we go far enough."

"Missee Lee," said Titty. "Pirates."

"So long as we get ashore," said Susan, "we'll be all right. But what'll the others do if they don't know where we are?"

"They'll get picked up by a liner," said John. "And then they'll come and look for us. Captain Flint'll guess what's happened."

"But if he doesn't?" said Roger.

"Ration of chocolate," said Susan hurriedly.

*

That night seemed to last for ever. Hour after hour they drove on in the dark, stern first, the little *Swallow* lurching up over each sea and diving down into the following trough. Susan and John between them used up half a box of matches trying to relight the lantern and then gave up. From time to time John flashed his torch on the compass and saw that they were still being driven towards the coast. The rope trailing from the bows kept them head to the wind more or less, but splashes came aboard from time to time. The strong wind blew the words from their mouths, so that they could only make themselves heard by shouting into each other's ears. But they soon gave up even trying to talk. Titty did her best to shield the parrot. The whimpering Gibber, bundled into his sleeping-bag, lay in Roger's arms. Hour after hour they huddled in the bottom of the boat, bumping against each other as she lurched, bumping so often that the bumps did not even keep them awake. Tired out, they dozed, waked, baled and dozed again in the darkness and the wind.

*

The wind dropped suddenly, so suddenly that it was like coming indoors out of a gale. The sea eased. For the first time for hours they felt that they could move without the fear of being flung out next moment into raging water.

"Is it over?" said Titty.

"Pieces of eight!" screamed the parrot.

"Has he been talking for a long time?" asked Roger.

"We wouldn't have heard him before," said Susan. "You didn't hear me when I was fairly shouting at you."

"Shut up a minute," said John. "Listen!"

"What is it?"

"Listen! . . . Breakers. . . . Over there. . . I thought I heard them before. . . ."

They listened. Yes, there could be no mistaking the dim, swaying roar of waves breaking on the shore.

"Land," said John. "Quite near."

"I wish we knew where we were," said Susan.

"We knew last night," said John. "We were right in the steamer track. But of course that

FIRST SIGHT OF CHINA

storm upset everything. That's why he wanted the sea-anchors out, partly, so that we'd stay where we were and keep together. But with ours going, of course, we've been moving all the time."

"I bet theirs went too," said Roger.

"They may be quite near," said Titty.

"They'd have shouted," said Susan.

"We wouldn't have heard them in that wind," said John.

"Let's try now," said Titty.

They hailed, all together. "Ahoy! . . . Ahoy . . . oy . . . oy!"

There was no answer.

"Pieces of eight!" shouted the parrot.

"Funny, Polly shouting in the dark," said Titty.

"It isn't dark," said Roger. "Look over there."

"Dawn coming," said John.

"John," said Susan suddenly. "I smell cinnamon."

"I smell all sorts of smells," said Roger.

"I believe we're quite close in," said John. "Lucky the wind dropped when it did."

They turned from looking at the faint light in the eastern sky.

"There's something showing," said Roger.

"Hills," said Susan.

"China," said Titty.

"If only we were all together," said Susan, and then . . . "We'd better have something to eat while we can. . . ."

Dawn in the tropics comes up as fast as dusk comes down. While they were eating rations of dates and chocolates it flared up out of the east. They stared at the shore and at each other, strangers all after that night of storm. They saw a coast-line of brown hills that, as they watched, turned to rose-grey above a belt of green forest. John, cramming the last of his chocolate into his mouth, turned to the bows and presently, hand over hand, quite easily now that there was no pull on it, was hauling in the rope from the sea-anchor.

"Hullo," he cried as he came to the end of it. "It wasn't my fault after all. It was the anchor itself that bust, not the rope." He held up the remains of the sea-anchor, a wooden ring with rags of grey canvas hanging from it. "Canvas rotten. Or perhaps some sparks burnt a hole and started it fraying. Well, if ours went, very likely theirs went too." He looked out hopefully again over the sea. There was not a thing in sight. He made up his mind.

"Look out, John," said Susan.

"Sorry," said John, who was tugging to get the oars clear of the mast and sail. "I'm going to row in."

Where the land was nearest to them there was a patch of green forest with a great cliff behind it rising high into the sky. To the left the land was much lower. To the right the trees seemed to be growing out of the sea. The hill behind them, not so tall as the cliff, had the shape of a great cat with its head resting on its paws. John got out the oars, put the rowlocks in their places, pulled the boat round and glancing over his shoulder, began to row.

"Where are we going to land?" asked Roger.

"Those trees under the cliff," said John. "Nearest place."

"Couldn't we sail?" said Titty.

"Not enough wind," said John. "Rowing's better, and with the sunrise behind us, we've got a good chance of getting ashore without being seen."

"But don't we want to be seen?" said Roger.

"Let's have a look at the people first," said John. "If they look beastly we can sheer off."

"They wouldn't do anything to shipwrecked sailors," said Titty.

"I do wish the others were in sight," said Susan.

John rowed on, stopping only for a moment at a shout from Roger. "There's a road going up that cliff. . . . Let's have the telescope."

They all searched the dark face of the cliff and saw what Roger had seen, a scratch sideways and slantways across the rock, another scratch above it, and yet another, a track, or at least a path. And a path meant people.

"Captain Flint did say we'd be picked up if we stayed where we were," said Roger.

Susan looked doubtfully out to sea, rolling green water stretching to the sunrise.

"We can't get back there," said John. "We'll try here, and if people are beastly we'll just have to dodge along the coast."

"I can't see any people anywhere," said Titty, who had been having a turn with the telescope, though it was hard to keep it steady as the little *Swallow* rose and fell.

"All the better," said John, and settled again to his rowing.

Nearer and nearer they came towards the cliff.

"There's a bit sticking out to meet us," said Roger. "That bit with the trees."

"That's what I'm going for," said John. "Got to find a place where we can land without smashing her up."

"Pull left," said Susan a few minutes later. "I say, John, it's a promontory. . . . There's quieter water behind it."

John pulled his left. Palm trees, other trees the names of which they did not know, were close to them, and below the trees were dark rocks and stony beaches on which the swell from the sea crashed in thunder and white spray. He must keep clear of that. He rowed on, keeping his distance from the shore, and then, coming to the end of the trees, began to turn in towards the cliff. Suddenly they were in smoother water.

"Gosh!" exclaimed Roger. "It's not a cape. It's an island."

They could see now that there was a wide channel of smooth water between the trees and the cliff.

"Good," said John. "There's our place. . . . Keep a lookout for rocks under water." He pulled suddenly with his starboard oar, and headed in for a little beach.

"Let me get in the bows," said Roger.

John waited a moment while Roger scrambled into his usual place. Then he rowed on. Susan was watching the water on one side, Titty on the other.

"Pull right," shouted Roger, and as John did so, Titty saw a black knob of rock slip by in the green depths.

"Pull left," shouted Susan, and John dodged another.

"Look here," said John. "If she bumps we must all be ready to hop overboard and take her up. Whatever happens we mustn't get her stove in."

But only a moment later there was a gentle scrunch and Roger was ashore. Gibber, whom Roger had let out of his bag, climbed over everything and everybody and was ashore a moment after Roger. John stepped out into a foot of water.

"Pretty near high-water mark," he said. "But we'll get her up as far as we can."

All four heaving together pulled *Swallow* her own length up the beach. John laid out her anchor among the roots of the trees.

"China," said Titty.

John looked carefully round. "Even from the top of the cliff nobody can see her in here," he said.

CHAPTER IV

WHAT HAPPENED TO *AMAZON*

I

"TALKEE ENGLISH BIMEBY"

WIND and the darkness had come together. There was a biggish sea running but the little *Amazon*, lying to her sea-anchor, was riding it well. Nancy and Peggy, tired after the shock of the fire, were sleeping fitfully in the stern. Captain Flint, with a corner of the centreboard digging into his back to keep him awake, was looking in the direction where he had last seen it for a glimmer of *Swallow's* lantern. There was not a sign of it, but that did not disturb him much. In a hard wind, in a tossing boat, the lantern might very easily have gone out and John would have found it by no means easy to light it again. There came a lull. He listened for a hail from John and then hailed himself, "*Swallow*, ahoy!"

Nancy and Peggy woke with a start, heard him, looked round in the darkness and hailed with him, "*SWALLOW*! AHOY!"

And then the wind freshened again and was blowing as hard as ever.

"No good," said Captain Flint. "They couldn't hear us and we couldn't hear them."

"I say, Uncle Jim, why aren't they close to us?"

"Where's their lantern?"

"Gone out. Lucky ours hasn't. Have they got torches?"

"John has, anyway," said Peggy.

"Well, now's the time to use it," said Captain Flint.

"I say, you do think they're all right?"

"Better off than we are," said Captain Flint. "No centreboard case to prod into their ribs."

"*Swallow* did capsize once, but that was only because of a rock. . . ."

"She didn't capsize then, you tame galoot. Don't you remember? She just holed herself and sank and her mast went clean over her bows."

"She wouldn't capsize without her mast and sail up," said Captain Flint. . . . "Anyway, not if they kept down in the boat, and John would see to it that they did. And there are no rocks out here. She'll be all right. Shut up, you two, anyway. Go to sleep, it's no use yelling in a wind like this. You go to sleep till dawn and we'll find them then. . . ."

"But they were only a few yards off. . . ."

"Shut up," said Captain Flint. "There's nothing to be done till daylight."

*

A second time Nancy and Peggy were waked by a roar from Captain Flint.

"AHOY! SHIP AHOY!"

They started up and stared about them, blinking at the hurricane lantern that Captain Flint was holding up and waving. Had he caught sight of *Swallow's* lantern? Had he seen the flash of a torch?

"AHOY! . . . SHIP AHOY!" he shouted.

"Where?" said Nancy. "What is it?"

"Chinese fisherman, probably," said Captain Flint. "No sidelights, of course. AHOY!" he shouted again.

"There," cried Peggy. "Look . . . look . . . She's right on us."

A dim light was swaying towards them.

"SHIP AHOY!" roared Captain Flint, and then, "Why doesn't that idiot, John, show a torch? They may easy run him down if they don't see him."

The light, swaying towards them over the seas, brightened. There was a shout. Captain Flint shouted back. Suddenly, thirty or forty yards away, a door opened. They saw people, black shadows flitting across a square patch of light. They heard the crash of water under the bows of a ship.

"You take the lantern, Nancy," said Captain Flint. "Ship the rowlocks, Peggy. Don't stand up. . . ."

Nancy, kneeling on the floorboards, holding firmly to the middle thwart with one hand, held the lantern above her head with the other. Captain Flint had begun by jerking the oars loose and then, seeing how close the ship was, he grabbed the painter and began coiling it, coil after coil, making ready to throw.

"She's seen us," he said.

A voice shouted out something in an unknown language. Lanterns were moving on the deck of the strange ship. A splash from her bow wave came aboard.

"Heave to and give us lee," yelled Captain Flint.

The black wall of the ship's side towered above the *Amazon*. Then as the little boat lifted on a sea, they caught a glimpse of the deck, a path of light from a cabin door, a faint shifting glow on a dark sail, the black knobs of heads looking over bulwarks with the light dim behind them.

"Stand by for a rope there," Captain Flint roared. They saw his right arm with the coil of rope swing back and then shoot forward again. They heard a shout above them. There was a violent jerk.

"Crazy lunatics," yelled Captain Flint. "You'll have us stove in."

There was a crunch as the little boat swung in against the larger vessel which, though she had checked her way, was still slowly forging ahead. The next moment Nancy's lantern was knocked from her hand as someone landed heavily aboard. She found herself lifted, grabbed from above and somehow on all fours on the deck of the ship. In the dim light of lanterns she saw half-naked figures at the rail. "Hey . . . la." There was a shout and Peggy was dumped beside her. She heard Captain Flint shouting to people to take care. The next moment he too came almost flying over the rail. He scrambled to his feet. . . . "Look out, you. . . ." He could not get near the rail. There was a shout from below. A dozen men started yelling all together, "Hey . . . la . . . Hey . . . la. . . ."

"Look out," shrieked Nancy. "You'll smash her."

Amazon was coming over the rail, tipping sideways and emptying oars, mast, sail, ration box and everything else that was in her down on the deck.

"Yi!" Somebody squealed as something heavy came down on a bare foot.

"Where's your skipper?" said Captain Flint. "There's another boat close by." He took a torch from his pocket and began flashing it in hopes of an answering signal from John.

A moment later the torch was snatched from his hand.

"Who's the skipper here?" he asked angrily.

"*Swallow*, ahoy!" shouted Nancy.

"*Swallow*, ahoy!" shouted Peggy.

"AHOY!" roared Captain Flint.

There was a terrific hubbub of other people all shouting at the same time, clearing the tangle of *Amazon's* gear. It was instantly stilled by an order from somewhere aft.

"Gosh!" exclaimed Captain Flint. "The scoundrels are going to sail on. Hey! I tell you there's another boat. . . . Another boat. . . . Where's your skipper? . . . Doesn't any of you talk English?"

"Talkee English bimeby." A voice sounded almost at his elbow, and then gave another order. A voice answered out of thc darkness aft. Men ran to obey. Somewhere forward there was the flap of a sail filling suddenly with wind.

Captain Flint, roaring, rushed aft. "Heave to, I say. . . . There's another boat!"

There was a crash. Then a rush of bare feet, a scramble, curses, a thud. Half a dozen men bumped something along the deck. In the light of a lantern Nancy and Peggy saw that the something was Captain Flint. Men had him by the feet and by the shoulders. They hove him up and swayed towards the bulwarks.

"NO!" shouted Nancy.

Another moment and Captain Flint would have

been thrown overboard. But Nancy's "NO!", a single, violent, determined word, shouted close beside them, startled the men. That moment saved him. A quiet voice, the same that had been giving orders, spoke again. There was a moment's grumbling, and the men, hauling Captain Flint with them, disappeared through an open door under the foredeck. The ship was sailing. The deck was dark once more.

"They've killed him," said Peggy.

Nancy grabbed Peggy's hand and hurried her along, feeling through the dark towards the place from which the orders had come. She crashed into something, almost fell, tripped over a rope, saved herself and stumbled on.

She was stopped by hearing the voice immediately in front of her.

"Talkee English bimeby."

"You've killed him," she stormed. "And what about the *Swallow*? There's another boat."

"Not dead. . . . Him mad," said the voice.

"There's another boat," cried Nancy. "You must pick her up. We can't go on without them. . . ." She stamped her foot.

The voice spoke again, not in English. Hands seized them both by the wrists, and, stumbling in the dark, they were run forward along the deck. A door was opened. They were pushed into a small cabin lit by a lantern hanging from a beam. The door was closed behind them. They were alone.

Round three walls of the cabin there was a low bench, with a wide shelf three or four feet above it. People could have slept on the bench or on the shelf. In one corner lay a

"NO!"

bundle of rugs. Peggy went to look, turned back, and sat down as far from them as possible.

"Nancy," she said. "I . . . I'm going to be sick."

"No, you aren't," said Nancy hurriedly. "Not in here."

She tried the door and found it fast. "No," she said, "you jolly well aren't. . . . Nothing to be sick about. . . . Ow, I did fetch myself a crack. . . ." She limped across the cabin and sat down by Peggy.

"Captain Flint's dead," said Peggy.

"Of course he isn't," said Nancy.

"And what about the *Swallow*?" said Peggy.

"Not prisoners, anyhow," said Nancy. "And we are. Do you know what that thing was I bumped into on deck?"

"No."

"Cannon," said Nancy. "At least I'm almost sure. . . . What's that tapping?"

"Somebody hammering."

"Shut up. . . ." Nancy listened. Outside there was the noise of the wind, the crashing of sea, the creaking of the masts. This noise was nearer . . . tapping, somewhere inside the ship . . . below . . . Tap . . . Tap . . . and then again Tap . . . Tap . . . Tap. . . ."

"Just a rope," said Peggy.

"It's under our feet," said Nancy. "Wait. . . . Listen. . . . Long and two shorts. . . . Long and two shorts. . . . It's Uncle Jim. . . . It's the calling-up signal. Who says he's dead?" She knelt on the floor and began tapping with her knuckles. Short, two longs. . . . Short, two longs. . . . The other tapping stopped, and then began again.

Peggy, forgetting that she had felt sick, flung

herself on the floor beside Nancy. The tapping was certainly coming from somewhere below them, but a little further forward in the ship. Slowly a question came through. Nancy tapped an answer.

"What did he say?" asked Peggy. "He's going too fast for me."

"He's all right," whispered Nancy. "I've told him we're all right too. . . . Shut up. . . . What's that? He's off again. 'Keep . . . your heads . . . sorry . . . I . . . lost . . . mine. . . . Good thing really they didn't get the others. . . . They will be picked up by a decent ship. . . . Bad luck our meeting fishermen. . . .'" Nancy banged the floor and violently tapped a message back. "I'm telling him about the cannon," she translated to Peggy.

She paused and listened.

There was a short reply.

"He says, 'Bunk.' . . . But it couldn't have been anything else."

There was more tapping from below, this time a long message.

"Let . . . them . . . take . . . us . . . into . . . port. . . . Then . . . we . . . get hold . . . of somebody . . . telegraph . . . warn . . . all shipping . . . look out . . . for . . . them. . . . I . . . know . . . exact . . . position. . . . Probably . . . these . . . chaps . . . hurry . . . to . . . get . . . home."

Nancy tapped again. "I . . . can . . . not . . . smell . . . any . . . fish. . . ."

"May be trader," the answer came back.

Nancy began again, banging on the floor. "If I don't look out I'll be taking all the skin off my knuckles." She banged away with her left hand instead of her right and, in the middle of a message, stopped short. Neither she nor Peggy had heard the door open, but, under the light of the lantern, a Chinese with a cartridge-belt and pistol-holster slung over his short jacket, and a black skull-cap on his head, was standing looking down at them.

They scrambled to their feet.

The Chinese bowed, waved them towards the bench on one side of the cabin and himself sat down facing them.

"Captain," he said, bowing.

For once Nancy did not know what to say. How long had he been there? Did he know they had been talking with Captain Flint?

The door opened and another Chinese came in, carrying a short bamboo pipe which he handed to the seated captain. The captain put it to his lips. The other Chinese lit it for him and went out. The captain pulled at his pipe and blew out a little smoke.

"How come?" he said at last, showing with a wave of his pipe that he meant, "What had they been doing to be out at sea in a small boat?"

Nancy eagerly explained. She began talking very fast, telling of the voyage, of the burning of the *Wild Cat*, of the two little boats, of their hopes to be picked up . . . but, as she talked, watching the expressionless face of the Chinese, her words came more and more slowly, more and more loudly, more and more clearly. . . . She repeated a sentence. . . . She hesitated for a word. . . . She stopped.

"Talkee English bimeby," said the Chinese.

"He doesn't understand," said Peggy.

"I know that," said Nancy desperately.

"Try pictures," said Peggy, and rummaging in a pocket brought out the stump of a pencil.

Nancy took it and looked for something on which to draw. The Chinese watched her. He smiled. He clapped his hands. The door opened. The captain spoke in Chinese. A minute later a man came in with a thin board of white wood, which, at a sign from the captain, he gave to Nancy. Nancy, putting the board on the bench beside her, drew the schooner, *Wild Cat*, as she had so often drawn her on letters for home. Then she drew the schooner again with flames licking up the masts. Then, with tears in her eyes, she drew the stern of the *Wild Cat* just before it went under, and the two small boats, with the crew watching the end of their ship. Then she drew the two little boats alone at sea. . . . Then she drew one boat all by itself. She took the board to the captain and, with her pencil, pointed to the pictures one by one.

The captain seemed to understand. When, last of all, she pointed to the picture of the *Swallow*, left alone, he looked aft and pointed with his pipe as if he could see through the cabin wall and the dark to the little boat tossing far astern.

"Yes, yes," cried Nancy, and showed that she wanted him to turn back and go and search for the others, but he held out his hands in a gesture that could not be mistaken. There was to be no going back. Nancy started talking again. He waited until she gave up.

Then he pointed as if through the floor of the cabin.

"Him mad," he said.

"But he isn't," cried Nancy.

"Him mad," he said again and then, pointing at Nancy and Peggy, he said, "Plisoners. . . . Talkee English, bimeby. . . ." He stood up, bowed and went out of the cabin into the darkness.

"Pirates," said Nancy. "I told you so."

"It'll be all right if he's taking us to someone who talks English," said Peggy.

The door opened for a moment and a Chinese came in with the bundle of sleeping-bags from *Amazon*. He went out.

Nancy tried the door. It was again fastened from outside. She started banging on the floor again to tell Captain Flint what had happened. She got no answer.

"He's gone to sleep," she said. "We'd better do the same. We can't do anything else."

"What time is it?" asked Peggy.

"Middle of the night I should think," said Nancy. "Go on, Peg. You get all the sleep you can. I'm taking this corner. . . . Gosh, I do hope those others are all right. . . . But, I say, they'll be pretty sick at being picked up by a liner when they hear what's happened to us. I knew at once. I was dead sure that was a cannon. . . ."

II

THE PIRATE JUNK

"Chiu fan!"

Nancy and Peggy stirred on their benches. What had happened to their comfortable cabin in the *Wild Cat*? Why were they not sleeping in their bunks, one above another? Where were they?

"Chiu fan!"

A Chinese was standing in the doorway, pointing to a large bowl of rice he had put on the floor. As soon as he saw that they were awake he went out, closing the door behind him. Nancy rubbing a painful hip-bone, sat up.

"Breakfast," she said. "Show a leg. It's morning. I don't believe I've been asleep five minutes. I say, it's not blowing like it was."

Though the door was closed, light was streaming through a small square window which must have been shuttered during the night.

Four chopsticks, like long pencils, were stuck in the rice, but after a trial or two, they found they were too hungry to use them, and taking turns with the bowl, scooped rice into their mouths with bent forefingers.

"Wonder if Uncle Jim's got his," said Peggy.

At that moment they heard the call sign, tapping away from somewhere in the bottom of the ship. Nancy answered. In a few minutes they had learnt that Captain Flint had had a good breakfast, that he could not see out, that he was pretty sure the ship was a trading junk, and that as soon as they got to port the captain would get into trouble for shutting him up. Captain Flint, for his part, had learnt that they too were filling up with rice, that Nancy was sure the ship was not a trader, that she had hurt her knee by bumping into a cannon, and that the reason she had stopped signalling last night was because the captain of the junk had caught her at it. "What about *Swallow*?" Nancy tapped.

"Cannot do anything till we get to port," came the answer. "No wireless aboard these traders."

"Pirates," tapped Nancy.

"O.K.," tapped Captain Flint.

They had just finished the rice when the man came in again with two smaller bowls on a tray. He put the tray on the floor and took away the empty rice bowl and the chopsticks.

"Tea," said Nancy, sniffing.

"Pretty weak," said Peggy. "And no milk."

"No sugar," said Nancy.

All the same, the rice had made them thirsty and the tea, if not sweet, was wet. They drank, made faces, and drank again. Presently the man came in, looked into the empty bowls and made them understand that he wanted to know if they would like some more.

"No, thank you," they said, shaking their heads.

He went away, but, this time, left the cabin door open and, hooking it back, showed that he was not doing it by mistake.

"Come on," said Nancy.

*

They went out into brilliant sunshine. The sea had gone down. Everywhere were green waves with little rippling white crests. There was no land in sight, nor any other vessel. They were on the deck of a large Chinese junk. Above their heads was the huge brown mainsail, ribbed across by bamboo battens. In some places the sail had been patched. Flourbags had been used for the patches and it was odd to read on them the names of English or American millers. Sitting on the yard, steadying himself with an arm round the mast, was a half-naked sailor. Nancy looked for the flag. There was none, but a long wisp of a scarlet pennant floated out from the masthead. Forward, above the cabin in which they had been shut up, they could see a smaller sail of the same kind. There was another, high above the poop-deck. On each side of the deck there were three large lumps covered with brown matting, and on the starboard side there was *Amazon*, firmly lashed against the bulwarks.

"She's all right," said Peggy.

But Nancy was looking at those odd-shaped lumps.

"Guns," she said. "Cannon. I told you so."

"No," said Peggy.

"Galoot," said Nancy. "Use your eyes. . . . I bet that's the one I bumped into. You can see a bit of it peeping out."

Half a dozen Chinese, naked to the waist, were sitting on the deck, playing cards. They looked up, but soon had seen all they wanted, and went on with their game.

"They don't mind us being out," said Nancy. "Look! There's the captain, by the steersman. Let's go up there and get him to let Uncle Jim out too."

The captain, in his black skull-cap, was sitting on a little stool built against the low rail. He was watching the helmsman swaying to and fro on an enormously long tiller, and glancing now at a compass and now at the horizon far ahead.

Nancy lost no time in saying what she had to say. Why was Captain Flint not on deck? Where was he? Would the captain please let him out at once?

The captain waited till she was out of breath. He smiled politely and said, "Talkee English bimeby."

Nancy started again, slower. The captain must have understood what she wanted, for he said, "Him too much stlong," smiled happily, and repeated, "Talkee English bimeby."

"Can't be helped," said Nancy to Peggy. "They got a fright when Uncle Jim went savage last night. But we're going somewhere where he'll be able to talk English and explain. Perhaps they aren't pirates after all. . . ." Her voice was almost regretful. "Those guns. . . . Perhaps they have to carry guns in case of meeting Missee Lee."

"Where's all the crew?" said Peggy. "There were dozens last night. And now there's nobody except the captain and the steersman and those men playing cards."

"And the look-out," said Nancy, pointing to the masthead.

As she said it, there was a shout. The look-out had scrambled to his feet and was standing on the yard with one arm stretched out like a signpost, while he clung to the mast with the other.

"Land, I expect," said Nancy.

"I can't see anything."

"I can't either."

But they saw that the captain had spoken to the steersman. The big junk changed course until the look-out, high overhead, was pointing directly over the bows. The card-players on deck were gathering up their cards. Men were pouring out from a door under the poop-deck. Some went to the foot of the foremast, some stayed at the foot of the main. Some came up on the poop. All were staring forward at that distant line where sea and sky met.

Nearly half an hour later they saw what the look-out had seen, a small knob on the horizon. The junk sailed on and presently more land appeared stretching away on either side of the knob. The junk sailed on. They could see a long line of rocky coast with hills behind it. The men now kept turning to look at the captain, who sat there, watching the land grow nearer. Suddenly he spoke. Men were busy with the foresail sheets and with the sheets of the little mizen above the poop-deck. The junk lost way.

"Gosh!" said Nancy. "They're heaving to. Whatever for? Just when we're in a hurry to get to a harbour."

The junk was hardly moving. From the way in which all the men kept staring now at the land and now at the look-out perched like a monkey at the masthead, it was clear that they were waiting for something. Nancy and Peggy stared at the land like everybody else.

"Wonder if he knows?" said Nancy at last and pulled Peggy by the sleeve.

They went forward through the Chinese sailors, who seemed hardly to notice them, and into the cabin where they had slept. They had hardly crossed the threshold before they heard an anxious question being tapped from down below them.

"Wind dropped?"

"Hove to," Nancy tapped back. "In sight of land."

"Damn!" tapped Captain Flint, paused a moment and tapped again. . . . "Bother!"

Nancy laughed.

"They've seen something," said Peggy.

Nancy stamped on the floor of the cabin by way of saying good-bye, and ran out. What was everybody looking at? Far away, sails were passing close under the land . . . junk sails . . . one, two, three, four junks, a little fleet sailing along the coast. An order rang out. Foresail and mizen were brought across. All three sails of their own junk were pulling again. They were heading in.

"Giminy, but she can sail," said Nancy, as the spray flew from under the bows. "And there isn't all that much wind, either."

"Look, look. . . . I told you they were guns."

Gun after gun was being cleared of the matting that had covered it. Sweating, half-naked Chinese were ramming things into the brass muzzles, and pouring black powder into the touch-holes. They were joking with each other and patting the old brass guns as if they loved them.

"Gosh," said Nancy. "She *is* a pirate . . . sailing to cut them off. That must be a cape, that bit we saw first. They'd have to tack to get back. Look at the way we're heading, keeping to windward of them. We've got them. . . . Here, I say!"

She and Peggy found themselves suddenly seized, run across the deck and pushed into their cabin. The door was fastened, and a shutter from outside slammed on the window.

"What a beastly shame." A little light came through cracks between the shutter and the frame of the window, but it was impossible to see out. Nancy began to tap a message to Captain Flint, but he interrupted her at once by tapping back.

"Shut up," he tapped. "I'm trying to make up on lost sleep."

"What's going to happen?" asked Peggy.

"We're going to miss it, anyhow," said Nancy, and hammered at the door.

Nobody came. The excited chatter on deck had come to an end. There was silence, except for the rushing of the junk through the water and the quick splash, splash from under her bows. They waited, Peggy more and more worried, Nancy angrier and angrier. "We may never have another chance in all our lives," she said.

An hour passed. There was not a sound on deck. It was as if they were sailing on a deserted ship. Then, at last, they heard an order.

BANG!

A gun had been fired from the foredeck, above their heads.

Peggy grabbed at Nancy's hand, as Nancy at the shuttered window was searching for a crack through which to see.

BANG! BANG! BANG!

Three guns went off from the deck just outside.

Peggy choked with a sob.

"Don't be a tame galoot!" said Nancy fiercely. "We're firing. You've got nothing to worry about. That's guns, not thunder!"

Minute after minute passed and nothing happened except that once they heard the running of bare feet overhead. Suddenly they heard someone shouting, not aboard the junk but not far off. An answer was shouted from close by their cabin door. They heard orders given and a sudden stampede along the deck. There was a tremendous groaning crunch.

"Rammed one of them," said Nancy. "No. We must have grappled. Oh, Giminy, giminy, I wish I could see out."

There was a noise now like that of a crowd at a boat-race. A huge booming voice sounded above the din which quieted to a sort of twittering.

"Our captain's got a megaphone," said Nancy.

The next noise was of luggage coming aboard. There was talk, some laughter, the slam of a hatch. Then there was the noise of straining ropes, an order, the crunch of ship against ship. Then, once more, the ordinary noise of a vessel moving through the water, and some cheerful chattering on deck.

A tapping came from below.

"Got a stable companion," tapped Captain Flint. "Funny fellow. . . . Chinese. . . . Gibbering with fright. . . . Called me Missee Lee. . . ."

"We are locked up again," tapped Nancy. "I was right. I knew they were pirates."

"Who?" tapped Captain Flint.

Some time later, a Chinese, grinning happily, brought them some rice and chopped chicken. Through the open door they caught a glimpse of a high coast, rocks dropping sheer to the sea, or into green forest along the water's edge. They were not allowed on deck again, but after the man had brought them some tea, Nancy made him understand that they were asking at least to have the shutter taken from the window. He went off, fastening the door behind him, but presently someone came and opened the shutter from outside. Even so, they could not see much through that small square hole. It was only looking sideways through it that they could get glimpses of the coast and knew that they were still sailing close along it.

The afternoon wore on. At dusk the motion of the junk changed and they knew that they were in smooth water. Less and less light came through the little window. It grew dark and Nancy was thinking of banging on the door in the hope of getting someone to bring them a light.

Suddenly there was a lot of cheerful shouting, the noise of oars in the water, and a lot of loud bangs.

"Guns again?" said Peggy.

"Fireworks," said Nancy. "We've got there, wherever it is."

There was the creaking of a windlass and then a heavy splash. "Anchoring," said Nancy. "Can't see any lights ashore, but they've got a lot on deck."

A boat bumped alongside and then another. There was a lot of talk on deck. People were moving about the ship.

"Gosh, what *are* they doing?" said Nancy. "They're putting *Amazon* over the side. They'll have every bit of varnish off. I just got a squint. . . ." She banged furiously on the door, but nobody took any notice.

Suddenly they heard Captain Flint tapping a message. "Nancy. If they ask questions leave the talking to me. You may be right. I've had a visitor. Called himself a Taicoon. So I said I was Lord Mayor of San Francisco. Just in case.... Give him something to think about...."

"But why?" Nancy began hammering at the deck.

Peggy stopped her with a tug. She looked round. People were watching from the open door. The man who had brought them their food came in and hung up a lighted lantern. The doorway was filled by a very tall man, in blue silk robes that glinted in the light of the lantern. He wore a blue skull-cap with a scarlet button that grazed the lintel as he came in, and a bird-cage with a white canary in it dangled from one hand. The captain of the junk came in after him.

"Taicoon, Chang," said the tall man.

"Nancy Blackett," said Nancy. "And this is Peggy."

"Melican?" he asked.

"English," said Nancy.

"Melican man with two English wives."

And at that moment the noise of tapping from below grew louder. Captain Flint was growing impatient.

The tall man listened. "Plisoners," he said. "No belong talkee." He turned to the captain of the junk. They heard the words "San Flancisco." "Tomollow all come my yamen," he said to Nancy, and then the two of them went out.

"Gosh," said Nancy. "We oughtn't to have let him catch us Morsing."

"They've shut the door," said Peggy. "And the window."

Nancy tapped the call sign but got no answer.

A moment later they heard Captain Flint's voice outside. "You take me Melican consul plenty quick. . . . Chop chop. Savee?" and then, clearly meaning them to hear, "Things'll be fixed up somehow."

"Can't you take us too?" shouted Nancy.

There was the sound of something like a struggle. Then Captain Flint's voice shouting from further away. "You sit tight and don't worry. Bound to get some sense out of somebody." Then came the sound of oars.

"Taking him ashore," said Nancy.

"What shall we do?"

"Sit tight, of course," said Nancy. "It'll be all right as soon as he's seen the consul or the harbourmaster."

"But if they're pirates?"

"Oh, shut up, Peggy. It'll be all right, anyway."

A little later the captain came in again, and with him a man with bowls of rice and soup.

"Man fan," he said.

"Why can't we go ashore?" asked Nancy furiously.

"Him too much stlong," he said. "Him mad. More betta in plison." He tapped with a knuckle on the cabin-wall. "Talkee," he said. "Taicoon say no belong talkee. San Flancisco go plison. You see him tomollow." He bowed, smiled and went out. The door closed behind him and they heard the noise of its fastening.

Nancy suddenly laughed. "He's been in prison before," she said. "Don't you remember? Over grabbing a policeman's helmet on boat-race night. He won't mind. And we're all right too."

"What about John and Susan and the others?" said Peggy.

"Been picked up by a liner long ago," said Nancy. "Sitting in a row at the captain's table and being fussed over by a lot of stewards and stewardesses and first-class passengers, poor beasts."

There were noises of boats coming alongside, and boats going off again. The noises came gradually to an end.

"Everybody's gone ashore," said Nancy.

"Not everybody," said Peggy.

They could hear soft footsteps walking up and down.

"Sentinel," said Nancy. "Night watchman. . . . Oh well, who cares? One more night in here. Let's have supper and go to bed. It'll be all right in the morning."

III

BRIEF HOUR OF FREEDOM

Going to bed was easy. It meant no more than wriggling into their sleeping-bags and hopefully feeling for soft places on a hard bench. Going to sleep was much more difficult. In spite of everything, pirates or no pirates, even Nancy more than half expected that Captain Flint would meet someone who really did know English and that at any minute she would hear the noise of a boat coming off to bring them ashore. For a long time they lay awake listening to the pad pad of the watchman on deck, listening for land noises, wondering what was going to happen and, now that twenty-four hours and more had passed, living as if for the first time through the burning of the *Wild Cat*. They slept and woke to hear a new noise. The pad pad of the watchman had come to an end. Instead they heard the squeaking and scurrying of rats, and Peggy would not be satisfied until they had got up and searched all round the cabin by the light of the hanging lantern to make sure that, though the rats might spend the whole night dancing on the decks and down below, there was no hole by which they could get in to join the prisoners.

They had no idea what time it was when they woke next morning. Light was coming through cracks in the shutter outside the window and under the cabin-door. The lantern had burnt out. They listened. They thought they could hear voices far away, and the calls of birds, the squawking of jays and the high whistling note of a kite. But aboard the junk there was not a sound that they did not make themselves.

"I wish we hadn't eaten all the rice," said Nancy, looking in the empty bowl.

"Can't we get out?" said Peggy.

"See what that watchman says about it," said Nancy, and started banging at the door.

There was no answer.

"If he's gone ashore too. . . ." said Nancy, as she hammered at the door again and began feeling round the edge of it with her fingers.

"They can't have forgotten us," said Peggy.

"They've no right to shut us up," said Nancy.

"What are you doing?" asked Peggy a minute or two later.

"There's something here I can jiggle," said Nancy, who was poking with her scout knife between the door and its frame. "I moved it a quarter of an inch."

"Better not," said Peggy. "They'll be pretty furious if we break anything."

"Their own fault," said Nancy, who was now working hard, poking her knife through the crack and then using it as a lever. "It's moving, whatever it is."

"What'll we do if we do get out?"

"Walk about on deck," said Nancy. "Why shouldn't we? And if we see anybody we yell to them to hurry up with our breakfast. Look here. The thing's stuck. Come and shove your weight against the door."

"What's the good?" said Peggy.

"Don't be a galoot," said Nancy. "It was you who thought of getting out. Now we're going to. No. Don't just lean. Shove. There. I shifted it another quarter inch. Give it a good shove. . . . No. . . . Not like that. . . . Barbecued billygoats, it isn't a china cupboard. If it busts, it busts. Come on. One, two, three!"

There was a noise of splitting wood, the door flung open and the two of them landed in a heap on the deck outside. Nancy, with her head on the deck, saw, two yards in front of her, a pair of huge bare feet with enormous toes. She scrambled up in a hurry. Slumped on the deck, with his shoulders against the bulwarks, lay their Chinese guard. His head had fallen sideways. His mouth was open. A little box and a tiny metal pipe with a bamboo stem lay by his side.

"Hey," said Nancy. "We want breakfast!" She leaned over the man, sniffed, made a face and shook him by the shoulder.

The man grunted as she let go of him, but did not speak. He did not even open his eyes.

"Opium, I expect," said Nancy. "Smells horrible."

"He's dead," said Peggy, shrinking back into the door of the cabin.

"He isn't. Didn't you hear him grunt? You can see him breathing. Hey, you!" she shouted, bending down once more.

There was no answer. Guard or night watchman, whatever he was, the man lay hopelessly asleep.

"Pig!" said Nancy. "Well, at least we can see things. I say, it isn't a harbour at all."

The junk was lying in the mouth of a river. Green forest stretched along the nearer shore, with hills behind it. On the other side a high bare cliff rose into the sky. A few hundred yards up the river they could see some brown buildings, partly hidden by trees. A long way upstream other junks were at anchor.

"There may be a proper harbour further up," said Nancy. "That looks like a fort. And one on the other side under that cliff. And look at all those logs. There are people about somewhere."

"I can't see any," said Peggy.

"I can hear them. Somewhere in behind those trees. Sounds like a monkey-house. And listen to that gong."

"Are those people coming along the top of the cliff?"

"I wish we had a telescope," said Nancy. "Gosh! We made a bit of a mess of that latch. Their fault, anyway, fastening us up."

"Can't we mend it before someone comes?" said Peggy.

"And fasten ourselves up again inside?" said Nancy. "Not me." She looked over the side. "Come on. Let's have a squint at *Amazon*." She went up on the poop and looked down into *Amazon*, floating astern at the end of her painter. "Beasts!" said Nancy to herself. "They might at least have put the bottomboards straight. All lying cockeye. Pretty strong current. Look at it swirling under her bows. . . . Oh, here you are!" Peggy had made a dash across the deck, without looking at the sleeping man, and was on the poop beside her.

"I wish someone would come," she said.

"Lend a hand with the painter," said Nancy. "We'll bring *Amazon* alongside. I'm going down to put those bottomboards straight and get some of the water out. They gave her an awful bump bringing her aboard."

Nancy unfastened the painter from a bollard on the poop and towed her along, coming down again on the middle deck, followed unwillingly by Peggy.

"Keep her just like that," said Nancy.

Peggy took the painter, looking nervously over her shoulder at the body of the watchman. Nancy climbed over the bulwarks between two of the cannon, found a hold for her feet, then another, and dropped down into her own old ship.

"Jibbooms and bobstays, what a beastly mess,"

she said. "Lucky we wedged the baler under the stern sheets."

She began scooping out the water.

"Nancy," came Peggy's voice from overhead. "I can't stay on board with it . . . with him. . . ."

"All right," said Nancy, tossing out water as fast as she could. "Come down and bale."

Peggy climbed over the bulwarks and came down. Nancy took a waving foot and planted it for her. Peggy dropped down into the boat.

"Now," said Nancy. "You bale, and I'll get things straight. Put your weight on that side. I'll get that bottomboard out of the way. Go ahead. I don't believe she's leaking really badly. Perhaps they just got a lot in when they put her over. Get her clear and we'll see if it's coming in anywhere. . . . PEGGY! What did you do with the painter?"

"I'm sure I made it fast," stuttered Peggy.

"Well, it isn't fast now."

Already the little *Amazon* had drifted clear of the junk, her long painter trailing on the water.

"Rowlocks!" cried Nancy. "Oars!" and then, "Great jumping Giminy, they're aboard the junk."

"We're going out to sea," said Peggy. "Oh, if only we'd stayed in the cabin."

Already the current was sweeping them out of the mouth of the river. The feathery tops of palms along the nearer shore were moving fast across the hills behind them.

"Get amidships," said Nancy. "And bale. Go on baling. I can paddle her with one of the bottomboards. . . . From the stern. Be quick. Don't tip her over. The more water you get out the steadier she'll be. We've got to get back."

"We're moving like anything," said Peggy.

"Of course we are. Don't be a tame galoot. You bale and go on baling."

With one of the bottomboards she set to work to drive *Amazon* upstream, back to the junk. That high, carved, painted stern was already far away and growing further. Nancy dipped her bottomboard, pushed as hard as she could, lifted, dipped and pushed again. *Amazon* wallowed round in circles, all the time drifting out towards the open sea. Nancy tried another way. With one hand on one end of the bottomboard and the other arm against the middle of it, keeping the awkward thing sideways as if it were a paddle, she managed to keep *Amazon* at least heading in the right direction.

"We're still going the wrong way," said Peggy.

"Shut up," snapped Nancy. "You bale. Yapping doesn't help."

"Someone's seen us," said Peggy. "I heard a shout."

"They'll have to bring a boat," said Nancy. "Go on. Don't stop baling."

Peggy baled. Nancy worked the bottomboard as well as she could, putting all the strength she had into each stroke. She glanced to the left. That high cliff over there had ended. Nothing that way but sea. She looked at the wooded shore on her right. The trees there were still slipping in the wrong direction. There was no hope of getting back to the junk, but she might be able to get to that shore before it was too late. She changed her plan and instead of trying to drive *Amazon* upstream tried to work her across the current and nearer to the trees. Along there the stream might not run so fast. But all the time those trees were sweeping past. She took one of them for a mark and drove towards it, but presently had to take another and then another.

"We're nearer than we were," she panted at last.

"There's someone running through the trees," said Peggy.

"We're going to do it," said Nancy. "If my arms don't break first."

Quite suddenly she knew that they had done it. They were much nearer to the shore. The current was weaker. She looked for a likely place to land. There was a gap, where a creek seemed to go in among the overhanging branches of queer trees with monstrous fleshy leaves. With a last effort she drove *Amazon* towards it.

"She's nearly dry," said Peggy.

"About time," said Nancy.

They were in still water. Great leaves drooped towards them. Peggy grabbed a branch and pulled. *Amazon* slid on, trees on either side of her. She grounded.

"Can't pole her up with no oar," said Nancy. "Hop out."

They splashed over the side and sank to the knees in mud. They hauled the boat with them, till they found firmer ground under their feet.

"Narrow squeak," panted Nancy. She took the painter and made it fast round a tree. "She won't get away this time," she said.

"I'm awfully sorry, Nancy," said Peggy.

"Over now," said Nancy. "I wonder what sort

of a slip knot you made. Anyway, we've landed on the coast of China."

There was a noise of running feet. Three Chinese pushed their way through the trees, grabbed Nancy and Peggy and, in a moment, tied their hands behind their backs.

"All right, all right," said Nancy. "We weren't trying to run away. We want our breakfast. Laugh, Peggy, you goat. Don't let them think we mind."

The Chinese, chattering among themselves, hurried them off through the trees in the direction from which they had come.

CHAPTER V

"HIC LIBER EST MEUS"

Looking about them, the crew of the *Swallow* could see nothing but the green curtain of tropical forest that shut in the little bay where they had landed.

"What about getting our things ashore?" said Susan.

"Better explore first," said John. "We may want to push off again in a hurry."

"Are we going to explore before breakfast?" said Roger.

"We jolly well are," said John. "You've been stuffing dates and chocolate already."

"Gibber's hungry, anyway," said Roger. "I'm going to get him some of those bananas."

"All right," said John. "What are you doing, Titty?"

"We'll take Polly with us," said Titty, who was getting the parrot cage out of the boat.

"I'll just get my compass," said John. "Gosh!" he exclaimed a moment later. "There's the sextant and the nautical almanac. I put them in the wrong boat. And Captain Flint'll be wanting them."

"Not if he's been picked up by a liner," said Susan.

"But if he hasn't," said John. "I wish. . . ."

"Never mind," said Susan. "You can't give them back to him now."

"I know, but I wish I could," said John. He looked carefully at his compass. "That wind was south-east. They'll be coming from somewhere over there if they've been blown in the same as us. Come on. Let's find a good place to look out from. Go quietly, everybody. If there are natives about we'd better have a look at them before they know we're here."

He had another look at the compass, and then, holding it in his hand, led the way into the trees. Roger followed him with Gibber on his lead. Titty with the ship's parrot came next and Susan last. It was not easy going. Tangled climbing plants hung from tree to tree like network put there to stop them. Here and there they climbed over rocks covered with green slippery moss. Here and there between the rocks were patches of swampy ground. They walked warily after Susan had warned them to look out for snakes. They saw lizards, but no snakes. Huge butterflies flitted past them. Strange birds screamed overhead, and grasshoppers or locusts made a noise like sticks being drawn along a paling.

Suddenly John stopped short. The others tiptoed up to him.

"A path," he said.

"That means people," said Titty.

"It's sure to go somewhere," said Roger.

They had struck the path at a bend. John had a look at his compass. "North-west one way," he said "and nearly east the other. We'll go east and get a look out to sea. Funny. I didn't see a sign of buildings along that shore."

"Keep together," said Susan.

"What about making a blaze," said Titty. "In case we have to get back in a hurry?"

"Good for you, Titty," said John. "I ought to have thought of it."

Titty had already got out her knife and was carving a blaze in the side of a tree. A thick syrup oozed from the bared wood and before she had finished huge butterflies were sucking at it, even brushing her fingers with their fluttering wings.

"That's good enough," said John. "Come on."

It was easy going now. Someone else had cut the climbing plants for them. Someone else had cleared the tropical undergrowth. Stumps at the side of the path showed where someone else had cut the trees. They hurried along, now and then getting a glimpse of shimmering water on their right. Suddenly they found themselves close above the shore, with solid rock beneath their feet and the sea once more open before them.

"Gosh, what a chair," said Roger, ran forward, hove himself up and sat down in it.

It was a huge armchair carved out of the rock. Its arms ended in dragons' heads and a prancing dragon, in shallow relief, was carved on the back of it.

"Pretty knobbly to lean against," said Roger. "But it's a grand place for a look-out post."

The four of them stared out to sea.

"Straight into the sun," said John. "It's no good. If there was a boat out there we couldn't see it. We'll come back here later. That path doesn't go any further. We'd better go and see what there is at the other end of it. Come on, Roger. Off that throne." And he set off back along the path.

They came to Titty's blaze, now marked by a cloud of blue butterflies. John walked more slowly, stopping every now and then to listen.

"We don't want to run into anything before we know," he said.

"What do we do if we hear someone coming?" asked Roger.

"Hop off the path and lie down," said John. "And don't leave a trail like an elephant's. Get out of sight like a snake."

"Snakes don't hop," said Roger, but Titty was the only one who heard him.

"It's quite a small island," said John. "We must be nearly at the other side. Hullo . . .!" He stopped short.

"What is it?" asked Roger.

"'Sh!" said Susan.

"House," whispered John. "You stay here and be ready to bolt."

"Do take care," said Susan, but John was already out of sight round a bend in the path.

Titty and Roger stood where he had stood. Susan joined them. They saw John going cautiously on. Where the path came out from among the trees they could see a carved red dragon on the corner of a roof of bright green tiles, and beyond it dark water under the great cliff they had seen before landing.

"Come back a bit," said Susan. "John said we were to be ready to bolt. Don't let go of Gibber's lead."

Minute after minute passed. John came back on the run.

LODGING FOR THE NIGHT

"Nobody there," he said. "It's a queer kind of house. I've been into it. And the path goes right down to a jetty. But there are no boats. And there's no other path from the house, only this one."

"Come on, Gibber," said Roger. "It's safe to go ahead."

The house, when they came up to it, was indeed a queer one. It had a red dragon at each end of the sagging ridge of its roof. There were red dragons at the four corners. The roof overhung the two steps that ran the whole width of the house. Behind the steps was a verandah, and behind that the house was open except for a low wall with an opening in the middle as if for a door. There was a wooden pillar on each side of the opening, so that it looked as if the whole front of the house was made up of a doorway with no door and two big windows with no glass.

"Only one room," said Susan.

"There's a sort of inner room built on behind," said John. "It's more like a summer-house than anything."

"Why's nobody living here?" said Susan.

"The people may have died of plague," said Titty.

"Rot," said John. "It's probably only a summer-house. Not big enough for anything else."

They went in, treading on tiptoe and whispering as if the owner of the house were asleep there and they did not wish to wake him.

"Somebody *is* living here," said Susan who, the moment her eyes had grown accustomed to the shadow, had seen an open cupboard in a corner of the room. "Primus stove . . . kettle and two cups

. . . and a can of paraffin. . . ." She unscrewed a cap and sniffed.

"Somebody jolly well is living here," said Roger. "English too. Look at this."

In a corner of the room furthest from the entrance there was a low wooden table and a carved stool. Roger was fingering some books on the table.

"Somebody doing Latin lessons," he said.

"This box is full of tea," said Susan, still at the cupboard.

"Look here, Susan," said John. "Cambridge University Tutorial. It's Virgil's beastly Aeneid."

"And a Latin-English Dictionary," said Titty.

Roger was looking at a thin exercise book. "Translation," he said. "Just begun. I know that bit. . . . It's where Father Aeneas starts spouting . . . . We had it last term I was at school."

"If they're English people we're all right," said Susan. "What's in there?" She was looking through into a small inner room that opened out of the first.

The others, leaving the books, joined her. Somehow, not one of them crossed the threshold into that inner room. A little light came into it through a pattern of square holes left in the side walls and they could see that it was empty except for an enormous red-painted chest on which was standing an upright, oblong block of wood, split half down, painted red, with Chinese characters on it painted in gold.

"It's a sort of altar," said John.

"Ought we to be here?" said Titty.

"Why not?" said John. "If it's all right for

people to sweat at Latin here, it's all right for us."

Roger had gone back to the books. "English or Chinese?" he said. "Look at this. She's written her name down often enough." They looked over his shoulder at the flyleaf of the Virgil and saw a name written again and again.

Li
Miss Lee
Miss Lee, B.A.
Miss Lee, M.A.
Miss Lee, Litt.D.
Dr. Lee, M.A., Litt.D., etc.

They stared at a lot of Chinese characters written at the side.

"Miss Lee," said Titty. "Don't you remember what the harbourmaster said?"

"Oh rubbish," said John. "He said the Chinese used her to frighten their children with. And that was Missee Lee, not Miss. Who's going to be frightened of a girl doing lessons?"

"But what's all that Chinese?"

Li	李
Miss Lee	李小姐
Miss Lee B.A.	李小姐 (文学士)
Miss Lee M.A.	李小姐 (硕士)
Miss Lee Litt. D.	李小姐 (博士)
Dr Lee M.A., Litt. D., etc.	李小姐 (硕士, 博士)

"We'd know Chinese if we were brought up in China," said John.

"She doesn't know much," said Roger. "She's only got the first four lines. All our chaps put another line at the end, and a picture."

He showed them at the beginning of the dictionary the Latin rhyme with which students warn people not to steal their books.

> "Hic liber est meus,
> Testis est deus
> Si quis furetur
> Per collum pendetur."

"It's no good without the last line," said Roger.

"Anyway," said Susan. "If it's a girl doing lessons here she won't mind us using the house. We'd better bring the things from *Swallow*."

"Let's sail her round," said Titty.

"Better where she is," said John. "For one thing, nobody can see her there. And we might want to bolt in a hurry. And anyhow, we'll have to watch on that side of the island for Captain Flint and the others."

"We are going to sleep here tonight," said Susan. "One night in *Swallow's* enough and we've got no tents. All hands to fetch the things."

"Let's just have a look at the jetty," said John.

The path went down from the house to a pleasant little bay with a stone jetty, a very tempting place to bring a boat. But John had already looked across the water to the steep cliff on the other side. There, too, at the foot of the cliff he had seen a landing place, and had seen a track zigzagging up the cliff behind it. He pointed it out to Susan.

"No houses," said Susan. "And I can't see any people."

"Let's go out on the jetty," said Titty.

"Don't leave the trees," said John. "We don't want to be seen by anybody till we've seen what they're like."

"We'll bring our things into the house," said Susan.

"All right," said John. "Let's go and get them. Where's Roger?"

They turned back and met Roger coming out of the house.

"I've put in that line she didn't know," he said. "She ought to be jolly pleased. I've done the picture too."

"Roger!" exclaimed Susan. "In someone else's book."

"I haven't made a mess of it," said Roger. "She'd have put it in herself if she'd known it."

Susan hurried up the steps and into the house. John and Titty followed her. The dictionary lay open. The rhyme on the flyleaf was now complete:

"Hic liber est meus,
Testis est deus
Si quis furetur
Per collum pendetur."

and then in Roger's handwriting:

"Like this poor cretur"

There was a picture underneath it.

"Have you got an indiarubber, Titty?" asked Susan, grimly.

"My pencil's a copying one," said Roger.

Hic liber est meus
Testis est deus
Si quis furetur
Per collum pendetur
Like this poor cretur

"So it is," said Susan, bringing the dictionary to the front of the house where there was more light. "We can't ever get it out."

"It'll make an awful mess if you try," said Roger. "And anyway, I've done it very carefully." He looked sideways at his own drawing and could not help chuckling.

"But it's not your book," said Susan.

"Roger," said John. "You're not fit to be counted able seaman. You're just an ass. A silly ass, and you may have dished the lot of us. If that girl's cross about your making a mess in her book it'll serve you jolly well right. But it'll be beastly for all of us. It's done now. Come on and help to carry things."

No more was said about the dictionary, even by Roger, though for some time, until he forgot about it, he was telling himself that everybody was very unfair. It was a jolly good drawing, anyway, and anybody would be pleased to have it.

One journey was enough to bring from the boat everything they had saved from the *Wild*

Cat. John carefully stowed Captain Flint's sextant and the nautical almanac in a corner of the larger room. Susan began to arrange the sleeping-bags to turn the place into a dormitory. Roger, keeping well away from the table with the books, though he rather wanted to have another look at his drawing, prowled round, and Susan was just going to tell him to keep away from the cupboard when he brought out his hand with a small tin box he had found behind the kettle.

"What's this?" he said, opening it and sniffing. "Little squares of jelly."

"You're not to eat one," said Susan.

"Not going to," said Roger. "You may. It's methylated. Solid."

Susan took the box from him, sniffed at the little cubes and looked at the lid. "Meta Fuel," she read. "And it came from Singapore," she added looking at the label on the outside.

"They *must* be English people," said Titty.

"I'm going to make tea," said Susan. "If this stuff'll work for lighting the Primus."

"Somebody else's Primus," said Roger.

"That's altogether different," said Susan. "I'll clean it afterwards. If the people were here they'd make tea for us themselves."

"Hurry up," said John. "We ought to be looking out to sea."

"They'd better have a proper meal," said Susan.

Already she had shaken the Primus stove and found that it had some oil in it. She took two of the little cubes of Meta and put them in the place for the methylated spirit. She found a cleaner and cleaned the nozzle. She put a match to the Meta. The little cubes melted and turned into something exactly like spirit, with a blue dancing flame. They watched till the flame began to die down, when Susan closed the valve and gave a few strokes with the pump. The Primus started up with a joyful roar.

"What about water?" said Roger.

"Quick, quick. Go and look for it," said Susan.

"There's a trickle running down by their landing place," said John. He took the kettle and ran off. He brought it back full. "It's fresh all right," he said. "There must be a spring somewhere."

Ten minutes later the kettle had boiled and Susan was making tea by dropping in a handful of tea-leaves and stirring them round with the spike of her scout-knife. John was opening a tin of pemmican from the box of iron rations. Titty was getting out the biscuits. "Two each," said Susan over her shoulder. Roger was counting the slabs of chocolate that were left.

"We've left the mug in *Swallow* with the water-beaker," said Titty.

"Two cups here," said Susan.

"Jolly little ones," said Roger.

"Big enough," said Susan.

"And someone else's," said Roger. "Like the Primus, and the methylated, and the tea, as well as that beastly dictionary."

*

There were no spoons, knives or forks in the cupboard but only a bundle of chopsticks, which set them wondering again whether the owners of the house were English or Chinese. But they had not had a square meal since they had eaten curry and sucked oranges in the shade of the *Wild Cat*'s mainsail. Fingers are as good as forks for putting food in hungry mouths, and not even John's hurry to get back to the seaward side of the island prevented the shipwrecked sailors from making a square meal now. John made a square meal himself, but long before the others had finished and Roger had said that he thought he could last for a bit after that, John had gone out to the verandah to see if he could see anybody moving on the cliff road or at the landing place across the water, and looked in two or three times to see if the others were ready.

"I'll just clean the Primus and the cups and the kettle," said Susan at last.

"Oh, look here, Susan," said John. "We ought to be watching already, and I've got to make sure there's nobody at the other end of the island. Leave the things till we come back."

"It won't take a minute," said Susan, and he knew that it was no good arguing.

"All right," he said. "Go along the path to the stone chair as soon as ever you're done. Keep together. I'll meet you there. I'm going round by the shore. . . . All right. I'll keep along the edge of the trees. Somebody's got to make sure, and it'll take longer if we all go. But do buck up."

"We'll be at the stone chair before you are," said Roger.

"I bet you will," said John. "No path the way I'm going."

And John had another look round the outside of the house and then, keeping as near the shore as he could without leaving the trees, set out to work his way northabouts round the island.

*

With John gone, Susan was in as much of a hurry as he had been. She posted Roger on the verandah to keep a look out in case anybody might be coming across from under the great cliff. Chinese or English, she did not want to have to deal with them alone. The moment everything was put away as nearly as possible as she had found it, she had a look round the room, thought of rolling up the sleeping-bags, decided that the dormitory effect was neater, put some chocolate in her pocket in case of need, and set off with Roger and Gibber, Titty and the parrot, along the path through the trees.

"I knew we'd get there first," said Roger as, once more, he sat himself in the big stone chair.

"It may take him a long time to get round," said Susan, already listening for the noise of John forcing his way through the trees.

"It's as if ships had never been invented," said Titty, looking out over the empty sea.

To the left a line of forest with a hill behind it ran out to a distant point. To the right and in front of them shimmering water stretched from below their feet to the horizon. There were no sails, no boats, no plumes of smoke from passing steamships. It was hard to believe that only yesterday they had been somewhere out there watching the end of the *Wild Cat* and that even now, somewhere out there, Nancy and Peggy and Captain Flint must be afloat in *Amazon*, sailing in to look for *Swallow*, unless indeed they had been picked up by a liner on the way to Shanghai or Yokohama or Hong Kong.

They did not hear John's coming until the moment he came.

"Jolly good Indianing," said Roger.

"I've been right round," said John. "Nobody on the island. No more paths. Only that one coming here from the house. So that's all right. It looks as if there's a creek or something between that cliff and the land over there where there's a lot of forest between the hills and the shore. You can see the trees along the shore, looking pretty far away, and then the cliff, and the trees at the bottom of the cliff look much nearer. But you can't be sure. I couldn't see any houses or people anywhere."

"What are we going to do?" said Susan.

"We've got grub," said John. "We're all right for a bit. What we've got to do is to keep a look out. As soon as Captain Flint saw we'd gone he'd guess what had happened. He'd know just which way we'd drift. He'd have a shot at coming after us. He's got a compass. He wouldn't want the sextant for that. . . . Gosh, I wish I'd remembered it when we were towing him to *Amazon*. Of course the other thing is, *Amazon* may have started drifting too. They may be quite near. They may be sailing along the coast looking for us."

"Pretty awful if they sailed past," said Titty.

"We've just got to keep a look out," said John.

"It's a lovely wind now if they're sailing *Amazon*," said Titty.

"Gone north-easterly," said John. "There's no

swell any more. We're sheltered by that point. But it's a good wind to bring them in."

"We may see them any minute," said Susan.

"But if they were picked up by a liner like Captain Flint said?" asked Roger.

"They couldn't do much till they got to port," said John. "But he'd know just where to look for us as soon as he could get a tug or something."

"Any ship we see may be them," said Roger, looking out eagerly to sea where there were no ships at all.

"Couldn't they wireless to coastguards?" said Susan.

"There won't be coastguards here," said John. "Anyhow, we're all right. We've got grub. We've got that house to sleep in. We'll just hang on and keep a look out all the time it's light."

"But the people the house belongs to may come back," said Susan.

"With luck they won't," said John. "And they may be decent if they do. But it'll be much better if Captain Flint and the others find us first."

All day they watched from the rock with the stone chair. As the day wore on and the sun moved round it was easier to look out over the sea. They grew sleepy, and each took a turn at being coastguard while the other three lay down in the shade close by. It was hard to keep awake after that night of tossing in the *Swallow*, but it was almost as hard to keep asleep. Birds, butterflies, the restless Gibber and worried dreams woke them one after another. The day wore on. The sun passed overhead and began to dip towards the land. Hour after hour they watched. The swell had gone. The sea was no more than rippled by a wind that would have suited *Amazon*. But the hours passed and there was never a sign of her.

It was not until nearly dusk that they saw a sail.

Roger, sitting in the stone chair was the first to see it. He jumped up and stood on the chair.

"Sail-ho!" he shouted. "Wake up, John!"

Everybody was awake in a moment. Roger was pointing.

"Brown," said Titty. "It's not *Amazon*."

John had the telescope. "Three masts," he said. "It's only a junk. . . . Coming this way," he added a moment later. "It's nearer that point than it was."

"If it's a junk we don't want to be seen," said Susan.

"You never know," said John. "We'd better lie low. . . . It *is* coming in."

"It's going to be dark in a minute," said Susan. "We ought to get back while we can see the path."

"All right," said John. "Hang on just a minute. She's sailing right along that shore. There must be a creek where I thought. There may even be a harbour."

"No lighthouses or buoys," said Titty.

"There must be something in there or that junk wouldn't be coming in."

"We shan't be able to see if we wait any longer," said Susan.

It was already growing dark. The brown sails of the junk were moving slowly against a green background of forest.

"She's coming in all right," said John.

"Hullo! They're hanging up lanterns," said Titty.

"Come along," said Susan. "Come on, Titty. Shall I carry Polly? Don't let Gibber go off again."

They took a last look at the junk, and then, a little downhearted just because it was a junk and not *Amazon*, thinking of Captain Flint, Nancy and Peggy, still drifting about at sea, or being carried in a liner further and further away, they hurried back along the shadowy path. They came to the house. Susan groped for the hurricane lantern. John was ready with a match.

"Keep the lantern right at the back," said John. "So that nobody could see it from the mainland."

Susan took the lantern to the table and nearly dropped it. "Roger!" she cried. "What have you done with those books?"

"I haven't touched them," said Roger. "You touched them last when you said I oughtn't to have put in that picture."

"They've gone," said Susan.

They looked hurriedly round. Everything else was exactly as they had left it but the Virgil, the dictionary and the exercise-book had disappeared.

"Someone's been here and taken them," said Titty.

"It couldn't be Gibber," said Roger. "He's been with me all the time."

"Someone's been," said John. "Someone knows we're here." He ran out and stared into the darkness towards the great cliff. There were no lights to be seen.

Suddenly, almost as if from behind the cliff, there was a sharp bang, followed by another and another, and then by a whole lot. The others ran out.

"What's that?" cried Titty. "Fighting?"

"Guns," said Susan.

"It's like the Fifth of November," said Roger.

"Firecrackers," said John. "There *must* be a harbour somewhere in there. It's that Chinese junk coming home. Good catch of fish or something. That's all her friends giving her a welcome. Gosh! I wish I knew who took those books."

"We can't do anything about it," said Susan. "They haven't touched our things. Ration of sardines all round. Ration of dates. And then bed. Nobody'll come now. But we'll have to be ready for them in the morning."

CHAPTER VI

IT'S THEM!

THEY woke soon after dawn after a restless night. Wriggling their bones because a sleeping-bag is not much of a mattress when you sleep on a wooden floor, they scrambled up, and remembered the visitor they had not seen.

"It's no good looking at the table," said John. "The books have gone."

"I thought perhaps I'd dreamed it," said Titty.

"I wish you had," said John. "What I can't understand is why whoever it was didn't touch anything else."

"Somebody get the kettle filled," said Susan, who was already busy with the Primus.

Roger was off in a moment. John and Titty followed him, round the queer Chinese house where they had slept, and down among the trees towards the place where John had found that trickle of fresh water. Roger running ahead with the kettle, stopped short and came darting back.

"Man in a boat," he said. "Coming this way."

"Crouch!" said John, and all three of them dropped into hiding.

"What sort of a man?" whispered Titty.

"There he is," whispered Roger. "Look at his hat."

The man was sitting in the stern of a long, brown punt. He was not hurrying. Working a paddle only now and then, he was moving crabwise across the channel between their island and the great cliff on which the morning light showed up that climbing track. His hat, yellow and round, going up to a point in the middle, seemed as big as an umbrella. Along the gunwale of his punt was a row of ten or a dozen black lumps. Suddenly one of them stirred and spread and shook black wings.

"Cormorants," breathed Titty.

Just then, close to the punt, they saw the long head and neck of a cormorant with a fish in its beak showing above the water. The bird came alongside, and the fisherman scooped it into the punt with a net.

"He's emptying it," said Roger, as they saw the fisherman holding the cormorant while another three or four fish fell from its open beak.

"There's another," said Titty.

"'Sh!" said John.

Another cormorant came up by the punt, was scooped out, emptied and set on the gunwale to flap and dry its wings. The punt was coming nearer. The fisherman laid down his paddle, prodded over the side with a long bamboo, found bottom and began poling his punt over the shallows close along the island shore.

John made up his mind.

"He's harmless enough," he said. "Just a fisherman."

"He might give us some of those fish," said Roger.

"He doesn't look as if he knew English," said Titty.

"He isn't a pirate, anyway," said John. "I'm going to hail him. Come on."

They stood up.

"Ahoy!" called John.

There was a sharp echo from the opposite cliff. The fisherman, standing in the stern of his punt, slowly poling it along, looked at the cliff, looked towards the island and saw John, Titty and Roger standing there and waving to him.

The punt swayed violently. For a moment they thought the fisherman was going to capsize her. He shouted something. He steadied himself, shouted again and, instead of bringing his punt in, drove it into deeper water, dropped his pole, took his paddle and paddled away as if for his life.

"Ahoy! Ahoy!" shouted John and Roger.

"We're friends," shouted Titty.

He only paddled the faster.

"What's he frightened about?" said Roger.

"Did you hear what he shouted?" asked Titty.

"Something or other in Chinese," said John.

"He said something about Missee Lee," said Titty. "I heard 'Missee Lee' quite plainly, twice."

"You couldn't have, really," said John. "When people talk a foreign language it sounds just like one long gabble."

"No need to hide now," said Roger. "Let's go out on the jetty."

They went out there, and stood watching the fisherman until he was out of sight.

"Do you think he took the books?" said Roger.

"I don't believe he knew anybody was here," said Titty.

"The person who took the books," said John, "may have come from straight across. You can

CORMORANT FISHER

see there's a landing place. Or he may have come from the same place as that fisherman."

"It wasn't a he," said Roger. "Look at this." He held out a long tortoiseshell pin with a green knob on the end of it. "It was lying just here. She must have dropped it getting into her boat."

"Sort of hairpin," said John. "Look here. Susan'll be raging. What about that water?"

They filled the kettle and took it back to Susan and told her what had happened, and showed her the pin.

"Which way did he go?" asked Susan.

John pointed. "He went across and then along under the cliff. He'll have gone to that harbour round the corner, where people were letting off fireworks last night."

"Oh well," said Susan. "He'll tell the harbour people, and they'll send a boat." She put the kettle on the stove. "John, you open three tins of sardines."

"It was somebody else took the books," said Roger, looking at the pin with its big green knob.

"We'll put it on the table where the books were," said Titty. "So that she'll find it when she comes again."

"You know what it means?" said John, licking sardine oil from his fingers before going on to pemmican and dates. "Some of us'll have to stay here, in case people come."

"They're sure to now," said Titty, "when the cormorant fisher tells them he's seen us."

"I know," said John. "But what about looking out for *Amazon?* Some of us'll have to keep watch on the other side of the island as well."

"Titty and Roger," said Susan at once. "If they see *Amazon* or anybody coming in from the sea they'll have plenty of time to slip back here for us. But if people come here, we've got to explain about using their house and the Primus and everything. At least I have. And if people come from the harbour John ought to be here to tell them where they ought to send a ship to look for the others."

"I'll stay here," said Roger.

"No good Titty being there alone," said John. "There ought to be two of you . . . one to signal to *Amazon* and one to bolt back and fetch us."

"Oh, all right," said Roger. "Three of us. I'll take Gibber."

"And I'll take Polly," said Titty, putting a fresh supply of parrot food in the feeding-box in the cage, and putting a handful in her pocket in case of need.

"Have a look at *Swallow* and see she's all right," John called after them as they went off along the path dappled with shadow and sunlight under the trees.

They came to Titty's blaze, now covered with dead butterflies and moths drowned in the syrup that had oozed out of the tree. Their own trail was clear enough. Anybody could see by the cut climbers and trampled undergrowth that people had passed that way. They hurried down to the cove to find *Swallow* lying as they had left her, except for a large green lizard with a blue head that was sunning itself on the gunwale.

"Regular dragon," said Roger. "Let's keep it."

But the lizard gave him no chance. There was a quick green flicker down the side of the boat and the lizard was gone.

"Come along," said Titty. "We'll see lots more and we ought to have been at the stone seat hours ago."

"We'll never see a bigger dragon than that," said Roger.

They forced their way back to the path and hurried on till they came to the stone seat.

"We needn't have hurried," said Roger. "There's nothing in sight."

There was a dead calm. The sun blazed on a deserted sea. Away to the left green forest and the long hill behind it was reflected in the glassy water. They lay by the stone chair, watching. The ship's parrot went on with its breakfast and Gibber was eating some green bananas from the tree that Roger had found when they landed. An hour passed, perhaps more. Suddenly, far away, they heard the beating of a gong and a faint noise of shouting.

"It isn't exactly harbour noises," said Titty.

"No cranes," said Roger. "And no dredger, and no pile-driver and nobody banging rust off the side of a ship."

"Just people," said Titty. "I wish we could see what they're like."

"We've seen one, anyway," said Roger. "That man with the cormorants. Gosh! I never thought we'd see anybody really fishing with them. Do you remember when we tried to be cormorants when we saw them on the lake?"

"That was a million years ago," said Titty. "It

was before the first time we went sailing in the *Wild Cat.*"

"Pretty beastly not having her any more," said Roger.

"Yes," said Titty.

"And having to go home in a steamer after all," said Roger. "But we've still got *Swallow.* And Nancy and Peggy have still got *Amazon.* And Captain Flint's still got the old houseboat."

"It isn't the same thing," said Titty.

"He'll buy another schooner, I bet," said Roger.

But Titty said nothing. *Swallow* and her crew were all right. They soon would be, anyway. But where were the others? What if no one had picked them up and all day yesterday and all night and even now *Amazon* was lying out there under the blazing sun, with no land in sight, and their rations getting shorter and the water getting used up. How did that poem go? "Water, water, everywhere, nor any drop to drink." John and Susan had never said that there was any danger. But she had seen their faces when they were talking to each other. She stared out to sea and shook her head because of a mist in her eyes. There was a blinding glare off the water. It was easier to look at the green trees and brown hills. . . .

"Ahoy!" she shouted suddenly at the top of her voice.

"What is it?" cried Roger, startled.

"Look, look," she almost whispered. "Is that *Amazon*, or isn't it?" She was tugging at her pocket to get out the telescope. "Over there. . . . Without her mast. . . . Between us and the trees."

Never had the telescope been so hard to focus. She got it right at last.

"It's them! It's them! I can see Peggy and Nancy. . . . But she isn't rowing. . . . She's paddling . . . . Captain Flint isn't there. She's paddling like mad. . . . But, I say, they're going away, not coming in. Stern first. There must be a current. Quick. Let's get *Swallow*. . . . No. . . . Roger. . . . I'll look after Gibber. You bolt for John and Susan. I've got to keep her in sight."

"Let me look," demanded Roger.

She grabbed Gibber's lead and gave Roger the telescope. Roger took one look through it, pushed it at Titty and was gone, elbows out, head back, running as if in a race at school.

Titty wriggled her arms into the canvas slings that let her carry the parrot-cage on her back and have her hands free. She stared through her telescope. Yes, there was *Amazon*, with Nancy frantically paddling, moving stern first out to sea.

"Ahoy!" Too far away. Peggy had her back to her and she could see by the splashes how Nancy was paddling. How soon would John be at the cove? He would want help to get *Swallow* out. It had taken all four of them to pull her up. But till the very last minute she must keep *Amazon* in sight. And then she saw that *Amazon* seemed nearer to that distant shore. Nancy must have worked her out of the worst of the current. She was no longer going backwards. She was getting nearer to those trees. And then, just as Titty heard John and Roger shouting together, *Amazon* disappeared. She had seen *Amazon* with the trees behind her. Now there were only trees. Creek or something, thought Titty, and, with her eyes on the place where *Amazon* had been, she remembered a dodge from old days. She took marks. "Coming! Coming!" she shouted. Just over that place was a tall palm-tree high above the rest, and over that there was a dip in the skyline of the hill behind the forest. She looked at them again to make sure and then, with the parrot-cage jolting on her back, the parrot screaming and Gibber scurrying and leaping beside her, she ran to join the others.

"Look here, Titty," said John, the moment she reached the little cove. "Are you dead sure? It wasn't only Roger who saw them?"

"You know what Roger is," said Susan.

"We both saw them," said Roger.

"I know it's them," said Titty. "Nancy and Peggy in *Amazon*. Something had gone wrong and Nancy was paddling her, not rowing. They were drifting stern first, but they worked her into the trees and then I couldn't see them any more."

"Have you got marks to find the place?"

"A tree and a dip on the skyline."

"That's all right. We'll go after them. You see there's something happening on the cliff. There were people on the top and then we saw them coming down. They'll be coming across."

"We can get back to meet them," said Susan. "Finding Captain Flint and the others matters most."

"We didn't see Captain Flint," said Titty.

"If you're dead sure you saw the others Captain Flint won't be far off. The same thing must have happened to them that happened to us. Perhaps we've been quite near each other all the time. Anyway, it'll be all right now. Get hold of the gunwale, opposite Roger. Susan and I'll take the stern. Now then. Lift!"

They all lifted together. "Come on," said John. "One more heave and we'll have her afloat."

Swallow's stern was floating. Her stem still rested on the shore. They climbed aboard, Titty first with the parrot-cage, then Susan, then Gibber, then Roger, and, last of all, John pushed her off and came in over the bows as she floated away.

"Rowlocks!" said John. "Oh, well done, Roger. You come in the bows now and look out for rocks."

"Oh bother," said Titty. "If only it wasn't a dead calm."

"Can't be helped," said John.

"Let me take an oar," said Susan.

"I'll get her clear first," said John. Already he was turning her round and working her slowly out of the cove. "No good getting her stove in," he said to himself, "and not getting there at all."

Outside the cove he rowed along the island shore to put her near the place where the stone seat was, so that Titty could pick up her marks exactly as she had seen them first.

"There's the stone chair," said Roger.

"Now, Titty," said John.

"Not in line yet," said Titty. "The dip in the skyline's a long way right of the tree."

John rowed on.

"Getting nearer," said Titty. "They're coming into line. . . . Now."

"We'll keep them so," said John. "You watch them and be compass. If you'll take an oar, Susan, we'll heave her along. I'll row in the bows. Roger, you go aft. Susan on the middle thwart. And do keep Gibber out of the way."

In another moment they were ready. "Now then, Susan," said John.

"I say," said Titty, after a few minutes, "it looked as if there was a pretty strong current between us and that shore."

"You watch the marks," said John. "You'll soon see if we're being swept off our course."

"What sort of people were coming down the cliff?" asked Roger.

"Couldn't see," said John. "You had the telescope."

"How many people?"

"Don't know."

"More than one?"

"Yes."

"More than two?"

"Don't talk," said John. "We've got to row."

"Well, how many?"

"A good lot," said John.

"Forty or fifty," said Susan. "And there was a lot of queer whistling."

"That fisherman's stirred them up," said Roger. "Or it may be the person who took those books and saw that Susan had been using their Primus."

"They'll know we're coming back," panted Susan. "We've left our sleeping-bags and things."

"Pull, Susan," said Titty. "The gap's slipping away from the tree."

"Current," said John, looking at Titty's hand, which, like a compass needle was pointing always in one direction, towards the place where *Amazon* had disappeared into those distant trees.

"Pull, Susan," said Titty again.

"Never mind about the compass-pointing," said John. "No good if we're in a current. We'll have to go crabwise. You just keep telling us when the marks are in line and when they're not."

"They're not," said Titty. "The gap's open to the right. It's still moving to the right. . . . Now it's stopped. . . . Now it's moving to the left. . . . In line."

"It's going to be a pretty tough pull," said John.

"They'll see us coming and wait for us," said Roger.

"They won't go far from *Amazon*," said Titty.

"It's going to take a long time," said John. "Those people coming down the cliff are going to be on the island before we get back."

"It doesn't matter," said Susan. "Nothing matters, if only we're all together again."

"I bet they thought we were drowned," said Roger.

"Gap's moving away again," said Titty. "Pull, Susan."

"Hullo," cried Roger. "I can see that junk that came in last night. There's a river in there."

"That's why there's a current," panted John.

"There's a sort of square tower a bit above the junk," said Roger. "And one on the other side. . . . And more junks further in. But, I say, I can't see anything like a harbour."

"No, don't look, Susan. Keep on pulling," said John.

"How are the marks?" he asked a few minutes later, seeing Titty glancing away from them towards the mouth of the river.

"All right," said Titty, finding them again. "In line, I mean."

"They might wave a flag or something," said Roger.

"Perhaps they haven't seen us yet," said Titty. "What'll they say when they do?"

"I know what Nancy'll say," Roger grinned.

"What?"

"Barbecued billygoats," said Roger.

"Oh, do shut up," said John, and even Roger, looking at the sweat pouring down John's face, was silent for a long time. He looked at Susan. She was rowing with her eyes shut, pulling, pulling with all her weight.

"Let us row for a bit," said Titty.

"No," said Susan.

"The gap's open to the left," said Titty.

"Good," said John. "We must be getting out of the current. Easy a bit, Susan. Nearly there. Can you see where they went in?"

"Not yet."

At last they were able to head straight for the shore. With every moment they were nearer to the trees.

"I can't see the dip in the hill any longer," said Titty. "Only trees. But I can see where they went."

John looked over his shoulder. "I'll paddle in," he said. "Well done, old Susan. Roger, you go to the bows again."

"Good," said Roger.

"Mangoes," said John. "Pretty nearly awash. We've been a long time. Bother that beastly current."

Already he was rowing in between queer huge-leaved trees. There was a din of insects.

"*Amazon* ahoy!" shouted Roger. "There she is. But there's no one in here."

"They'll be close to," said Susan.

"Let's do a hail all together." said Roger.

"Wait just a minute," said John.

Swallow slid on into the little creek where *Amazon* was lying, her painter fast to a tree and her stem pulled up on swampy ground.

"Can't we find a drier place to land?" said Susan. "Look at the holes they've made with their feet."

"They must have been in a hurry," said John. "There's a better place. Take your shoes off, Roger.

"They *are* off," said Roger indignantly. He had begun taking them off as soon as he had seen where *Amazon* was tied up.

"Ready, now." John gave a hard pull. They felt *Swallow's* keel sliding through soft mud. She stopped. Roger jumped clear and landed on a huge tree-root. He grabbed her bows. In another moment John too was ashore and looking at *Amazon*.

"They've taken their oars," he said. "Hidden them probably."

"Nancy wasn't rowing," said Titty.

"She must have lost her oars," said John. "Using a bottomboard. Look at the mud on it. She must have done that coming in here."

Susan and Titty came ashore.

"You can see where they went," said John. "Funny. No hoofmarks of Captain Flint. But a lot of others. Barefooted."

"He wasn't with them," said Titty. "They'll have gone to fetch him."

"That's the way they went," said John. "There are their tracks. They've gone along the shore. Towards the mouth of the river." He thought a moment and made up his mind. "Look here, we'll go after them. Titty and Roger stay here and look after both boats."

"Oh, I say," said Roger.

"Somebody's got to."

"Much better," said Susan. "And there's Gibber and Polly. Look after the boats between you. We'll bring the others. We'll have to go back to the island, anyhow, to fetch our things and explain about using that house."

"Aye-aye, sir," said Titty.

"But be quick," said Roger. "We want to see them too." John and Susan, following the tracks in the soft ground, hurried off and were instantly out of sight among the trees.

CHAPTER VII

THE SHADOW OF A MONKEY

FOR a long time, Roger and Titty did as they had been told. They tidied up *Amazon* and put her bottomboards back into place after cleaning the mud from the one that had been used as a paddle. Roger put his shoes on. They hung about, listening and waiting in the green shadow of the trees where they could see almost as little as if they had been shut up in a room.

"Look here," said Roger at last. "This is a bit hard on Gibber. He'd like to explore and I don't see why we shouldn't so long as we stay close to the boats."

"They'll be back any minute," said Titty. "They must have found the others by this time."

"We'll hear them coming," said Roger.

"We must keep close to," said Titty.

"Just far enough to find some more bananas for Gibber," said Roger.

"Hi, wait a minute," said Titty. "I can't leave Polly. Help me to hitch his cage on. It's all very well for you with two spare hands."

Roger held the cage while Titty wriggled her arms through the carrying loops. Then, with the cage on her back and both hands free to push aside bamboo shoots and the clinging tendrils of the climbing plants, she followed Roger. The two boats were well tied up. There could be no harm in going just a few yards from the shore.

It might be the only chance of exploring just here. Susan had said that as soon as they had found the others, they would be going back to the island.

"Don't let's go any further," said Titty almost as soon as the boats, left behind them, were hidden by the tall undergrowth.

"Let's find somewhere to sit down," said Roger. . . . "No, Gibber. To heel!" He gave a gentle tug at the monkey's lead, and Gibber seemed to understand and kept close to his master.

They stopped where a sort of pine tree had shed its needles on the ground and so had made a little clearing round itself.

"This'll do," said Titty. "No further." She began to wriggle out of the loops of the parrot-cage. With one shoulder free, she stopped and listened.

"They're coming back," said Roger, and put a hand to his mouth to shout "Ahoy!"

"Sh!" said Titty. "Don't yell. That's not the way they went. We'd better get back to the boats."

"People, anyway," said Roger. "Quite near. I'll just scout and see."

Titty wriggled the loose loop back on her shoulder and followed Roger and the monkey.

"Come on," said Roger over his shoulder, pushing his way through the undergrowth.

"I don't believe we ought," said Titty.

They heard voices again.

"It's not them," said Titty. "Come back."

"I must just see," said Roger.

"Roger," said Titty, but did not dare to shout, or even to talk above a whisper. Bother Roger. She pushed after him, and almost fell over him, crouching with Gibber at the very edge of the belt of forest. She dropped beside him.

They were looking out on open country, with rocks and tussocks of coarse grass, that stretched almost to the foot of the brown hill they had seen from far away rising above the trees. A long row of Chinese, twenty or thirty yards apart, were slowly moving forward, in hops, never standing up but getting along with bent knees, a hop, a crouching search for something, and then another hop. Their yellow bodies were naked to the waist. Their short blue trousers flapped above their ankles. They had wide conical hats like straw-coloured lampshades.

"Like yellow frogs," whispered Roger.

"Keep down," whispered Titty.

"Gosh, that one gave a good hop. Ow, look out. He's coming close by."

"Keep still."

"I am keeping still. Hop. There he goes again. Look at his shadow."

One of the Chinese, blue-trousered, straw-hatted, yellow-bodied, was no more than a dozen yards from the lurking watchers. He hopped, crouched and suddenly snatched into a tuft of grass and put something into a little yellow box that he had in his left hand. The sun was behind him and each time he hopped his queer black shadow flopped forward over the ground. He came on, crouching, hopping and snatching suddenly at the grass. Sometimes he seemed to get nothing. Sometimes, after a snatch, his right hand swept across to meet his left, and there was a sharp click as the little box closed on whatever it was he had put into it. Every moment Titty

TWO SHADOWS JERKED FORWARD

thought he was going to turn directly towards them. But he never turned. It was as if he had a line to follow. Beyond him was another Chinese doing exactly the same, and beyond him another and another.

He was only a few yards away. Titty could not bear to watch him. She held her breath and looked down at the ground where she was kneeling. Once let him get well past and, whatever Roger might say, they would go back through the forest to the shore and the boats. Suddenly she heard Roger gasp. She looked up and followed Roger's pointing finger.

"Got away," whispered Roger. "Lead and all."

Gibber, his lead trailing on the dry grass, was out in the open and following the Chinese. Gibber had found something new to copy. As the Chinese crouched, so did Gibber. As he hopped forward, so did Gibber. As he searched a tussock of grass the monkey did the same. And now, each time the Chinese hopped, not one but two shadows jerked forward over the ground.

Titty and Roger could not breathe. They could not shout to call Gibber back. They could do nothing. And the monkey, more and more interested, copying every movement of the man, was coming nearer and nearer to him, perhaps trying to see what it was that he ought to be snatching from the grass. Hop, hop. The leaping shadows were almost side by side. Hop, hop. They were almost touching. And suddenly the Chinese, crouching, searching, hopping, saw the monkey's shadow jerk forward with his own. He looked over his shoulder straight into Gibber's face, screamed, jumped up, dropped his little box and then, seeing what it was, made an angry grab at the monkey. Gibber was as startled as the man and jumped away. The man kicked at him, missed him, saw the lead trailing across the grass, set his foot on it, seized it and jerked the monkey backwards.

"Hi! Stop that! He's my monkey," shouted Roger, dashing to the rescue.

The man stared, caught Roger by the arm, looked round for his little box and found Titty facing him in a fury. "Let go of him at once," she said. The other hoppers and searchers were running towards them and in two minutes there were Chinese all round them, chattering, staring at them, fingering their clothes, and pointing at the green parrot in the cage on Titty's back.

Suddenly one of the Chinese pointed at himself. "One time number one boy," he said. "One time number one cook big steamer. Talkee English velly good. You Melican missee? Melican boy?"

"English," said Titty.

"Make him let go my monkey," said Roger.

The one-time cook spoke to the others, took Gibber's lead from the man who had caught him and gave it to Roger.

"You come talkee Taicoon Chang," he said.

There was nothing to be done but to obey and Titty and Roger found themselves hurrying along in the middle of the Chinese.

"What about the others?" said Roger. "And the boats?"

"I know, I know," said Titty. "They'll be pretty mad. But they'll see which way we've gone and Captain Flint'll know what to do."

"Shall I shout?"

"No," said Titty. "If they're friends there's no need and if they're enemies it's no good getting everybody grabbed as well as us."

"They've got an awful funny smell," said Roger.

"Just foreignness," said Titty.

"But pretty decent grins, some of them," said Roger. "What do you think they've got in those boxes?"

He touched the little bamboo box in the hand of one of the Chinese who was walking beside him.

"Berries?" he asked.

The man stared at him, but seemed to understand what he meant. He held the little box close to Roger's ear and shook it gently.

"Sounds like matches," said Roger.

The prisoners were being hurried along, not towards the mouth of the river, but in the opposite direction, towards the point that they had seen when looking out from the stone chair on the little island. They were moving over open country further and further away from the belt of forest that ran along the shore. The ground was rising. Presently they could see the glitter of water through the tops of the trees to their right, and suddenly straight ahead of them the ground fell sharply. They were looking down towards another belt of forest and beyond it the long line of the open sea. On the slope before them were some scattered pine-trees. Under the pine-trees there were men with cartridge-belts slung about their naked shoulders and rifles in their hands.

At the sight of them the Chinese who had captured Roger and Titty broke into a run, their prisoners with them. The men with rifles looked round and made angry gestures. The Chinese with Roger and Titty stopped running and went forward on tiptoe as if afraid to make the slightest noise. They came to the pine-trees. The guards who were standing about stared at Titty and Roger.

"Look at that chair," said Roger, pointing to a carved wooden chair with crimson cushions in it and long bamboo carrying poles at each side.

Suddenly they were looking down into a hollow, where was a group of about a dozen Chinese. There was a flood of bird-song, larks singing as if to see which could sing the loudest. They saw a lot of bamboo bird-cages. And then, as they came nearer they saw that the men standing round were respectfully watching a man in a pale blue robe with a blue skull cap that had a red button on the top of it. He was crouched low to the ground, whistling to something close in front of him.

The Chinese who had told them he had been a number one cook in a big steamer tiptoed nearer to Roger and whispered.

"What?" whispered Roger.

"Taicoon," whispered the man. "Taicoon Chang. Velly gleat man."

"What is a Taicoon?" whispered Roger.

"Chieftain, I expect," whispered Titty.

All the hoppers and searchers, except the one-time cook and the man who had been startled by Gibber's shadow, now began to hang back, and presently stopped. The other two tiptoed on with their prisoners until, close to the bird-cages, they joined the circle of men who were watching the Taicoon, Chang.

The Taicoon had his back to them and was taking no notice of anybody or anything except a nearly white canary, that was perched on a bare twig stuck into the ground. Two more such bare twigs, about a yard apart, were sticking up between the Taicoon and his canary. The Taicoon whistled softly and held out a finger with something on the tip of it.

Suddenly the canary fluttered from its twig to the next, a yard nearer to the Taicoon.

The onlookers breathed a sigh of admiration.

The Taicoon made a sharp movement with one hand behind his back and they were silent. He whistled again. The canary fluttered its wings and flew to the next twig. Again the Taicoon whistled, and the canary left its twig, flew to his finger, perched on it and took whatever it was that had been waiting there for it.

"Ah!" sighed the onlookers and the Taicoon looked round, his face alight with joy. He caught sight of Titty and Roger. The smile left his face. He made to stand up. Two of the others darted forward to help him to his feet. He scowled at them and stood up slowly, his eyes all the time on the canary that was sitting on his finger. He was the tallest man there. He put a question in Chinese. The one-time cook, and the man who had caught Gibber began talking both at once. He stopped them and signed to the one-time cook, who poured out a flood of Chinese, pointing now at Gibber, now at Roger and now at Titty.

Then he stopped talking and the other man

began. Suddenly he crouched on the ground and pointed to his shadow.

"He's telling how Gibber . . ." began Roger.

"Shut up," said Titty.

Suddenly she saw an angry frown on the face of the Taicoon.

"Look out, Roger," she cried. "Gibber . . ."

Just in time, Roger pulled at Gibber, who, at the end of his lead, was reaching towards one of the cages of singing larks. At that moment the Taicoon saw the parrot-cage on Titty's back. He said something, and Titty found two of the Chinese pulling at the cage. They could not very well take it from her because it was fixed on her back like a knapsack. She wriggled out of the loops, took the cage herself, and held it so as to let the Taicoon have a good view of the ship's parrot.

"Make him say something," said Roger.

Titty chirped at the parrot, and the parrot put its head on one side.

"Pretty Polly," said Titty.

"Pieces of eight," shouted the parrot.

"Very good bud," said the Taicoon, and then, seriously, "Where you come flom? My captain hide you?"

Titty was making up her mind how to answer him when the Taicoon, forgetting his question, pointed to the canary sitting on his finger and then to the door of the parrot's cage.

Titty opened it, and the parrot, using his beak as well as his claws, swung himself to the door and looked out. Titty offered her hand and the parrot stepped from the door of the cage to her forefinger.

The Taicoon beamed. Then he pointed at the twig on which the canary had been sitting at first. Titty made the parrot step from her finger to the twig. She looked round. The Taicoon beckoned and Titty went and stood beside him. The great man whistled just as he had whistled to his canary. The parrot opened and shut its wings two or three times, and suddenly flew away with a loud cheerful scream.

"Velly solly. Velly solly," said the Taicoon. His face had turned so melancholy that Roger for a moment thought he was going to cry. He was looking from one to another of his cages of larks as if he were trying to make up his mind to give one of them to Titty to make up for the loss of her parrot. "Velly, velly solly," he said again.

Titty was watching the ship's parrot. It flew up, a green flash in the sunlight, up and up, circled above the tops of the pine-trees and then, suddenly, swooped back, perched on Titty's hand, screamed "Pretty Polly!", put its head on one side, half closed an eye, and began to tidy the feathers of its breast.

"Ah!" sighed the Taicoon.

"Ah!" sighed all the other Chinese standing round.

Titty made up her mind. A man so interested in birds could hardly be an enemy. "Roger," she said, "I'm going to tell him about the others."

"Well, he talks English," said Roger.

"Please," said Titty. "Our brother and sister are somewhere over there. . . ."

"Blother and sister," said the Taicoon bird-fancier. "Blother," pointing at Roger. "Sister," pointing at Titty.

"No," said Titty. "Another brother and sister."

"Not your blother," said the Taicoon, putting his canary into its cage.

"Both my brothers," said Titty desperately. "And a sister. And the rest of us. . . . Two more girls. . . . Sisters. . . . And their uncle. . . ."

"Sister to both blothers?" said the Taicoon.

"Yes," said Titty. "But two other sisters . . ."

The one-time cook put in a word.

"You come from Melica?" asked the Taicoon.

"England," said Titty. . . . "And America. . . . We were ship-wrecked. Our ship was burnt. We were in two boats. . . ."

"Two ships?"

"Two boats . . . little boats. . . . We were in one and Captain Flint and the others, the two sisters, were in the other. We got ashore yesterday and today we saw them. . . . We came and found their boat. . . ."

At last the Taicoon seemed to understand. "Captain James Flint?" he said. "Velly fat man? Velly stlong man? Velly mad man? Two wives? Lord Mayor San Flancisco. Pick up at sea? I got him."

"Where? Where?" asked Titty.

"You see him plesently," said the Taicoon. "My plisoners. All together. Velly happy. And now we feed my buds. I take you with me. . . ." He beckoned, and a Chinese came and stood listening while the Taicoon spoke to him. While he listened the man was fingering a queer instrument like two bamboo flutes joined together. The moment the Taicoon had stopped speaking, the man put the instrument to his lips and began whistling on it, a queer high-pitched, ear-splitting whistling on two notes.

"He's signalling," said Roger.

The man stopped, and from up in the hills came an answer, a thin high whistling like a curlew far away.

The Taicoon had turned to his bird-cages. The one-time cook grinned. "Taicoon Chang velly kind man," he said. "He send for donks," and, to make his meaning clear put a hand to each of his ears and lifted them as if to show that his ears were very long.

"What's going to happen?" asked Roger.

"I think he's got Captain Flint and Nancy and Peggy," said Titty. "But it's no good talking. We'd better keep quiet."

"But what did he say about San Francisco? I thought . . ."

"Captain Flint's been up to something," said Titty. "You keep quiet. . . . And don't let Gibber get near those bird-cages."

"They've got some bananas," said Roger, pointing to a huge cluster of ripe bananas from which the Chinese were helping themselves. "And Gibber's pretty hungry. And so am I."

The Taicoon, wanting Titty to admire his birds, turned at that moment, saw where Roger was pointing and laughed. One of the men with rifles offered the bunch of bananas to Roger, who took one for himself and broke another off for Gibber. The Taicoon gave an order. One of the men who had been searching the grass handed him his little bamboo box. The Taicoon carefully opened the lid. Something showed over the edge. He took it between finger and thumb and offered it to the parrot.

"It's a grasshopper," said Roger. "Look out. Polly's dead sure to nip his finger."

But the parrot was more interested in the grasshopper. He cocked his head on one side, balanced himself on one leg on Titty's finger, reached out and took the grasshopper and put it in his beak. He spat it out the next moment.

Titty, seeing the Taicoon's disappointed face, was in a hurry to explain. "I'm very sorry," she said. "Polly didn't mean to be rude. He just isn't accustomed to grasshoppers. This is what he eats." The food-box in the parrot's cage was empty, but Titty dug in a pocket and brought out a handful of parrot food and showed it to the Taicoon.

The Taicoon looked at it, separating one seed from another and nodding his head. He pointed to his canary and to the millet seed in its feeding trough. Then he pointed to the grasshopper and shook his head. It was clear that the canary, like the parrot, was not an eater of grasshoppers. Titty with a question pointed to the larks. The Taicoon took a grasshopper from his box and in a moment one of the larks was gulping it down. Titty and the Taicoon smiled at each other. The Taicoon took a sunflower seed out of Titty's handful and offered it to the parrot. Titty's heart stood still for a moment, for she did not know how Polly might behave. But the parrot took the sunflower seed, and even allowed the Taicoon to scratch the small feathers at the back of its head. The Taicoon was delighted. He talked away in a sort of pidgin English of which Titty understood one word in ten, and Titty talked to him in English of which the Taicoon understood about one word in twenty. But this did not matter. There were the birds. In Titty, the Taicoon felt he had found another bird-fancier, and while Roger and Gibber were having a good time with the bananas, the Taicoon and Titty were moving from cage to cage feeding the larks and not exactly talking but somehow managing to show good will.

And then, suddenly, everything changed.

There was a new burst of whistling, this time not from the hills but from somewhere up the river, a loud insistent whistling.

"Missee Lee," said the Taicoon, stood up and looked at the man with the queer instrument who was standing rigid, listening.

The whistling stopped, and the man began talking to the Taicoon as if he were repeating a message. The Taicoon frowned and stared at Roger and Titty as if he were seeing them for the first time. The guards and the other Chinese were looking worried as if they had been found out in something they ought not to be doing.

"You go Missee Lee's island?" said the Taicoon.

"We were on an island," said Titty.

"You go Missee Lee's temple?"

"Was it a temple?" said Titty. "I'm sorry. We really didn't know."

"Missee Lee know evellything," said the Taicoon. "Tomollow you go see Missee Lee. Plisoners. All my plisoners go see Missee Lee tomollow. Why you go to Missee Lee's island?"

The far away whistling began again. The Taicoon stamped his foot and spoke to his own signaller. The moment the whistling stopped, the man whistled a short answer.

"Missee Lee know too much," said the Taicoon and then, with a flap of the hand as if to change the subject, he turned once more to the business of feeding grasshoppers to his larks.

"What's happened?" asked Roger when he got a chance.

"I don't know," said Titty. "But it's something to do with Missee Lee. That was her island we were on. And that house. . . ."

"Oh Gosh," said Roger. "And I drew a picture in her book."

CHAPTER VIII

TEN GONG TAICOON

THE day wore on. The Taicoon and his prisoners had drunk unsweetened tea from little bowls without handles and had eaten queer sticky sweetmeats handed round in a bamboo basket. The hoppers and searchers had been sent off again and had come back with fresh supplies of insects. More than once Titty had been on the point of asking the Taicoon to look for John and Susan, but had thought better of it. The Taicoon had said clearly enough that he had got Captain Flint, Nancy and Peggy. And then there had come that message that had made the Taicoon pretty cross, about Missee Lee wanting to see his prisoners. Did that mean that John and Susan had gone back to the island and that they were in Missee Lee's hands already? And who and what was Missee Lee, with her Virgil and her Latin-English Dictionary and her orders that the Taicoon had to obey? Titty gave it up. The Taicoon had said that they were going to see Captain Flint. He would know what to do and Titty decided to wait until she saw him. In the meantime there was nothing to be done but to keep the Taicoon in a good temper, and to hope that Captain Flint would turn up pretty soon. "Presently," the Taicoon had said, and that was a long time ago.

There was a sound of voices and running feet. Titty, who was letting the canary peck millet from her finger, looked hopefully up. "Here they are," she said, but over the edge of the hollow came not Captain Flint and the others but a lot of the hoppers and searchers together with two men who were leading a couple of donkeys with wide wooden saddles, painted in red and blue and gold and hung with leather tassels.

There was a general stir. The Taicoon got to his feet. The grasshopper hunters were picking up the bird-cages. The guards were slinging their rifles on their backs. Four bearers were bringing the carved chair with the crimson cushions down into the hollow. A man was busy unfurling something that looked like a banner.

The Taicoon bowed politely to Titty and pointed to one of the donkeys. He bowed to Roger and pointed to the other.

"Gosh!" said Roger, who knew a lot more about boats than about riding.

"We've got to do it," said Titty hurriedly. "And we've got to keep on somehow. They'd laugh like anything if we fell off."

She was just thinking about getting the parrot's cage on her back when the one-time cook took it from her. "Cally pallot," he said. The donkey was close beside her. She felt someone take hold of her by the ankle and the next moment she found herself hove into the air and sitting on the saddle. She looked round to see Roger also mounted, looking very grave, with his legs sticking straight out on either side. The Taicoon was sitting in his chair, his white canary in a cage on his knee. The man had unrolled his banner, green, with an orange tiger with black stripes prancing upon it. The one-time cook explained. "This Tiger Island," he said.

"Belong see plenty more buds," said the Taicoon and gave an order.

The procession was on its way, marching up out of the hollow. First went the man with the tiger banner. Then some of the guards with rifles. Then the grasshopper-hunters, carrying the bird-cages so that the Taicoon could keep his eyes on them. Then, four bearers carrying the Taicoon in his chair shoulder high. Then came Titty, clutching at the high pommel of the wooden saddle, with the one-time cook walking at the donkey's head carrying the ship's parrot in his cage. Then came Roger, on his donkey, led by another of the men. Gibber was running alongside at the end of his lead but thought better of it, caught hold of the donkey's tail and swung himself up behind Roger, gibbering angrily at the donkey which had only just missed him with a hind leg. Then came the rest of the guards. The Taicoon, Chang, of Tiger Island, was going home after giving his birds an outing.

They came up out of the hollow and marched across the open country towards the rocky shoulder of the hill. Presently they were moving along a well-marked track. Some of the Chinese started something that could not be called a song but was meant to help the feet. It was a sort of chant, something like the "Hi . . . yah . . . hee . . . yo . . ." of the coolies in the last port at which the *Wild Cat* had put in. But, though it may have helped the marching men, it did not ease the jolting of the donkeys. Titty found herself thinking in time with the chant, which was out of time with the jolting of her donkey. She began to wonder how soon she would have to roll out of that uncomfortable saddle just to keep her backbone still in one piece. She looked at Roger. He stared back with serious eyes. He could not manage a grin. He had just bitten his tongue.

The track came to the edge of the grass country and began to climb along the side of the hill. Keeping her teeth firmly clenched for fear of accidents, Titty, painfully jolting in her saddle, looked down on the strip of bare country to the belt of forest, to the water beyond it, to the great cliff beyond the water and the green speck of the little island where they had slept last night. She could see a wide river with faraway junks at anchor. Under the cliff, near the mouth of the river, was something like a fort, and on the nearer shore too there was a building on the water's edge partly hidden by the trees. Somewhere down there were John and Susan. Between the jolts she wondered what had happened to them? What had they thought when they came back to the boats and found that she and Roger had disappeared? Had they gone back to the island? Had they been found by Missee Lee? Had they made Missee Lee send out that whistling signal about prisoners? What would they be thinking? If only it had been possible to let them know that Captain Flint and the other two were somewhere close at hand. Oh well (jerk) Captain Flint (jolt) would be jolly (jerk) glad (jolt) to know that (jolt) none of them had been drowned. (Ow, she was nearly off that time.) But if only John and Susan were there too.

And then she saw them, two white specks moving on the scorched grassland far below.

"Ahoy," she shouted, with a hail that was meant to be a long one but was cut off short as a jolt of the donkey crashed her teeth together.

The Taicoon turned in his chair. The procession stopped.

"It's John and Susan," cried Titty, "down there."

"Ahoy," yelled Roger.

One of the small white figures waved a hand.

"Our brother and sister," explained Titty to the Taicoon.

The Taicoon frowned. He gave an order, and two of his guards, their rifles swinging on their backs, went off, leaping and running, straight down the side of the hill. The four bearers lowered his chair and stretched themselves on the ground. The others rested, watching the two white figures walking side by side to meet the guards. The brown figures of the guards and the white figures of John and Susan met. The four came together to the foot of the hill and began climbing the steep slope to the road where the procession was waiting for them.

"Not tly to lun away," remarked the Taicoon.

"Of course not," said Titty. "They've seen us." And then the dreadful thought struck her that perhaps she had made a mistake in pointing them out. But no. Nothing was worse than not being all together.

John and Susan, with the two guards, were climbing wearily up towards the road. Their faces were covered with dust except where they were streaked with sweat.

"Oh Roger, Roger," panted Susan. "And Titty

. . . .” John went straight up to the Taicoon. “Please,” he said. “We want help at once. A man and two girls have been captured by pirates. . . .”

The Taicoon stared at him, not understanding.

“But he's got them himself,” said Titty. “We're going to see them now.”

“But we've seen them,” said John. “They were carrying Captain Flint along in a cage like a hen-coop, and Nancy and Peggy had their hands tied behind their backs. And our boats have gone. . . .”

“You been Missee Lee's island,” said the Taicoon.

“That *was* her dictionary,” said Roger. “And her Primus.”

“Plisoners,” said the Taicoon briefly. “You see Missee Lee tomollow.” And then, suddenly, a new idea struck him. “More buds?” he asked, looking to see if John and Susan were carrying parrot-cages on their backs. “No buds,” he said sadly, and then, “Melican?”

“English,” said John.

“San Flancisco, Melican,” said the Taicoon, frowning, gave an order and set the procession once more on its way.

“Susan,” said Roger, “would you like to ride my donkey?”

“No,” said Susan. “We've walked miles and miles looking for you and we may as well go on now. Why didn't you stay where we left you?”

“Never mind that now,” said John. “If they had they'd only have been bagged by the people who took the boats.”

CHANG AND HIS PRISONERS

There was not much talking among the prisoners. Titty and Roger, on the jolting donkeys, dared not open their mouths and John and Susan were too tired and bothered to answer questions that had not been asked. But, when the road stopped climbing and over the top of the hill began to dip and they caught a glimpse of forest, and water below them, and walking was not such hard work, Titty and Roger learnt something of what had happened to the others. They heard how John and Susan had come almost to the fort at the riverside only to see Captain Flint and the others going up into the hills as prisoners. They heard how they had seen a fleet of small boats coming down the river, how there had been a lot of strange whistling, how they had seen boats round the little island they had left and how on coming back they had found *Swallow* and *Amazon* gone and how they had spent hour after hour searching, half thinking Titty and Roger had been taken with the boats, half hoping to find them because of their tracks in the belt of forest. They heard how in the end John had decided that the only thing to do was to follow Captain Flint and give themselves up, and then, how they had hoped, when they saw Titty and Roger on donkeys, that they had fallen among friends.

"Tiger Town," said the one-time cook walking at the head of Titty's donkey. The road was dropping from the rocky bare hillside towards green rice fields and bamboo woods. They could see a brown wall and green roofs.

"Not much like a town," said Roger.

The procession broke into a trot, the men running, John and Susan wearily running with them, Titty and Roger painfully jolting on their wooden saddles. Another road joined the one they were on, which now ran straight between the rice fields to a high brown gateway in the wall. As the man with the tiger banner passed under the gateway, the procession slowed to a walk, and a great gong or bell boomed overhead. Boom. . . . Boom. . . . Boom . . . . Four, five, six, seven, eight, nine, ten. . . . Men with rifles presented arms.

"That must be a salute," thought Titty. "Head of everything?" she asked, pointing to the Taicoon, swaying before her in his chair. The one-time cook did not understand her. "King?" said Titty. "General?"

The one-time cook looked almost frightened. He shook his head. "Chang, velly gleat man," he said. "Chang, ten gong Taicoon. But. . . ." He lowered his voice . . . "Missee Lee number one. Missee Lee, twenty-two gong Taicoon."

"Is she here?" asked Titty.

The one-time cook shook his head.

"Look at that," cried Roger. "And I thought we'd never see a bigger one."

Titty looked round, saw where Roger was pointing, and in her surprise, almost forgot the pains of donkey-riding. The huge head of a dragon was lying, as it were, on one cheek, just inside the gateway. Two men were working on it with a paint-pot, brightening up the red paint. Another was sticking silver scales on its neck. A row of women were busy stitching at something like a carpet that was stretched along under the wall.

The one-time cook laughed. "Makee dlagon shipshape," he said, "Leady for Dlagon Feast."

"It's for a carnival," said John. "I've seen pictures."

But, if the dragon interested the prisoners, they themselves were much more interesting to everybody else. Only one man stuck to his work with the paint-pot. The other and the women, who had been sitting at their work, got up and followed them. Children playing in the dust raced after them, pushed close to the donkeys and tried to touch the prisoners.

"It's like being a circus," said Roger.

They went on through the green-roofed village to another gateway.

"Taicoon Chang's yamen," said the one-time cook.

Again a gong sounded ten times. Men with rifles ran out to meet them. They passed through into a dusty courtyard with one-storey houses all round it. At the far corner of the yard a small crowd was standing before one of the houses. A man in a black skull-cap, with a revolver slung from a belt about his middle, left the crowd and came to speak to the Taicoon, who was getting out of his chair which had been set down before a large house on the opposite side of the courtyard. The Taicoon, listened and pointed to his prisoners. The grasshopper hunters were carrying the bird-cages into the house. The Taicoon, with his canary, turned to follow them. He stopped a moment and spoke to Titty.

"He show you San Flancisco," he said, nodding towards the crowd. "Then we go hear my buds. No belong sing when sun go down." He turned away and went up the steps into the house.

The man with the revolver beckoned and walked across the courtyard. John, Susan, Titty and Roger followed him. He shouted an order and the crowd made room, though hands shot out from all sides to feel the prisoners' clothes. They were looking at a grille or iron bars, like the front of a cage at the zoo. For a moment they could see nothing behind the bars, but then, looking into the darkness at the back, they saw Captain Flint, sitting on the ground, asleep, with his back against the wall.

"Hey! Captain Flint!" cried Titty.

Captain Flint opened his eyes, leapt to his feet and in a moment was at the bars.

"Gosh!" he said. "You got ashore all right. John, Susan, Titty, Roger. All the lot of you. Bless my soul and I haven't had a minute without wondering what I was to say to your mother. That fine lad, standing behind you, picked us up and wouldn't stop to look for you. And it blew that night. Were you picked up by another of'em? We're in a fix yet, but who cares what happens now?"

"Where are Nancy and Peggy?" asked John.

"In the lock-up," said Captain Flint.

"Hi! Captain!" Nancy's voice came from somewhere close by. And then, "Barbecued billygoats! Jibbooms and bobstays. Ten thousand million cheers! Shiver my timbers! KEEP STILL, PEGGY! It's the Swallows. Here."

The Chinese with the revolver was smiling upwards. They looked up and saw Nancy's face behind the bars of a small square window above their heads.

"Where's Peggy?" said Roger.

"You can't see her just for a minute," said Nancy. "I'm standing on her shoulders. Don't jiggle about," she added, looking down. "It's the Swallows, the whole lot of them. . . . Ow!"

Nancy vanished.

"Peggy, you tame galoot, I nearly broke my leg."

"Well, let me see." They heard Peggy's voice.

A moment later they saw her face at the window, but not for long. By the way that Peggy's face was bobbing up and down they could tell that Nancy was not keeping very still.

"Didn't I tell you she'd say 'Barbecued billy-goats'?" said Roger.

"Ask them how they got here." They heard Nancy's voice.

"We landed on an island," said Roger.

"We did lots better." They heard Nancy's voice again. "We got picked up by pirates. We were in a pirate fight. Oh, look here, Peggy, I can't tell them unless I can see their mugs. . . ."

Peggy disappeared, and a moment later Nancy was at the window again, explaining. "Guns. . . . A battle. . . . Captain Flint had a row with them because they wouldn't stop to look for you. They knocked him out. That's our captain . . . the captain of the junk. They left us in the junk all night and we got away in *Amazon* . . . we didn't mean to but . . . well, somebody forgot to make a clove hitch. . . . We just drifted away. . . ."

"We saw you," said Roger.

"And then we got caught again and they

brought us here. They carried Captain Flint in a cage."

"But he's still in a cage," said Titty.

"That one was worse," said Captain Flint from behind his bars.

"What are we going to do?" said Susan.

"Look here," said Captain Flint, talking fast, and almost in a whisper. "If they ask you questions, the pirates, don't tell them too much." His face was close to the bars. "You keep mum."

"They said you were Lord Mayor of San Francisco," said Roger.

"And so I am," said Captain Flint, and whispered again. "It's a good long way off. Take some time for them to send a message there to ask for a ransom. We don't want them trying Hong Kong and having some fool of a consul cabling home and stirring up your mothers."

"But we'll get home," said Susan.

"Of course we will," said Captain Flint. "We'll be all right now we're all together."

Roger suddenly shook a bar of Captain Flint's cage. "Why don't you let him out?" he said angrily to the junk captain with the revolver.

The junk captain looked grave. "Him mad," he said. "Him velly too much stlong. Him velly near kill my sailor."

"Gosh!" said Roger, and looked with a new respect at Captain Flint.

"Look at the little beasts," said Nancy from her window. "Shiver my timbers but I'd like to get a hand on them."

Three small Chinese boys were standing just far enough from the bars to make it impossible for Captain Flint to reach them. All three were doing the same thing, grinning from ear to ear and hitting the backs of their necks with the edge of a hand. At that moment they thought of something better. One did a good imitation of chopping off his fingers. Another bent his head while the third swung his arm up and brought down his hand, edgeways, as if to cut off the other's head.

"Little beasts," growled Nancy. "They've been doing that sort of thing ever since we got here."

"Just cheering us up," said Captain Flint. He roared like a tiger and the three small boys started back and then, keeping safely out of reach, went through their performance again.

"Look here, Skipper," said Captain Flint, looking at the man with the revolver, the one whom Nancy had called "our" captain. "When are you going to let us out?"

The man smiled gravely and put a hand to his ear.

"Look here, Captain, dash it all, Admiral if you like, when are you going to let us out?"

"Talkee English, bimeby," said the captain.

"That's all we can get out of him," said Nancy.

"And I couldn't get much more out of the big boss with the bird," said Captain Flint. "Wish I'd picked up more Chinese when I was fooling about in Java years ago. There's something funny about this lot. The big boss wasn't more than half pleased with the captain for bringing us along last night. He was thinking of getting rid of us out of hand until I told him who I was."

"Lord Mayor," murmured Titty.

"It was San Francisco that did it," said Captain Flint.

"He isn't the big boss," said Titty. "Not really. It's Missee Lee."

"I'd guessed as much," said Captain Flint.

"We're going to see her tomorrow," said Roger.

"Good," said Captain Flint. "Cheer up, John, old chap. And you, Susan. If only we can find somebody who really does talk English we ought to be all right."

There was a stir among the crowd and looking round they saw that the Taicoon, Chang, head and shoulders taller than his guards, had come out of his house and was crossing the courtyard towards them. He came straight up to Titty and tapped her on the shoulder. "Come walkee quick time," he said. "Hear plenty fine buds."

"Can't you let us out?" said Nancy.

The Taicoon looked up at the little barred window.

"Couldn't we all be together?" said Titty.

"They lun away," said the Taicoon.

"We didn't mean to," said Nancy.

"They won't run away now," said Titty. "We none of us will. Can't you see Susan's tired out?"

The Taicoon may have understood something of what she was saying. Or it may have been that he was in a hurry to show Titty his birds. He signed to the captain, who unfastened the door under Nancy's window. In a moment all six of the Swallows and Amazons were shaking hands together.

"But Captain Flint?" said Roger.

"Too much stlong," said the Taicoon. "Him

belong plison. Tomollow see Missee Lee." He smiled at Titty. "Now you come see fine buds."

Together, the Taicoon, his blue skull-cap with its scarlet button high above the crowd, and Titty, looking doubtfully back over her shoulder, went off across the courtyard. Another door had been opened and John, Susan, Nancy, Peggy and Roger were being shepherded towards it. The one-time cook was going with them carrying the ship's parrot. There seemed to be an argument about Gibber. Behind his bars she saw Captain Flint wave a cheerful hand.

"What's going to happen to them?" she said.

"All sleep one house," said the Taicoon. "To-mollow all plisoners see Missee Lee. All eat man fan with Taicoon. . . . Supper. Perlaps tomollow no supper. No heads. No wantee chow."

Not very cheering, thought Titty, but the Taicoon did not seem to think it mattered.

"Fine buds in Melica?" he asked.

"Lots and lots," said Titty.

CHAPTER IX

PIRATE SUPPER

THE Taicoon led the way up the steps into his house. Titty looked round at walls hung with a strange mixture of guns, swords and pictures of birds painted on silk. Chang clapped his hands. A man came running in, listened to what Chang had to say, and ran out again. They went on through a larger room with a long table in it and out on a wide verandah into a babel of bird-song. The evening sun, slanting low over a garden, was lighting up row upon row of bamboo cages, and the birds were singing each against all.

The Taicoon, smiling happily, passed from cage to cage, inviting Titty to listen. He seemed able, in all that din of song, to pick out the voice of any bird he chose, and to shut his ears to all the rest. Titty could hear them only as an orchestra all making a noise at the same time. The Taicoon would stop by a cage, point to a bird and cup a hand over one ear. His blue skull-cap with its scarlet button would nod slowly, and he would look round at Titty, asking for applause. Then he would move to another cage and do the same. "Bud like him in Melica? Bud like him in San Flancisco?" And Titty wished to goodness Captain Flint had chosen to make himself Lord Mayor of a place she knew a little more about.

There seemed to be hundreds of birds, larks and thrushes mostly but many that she did not know at all. And the Taicoon kept stopping now by one and now by another. "Lovely, lovely," Titty kept saying and wished she could think of something else. She clapped her hands together when she saw the Taicoon wanted her to be particularly pleased. That was easier. What was the good of saying anything when you could hardly hear yourself speak?

The queer thing was that, happy though the Taicoon seemed in showing off his birds, she knew he had something on his mind. They were only half-way along the rows of cages when, after listening to a bird, he stood for a moment, looking far away towards the setting sun. He looked down at Titty.

"Captain James Flint," he said slowly. "San Flancisco. . . . Melican. Why for you not Melican too?"

"I'm English," said Titty.

"Better you Melican," he said, and then, "Missee Lee see plisoners tomollow. Missee Lee chop heads. . . ."

"Not if she knows English," said Titty cheerfully.

A new idea struck the Taicoon.

"Melican bud," he said. "Pallot." He seemed to be trying to offer some sort of comfort. "If Missee Lee chop heads. . . . Melican bud come live here. Taicoon Chang take care of him." And then, not waiting for an answer, he shrugged his shoulders as if casting off whatever was in his mind, and turned again to his bird-cages.

The sun went down behind the hills in the west and the chorus of the birds died away. "No sun, no sing," said the Taicoon. In the quickly deepening shadow he went back along the verandah and stopped by some cages of white canaries like the one he had had with him all day. He opened the doors of the cages and brought out one bird after another for Titty to admire. Titty wished she had not said "Lovely" so often already. But she liked the canaries and, even if no other word but "Lovely" would come into her mouth, at least she was able to say it as if she meant it. When the Taicoon shut up the last canary and turned to lead the way back into the house he was talking happily as hard as he could and Titty mostly not understanding what he said was getting along quite well by saying "Yes" every now and then.

Big paper lanterns had been lit in the house and, when she came into the room with the long table she saw Nancy and Peggy, John and Susan, looking much less tired and more like themselves, standing in a bunch, while half a dozen Chinese, all with big revolver holsters slung at their sides, were looking down at Roger who was trying to talk to the one whom Nancy had called "our" captain. Roger ran to meet her the moment he saw her.

"Jolly decent," he said. "A woman in trousers brought us a basin with hot towels to wipe the dust off our faces."

Titty wished the Taicoon had thought of doing as much for her.

The Taicoon waved a hand towards the other Chinese.

"My captains," he said, and explained, "Captains of my ships."

He took his seat in a carved and cushioned

chair at the middle of the long table. He made Titty sit at his right hand, John at his left. Roger plumped himself on a chair next to "our" captain to whom he had been talking. Nancy, as an old acquaintance, worked herself next to her captain on the other side. Prisoners and pirates sat down to supper together. No one could have guessed, to look at them, that there had been any talk of chopping heads. The pirates smiled at their neighbours, loosened their belts and put their pistol-holsters on the table. Opposite each chair was a plate, painted with birds, and a pair of chopsticks. Titty saw that Roger was wasting no time but was busy making "our" captain show him how to hold them.

"Thumb and finger for one," he called to Titty. "And the other between two fingers. All in the same hand. And then you use them like crabs use their claws."

Titty caught Susan's eye. "What about Captain Flint?" she asked.

"They were bringing him his supper," said Susan.

The Taicoon understood. He spoke to one of the servants, and smiled at Titty. "San Flancisco all light," he said. "Chow allee same Taicoon."

Green and gold bowls were set before them. Titty looked warily into hers. Clear soup, with a lot of pale rice at the bottom of it. But no spoon. She looked round, hoping that someone else would begin and show her what to do. She saw the Taicoon lift his bowl and drink from it. She did the same. Then she saw that the captains were not drinking quietly like the Taicoon. They sucked the soup noisily and smacked their lips. Guests, of course. That must be the proper thing to do. They were politely showing how good they thought the soup. So Titty sucked the soup in as noisily as she could and licked her lips. She saw Susan looking at her in horror. But John was following the example of the captains. Nancy outdid them all. Roger choked and was politely patted on the back. That was all right. But what about the rice in the bottom of the bowl? There the Taicoon showed her the way. Taking both chopsticks and keeping the ends of them together, he put the edge of the bowl to his lips and with a quick, sweeping, circular motion swirled the wet rice into his mouth. That, she found, was none too easy, and she was very glad when one of the captains simply threw his head back and tipped what was left of his rice straight down his throat.

Much larger bowls were now being put on the table, and the guests began to help themselves, taking things now from one bowl and now from another.

"Shark's fin," said the Taicoon, putting a bit on Titty's plate.

There were all kinds of things in the bowls. There were noodles, and little bits of fried meat, and little bits that might have been fish or might not, soaked in sauces that made Titty's eyes water and made Roger secretly put out the tip of his tongue to cool it.

Suddenly Titty saw Roger staring at her across the table, at her and at the Taicoon. The Taicoon, who had just used his chopsticks to put something in his mouth, had picked a titbit off his plate and, smiling politely at Titty, was poking it at her face. Titty looked at it and at him. There was nothing else to be done. She opened her mouth. The Taicoon popped the titbit in. Titty chewed it up, wishing she could spit it out instead, and then, seeing the Taicoon's face, smiled at him, smacked her lips and said, "Thank you."

It was as if a signal had been given. Looking right and left along the table, Titty saw that all the captains were doing the same for their next-door neighbours.

"Here, I say," said Roger, but, when he saw what was happening even to Susan, opened his mouth and smacked his lips like the rest of them.

More and more bowls were brought to the table and every now and then a piled plate was carried out of the room, when the Taicoon would point out to Titty what was happening, and would say, "San Flancisco chow" and Titty would smile back at him and say, "Thank you very much."

At last, one after another, the pirate captains made loud noises of having eaten too much. Little cups of pale tea were brought in. Nancy's captain pushed a bowl of meat-balls towards Roger. But Roger, even Roger, could eat no more and explained that this was so by tapping first the table and then his stomach to show that he was tight as a drum. The captain laughed and did the same, and presently all the pirate captains were tapping the table and tapping their stomachs while their host, the Taicoon, Chang, rolled in his seat with happy laughter.

And then, unexpectedly, Titty, tired out, found her head nodding forward. She hurriedly held it up, smiled at nothing, and nodded again. The Taicoon, sitting beside her, laughed, tossed down his cup of tea and rose from his chair. The captains stood up. The Taicoon spoke to a servant. Two guards with rifles came in and waited at the door. It was clear that the party was over.

One by one the prisoners shook hands with the Taicoon and said, "Thank you". The Taicoon said, "Velly pleased". The pirate captains smiled and bowed. Then, while the prisoners were walking to the door, they sat down again at the table. Servants were bringing in more cups of tea, and little bamboo pipes with metal bowls. Suddenly the Taicoon shouted a question after his guests.

"Lord Mayor San Flancisco," he asked. "Him velly lich man?"

No one knew what to answer. Captain Flint certainly wasn't. Ought they to say he was very rich or not?

"Velly gleat man?" said the Taicoon, putting his question differently.

"Very great," said Nancy.

And the Taicoon, leaning on the table, began to talk with his captains.

*

They came out with their guards into the cool of the courtyard.

"Barbecued billygoats," said Nancy. "Just think of grubbing with a pirate chief."

"That you people?" A voice came out of the dusk, and, before the guards could stop them, they raced across to talk to Captain Flint.

"Gosh," said Captain Flint. "They gave me such

a supper that I began to think they were going to hang me in the morning."

"Are you going to sleep here?" asked Susan.

"I'm all right," said Captain Flint. "There's a comfortable hole at the back. I've slept in worse places before now. What about you?"

"Much better than where we were," said Nancy.

"They've put Gibber where they were," said Roger. "But they gave him some more bananas."

"I say, Titty," said Captain Flint. "How did you get so pally with the big chief?"

"Birds," said Titty. "It was Polly did it really."

"He didn't let out anything when he was talking to you?"

"Not exactly." Titty hesitated. "He said that he'd look after Polly if Missee Lee cut off our heads."

"Nobody's head's going to be chopped off," said Captain Flint.

One of the guards said something in Chinese.

"We'd better go," said John.

"Don't worry about anything," said Captain Flint. "We'll get some sense out of somebody in the morning."

*

Light was coming from an open door. The guards hurried them towards it. "Come on, Titty," said Roger. "You haven't seen it."

The guards waited outside the door when they went in. In an empty room, hung with bamboo matting, a Chinese woman was standing by a huge pile of silk cushions.

"Taicoon," she said, and they knew that Chang must have sent them.

"Polly's in a room at the back," said Roger.

The Chinese woman bowed and went out. The door closed behind her. They heard the guards walking away.

Roger ran to the door. It was locked.

"Prisoners all right," said Nancy. "But Giminy what a lark. I say, John. Do tell us what did happen to *Swallow*."

"Tomorrow," said Susan. "Don't let's waste time talking now. Titty and Roger must be nearly dead."

"All right, Mister Mate," said Nancy. "So are we and so are you. We'll just grab cushions and camp down."

CHAPTER X

ON THE ROAD AGAIN

THE lanterns had gone out during the night but thin slivers of sunshine came through cracks in the shutters into the room where the six prisoners, awake and fresh after a long sleep, were squatting on cushions and piecing together their tales of what had happened. Roger had told the story of Gibber and the hunters for grasshoppers. Nancy had told of what happened aboard the pirate junk. John and Susan, with interruptions from Roger, had told of the house on the island, the books that had vanished, and of how, when they set off after Titty had sighted the *Amazon*, there had been people coming down the cliff.

"I wonder what happened to the boats," said Nancy.

"I don't know," said John. "There was a whole fleet of sampans coming down the river when we were looking for you. And then there were more of them by our island. They've probably collared all our things . . . Captain Flint's sextant. . . . My barometer. . . ."

"The sleeping-bags," said Susan. "My first-aid box. . . . They've got every single thing we didn't have in our pockets."

"We've lost all ours," said Peggy.

"If they're going to chop our heads off it won't matter," said Roger. "I mean, not having the things won't matter. Not our heads." He felt his neck as if to make sure his head was still firmly in its place. "Oh well," he added, "Captain Flint won't let them. But I do think they might give us some breakfast."

Boom!

It was the gong that they had heard the night before. Ten thrumming strokes. They had already heard a good deal of moving about and talking in the courtyard. Now they heard the noise of marching feet and, suddenly, close to them, the voice of Captain Flint, singing:

"Farewell and adieu to you fair Spanish ladies,
Adieu and farewell to you ladies of Spain.
For we're under orders for to sail to old England,
But we'll jolly soon see you fair ladies again."

They rushed to the shuttered windows and tried to look through the cracks. They could see that people were passing. John was the only one to catch a glimpse of Captain Flint.

"Gosh," he said. "They've got him in the hencoop again."

"He's saying 'good-bye'," said Nancy. "They're taking him away somewhere."

"He's changed the last line," said Titty.

"He can't mean they're sending him off to England without us," said Peggy.

"Galoot," said Nancy. "What he means is that we're going too. Soon see you again. That's what he means."

Captain Flint was still singing, further away now, but he was singing the same verse.

"Quick. Quick," said Titty. "Let's answer, to

show we're all right. . . . We'll rant and we'll roar. . . ."

"Come on," said Nancy and they all sang together:

"We'll rant and we'll roar like true British sailors,
We'll range and we'll roam over all the wide seas
Until we strike soundings in the channel of old England
From Ushant to Scilly is thirty-five leagues."

There was no answer. Captain Flint, in his hencoop, had been carried out of the gateway and away.

"I say," said Titty. "British. . . . We ought to have made it American because of his pretending to belong to San Francisco."

"Oh rot," said Nancy. "He said 'England' himself. It's only a song. They won't make head or tail of it, anyway. And Ushant and Scilly in the last line will muddle them up."

*

Steps sounded outside and fumbling at the door. It opened and two of the servants whom they had seen at the Taicoon's supper came in with trays, on which were bowls with rice and chicken, a bundle of chopsticks and a much smaller bundle of little splinters of bamboo. They set the trays on the floor and went out. Two guards with rifles were outside the door, and, when Nancy made as if to go out, stopped her at once.

"Oh well, here's breakfast, anyway," she said. "We'd better eat it," and the prisoners set their cushions round the trays and hungrily began.

"Bother these chopsticks," said Roger, taking a bit of chicken in his fingers.

"We'll have to learn," said Susan. "It was awful last night. . . . How *do* you hold the things? Oh, never mind. . . ."

They heard a laugh. A shadow fell across them. The one-time cook was standing in the doorway and behind him the two guards were watching them with wide grins.

"Stowee chow chow plenty quick," said the one-time cook. "Taicoon. . . ." He waved his hand to show that the Taicoon had gone away. "San Flancisco. . . ." He waved his hand again. "All go Missee Lee yamen plenty quick." He lifted both hands to his ears and made a terrific braying noise.

"Gosh," said Roger. "Donkeys again. And I'm still sore."

"We walked on our own hoofs yesterday," said Nancy.

"So did we," said Susan.

"You don't know what those donks are like," said Roger. "I wish we were walking today."

"Hully up," said the one-time cook, squatting beside them on his heels.

They hurried up as best they could, sweeping the rice over the rims of the bowls, playing catch-as-catch-can with the bits of chicken, emptying the bowls down their throats. Before they had done, the one-time number one cook went off again, pretending to lift his ears.

"He's gone to fetch those donks," said Roger

grimly.

"Well, buck up," said Susan. "Don't stop to talk about it. Nothing makes people so cross as other people being late."

They drank their tea. Susan and Peggy put all the empty bowls one inside the other. They made six neat piles of the cushions. They even did a little washing in a huge earthernware basin full of cold water they found in an inner room.

"No toothbrushes," said Roger.

"That's what those little bits of bamboo are for," said Susan who had been looking at the little bundle that had been brought in with their breakfast.

"Toothpicks," laughed Nancy. "No getting out of it, Roger. Go ahead. We won't have any toothbrushes till we get to an English ship or a proper town."

"Well," said Roger, "if they're going to cut our heads off I'm not going to bother." He looked anxiously at Susan.

"I'm going to, anyway," said John.

"So'm I," said Nancy. "If they're going to be beastly to us, I want clean teeth to gnash at them."

They were using the toothpicks and laughing at each other using them when the Chinese woman who had brought them the cushions the night before came in with a bowl of sunflower seeds. She took it to the parrot's cage and then looked from Nancy to Susan, from Susan to Titty and from Titty to Peggy. Titty darted forward, took the bowl and thanked her. "It's the Taicoon again," she said. "He's sent some food for Polly."

"Oh I say," said Roger. "Gibber can't go till he's had his breakfast."

There was a stamping in the courtyard outside and they caught a glimpse of brightly painted saddles.

"All leddy?" asked the ex-cook from the doorway.

"Come on," said John.

"Put a grin on, Peggy," said Nancy.

Titty was hurriedly pouring the sunflower seeds into the parrot's feeding-box.

Roger looked from one to another, and then ran out of the door, dodged between the rifles of the guards, bolted through the men who were waiting with the donkeys, and raced up the courtyard to Nancy's and Peggy's prison of the day before. At the small window where they had seen Nancy's face, Gibber, who had managed to climb up inside, was peering out.

"Come on, Gibber," said Roger. "You're coming too. But you've got to have some breakfast first." He began looking for the way to open the door.

"Monkey belong stay here," said the ex-cook who had hurried after Roger. "You belong see him, bimeby."

"But he hasn't had any food," said Roger, opening and shutting his mouth to show what he meant.

"Plenty chow-chow," said the man and led Roger back towards the crowd with the donkeys. Titty was coming out with the parrot in his cage. The ex-cook shook his head. "Pallot belong stay here," he said. "See him, bimeby."

"That's all right, Titty," said John. "It means we're coming back again."

"Pallot all light," said the ex-cook, taking the cage from Titty to carry it back into the house.

"Pieces of eight," screamed the parrot.

"What him say?"

"Pieces of eight," said Titty. "Money."

The ex-cook rubbed his hands. "San Flancisco plenty lich man," he said.

*

Two minutes later they were off, the six prisoners sitting on those gay but painful saddles, with a man leading each donkey, a dozen guards with rifles walking beside them, and a crowd of onlookers jostling each other to get a better view. They left the courtyard and, busily trying how best to sit their donkeys, came to the outer wall where they had another view of the dragon, lying like a cast snake-skin on the ground while men and women crouched and worked at it. Most of the crowd went no further but stopped to see how the work on the dragon was going on. Only some of the small boys followed them out under the gateway, and turned right with them along the wall, grinning up at them, chopping off fingers with imaginary knives and cutting off heads with imaginary swords.

"Don't look at them," said Susan.

"Nasty little beasts," said Nancy.

"I'd like to bat one of them," said Roger.

"What does it matter," said John, "if they like cutting off their own heads."

They left the wall and set out on a broad

beaten track slanting up towards the ridge that they had crossed the day before. All but two of the small boys stopped and turned back. These two, the noisiest of the lot, ran along beside the guards, jeering, shouting, pointing at the prisoners and making signs of head-chopping. Suddenly the ex-cook, without saying a word, let go the leading-rein of Titty's donkey, grabbed the two boys, banged their heads heartily together, and was back again by the side of the donkey. The two boys, each, no doubt, blaming the hardness of the head that had bumped his own, went for each other, fell on the ground and were left fighting in the dust.

"Velly plitty countly," said the ex-cook, placidly waving his hand. "Allee same Melica?"

"It's lovely," said Titty, keeping her teeth clenched together because of the jolting of the donkey.

"Giminy," she heard Nancy say. "My spine's coming through the top of my head."

"You wait," said Roger. "They haven't trotted yet."

And as he said it, someone shouted an order. There was no more talking for a bit. The guards were running, their rifles leaping on their backs. The donkeys were trotting, galloping, trotting again. The prisoners were hanging on with both hands, their legs, spread wide by the saddles, kicking loose in the air. The cutting off of heads hardly seemed to matter now. How soon, how soon would the donkeys slow down into a walk?

They slowed down at last and the prisoners looked at each other. All had serious faces. All were trying to find softer spots in their saddles. But nobody had fallen off. The ex-cook was again inviting Titty to admire the scenery.

Moving along the side of the ridge they could see away to the right the feathery tops of bamboo woods, glimpses of water and more forest beyond them. Far ahead they could see more water and beyond that, range upon range of blue hills.

"It's an island," Nancy called over her shoulder.

The ex-cook said a name in Chinese. He translated it. "Tiger island. Velly fine island."

"That's why the Taicoon had a tiger on his banner," said Titty.

For some time they went on at a fast walk. The road began to bear to the left over the shoulder of the ridge and suddenly they were looking down on the river, the mouth of which they had seen the day before. There, on the further side, was that great mass of rock, with cliffs falling to the water's edge. Further up the river the cliffs were not so high, and the great rock sloped gently down towards green fields and trees almost on the level of the water, white walls, green roofs, a tall queer-shaped tower, a flagstaff, a widening of the river where junks were lying at anchor, and, beyond all this, a glimpse of yet more water on the further side of the trees.

The ex-cook pointed.

"Dlagon Island," he said, and dropped his voice. "Missee Lee. . . . Twenty-two gong Taicoon."

"Gosh!" said Nancy. "Another island."

The ex-cook heard her.

"Thlee Islands," he said and pointed down the river.

They looked, but Dragon Island seemed to be all in one piece.

"Perhaps he means the little island where we landed," said John. "It's hidden, round the corner, behind those cliffs."

But the ex-cook was pointing almost straight across the river.

"He must mean there's a way through," said John, "but you can't see it from here."

"Thlee Islands," said the ex-cook again. He said a name in Chinese, hesitated and found the word he wanted. "Tort. . . . Turtle Island. Taicoon Wu. Tiger Island . . . Taicoon Chang. Ten gong Taicoons. . . ." And then, drawing himself up and squaring his shoulders proudly. . . . "Thlee Islands. We . . ." He tapped his chest. "We Thlee Islands men and Missee Lee our Taicoon. Twenty-two gong Taicoon," he added, making as if to count on his fingers.

"I say," said Nancy. "You know our Taicoon. All the others run like rabbits for him. If Missee Lee's a bigger boss than him, she must be pretty good as a pirate." And then, as she looked before her and saw how the road dipped steeply down towards the anchorage she thought of something very different. "Giminy," she said. "If they begin to trot now we're done."

But for a long time they did not. The donkeys were allowed to choose their own pace till they were down among the trees and paddy-fields. Then, at a signal, donkeys and men set off just as hard as they could, as if to show that they had been hurrying all the way. The men ran, the donkeys galloped, and, in a cloud of dust, they came to a rough quay at the side of the river.

"Hully, hully," panted the one-time cook.

The prisoners found themselves being pulled off their donkeys. Staggering as if they had been long at sea, as indeed they had, though it had never made them so unsteady, they were hurried out on the quay and down into a wide, square-ended boat. The boatmen had been waiting for them and the moment prisoners and guards were aboard, they pushed off from the quay.

"Aren't the donks coming too?" said Roger.

"Doesn't look like it," said John.

"Good," said Roger.

CHAPTER XI

DRAGON TOWN

THE ferry-boat was moving. One ferryman had joined the other on a platform in the stern and the two of them, facing each other, were swaying a long sweep to and fro. The sweep was not straight, but had a kink in the middle of it.

"It works on that pivot," said John. "But why do they have an elbow in it?"

"Make it go cockeye," said Nancy. "First one side and then the other."

"Like sculling," said John, watching the blade of the sweep which turned one way when going from port to starboard and the other way when going from starboard to port.

The thought of sculling reminded them both of working their little dinghies with an oar over the stern in and out of narrow places on the lake at home in the far away north.

"Gosh, I wish they hadn't bagged *Swallow*," said John.

"And *Amazon*," said Nancy.

But being afloat, even if they were only crossing a river in a broad flat-bottomed Chinese ferry-boat, made everybody feel better. They were on water again, and moving, and they felt like fish that had been flapping about on dry land and had somehow got back into the sea. They forgot that they were prisoners, forgot the painful shape of Chinese donkey saddles, and, with the eyes of six experienced seamen, looked at the small sampans tethered to poles along the bank or lying astern of the big fighting junks in the anchorage, and admired the skill of the ferrymen working their long sweep.

"Why are we going along the shore instead of straight across?" asked Roger, pointing over the river to the landing-place on the further side, where there were men waiting on a jetty and they could see walls and roofs among the trees.

"Current," said John. "They'll work upstream before crossing. No good going straight and being swept too far down. Look how the water's swirling past those junks."

"Beast of a current," said Nancy. "Just you try working against it with nothing but a bottom-board."

"The junks have all got eyes," said Titty, seeing the big black and white eyes painted on their bows.

"See their way about," said Roger.

"I say," said Nancy. "That's our junk. Look at the guns poking out. They must have brought her up since yesterday. Drying the mainsail. Look, John. You see what I meant when I told you they had about a dozen sheets to each sail, one to every batten."

"Why don't they have the ferry at a narrower place?" said Susan.

"Current's worse in the narrows," said John. "Here they get a bit of slack water each side."

The ferry-boat was being slowly driven upstream twenty yards or so out from the shore. Already they were well above the landing-place.

On the opposite side they could see where a wall ran down to the water's edge. The town itself was hidden by trees and they could see nothing of it but a tower and a flagstaff.

"I say, there's a lovely creek over there," said Roger.

"And a baby junk in it," cried Titty. "Just like the big ones, only smaller."

"Perhaps that's where we're going to land," said Roger.

John looked at the curl in the water pouring down the middle of the river. "We aren't," he said. "They're beginning to work her out already. We'll hit the other side just about opposite where we started from."

The ferrymen were working harder now. They were chanting as, facing each other, one pulling, the other pushing, they swayed to and fro across the platform in the stern. The ferry-boat was moving out into the stream, still heading up, but being swept down faster and faster as it came out into the main current.

There was a sudden yell from Nancy. "Giminy!" she shouted. "Look! Look! There's *Amazon*, pulled up in that creek, and *Swallow* just beyond her."

"Where's that telescope?" said John.

Titty began fumbling at her pocket. "Better not," said John, remembering where they were. "They might grab it." Titty pulled out a handkerchief and blew her nose instead.

They had been staring at the little junk in the creek, bright in scarlets and blues with a streak of green along her bulwarks and green tops to her three masts. Just for one moment they were able to see their own little boats, and then, with a tug at their heartstrings, they lost sight of them as the ferry-boat moving across drifted down below the opening into the creek. A moment later even the green tops of the little junk's masts were hidden by the trees. They turned to see that they were dropping fast downstream towards the bigger junks at anchor.

"Hee . . . yo . . . hee . . . yo," chanted the ferry-men.

"We're going to hit that first one," said Peggy. "We are."

"Good work," cried Nancy, as, with a tremendous effort the ferryman drove their boat clear. They just missed the anchor hawser and swept past the big junk almost near enough to touch it, while men in pointed straw hats looked down on them and jeered as sailors always do jeer in harbour at other sailors who have narrow shaves of bumping their new paint.

"Hee . . . yo . . . hee . . . yo," chanted the ferry-men. The sweat was pouring in streams down their naked brown backs, and dripping from their faces on the wooden platform. But already the boat was sweeping past the last of the anchored fleet and was coming quickly nearer to the other side of the river. A sampan with some Chinese in long robes and others with rifles like their own guards, had left one of the junks and was racing them for the jetty.

"More prisoners," said Nancy, almost as if she were herself one of the pirates.

The sampan and the ferry-boat reached the jetty together. The men from the sampan scrambled ashore with their prisoners and set off at a run up from the landing-place towards a gateway in the brown wall of the town. Their own guards shepherded them ashore and, falling in beside them, marched them briskly after the others.

"Why isn't Uncle Jim here to meet us?" said Peggy.

"Probably smoking a pipe of peace with the pirates," said Nancy.

"Not if Miss Lee's like the Great Aunt," said Roger.

"She isn't," said Nancy. "She's a pirate. Don't be a galoot."

"If Captain Flint's found someone who can really talk English," said Susan, "he's probably getting a telegram sent home to say we're all right."

"But are we?" said Peggy.

"We're jolly soon going to be," said Nancy.

Through the gateway they passed into something much more like a town than Chang's village on Tiger Island. There were many more houses, for one thing, though there seemed to be very few people. The streets, between the low, green-roofed houses, were not paved, but just earth trodden smooth. Pigs were wandering about. There was the harsh trilling of grasshoppers in the trees. Dust rose about their feet. A big blue butterfly fluttered across the street above their heads. Here and there women were sitting in the open doorways. A small boy sitting in the dust and tootling to himself on a long bamboo flute, took his flute from his lips and stared at the prisoners as they went by. But, for a town, the place seemed empty.

IN THE COURTYARD

"There's an awful lot of people somewhere," said Roger. "Can't you hear them?" Suddenly he pointed. "They've got a dragon here too."

Here, as in Tiger Town, women squatting in the dust were stitching away at the partly unrolled body of a dragon. Its huge grinning head lolled on the ground. Part of the body lay like a narrow carpet where the women were working at it. The rest was like a carpet rolled up for storage.

"I say, it must be a mile long when they spread it all out," said Roger. "It's a new one. The head hasn't been painted yet. I say, I wish they'd let us stop and have a look at it."

There was no chance of stopping now. The guards hurried them along, and all the time, though there seemed to be no one about, the noise of a crowd grew louder and louder. Suddenly they turned up a short road that ended in a sort of three-storied tower with a gateway under it. Here they were stopped. Questions were being asked and answered by their guards.

"Passwords," said Nancy. "This is the real thing."

"Pretty fair scrum," said Roger, looking through under the arch.

"I do think Uncle Jim might have come out to meet us," said Peggy. "What's that clicking noise?"

Through all the noise of the chattering crowd there came a queer sound of clicking, now stopping, now going on again, as if people were dropping pebbles on a hard floor.

"We'll know in a minute," said Susan.

"Now," said Titty under her breath.

A guard gave a tug at her sleeve. She remembered quickly to keep grinning. With their guards all round them they walked through the gateway into a shouting crowd of Chinese. The din was like the noise of a street market. They were in a courtyard like Chang's, only very much bigger, sloping gently up to the steps of a big, steep-roofed building with a wide verandah in front of it. Up there, over the heads of the crowd, they could see two banners, one, the green banner with Chang's black and orange tiger on it, the other a banner with something like a huge grey tortoise on a scarlet ground. There were more buildings on either side of the courtyard. Some of these, too, had open verandahs three or four steps up, and there, above the level of the crowd, were men with shaven heads squatting on the floor busy flicking beads to and fro on wires strung in wooden frames.

"Look, Peggy," said Roger. "That's what that noise is."

"Abacus," said Titty. "There's a picture of it in *Petit Larousse*."

"I know," said Roger. "Doing sums."

"Hullo," said Nancy. "There's our captain."

They were glad in all that crowd of strangers to see a face they knew, even if it was the face of the captain of a pirate junk. Nancy made as if to go and speak to him, but was stopped at once by the guards.

"Our" captain was talking to one of the prisoners who had been brought ashore in the sampan. The man took a bag out of his sleeve and offered it to him. The captain did not take it but motioned to a man standing by him who took the bag and passed it up to another man waiting on a verandah above him, who turned it upside down, emptying a great stream of silver dollars on the floor in front of one of the squatting men. One of the dollars rolled off and came to Roger's feet. He picked it up, looked at it and gave it to a guard who passed it up to the man on the verandah. The man squatting on the floor quickly sorted the money into little heaps. He had a pair of brass scales in which he weighed each heap separately, pouring the money from the scale into a general pile. Each time he did this he flicked a bead across the abacus. When he had done he nodded and spoke to the captain. The captain and the man who had brought the money bowed to each other. The captain spoke to the guards who went off with the man towards the upper end of the courtyard.

"What was he doing?" asked Roger.

"Paying a ransom, I bet," said Nancy.

The captain, looking very pleased with himself, turned and saw them.

"Talkee English, bimeby," he said.

"Where's Captain Flint?" asked Nancy. "San Francisco," she added, remembering what the Taicoon had called him last night.

The captain pointed up the yard and led the way through the crowd, followed by the guards with their six prisoners. Where the crowd was thickest they found a barred enclosure like a lion cage at the zoo, divided into compartments. Outside the first of them the elderly man they had seen paying the ransom was eagerly talking to another elderly man behind the bars. The two of them, the man in the cage and the man outside, were exactly alike.

"Blothers," laughed the captain over his shoulder. He pushed on. The crowd parted before him and suddenly they were looking at Captain Flint. He was sitting on a narrow perch in a bamboo cage in which there was only just room for him. The cage was indeed very like a hen-coop, and it had long carrying poles, like Chang's chair. The captain smacked the head of a small boy who, with the long feathery tip of a green bamboo, was tickling Captain Flint through the bars.

"Why haven't they let him out?" said Nancy angrily.

"Oh, I say," said Titty.

Susan and John looked at each other. Their hopes that Captain Flint had been able to put everything right had faded suddenly away.

"Hullo," said Captain Flint. "Four, five, six. All complete except for the parrot and that blessed monkey. Had a good night? All well so far." He shifted on his narrow perch and rubbed a sore place. "I wish they'd buck up and let me out. It would take a parrot or a vulture to sit comfortably on this thing."

Nancy's captain was listening as if to strange music.

"Talkee English, bimeby," he said. "Talkee English. Talkee Melican. Missee talkee evellything."

"All right old chap," said Captain Flint. "But I'd like to be able to stand up." He shook one of the bamboo bars of his cage.

"Too much stlong," said Nancy's captain.

"What do you think's going to happen?" asked John.

"Blest if I know," said Captain Flint. "Keep smiling. That's the ticket."

"Have you had anything to eat?" asked Susan. She dug in a pocket and brought out a bit of chocolate. "It's a bit sticky," she said. "I meant it for Roger yesterday." She held it out and Captain Flint took it through the bars, winked at Roger, unwrapped it and sat on his perch thoughtfully chewing. The watching crowd roared with laughter.

"Oh, all right," growled Captain Flint. "Feeding the apes, eh? Like to see my celebrated gorilla act?"

"No, no," said Titty. "You'll only make them cross. And they've been quite all right so far . . . except about putting you in a cage," she added hurriedly.

"If only they'd let me have a word with somebody who really does talk English," said Captain Flint.

Suddenly the air shook with the throbbing boom of an enormous gong. The whole chattering crowd in the courtyard was silent, waiting as the waves of sound slowly died away. Again the gong boomed. Again it was as if the whole world throbbed like a pulse.

"Gosh," said Roger, looking round at Susan with startled eyes.

Again the gong boomed and again. Each time there was a long pause until the last wave of sound had died, and then, yet again, came that tremendous booming noise.

"Eight . . . nine . . .. ten . . ." Titty was counting. "It's for Chang. . . ."

But the gong was still booming. Again and again that single, powerful noise broke each new silence. It was as if someone were throwing pebbles one by one into a pool, waiting till the last ripples were smoothed away before dropping the next pebble in the still water. Eighteen . . . nineteen . . . twenty . . . twenty-one. . . .

"Missee Lee. . . . Twenty-two gong," said the captain, and went off through the crowd and up into the large building at the head of the courtyard.

For the last time the gong boomed and with that twenty-second gong-stroke, they saw that everybody was looking in one direction, towards the tall flagstaff that towered above roofs and trees alike. A huge black flag was rising jerkily to the top of the flagstaff and on it a monstrous golden animal seemed to dance as the light wind rippled the flag.

"It's a dragon," said Titty.

"I can see it isn't a skull and crossbones," said Nancy.

CHAPTER XII

TWENTY-TWO GONG TAICOON

As the throbbing of the last gong-stroke died away a sort of sigh that sounded like "Missee Lee" rose from the crowd. Everybody was looking towards the steep-roofed building at the head of the courtyard. Men with rifles came out on the verandah, thumped the butts of their rifles on the wooden floor, and waited. Presently an old man came out on the verandah and stood at the top of the steps, with a roll of paper in his hand. There was silence. He let the paper unroll, looked at it and called out a name. There was a stir in the crowd. A guard opened a gate in one of the cages, and the two brothers, the prisoner from inside the cage and the other who had paid over all those silver dollars, were led off up the steps to the verandah and into the building.

The hubbub of talk broke out again, and through it, all the time, they could hear the clicking beads of the accountants doing their sums.

"Believe it's a sort of settling day," said Captain Flint.

"We saw them weighing silver money," said Nancy.

"What did they weigh them for?" said Roger.

"To see somebody hadn't clipped the edges," said Captain Flint. "That used to be a great game in these parts."

"Do you think it'll be our turn next?" asked Titty. "I wish we could get it over. . . ."

"What are we going to settle with?" said Captain Flint. "We've got no bags of silver. Paying business this seems to be. But I'll do my best."

"Tell them we've simply got to get to Hong Kong or somewhere," said Susan.

"Don't let's hurry," said Nancy. "We'll never have a chance like this again."

"I like that," said Captain Flint. "You just try sitting in this cage."

There was another silence. The old man at the top of the steps was reading out another name. The two brothers came out smiling happily, bowing in all directions, even to the guards. Another prisoner was taken in. He came out and yet another name was read.

"It's like waiting to see the headmaster," said Roger.

"Our turn'll come all right," said Captain Flint. "No good worrying till it does. Look here, John, let's hear exactly what did happen that night. How did you get ashore? Were you anywhere near when that blighter picked us up and wouldn't stop to look for you?"

With help from the others, John told the story of that windy night, of how he had put the sea-anchor out and made sure that the rope should not chafe, of how he had fallen asleep and been waked by a splash and guessed that something had gone wrong, of how he had begun hauling in the rope ("We got broadside on and I knew I was wrong, so I let it out again, and after that she was dry enough.") He told of hauling in the rope next morning when the wind had dropped and finding the sea-anchor no more than a few rags at the end of it. "Wonderful what a warp over the bows'll do," said Captain Flint, "to keep a little boat safe in a big wind"; Roger told of the tannic jelly put on Gibber's scorched arm; Susan of the struggle to relight the lantern. Even Titty, as the story of that night's drift was being told, forgot her present worries, remembering them only in the silences when new names were being called from the steps, and junk captains and guards were swaggering up into the big building, or swaggering down again. Sometimes on coming down those steps prisoners and guards would go to the accountants squatting over the sums and clicking their beads. Sometimes the prisoners were marched straight out of the courtyard. Meanwhile the tale went on. "What was the first thing you saw?" asked Captain Flint. They told of the dawn coming up behind them out of the sea, and the hills, and the big cliff and the landing on the tiny island.

"And the first thing I found when we got ashore," said John, "was that I'd got your sextant and the nautical almanac in *Swallow*. I'd meant to put them in *Amazon*, but in all that rush. . . ."

Captain Flint half jumped up, and hit his head on the roof of his hen-coop.

"You've got my sextant! Good for you. And I thought I'd lost it for ever. Where is it now?"

"It's in Miss Lee's temple," said Titty.

John was just telling how they had found the stone chair on the island, and the little house where they had spent the night when a new name was called from the verandah.

"There's our captain coming," cried Nancy. "There. He's coming down the steps now."

The junk captain was hurrying towards them. He clapped his hands and shouted, and two enormous half-naked Chinese pushed their way through the already thinning crowd and joined him by Captain Flint's hen-coop.

The junk captain turned to Nancy. "Him too much stlong," he said.

The two big Chinese stood outside his cage, glaring at Captain Flint, bending their arms and making their muscles stand up. They slapped their knees. They beat their chests like great apes.

"What are they making faces for?" said Roger.

"Two can play at that," said Captain Flint cheerfully, and began making faces in return. He got off his perch, crouched with bent knees, took a bar of the cage in each hand, shook them and growled. "This is the gorilla act," he said. There was a gasp from among the watching Chinese.

The two big men hopped up and down. Captain Flint, growling, did the same.

"Don't make them angry," said Titty.

"Fun for their money," said Captain Flint.

"They're opening the cage," said Roger.

The cage door opened and Captain Flint came out and tried to stretch himself. Each of the two big Chinese grabbed one arm. The junk captain, again with a glance at Nancy, brought a pair of handcuffs from behind his back and clapped them on Captain Flint's wrists.

"Oh," said Titty.

But Captain Flint just jingled the handcuffs

as if they were ornaments and smiled at the Chinese.

"Stout fellows," said Captain Flint. "Too much strong. Look at them now. Pleased as Punch. It's just as well to make everybody happy. As for you, you son of a gun," he added, turning his head towards the junk captain, "if ever you get wrecked and I pick you up at sea. . . ."

The junk captain bowed politely. "Talkee English, bimeby," he said.

With jangling handcuffs Captain Flint walked off between the big Chinese, the junk captain walking beside them. They went up the steps to the verandah and were gone.

"It's going to be all right in a minute," said John.

"But they've put him in chains," said Titty.

"What else could they do?" said Nancy. "He *is* pretty strong, and anybody who saw him being a gorilla would think it wasn't safe to let him out."

"He didn't mind," said Peggy. "Didn't you see him wink?"

"So long as there's somebody who knows English," said Nancy. "Not this gabble that's no good for asking or explaining anything. If there's somebody who really does know. . . . And I'm sure there is. Our captain's been saying so all the time."

"Missee Lee knows English all right," said Titty. "Oh, I say. We've never had time to tell him about those books. . . ."

"Or about using her Primus," said Roger hurriedly.

Susan glanced at him but said nothing. There was no more talking among the little bunch of prisoners waiting with their guards beside the empty travelling cage, watching, watching for Captain Flint to come out again on the verandah at the top of those steps. They had expected him to come out at once. One word of explanation would surely be enough and he would come charging out to fetch them in, and the next thing would be to arrange for them to get to a proper port and go aboard an English ship. Minute after minute went by and still no new name was shouted from the steps and nobody went in or out.

Half an hour went by. Titty caught John and Susan looking at each other as if they thought that something might have gone wrong. Even Nancy was looking less confident. "I say," whispered Roger, "you don't think he's got in a row about that book. Shall I bolt in and tell them I did it?" "Keep quiet," said John, "and keep grinning."

At last they saw Captain Flint coming out.

"They've taken off those handcuffs," cried Roger.

But Captain Flint did not look as if anything was settled. He came down the steps with a grave, puzzled face, the junk captain beside him and the two big guards walking behind.

"He's free anyhow," said Titty.

But the little group came straight across the courtyard to the bamboo travelling cage. The junk captain stood at the door of the cage and bowed. Captain Flint bowed to him, stooped, went in and sat down on his perch. The door of the cage was closed once more.

"What is it? What is it?" asked Nancy.

"Why are they shutting you up again?" asked Roger.

"Are they sending a message home?" asked Susan.

"Is Missee Lee a she or a he?" asked Nancy.

"Doesn't she talk English after all?" asked Titty.

"Rum go. Rum go," said Captain Flint. "Blest if I know what to make of it. Jabbering Latin .... Asked if I knew Greek. Asked . . . Gosh! I've left school too long. . . . You people'll be all right if you keep your heads. Where were we going? What were we doing? That's all right. But Cambridge? Cambridge? Why Cambridge? Must have meant Cambridge, Massachusetts. . . . Well, of all the rum goes. What's that? Does she talk English? English? English? I should think she does. She knows more English than I do. . . ."

He was still muttering to himself when there was a sharp call from the steps. The junk captain gave an order to the guards and John, Susan, Nancy, Peggy, Titty and Roger found themselves being marched towards the big green-roofed building at the top of the courtyard.

"In for it now," said Nancy, confident once more now that the moment had come. "Look here, John. She's a she-pirate. Let me do the talking."

They were marched up the steps, across the verandah between men leaning on their rifles, into a large, cool room that for a moment seemed dark after the sunshine in the courtyard. At the far end of the room there was a small group of people on a raised platform one step up from the floor. They saw Miss Lee at once. A tiny Chinese woman

WAITING TO HEAR THEIR FATE

was sitting on a straight-backed chair. She had a black silk coat and trousers, and gold shoes that rested on a footstool. She was wearing a cartridge belt over her black silk coat and her fingers were gently tapping a large revolver on her knees. An old Chinese woman was standing behind her chair and every now and then flapped a fly-whisk to and fro above her head. At Miss Lee's right elbow, in a chair set a little way behind her own, sat a very old man in dark green, gold-embroidered robes, combing a thin wispy beard with fingers like a bird's claws. Next to him was sitting a big man whom they knew at once for the Taicoon, Chang, the bird-fancier. At the other side of Miss Lee sat a much smaller, stout man, with a brown, wrinkled face, and eyes screwed up like those of an old sailor. Some of the junk captains they had seen at last night's supper were standing about, and some others whom they had not seen before. All watched the little procession of prisoners as they crossed the shadows on the floor, in a silence that seemed all the quieter for the chattering of men and the clicking of beads that was still going on outside. It was an odd thing, but nobody in the room seemed to matter at all beside that tiny young woman with her gold shoes and her revolver seated in the big chair. Her eyes seemed to be half-closed, yet they felt that she could see even what they were thinking.

They were placed in a row at the edge of the raised dais, immediately in front of Miss Lee. Nancy's captain went up on the dais and joined the others behind the chair of the Taicoon, Chang.

Suddenly they saw that Miss Lee was smiling

at them. They found themselves smiling back. But already her smile was gone and she was speaking quietly to the old man sitting at her elbow. Chang and the others listened. Then the old man spoke, still combing his wisp of beard. Then the little wrinkled man on Miss Lee's left. Then Chang, who seemed to be disagreeing with what had been said. It was like watching people talking behind a window without being able to hear what they were saying. For the prisoners it was worse than that because they knew that the argument they were watching had something to do with themselves. Something was being decided about them, and they could not say a thing to help the decision one way or the other.

Miss Lee spoke again, glancing for a moment in their direction. The old man stopped combing his beard and spoke earnestly. The little man with the wrinkled eyes was nodding his head in agreement. Chang was scowling. Again Miss Lee was talking. The little man shook his head. The old man staring straight in front of him, was twisting together two or three of the long hairs of his beard. Chang's face changed. Suddenly he got up and crossed the dais towards the prisoners. His smile was as friendly as it had been when he and Titty had been feeding grasshoppers to his birds, but Titty, without knowing why, reached for Susan's hand. Miss Lee said a single word. Chang suddenly lifted both hands and dropped them. He went back to his seat. He spoke to one of his captains who bowed to Miss Lee and went quickly out.

"Our Taicoon's agreed to something," whispered Roger.

The discussion, whatever it had been, was over. That part of it at least. Once more, everybody on the dais was looking at the prisoners. Suddenly Miss Lee spoke in English.

"Who are you?" she asked quietly.

John looked at Nancy, Nancy at John. Nancy looked straight at Miss Lee, who was watching her through narrowed eyes.

"I am Captain Nancy Blackett," she said. "Amazon pirate when at home. . . ." She paused a moment to let that sink in.

"Pilate?" said Miss Lee. "Captain?"

"Rather," said Nancy. "And this is Peggy Blackett, my Mate."

"And the others?"

"This is Captain John Walker, Mate Susan Walker, and Able Seamen Titty Walker and Roger Walker."

"Pilates too?" asked Miss Lee with just the faintest hint of a smile.

"Not exactly," said Nancy. "Explorers."

"How did you come here?"

"We were all sailing round the world in the *Wild Cat*. She's . . . she was a schooner belonging to Captain Flint."

"And Captain Flint?" asked Miss Lee.

"Our Uncle Jim," said Nancy.

"Velly uncultured man," said Miss Lee, and turned to talk to the others in Chinese. "Go on," she said presently.

"The *Wild Cat* caught fire," said Nancy. "Roger's monkey . . ."

"It wasn't his fault," said Roger.

"Monkey?" said Miss Lee.

"Gibber went and dropped Captain Flint's cigar into the petrol-tank," began Roger, but was nudged by John and shut up.

Nancy went on with the story.

"She burnt right out and went under," said Nancy. "Then we were in our two boats . . . you've got them here. We saw them in the creek. . . . We tried to keep together but it blew a bit hard and their lantern went out and then a junk picked up Peggy and me and Captain Flint, and Captain Flint had a bit of a row because naturally he wanted the captain to stay where he was and look for the others, but the captain wouldn't."

Miss Lee spoke to Chang who spoke to Nancy's captain, who came across and pointed first to Nancy and then to Peggy. Miss Lee nodded.

"And the others?" she asked.

Nancy looked at John.

"Our boat just drifted ashore," said John. "The canvas of our sea-anchor was rotten."

Just then a new noise made itself heard above the chattering in the courtyard outside. It was Captain Flint, singing at the top of his voice. But the song was not one of the sea shanties they were accustomed to sing aboard the *Wild Cat*. It was something very different:

"Columbia the gem of the Ocean,
The land of the brave and the free,
The shrine of each patriot's devotion,
The world offers homage to thee."

Most of them did not know what it was but John and Nancy knew very well, and knew too what

Captain Flint was trying to say to them. Captain James Flint, Lord Mayor of San Francisco, was still being as American as ever he could.

The song sounded as if he were going rapidly further away.

Roger turned and bolted for the verandah. He was instantly grabbed by a guard and brought back.

"But it's Captain Flint," he said.

"They're taking him away," said Peggy.

The song was growing fainter.

"It's all right, Roger," said John. "He said we were to keep our heads. Don't get excited. Nothing to be worried about."

"It's all right, Roger," said Titty. "We'll be going back too. That's why they didn't let us bring Polly and Gibber."

Chang half rose from his chair, but Miss Lee stopped him by a single word.

They heard the song no more.

And now the old man at Miss Lee's elbow seemed to be suggesting questions for her to ask.

Miss Lee looked at John. "Were you coming here when you lost your ship?"

"No," said John.

"We jolly well would have been if we'd known," said Nancy.

"Why?" asked Miss Lee.

"Well, pirates," said Nancy. "Who wouldn't?"

"Do you know where you are?" asked Miss Lee.

"How can we know?" said Nancy. "We were shut up in the junk for a long time before we anchored, and we've never been in the China Seas before. We'd awfully like to know," she added.

Miss Lee looked closely at her, and then at John.

"We don't know either," he said. "We were blown a long way in the night and were close to land when the sun came up again. And then we got ashore on the island. We were nearer to it than to anything else."

Miss Lee talked to the old man while Chang and the others listened carefully. The old man spoke again. Miss Lee asked in English:

"Was your ship in sight of land when she was burnt?"

"No," said John.

After that there was a lot more talk on the dais while the prisoners stood silent beside their guards.

Suddenly Susan burst out. "Please, can't we send a telegram to say we're all right?"

Miss Lee and the others glanced at her and then went on with their talk as if she had not spoken.

"Not just now," whispered John.

Suddenly the prisoners saw that the council was over. The men were all bowing to Miss Lee. The old Chinese woman with the fly-whisk went out through a small door at the back of the room, through which they caught a glimpse of green trees and scarlet climbing flowers. Chang strode hurriedly through the room to the verandah followed by his captains. The old man with the wispy beard and the little man with the wrinkled face went slowly out talking together. The other captains followed them. Miss Lee signed to the guards and the six prisoners found themselves being stood in a row along one of the side walls.

BOOM! The big gong from over the gateway thundered once more into the air. BOOM! . . . BOOM! . . . BOOM!

"Twenty-two times," whispered Roger. "Bet you anything."

At the twentieth booming of the gong Miss Lee stepped down from her chair and walked slowly through the council chamber. At the twenty-first she was close to the verandah. As the throbbing of the twenty-second gong-stroke died away they could see her tiny figure at the top of the steps looking down into the courtyard. There was a tremendous roar of cheering. Miss Lee came slowly back into the council chamber, smiling to herself. She said a word and the guards marched out. Miss Lee was alone with her prisoners.

"And now," she said, "you will come with me and we will have a nice cup of tea."

She led the way towards the small door at the back through which the old Chinese woman had disappeared. Her prisoners, too astonished to speak, followed her without a word.

CHAPTER XIII

MISS LEE EXPLAINS

THEY followed her through that small door at the back of the council chamber and found themselves in a garden. Miss Lee turned right along a paved path and led them up some steps into a room something like Chang's except that no pictures of birds hung among the weapons on the walls. A single spray of a flowering shrub stood by itself in a tall blue-green vase on a black pedestal. Miss Lee did not stop here but went on through a passage, and into another room. They went in after her and stood gaping.

Walking into that room was like walking into Europe out of Asia. There were a couple of deep easy-chairs. There were cushions everywhere. There was a table with a reading-desk and a reading-lamp. There were bookshelves all round the walls. There was an English fireplace, with a coal-scuttle and fire-irons beside it, its mantelpiece covered with photographs. There was a coloured picture of some green lawns, big trees, and ancient buildings with water flowing past them. There was a varnished oak plaque over the mantelpiece with a shield painted on it with a lion flourishing a fore-paw in each of the four quarters. On the mantelpiece, among photographs of young women with large sprawly signatures, there were ornaments, matchstands, vases and such, mostly in white china and all decorated with that same coat of arms. On a little table in one corner there was a signed photograph, much larger than the others, in a black and gold frame, of a middle-aged woman with a firm mouth, clever, wise eyes, and white hair brushed back from her forehead. In another corner of the room was a hockey-stick. Beside the reading-desk, on the table, was an ash-tray on which were resting three little bamboo pipes, the only Chinese things in the room except for Miss Lee herself, who stood there in her black silk coat and trousers and her gold shoes, smiling quietly, enjoying the astonishment of her visitors. She unbuckled her cartridge belt and her pistol holster and hung them on a clothes hook behind the door as if she had been out for a walk and was hanging up a mackintosh.

"Now," said Miss Lee. "Dulce domum. Please make yourselves at home."

Roger was staring at a large photograph of a school hockey team. There was a back row of girls standing. "Pretty beefy," Roger murmured to himself. There was a front row of girls sitting down holding their hockey-sticks. Roger looked at Miss Lee and turned again to the picture. Third from the right. He looked at Miss Lee again, jogged Titty's elbow, and pointed to one of the seated figures.

"Yes," said Miss Lee. "Half-back."

"They look a jolly tough team," said Nancy. "Were you at school in England?"

"Gleat Marlow," said Miss Lee.

The door opened and the little old woman who had stood behind Miss Lee's chair in the council chamber came in, followed by a man with a tea-pot and a steaming kettle on a tray and another man with a trayful of cups and a dish of little cakes.

"My amah," said Miss Lee. "My nurse. My father sent her to England with me and she speaks English."

"How do you do?" said the little old woman. "Velly fine weather."

"How do you do?" said five of the visitors. Roger was the sixth. He said nothing. He hardly heard what was being said by other people. He had moved out of the way of the men bringing in their trays, and, in doing so, had seen the book that was lying closed on Miss Lee's slanting desk. It was a Latin-English Dictionary.

Miss Lee nodded, and the amah and the two men went out.

"We will have English tea," said Miss Lee. "Stlong . . . with milk. . . . And plenty of sugar. You are surplised?"

"Well, yes, rather," said John. "We didn't expect . . ."

"I will explain," said Miss Lee, sitting down at her table, pushing the reading-desk a little further to one side, and beginning to pour out tea. "Sit down. Take cushions. Sit how you like. On the floor. Like a Camblidge sing-song. Solly no more chairs. Tomollow. And now, tell me your names again." As each one took a cup of tea Miss Lee asked, "Your name, please," and when, with cups of tea and cakes they were sitting down, Peggy in one of the armchairs, with Nancy and Susan one on each arm, and John on the floor beside Roger who had gone down gladly because standing up or in a chair he would not have been able to keep his eyes from wandering back to the dictionary, Miss Lee pointed to each in turn. "John. . . . Su San. . . . Peg gee. . . . Nansee. . . . Tittee. . . . Loger. . . ." Not a word about that dictionary. Perhaps, thought Roger, she had not opened it. Well, he would have to tell her later.

They had left one of the armchairs empty. Miss Lee brought her teacup from the table, bowed to them slightly, sat down and began to talk.

"My father," she said, "was a velly gleat man. I will tell you how. There are thlee islands here, Dlagon, Turtle and Tiger. This is Dlagon Island. Now the men of these thlee islands have lived by what you call pilacy since the world began. They used to take junks and cargoes and plisoners. The owners paid velly well to get the junks back, paid for the cargoes, paid for some of the plisoners. . . ."

"What happened to the others?" asked Roger, cheerful again now that it was clear that the talk was not to turn on books.

John gave him a look, but Miss Lee, just making a slight motion of her hand, as if it were a sword hitting the back of her neck, went on:

"The old Taicoon, the chief of Dlagon Island, took my father out of a Foochow junk. That junk fought with guns and went down and the Taicoon picked my father out of the water. My father was a velly little boy but he hit the Taicoon with his fists. One of the men took my father to throw him overside but the Taicoon said, 'No. That is a good boy. Keep him and see what comes.' He thought someone would pay for him. But my father lost all his family when that junk went down. My father never knew who was his father but he lemembered that he was a mandalin, with peacock feather and gold button. The Taicoon had no sons and my father glew up in his house. He glew up velly good pilate. But in those days there was much trouble. Gunboats came to smash up pilacy. That was not so bad. Gunboats came but they went away again. But the worst tlouble was quallelling between the thlee islands. Tiger Island men fought Turtle Island men. Dlagon Island junks came back with plisoners and Turtle Island men fought to stop them coming into the liver. Velly, velly bad.

"Bimeby, when the old Taicoon died, the Dlagon Island men made my father their Taicoon. My father sent to Tiger Island and to Turtle and asked their Taicoons to meet him. Each one said 'Velly pleased,' but each one wanted to have the meeting on his own island. Nobody tlusted anybody. My father said, 'Better meet on a junk.' They said, 'All light, but whose junk?' At last they agleed to meet on that little island where you landed in your small boat. They met there and my father told them his plan to make things better. The Taicoon of Turtle Island said 'No.' Then there was fighting. The men of Dlagon Island and Tiger Island fought the men of Turtle Island. They won. The Taicoons met again, and agleed that my father was to be chief of the thlee islands, and each island was to work for all thlee. So no more fighting. My father did more than that. He made a law, never to take English plisoners to the islands. And after that there was no more tlouble with gunboats.

"All this was a long time ago when the old Empress was in Pekin. In those days many pilates all along the China Coast. Now my father was a velly gleat man. He said, 'Tax collectors are licher than pilates. Pilates had better turn tax collectors. No more pilacy. Thlee Islands men will plotect tladers flom pilates.' And my father built up a nice quiet business, good for evellybody. Evellybody velly pleased to pay a bit to Thlee Islands men for plotection. Nobody dare touch a tlader who paid Thlee Islands men. Thlee Islands men paid a bit to the mandalins to keep quiet and evellything went velly well. Of course they sank junks that had not paid and took plisoners, lich passengers, never poor ones, like your Lobin Hood. Good business, because lich men are in a hully to get back to their counting-houses, and pay quick. And afterwards they know better and pay Thlee Islands men for plotection. Some of my father's best customers were old plisoners. And no Chinese asks for gunboats, because he knows that if gunboats were to smash up the Thlee Islands men there would be no plotection for anybody. English are diffelent, so my father made that law. He made much money, and Thlee Islands men were happy and contented. Then came the Levolution. Lepublic. Yuan Shih Kai. . . . No matter. Mandalins go. Other men come. We paid the same squeeze and evellything went on as before.

"Now my father never forgot that his father wore the peacock feather and was a learned man. Himself, he had no time for learning. My mother died when I was a little girl. He had no sons. He was at the velly top of his plofession and he said

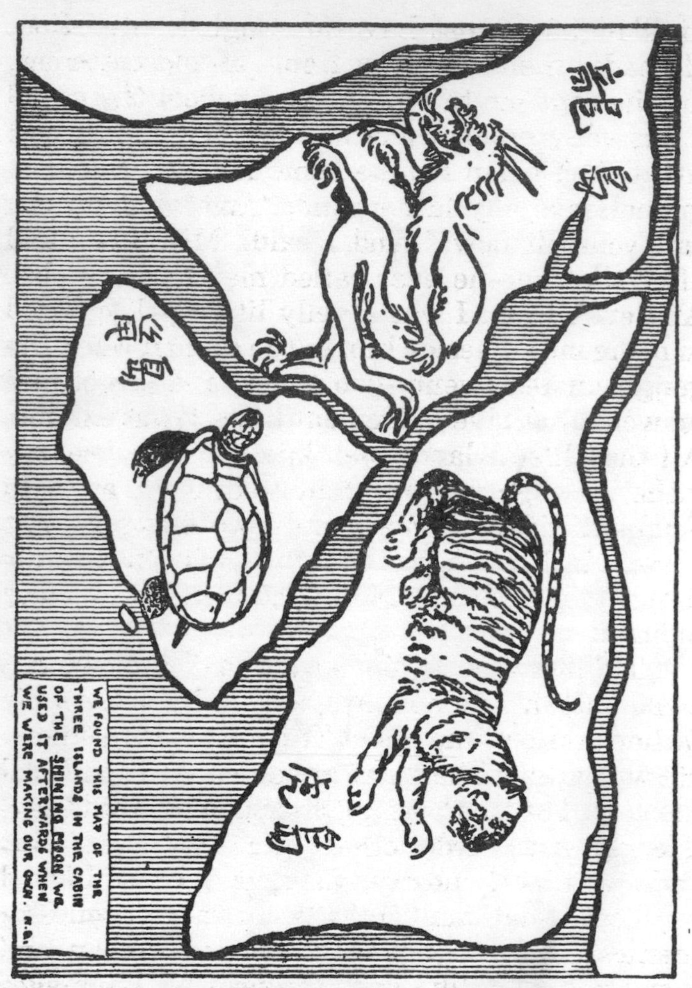
WE FOUND THIS MAP OF THE
THREE ISLANDS IN THE CABIN
OF THE SHINING MOON. WE
USED IT AFTERWARDS WHEN
WE WERE MAKING OUR OWN. R.B.
龍島
虎島

his daughter must have an English education. He had a fliend in Hong Kong, an old customer, and he sent me to him to go to school there and I was velly happy there and learned as fast as I could. And when I came home for the first time, for holidays, my father said, "And what do you call yourself now?" And I said, 'Miss Lee,' and after that no one ever called me anything else. And even when I was a velly little girl, he used to make me sit beside him in the council when the gong sounded twenty-two times, and sometimes he would not give judgement himself but ask me. All the Thlee Islands men knew Missee Lee, my father's daughter. And then he sent me away to England with my amah, and I went to school at Gleat Marlow. 'Work hard,' he said, 'but never forget that you are my daughter and your place is here.'

"England was so far away that I could not come back in the holidays, and in his letters my father said nothing about Thlee Islands business. He would say, 'The junks are doing well', or 'Good harvest', but that was all, and then he would say, 'He who would order others must first learn'. But there was leally no need for that, because I loved my books and went quickly up the school. The mistless there was a velly learned woman and I wanted to be like her. She lead all languages and lote books herself and she said that I was a velly good pupil and ought to pass examinations and go to Camblidge. My father agleed. And I forgot about the islands and worked hard and passed examinations. . . . Higher Certificate with Honours . . . and she told me that I should go to

Camblidge and be a learned woman, and I was velly happy. I thought I should go on passing examinations and perhaps spend all my life, like her, in learning and teaching. I went to Camblidge and listened to lectures and made fliends (there were many there who hoped to teach). And then in my velly first year, my father sent me a letter with only two words in it, 'Come home'. So I came home, by big steamer to Hong Kong, leading my books in my cabin, to lose no time, thinking of my examinations. A junk from the Thlee Islands came to Hong Kong to fetch me. I came home to Dlagon Island and I saw that my father was a velly old man.

"I could not leave him to go back to Camblidge. I stayed here, and he taught me all his business. He sent me out in the junks, so that the men should see I was my father's daughter and not afraid. He was velly ill. He said there was no need for me to go back to Camblidge. He said I had learned enough."

"Jibbooms and bobstays!" exclaimed Nancy. "No more schoolbooks and piracy instead. . . . I mean protection," she added.

Miss Lee looked at her sadly. "No more Camblidge," she said. "And I should never be able to go on with any examinations and become a Bachelor of Arts."

She paused and then went on with her story. "At last my father called a Thlee Islands Council. He was too weak to walk to his chair when the gongs sounded. They callied him. The chairs were set above the courtyard so that the fighting men of all thlee islands could be there. And

And I was there, and my father's old fliend, the counsellor, whom you saw today. (Roger's fingers strayed unconsciously to his chin.) There were new Taicoons now on Tiger and Turtle. You have seen them. My father spoke to them all and asked them what they would do when he died. The Dlagon Island men looked at my father. But the Tiger men looked at Chang, and the Turtle men looked at Wu, and my father saw that fighting might easily begin all over again. He laughed and he spoke to them all. He said that Chang was a velly good man and so was Wu. Then he told them the story I have told you, how the Thlee Islands came together and he said, better keep it so. He pointed to me, sitting beside him. He said he had taught me evellything he knew. He told them that I had gone to far countlies to learn more. He leminded them that they had heard me giving good judgements. And then he said that he could lead them no more. He made the men lift him and hold him up. He made me sit in his chair. And they sounded the twenty-two gongs for me, Miss Lee, with my heart in Camblidge. And when the last gong sounded, my father bowed towards me, and the old counsellor, and Wu and Chang, and they all swore that they would obey me, Miss Lee, as they had obeyed my father.

"That night my father said that it was his whole life that he had put into my hands. He said that all would be well with the islands while they were one, but that if I were to fail them, there would be qualleling and all he had built would be undone. And in the morning he was dead. He had chosen the place for his glave, on the little island where he had had that meeting with the other Taicoons many many years ago. We buried him there. That little house you found on the island is the temple we built over his glave. I go there sometimes to honour his glave and to be alone with my books. So you know now why I shall never see Camblidge any more."

There was a long silence. Then John spoke with, in spite of himself, a shake in his voice. "I hope you will forgive us for sleeping in the temple. We didn't know what it was, and, you see, we had been ship-wrecked, and there was nowhere else."

"Quite all light," said Miss Lee. "I think my father velly pleased."

"I used your kettle," said Susan. "And the Primus. I never thought we weren't coming back. And we left all our things there."

"We will get them when I go next to my father's glave," said Miss Lee. "No one else goes there without my orders. No one would touch them in the temple."

"We took some of your tea, too," said Peggy.

"Polly left husks on the floor," said Titty.

But Miss Lee was not listening. She had got up from the armchair and moved to the table. Roger scrambled up from the floor.

"Who wrote in this book?" asked Miss Lee, sitting down at the table and opening the dictionary on her slanting desk.

"I did," said Roger, very red indeed. "I'm very sorry. I did it without thinking."

"Not Latin," she said, "that last line, but velly good."

"Our chaps always put it in," said Roger,

whose face was like sunshine breaking through clouds. "I thought you'd just forgotten to finish it."

"Do you know any more?" asked Miss Lee.

"No Latin ones," said Roger. "Of course the men who haven't really started Latin sometimes put something in English."

"What do they write?" asked Miss Lee.

"Very dull," said Roger. "They just write:

'He who takes what isn't his'n
When he's caught shall go to prison.'"

"His'n," said Miss Lee. "Possessive emphatic .... His own. ... I see."

"We don't bother about Latin," said Nancy. "But we've got a rhyme like that to put in the beginning of books. We write:

'If this book should chance to roam
Box its ears and send it home.'"

"Why punish the book and not the thief?" said Miss Lee. "The one in the dictionary is better and Loger's last line and the picture make it a warning even for uncultured persons."

She thought for a moment, and went on. "Velly lucky you went to my father's glave. Velly luck Loger lote in my book. I will tell you. I sent my amah to fetch my books. She told me people had been at my father's glave. I sent men to kill. A fisherman saw you and he told Turtle Island men. They too were on their way to kill when I sat down to do some tlanslation and saw what Loger had litten in my dictionary. It was like a message flom my father's glave to say 'These persons are not thieves but students'. Quick, quick, I sent a message not to kill. Wu's men from Turtle Island saw you go across to Tiger. So I sent orders to Chang to bling all plisoners to my yamen today. Chang thought I knew evellything. So he blought all, even his Lord Mayor . . . whom I knew nothing about. Chang meant to keep him and say nothing because of my father's law."

"Gosh," said Roger. "Was that why he looked so mad when that message came? That whistling was signalling, wasn't it?"

Miss Lee smiled proudly. "When I was in England I was a Girl Guide," she said. She tapped with her fingers on the table, giving the call up sign in Morse. "No teleglaph in Chinese. So I made a signal code for Thlee Islands men. My father was velly pleased. We can talk from Dlagon Island to Tiger or Turtle and no one knows what is said, only the whistlers. Velly difficult because of Chinese language. I taught twelve men English letters so that they could whistle messages. . . ."

"How did you teach them?" asked Roger.

"Bamboo," said Miss Lee. "Velly uncultured men."

"Can we send a message somewhere to say we are all right?" asked Susan.

"No." Miss Lee frowned. "Bling gunboats," she said and shook her head. "You are English," she said. "All English . . . except your Captain James Flint, Lord Mayor of San Flancisco. . . ." She looked hard at Nancy.

"But we were picked up at sea," said Nancy. "We ought not to be prisoners at all."

"That captain who picked you up was one of Chang's men, a Tiger Island man. He knew my father's law. He knew velly well he ought to leave you alone."

"But what could he do?" said Nancy.

"Leave you dlown," said Miss Lee. "But Chang is a velly gleedy man. Chang wants to get lich quick. And when your Captain Flint told him he was Amelican and Lord Mayor of San Flancisco Chang said to himself 'Amelican is not English'. He knew I would not allow, but he thought quite safe to keep him and get a lot of money flom Amelica."

Miss Lee's six guests looked at each other uncomfortably.

"Chang hoped I should know nothing," Miss Lee went on. "He will make Lord Mayor San Flancisco lite a letter to Amelica and get plenty of money, and keep all that money for Tiger Island men."

"But now that you know?" said Nancy.

"Listen," said Miss Lee. "We all bleak my father's law together. I think my father velly pleased for me. I cannot go to Camblidge so I make my Camblidge here. Only my father's old counsellor not pleased. And Wu. They say English and Amelican are all one. Chang says quite safe to keep Amelican plisoner not English. I told them Chang could keep San Flancisco and that I would keep you. No one would know. No one would come to look for you. Chang agleed, but he wanted to keep Tittee. I said No. The others wanted to kill evellybody and keep my father's law and have no tlouble with gunboats. I said No. You stay in my yamen. Chang has San Flancisco."

"But if Uncle Jim writes to America," said Nancy, with something of a sparkle in her eyes, "won't that be just as bad as sending a message to Hong Kong?"

"No," said Miss Lee. "Amelica is far away. Chang thinks he will send a letter by a messenger. No one will know where it comes from or where the answer goes."

"But when he lets Captain Flint go?" said Susan.

"Chang says there will be no need to let him go. First get the money, then . . . No head, no talk."

"But that's beastly," said Roger.

"The money'll be a long time coming," said Nancy with a grin.

Miss Lee looked at her through half-closed eyes. "I think so too," she said.

"I mean it's a long way to America and back," said Nancy hurriedly.

"Chang's got my parrot," said Titty.

"And he's got Gibber," said Roger. "My monkey. In the prison, next door to Captain Flint's cage."

"Pallot?" said Miss Lee. "Monkey?"

"Ours," said Titty and Roger.

"I will send a message," said Miss Lee. "Too late for them to come today, but you shall have them tomollow. You will be my guests. You will be velly happy. I think it is lucky I saw Loger's liting in my book. I think my father velly pleased I have a class of students. Not quite Camblidge.

But we will study here. We will study evelly day. We will tlanslate Virgil. We will lead Caesar. . . ."

"But Peggy and I don't know any Latin," said Nancy.

"Neither do I," said Susan.

"I only picked up a little while Roger was doing lessons," said Titty. "I've never learnt properly."

"I will teach you from the beginning," said Miss Lee.

"But we've got to get home," said Susan.

"You will stay here," said Miss Lee. "And now my amah will show you where you will sleep."

She clapped her hands, and the old Chinese woman, who must have been waiting outside, hurried into the room. Miss Lee said a word or two in Chinese.

"My speak velly good English," said the old amah. "You belong walkee. My show you."

One after another, led by John, they shook hands with Miss Lee as if it had been an ordinary party. Then, almost stunned by what they had heard, they followed the old amah out of the room, out of Miss Lee's house, along the path to a small one-storey house on the further side of the council chamber. There were three or four small rooms in it besides a big one looking out into the garden. The old amah pointed to plank beds with cushions and quilts. She seemed to guess that in such things Susan was the one who mattered. She pulled Susan by the hand and showed her a Chinese bathroom, with a huge earthenware water kong and a dipper for dipping out the water. "Missee Lee think of evellything," she said, and pointed out a small packet with a printed label.

"Wright's Coal Tar Soap" and three or four big sponges on a bamboo rack above a row of towels.

"Thank you very much," said Susan.

"You belong live here. . . . My belong bling man fan . . . chow," said the old amah. "If you wantee piecee anything you belong clap hands . . . so."

She bowed to them all and left them.

*

"She can't mean to keep us for ever," said Susan.

"But she does," said Titty. "She said so."

"She's practically bought us," said John. "You heard what she said about keeping us herself and letting Chang have Captain Flint."

"Listen," said Roger. "That whistling again. She's telling Chang he's jolly well got to give up Polly and Gibber."

"Barbecued billygoats," said Nancy. "*We're* all right, unless she really means all that stuff about Latin. But what about Captain Flint? She knows he isn't American. I could see that. And when Chang finds out he'll be furious. They'll have his head off first thing. . . ."

"It's jolly lucky I did write in her dictionary," said Roger.

"We're not all right," said Susan. "What about Daddy? What about Mother and Mrs. Blackett at Beckfoot? What about Bridget?"

"Bridget won't mind," said Roger.

"Mother will," said Susan.

"Look here," said John. "Nobody's expecting to hear from us for ten days or a fortnight at least.

They won't begin worrying yet. It'll be all right if only we get away in time."

"But how?" said Susan.

"We're prisoners just as much as Uncle Jim," said Peggy.

"Let's see if we are," said Nancy. "We can get into the garden, anyhow, and there's another door at the back."

They tried the door and found that they could open it. They looked out into the great courtyard, empty now and silent, except for voices from the gateway where the guards, their rifles leaning against the wall, were playing cards, sitting on their heels. They turned back, closed that door and went warily out into the garden. Keeping out of sight of Miss Lee's house, they dodged through orange-trees, and found themselves looking down on steep terraces with winding paths. There were willow-trees drooping over a little pond in which they caught the golden glow of fish. There were trellises covered with purple and scarlet flowers. There were dwarf trees like pines and oaks. And far away, below the garden, they could see the water of the river and, in the distance, range upon range of blue hills.

"Look," whispered Roger.

On one of the paths below them two figures were earnestly talking. One was the aged counsellor and the other was Miss Lee herself.

"We'd better go back," said Susan.

They went back into their house and chose their rooms for the night, one for John and Roger, one for Titty and Susan and one for Nancy and Peggy.

"Three cabins," said Roger. "It's like being back in the *Wild Cat.*"

No one answered him, and Roger himself pinched his lip between his teeth. If only Gibber had not set fire to the *Wild Cat* they would not be prisoners now.

"It'll be all right in the end," said Nancy at last. "For Uncle Jim too. It always is."

The old amah came in with a man bringing them their supper, big bowls of rice with pigeon's eggs and bowls of congee soup. The old amah, who had nursed Miss Lee when she was a little girl, stayed and watched them. She began to treat them as if they were all small children, even John, and stopped first one and then another because they were not using their chopsticks in the proper way. "You belong live Missee Lee yamen," she said. "Belong chow-chow China fashion."

Long after they had eaten their supper and seen the trays of empty bowls carried away, Miss Lee came to look at them, but only for a moment. She gave them no chance of asking questions. She just looked at them with a pleased smile. "You come to me tomollow," she said, "and have bleakfast Camblidge fashion. . . . Ham and eggs. . . . Then we begin study. . . . Good night. Sleep well." She bowed and was gone.

"She looked at us as if we were pet rabbits," said Roger.

"Oh, well," said Nancy. "We ought to be jolly pleased. People don't cut off pet rabbits' heads."

CHAPTER XIV

CAMBRIDGE BREAKFAST AND AN S.O.S.

THEY were getting accustomed to sleeping in strange places. It was four days now since they slept for the last time in their comfortable cabins in the *Wild Cat.* They found the Chinese beds much easier than they had looked, and, after a good night's rest, woke early and ready for anything. Roger was up first for once, and there was a little trouble because he wanted to climb into the great earthenware water kong to have a bath. John grabbed him just in time and explained that the same lot of water had to do for everybody, and that the way to use it was to dip from it and empty the dipper over one's shoulders and head. Anybody could guess that who looked at the brown tiled floor and saw how it sloped from each side towards a channel in the middle that carried the water away and out through a hole in the wall. They were more or less dressed when the amah came in and Susan made signs of toothbrushing. The amah went off and came back with some bundles of bamboo toothpicks, and then waited to see how they used them.

A bell sounded and the amah bustled them out. "Missee Lee," she said. "You belong chow chiu fan . . . bleakfast . . . longside Missee Lee."

She led the way through the garden to Miss Lee's house and into Miss Lee's Cambridge study.

"Good morning," said Miss Lee who was pouring out coffee at the head of a trestle-table that had been put up at one side of the room.

Staring at the table, they said, "Good morning."

"Gosh!" murmured Roger.

"Sit down, please," said Miss Lee, and they sat down, three on each side. In the middle of the table was a large jar of Cooper's Oxford marmalade. In front of each of them was a bowl of porridge and from somewhere in the house came a smell of fried ham that made Roger sniff and sniff again.

"Knives and forks," said Roger.

"And spoons," said Titty.

"Evellything Camblidge fashion," said Miss Lee proudly. "Sugar, please? Please take milk."

"Jolly good porridge," said Nancy after her first mouthful. "Wouldn't Uncle Jim like some. . . ."

For a moment they all thought of Captain Flint, sitting behind bars, doing his best to eat rice with chopsticks. The thought spoilt the taste of the porridge.

"Chinese food is velly wholesome," said Miss Lee. "You need not wolly about your Captain Flint. Taicoon Chang will tleat him velly well till he gets his answer from Amelica."

"But he's in prison," said Titty.

"Velly uncultured man," said Miss Lee. "Why not?"

"What about Gibber and Polly?" asked Roger.

"Roger's monkey and Titty's parrot," John explained.

"Taicoon Chang will send them today," said Miss Lee.

"Oh good," said Roger, and with the thought

that Gibber and Polly were to join them, the thought of Captain Flint faded. It did not seem quite fair to him. But there was nothing to be done and there was no point in letting the porridge get cold.

The smell of fried ham grew suddenly stronger, and men came in, took the empty porridge bowls away and set a plate before each of them, with fried ham on fried toast with two very little eggs, fried, on the top of the ham.

Miss Lee said she was sorry about the size of the eggs. "Camblidge eggs are bigger. Velly small eggs. Velly small hens."

"Bantams, I bet," said Roger.

After the ham and eggs, Miss Lee invited them to take toast and marmalade. "We always eat Oxford marmalade at Camblidge," she said. "Better scholars, better plofessors at Camblidge but better marmalade at Oxford."

Anybody could see that Miss Lee was enjoying herself. The cartridge belt and the revolver hung behind the door were the only things in the room to suggest that the Miss Lee of Cambridge giving breakfast to her students was also Missee Lee, the pirate chief of the three islands, the terror of the China coast. She talked away about days boating on the Cam, about breakfasts with her tutor, about the head of her college and her old plans for a career of scholarship. It was hard to believe that in the courtyard close by they had seen prisoners behind bars, ransoms being paid, and busy accountants weighing silver dollars and working out with the help of the abacus the shares of the profits due to junk captains and crews and to Miss Lee herself. And when, soon after breakfast, they found themselves sitting at the table being examined as to how much Latin they knew, it was only the whistling of kites and the churr of cicadas in the orange-trees outside that reminded them that they were not at school at home in England.

Miss Lee began at the beginning of the Latin Grammar, with the declensions, and soon found that "Mensa mensa mensam" meant nothing whatever to Susan, Nancy or Peggy, though Titty struggled through with a little help. John and Roger went through the declensions with ease. "Now genders," said Miss Lee.

"'Common are to either sex
Artifex and opifex,'"

"How does it go on?"

Roger looked at John. John looked like someone trying to remember a dream.

"I used to know it," he said.

"Well, Loger?" said Miss Lee.

"'Conviva, vates, advena,
Testis, civis, incola,'"

Roger rattled off, hesitated a moment and went on:

"'Parens, sacerdos, custos, vindex,
Adolescens, infans, index. . . .'"

He stuck . . . "infans, index . . . um . . . index. . . .

"'Judex, heres, comes, dux. . . .'"

He stuck again. Miss Lee prompted him with:

"'Plinceps, municeps, conjux,
Obses, ales, interples. . . .'"

"I know, I know," said Roger.

"'Auctor, exul; and with these
Bos, dama, talpa, tigris, grus,
Canis and anguis, serpens, sus.'"

"I can always remember the dog and the two kinds of snake and the old pig," he added.

"John must learn that," said Miss Lee. "Now, do you know your verbs?"

But there is no need to describe the whole of that long, uncomfortable examination. Miss Lee looked more and more disappointed as it went on. Indeed, if it had not been for Roger, who had never thought that Latin would come in so useful, she might well have given up her idea there and then, in which case most likely the story would have ended at once and no one would ever have known what had happened to the crew of the *Wild Cat.* The little schooner and her crew would have vanished like so many other ships and sailors in those far off seas. But, though Susan, Peggy and Nancy had to start at the very beginning, though Nancy and Peggy showed that they thought it waste of time even to begin, though Titty had only picked up a few words, and though Latin had always been John's weakest subject, a lively rendering by Roger of a bit of Caesar's "Gallic War" saved the lot of them, and Miss Lee made up her mind to do the best she could with her uneven class.

"I think Loger will go to top," she said. "He

will sit here. Then John. John had better lead Latin Grammar till he lemembers it. Then Tittee. She was all long about the second declension but she knows the first. Then. . . ." She looked despairingly at the three others. . . . "Su-san, Nansee and Peggee. . . . Never mind. They will lead glammar hard and we will do tlanslation all together. They will soon pick up."

"Just try Roger in French," said Nancy, one time leader but now at the bottom of the class.

"Flench?" said Miss Lee.

"They never are any good at French at boys' schools," said Nancy.

"Flench," said Miss Lee, "is not a classical language. Now Gleek? Do Loger and John learn Gleek?"

But nobody knew any Greek except John, and he knew only the alphabet, which was wanted for mathematics.

"Latin first," said Miss Lee. "Pelhaps Gleek next year or the year after that. . . ."

"But we can't. . . ." Susan began in horror. She caught Miss Lee's eye and was silent.

"And now," said Miss Lee, "for tomollow. We shall be leading Virgil's Aeneid, Book Two. Loger and John will take the book and the dictionary and plepare as much as they can. Tittee, Su-san, Peggee and Nansee will take the Latin Glammar and will show me tomollow how well they can learn if they tly. You can go out in the garden. Dismiss."

"How soon do you think Gibber and Polly will be here?" asked Roger.

"They will come quite soon," said Miss Lee

and smiled at the only one of her pupils who had shown any kind of promise.

*

"This is pretty awful," said Nancy as they came back to their own house. "I don't care what anybody says, I'm not going to do any prep till this evening. What's the good of learning Latin, anyway? All very well for Roger."

"Let's have a look round that garden while we've got a chance," said John.

They went out and down the terraces, looked at the gold fish in the little pond, and, going on, found that the whole garden was enclosed by a wall too high and smooth for even John to climb. The only door in the wall was locked. The only other ways out were through Miss Lee's, or the council chamber, or their own house, into the great courtyard with its armed guards always at the gateway. There was a door into the courtyard just beyond Miss Lee's house, but that, like the door at the bottom of the garden, was locked.

"No good," said John. "We can't get out unless she lets us."

"Even if we did we'd have to get back to Tiger Island and rescue Captain Flint," said Titty.

"We'll think of a plan," said Nancy. "We'll just have to stick it for a bit. There's plenty of time before Chang gets a message to America and back."

They were in their house when Titty heard the scream of the ship's parrot and then a cheerful "Pieces of eight". They ran through the house and out into the great courtyard to see the one-time cook holding the parrot-cage in one hand and Gibber's lead in the other, coming in at the big gateway. A crowd that had gathered as he led the monkey through the streets was staring in, and the guards were making faces at the gibbering monkey.

"Numpa one bad monkey," said the ex-cook, grinning. "Him bite. Him lun away. Him pull donk ear. Him pull donk tail. Numpa one bad monkey." He let go of the lead and in a moment the monkey had run to Roger and was hanging round his neck.

Titty was already talking to the parrot. The ex-cook handed over a small sack that had been slung over his shoulder. "Pallot chow," he said. "Flom Taicoon Chang."

"Is Captain Flint all right?" asked Nancy. "Big man . . ."

The ex-cook laughed. "Him first chop," he said. "Him all light. Him give my chit. In pallot chow."

"What? What?" said Nancy. But the ex-cook had turned to join his friends, the guards at the gateway.

"Pallot chow?" said Nancy.

"Parrot food," said Titty. "That's the Taicoon. He liked Polly. He's probably sent a lot of sunflower seeds."

"But what had Uncle Jim to do with that?" said Nancy.

Back in the house, while Roger was tickling Gibber and talking to him as if he had not seen him for a year, Titty opened the sack and dipped out a handful of sunflower seeds and things that looked like big white beans.

CAPTAIN FLINT'S S.O.S.

"It's not quite the same as his ordinary food," she said. "But the Taicoon's tried to get it. I showed him some of Polly's food when we were there."

"Empty out that bag," said Nancy.

"What for? It'll make an awful mess," said Susan.

"I'll sweep it up," said Nancy, and took the bag and emptied it out on the floor, a heap of seeds under a little cloud of dust. She spread the seeds wider and wider, and then, suddenly, turned the bag inside out. A folded paper fluttered to the floor. Nancy pounced on it.

"Now," she said.

"What is it?" said John.

"Letter from Captain Flint of course, just to tell us he's all right."

She held out a drawing that looked like one of her own pictures, except that all the people in it had Chinese hats. It was a picture of a lot of Chinese, in procession, climbing a mountain road. Somehow or other some Chinese junks had found their way up the mountain.

"Read it aloud," said John. "What does it say?"

"REBBIGFOTSA. . . . Can't make head or tail of the beginning. He must be up to some new dodge. . . ."

"Let's look," said Titty.

"Pencil," said Nancy, and Roger handed over the copying pencil he had last used in writing in Miss Lee's dictionary.

"Not that," said Nancy. "If it's really secret, we'll want to rub it out."

Titty dug the stump of a pencil from her pocket

and Nancy hurriedly pencilled a letter under each of the little figures in the procession.

"What about the junks?" said Roger.

"Leave them," said Nancy.

"REBBIG FO TSAL EHT EES OT YRROS
EB DLUOW I THGUOHT REVEN SP REH FO
EDIS THGIR NO PEEK SNEPPAH REVETAHW
HTURT ELOHW EEL SSIM LLET RETTEB
GNIWERB ELBUORT DNA DNUOR LLA
SKOOL KRAD EKATSIM YM OCSIRF NI
SROYAMDROL SA SLAMINA HCUS ON SSOB
SIH DLOT NOTGNIHSAW EGROEG SIHT
AINROFILAC NI STNAP HSAW OT DESU
OHW SHGUOT SIH FO ENO NI DELLAC
EH NACIREMA DAER TONNAC FEIHC GIB
RETRONS A ETORW I NIAGA ROYAM DROL
RIEHT EES OT DETNAW YEHT FI KCIUQ
PU YAP DNA EMOSDNAH PU YAP OT
NEMREDLA YM ETIRW EM EDAM FEIHC
GIB SSERP POTS
SWEN YLIAD
DNALSI REGIT"

"That first word's Gibber the wrong way round," said Titty.

"I've seen that," said Nancy. "Up hill instead of down." And, stopping sometimes when she had run two words together, and finding out at once that the junks were meant as stops, and that each line went from right to left no matter which way the climbers seemed to be going, she read aloud:

"TIGER ISLAND DAILY NEWS. STOP PRESS. . BIG CHIEF MADE ME WRITE MY ALDERMEN TO PAY UP HANDSOME AND PAY UP QUICK IF THEY WANTED TO SEE THEIR LORD MAYOR AGAIN. I WROTE A SNORTER. BIG CHIEF CANNOT READ AMERICAN. HE CALLED IN ONE OF HIS TOUGHS WHO USED TO WASH PANTS IN CALIFORNIA. THIS GEORGE WASHINGTON TOLD HIS BOSS NO SUCH ANIMALS AS LORDMAYORS IN FRISCO. MY MISTAKE. DARK LOOKS ALL ROUND AND TROUBLE BREWING. BETTER TELL MISS LEE WHOLE TRUTH. WHATEVER HAPPENS KEEP ON RIGHT SIDE OF HER. PS. NEVER THOUGHT I WOULD BE SORRY TO SEE THE LAST OF GIBBER."

"Giminy," said Nancy. "It's an S.O.S."

"He isn't all right at all," said John. "They've found him out."

"Perhaps they've done it already," said Roger and did not explain what he meant.

"Look here," said Nancy. "We can't sit here doing Latin while Uncle Jim's having his head cut off."

"What are we to do?" said Susan.

"There's only one thing we can do," said Nancy. "We've got to make Miss Lee get him out."

"But how?"

"Ultimatum," said Nancy. "Tip her the black spot. It worked with Uncle Jim. It'll work with her. She's dead keen on these beastly lessons. We'll go on strike. We'll depose her. She can't be a schoolmarm if she's got no pupils. Tell her 'No Captain Flint, no lessons'."

"We'll want some paper," said Titty.

"Hop along, Roger," said Nancy. "You're the top of the class. You hop along and ask for some paper."

Roger, with the monkey in his arms, ran out into the garden. In five minutes he was back, blushing and looking very serious. He held out a sheet of ricepaper and something in a saucer.

"I say," he said, "she doesn't like Gibber. She says he is dirty. She says he's got fleas. And he hasn't, not since that last scrubbing. She is a bit Great Auntish after all. She says I must never bring him into her room. And he isn't to sleep in the house. He's got to go into one of those cages every night."

"Well, you've got the paper all right," said Nancy.

"She perked up like anything when I asked for it," said Roger. "She was very pleased, and said it would be a good thing to copy out some of those rhymes like Artifex and Opifex and the simple stuff you've got to learn. She was talking to the old man with a beard. I say, you know why his fingers look so long? His nails are as long as his fingers. I didn't tell her what we really wanted the paper for."

"It doesn't matter," said Nancy. "She'll know when we hand in the ultimatum. I say. Hadn't she got a pen?" She was looking at the saucer of black ink and at a bamboo writing-brush with its pointed tip of fine hair.

"She has a fountain pen herself," said Roger.

"Oh, well," said Nancy. "Let's get the thing written."

There was some argument about the wording. Nancy was all for making it hot and strong. Susan was for mildness. Titty pointed out that Captain Flint himself had said that they ought to keep on the right side of Miss Lee. Nancy said that all that mattered was to make Miss Lee take him away from Chang.

The rough copy, written by Nancy herself, with corrections by everybody, was done in pencil. The final copy was done by Titty, because she was the best hand with a paintbrush, using Miss Lee's ink for the sake of politeness.

Here is the ultimatum:

"To Miss Lee

We the undersigned point out that Captain Flint is one of us and it is all wrong to put him in one place and us in another. He is not used to cages. How can anybody learn Latin when their uncle is shut up like an animal in a Zoo? We will do our best to learn Latin (Nancy's original sentence was 'We'll stick to those lessons') if Captain Flint is here too. But we cannot be any good at it while (Titty's suggestion) our hearts are far away. Save Captain Flint and we will work like anything. But if not, not. (Nobody but Nancy liked that last sentence, but she was so pleased with it that they had to let it pass.)

Signed

CAPTAIN	Nancy Blackett (of the *Amazon*)
MATE	Peggy Blackett
CAPTAIN	John Walker (of the *Swallow*)
MATE	Susan
A.B.	Titty
A.B.	Roger

Members of the crew of the *Wild Cat* which was burnt through no fault of our own."

"Buck up, Titty," said Nancy.

"It's pretty difficult writing with a brush," said Titty who was kneeling on the floor painting letter by letter on the paper spread in front of her.

"You simply must buck up," said Nancy.

"I am," said Titty, working away with the tip of her tongue between her lips.

It was done at last and Nancy grabbed it.

"Look out," said Titty. "It's still wet."

"All right," said Nancy. "Let's have that brush. Giminy, what a thing to write with." She signed her name, put the name of her ship and gave the paper to Peggy. One by one they all signed and Titty held the paper in the sun to get the ink dry.

"Who takes it to her?" asked Roger. "Not me. I went in and got the paper."

"All of us," said Nancy. "Come on. And leave that monkey behind."

Going through the garden they met the old counsellor coming from Miss Lee's. He looked through them as if they were not there and turned in at the small door in the back of the

To Miss Lee

<u>We the undersigned</u> point out that Captain Flint is one of us and it is all wrong to put him in one place and we in another. He is not used to cages. How can anybody learn Latin when their uncle is shut up like an animal in a Zoo? We will do our best to learn Latin if Captain Flint is here too. But we cannot be any good at it while our hearts are far away. Save Captain Flint and we will work like anything. But if not, not.

<u>Signed</u>

CAPTAIN NANCY BLACKETT (OF THE AMAZON)
MATE PEGGY BLACKETT

CAPTAIN John Walker (of the Swallow)
MATE Susan
A.B. Titty
A.B. Roger

Members of the crew of the Wild Cat which was burnt through no fault of our own.

THE ULTIMATUM

council chamber. They went on and were stopped by the amah.

"You wantee see Missee Lee?" she asked.

They waited. The amah came out and led them to the door of Miss Lee's study.

"Please come in," said Miss Lee. "You want help with your grammar? If there is anything you do not understand, you may always come and ask."

"It isn't that," said Nancy.

"What is it?"

"It's about Captain Flint." Nancy gave Miss Lee the ultimatum.

"From all of us," said John.

Miss Lee laid the paper on her desk and read it through to the end. She looked at them through narrowed eyes.

"I can not," she said. "Wu and my counsellor want to keep my father's law. I am bleaking it, because I want my students. You are English, but I tell them it is safe because you cannot get away, because no one knows you are here, and because even if you could get away you would not know how to come back with gunboats. But they think better to chop off heads and have no trouble. Chang thinks it is safe to keep your Captain Flint because he is Amelican not English. . . ." Her eyes narrowed still more. "It is a bargain. Quid plo quo. I keep my students. Chang keeps his Amelican."

"But he isn't American," said Nancy.

"I did not think he was," said Miss Lee. "But Chang thinks he is. No matter. No hully. That man velly well in plison. He is a velly uncultured man and it is good for him to sit and think. Chang will keep him safe until his messenger goes to Amelica and comes back."

"But it's all wrong." said Nancy. "Chang's beginning to guess already."

"How do you know?"

There was a pause full of doubts. Captain Flint had told them to tell Miss Lee the truth, but he had not meant them to show her his letter.

"How do you know?" asked Miss Lee again.

"Better show her," said Titty. "It'll be all right if she says 'Honest Pirate' first."

"You won't give him away to Chang if we tell you?" said Nancy.

"He belongs to Chang already," said Miss Lee.

"I mean you won't . . . Look here. We'll have to take the risk. You've got the letter, John."

John handed over the paper with Captain Flint's message.

"A picture?" said Miss Lee. "Not velly good."

"Semaphore," said Nancy. "You said you've been a Girl Guide. Signals. You have to read them backwards."

"Chinese fashion," said Miss Lee and, working backwards, looking at the little figures, starting at the bottom of the hill and going to and fro to the top, she read the message through.

"The junks are full stops," said Nancy.

"I see you have litten the letters," said Miss Lee.

"So I did," said Nancy. "I forgot, but you could have read the signals, anyway, couldn't you?"

"I could," said Miss Lee. She read through the message again and gave it back to John.

She thought for a minute. Then she said. "It is his own fault. He lied to Chang and he lied to me."

"But if he hadn't we'd have been killed already, Peggy and me and Captain Flint."

"What then?" said Miss Lee. "You are not velly good students."

"But they will be," said Titty.

Miss Lee smiled. "Keep on the right side of Miss Lee," she repeated slowly.

"We'll try to," said Susan.

"Is this how you tly?" said Miss Lee, holding up the ultimatum. "No. I can do nothing. That man has cheated Chang. If I take him now I shall have cheated Chang myself. You are my students but that man is Chang's. If he has lied and Chang cuts his head off it is his own fault."

"But he's our uncle," said Nancy.

"He's our friend," said John.

And then Titty said something which, almost as soon as it was out of her mouth, she wished she had not said.

"It's the same as if it was Daddy," she burst out. "Think. Think. You couldn't learn Latin if you knew your father was a prisoner. . . ."

Miss Lee's tiny fingers stiffened. She stared at Titty, and suddenly her manner changed.

"Pelhaps not," she said gently. "I will talk to Chang. You may go now."

And five minutes later, they heard Miss Lee's whistler shrilling a message into the air.

"We've done it. We've done it," cried Nancy, as they listened and heard an answering whistler repeat the message faint and far away.

"It was what Titty said about Daddy that did it," said Roger.

"Jolly good thing you thought of it, Titty," said Nancy.

But Titty was feeding sunflower seeds to the ship's parrot and did not turn round.

CHAPTER XV

MISS LEE BUYS CAPTAIN FLINT

THERE was no lesson next day. "Chang is coming," said Miss Lee at the end of an almost silent breakfast. "I must talk with my counsellor. John and Loger can go on pleparing tlanslation and if Nansee, Su-san and Peggee know the first declension they can join Tittee in learning the second and third."

"Will he bring Captain Flint with him?" asked Titty.

"No," said Miss Lee.

*

"Bother the declensions," said Nancy when they were back in their own house. "Why should we learn the beastly things? Let's stick to what we said. No Captain Flint, no Latin."

"She sent off that message pretty quick," said John.

"He said we were to keep on the right side of her," said Susan.

"Come on," said Roger. "Nansee. . . . Let me hear the plural of mensa . . ."

He dodged just in time, but Titty agreed with John and so did Susan, and after Titty had fed the parrot and Roger had seen that there was plenty of food in the monkey's cage after taking him for a short run in the courtyard (when, as Roger put it, Gibber and the guards, chattering at each other, talked two foreign languages at once), Miss Lee's students did indeed try to work in the cool of the big room on the garden side of their house. But it was hard to think of dominus, domine, dominum when every minute they were listening for something else.

Most of the morning had gone and nobody had learnt much when the great gong set the air throbbing about them.

"Chang!" cried Nancy.

"It's the Taicoon!" said Titty.

"Come on," said Roger.

They ran through the house and out into the courtyard in time to see the Taicoon, Chang, carried in through the gateway, sitting in his chair with a lacquered bird-cage on his knee.

He saw the prisoners at once and, the moment he got out of his chair, beckoned to Titty.

"Velly good bud," he said, pointing to the bird, a lark this time instead of a canary. "Sing all way."

"He's a beauty," said Titty.

"How pallot?" asked the Taicoon.

"Very well," said Titty. "And thank you for his food. But where is Captain Flint?"

The Taicoon scowled. "Captain James Flint," he said. "San Flancisco. Him numpa one velly bad man."

He said no more. The old counsellor was coming down the steps from the council room. They greeted each other and went in together, the old counsellor talking, and the Taicoon listening, nodding his dark blue skull-cap with its scarlet button, his bird-cage dangling from his hand.

"I like that," said Nancy. "We know the Taicoon

means to get money for Uncle Jim and then cut off his head, and now he calls Captain Flint a number one bad man just because he's beginning to think that perhaps there won't be any money."

"What'll Miss Lee say to him?" said Peggy.

"If she wants to give us lessons she's jolly well got to do something," said Roger.

"Chang looked pretty wild," said John.

"Couldn't we get some grasshoppers for his bird?" said Titty.

"There's something like them chirping in the garden," said Roger.

"How long's he going to be in there talking?" said Susan.

"Good long time," said Nancy, pointing towards the gateway. The Taicoon's bearers had left his chair in the courtyard and were already settling down to play cards. "They wouldn't be doing that if they thought he was coming out in a hurry. Come on. Getting grasshoppers is better than waiting about not knowing what's going to happen."

They went through their house into the garden. At the other side of the orange-trees they stopped short. There, on the topmost terrace, were Miss Lee, the counsellor and the Taicoon, Chang, sitting in chairs, with little tables beside them, each with a tiny bowl of tea and a plate of sweetmeats.

"Gosh!" whispered Roger. "I thought they'd be in the big room."

"Come on," said Nancy. "They've seen us, anyway." The six prisoners went on down the terraces into the lower garden.

"He looks furious," said Titty.

"Titty," said Nancy, "hop back and bring out Polly. He'll see and it may put him in a good temper."

"Shall I get Gibber?" said Roger hopefully.

"No," said John. "Gibber's more likely to send him raving mad. But Polly's worth trying."

It was pretty awful going up the paths alone in full view of the three sitting there on the topmost terrace, but John had agreed with Nancy and Titty obeyed as she would have obeyed an order aboard ship. She waited a moment in the house, and put a fresh handful of parrot food into the feeding-box. "Come on, Polly," she said, "you've got to help." Then she picked up the cage and carried it out under the orange-trees. With one eye on Miss Lee, the Taicoon and the old counsellor, she crossed the terrace where they were sitting. The Taicoon was talking angrily and did not see her.

And then the parrot, stirred by this sudden journey, sang out "Pieces of eight" at the very top of its harsh voice. The Taicoon turned sharply. Just for a moment a smile showed on his face. Then he went on with what he had been saying to Miss Lee.

"Well," said Nancy, as Titty joined the others. "Did he see?"

"He heard," said Titty. "And he grinned."

"Good," said John.

"We all heard," said Roger. "It was what old Polly said. I bet he grinned because Polly talked about money. Probably made things worse. If only I'd had Gibber. . . ."

"You'd have had Miss Lee and the Taicoon and

the old man all raging mad together," said Susan.

Roger chuckled. "He might have copied the counsellor combing his beard." His own hand strayed to his chin as he spoke.

"Look out," hissed Nancy. "The counsellor'll think you're as bad as Gibber."

"I've got one grasshopper," said John. "Let's have something to put it in. Matchbox, Susan."

"I threw the box away when I used the last match," said Susan. "All our others are on the island with the iron rations."

"Shall I make a paper box?" said Peggy.

"Can you?"

"She's jolly good at it," said Nancy.

"All the paper's in the house," said Susan. "No. Stay here, Roger."

But Roger was off up the terraces at full tilt, glad of the excuse, because he wanted to get a nearer look at the Taicoon. Presently they saw him coming slowly back.

"Squabbling," he said as he gave a sheet of rice paper to Peggy.

"That means Miss Lee's really trying," said John.

Peggy folded the paper and cut it square with her scout-knife. Then she folded in the corners so that it became a smaller square. Then she folded again. It turned into a hat, a double-ended boat, a salt cellar.

"Bother," said Peggy. "I've forgotten how."

"No, you haven't," said Nancy. "Go on. You fold and fold and then unfold and cut bits out."

"It's not a very good one," said Peggy a few minutes later.

"It'll do," said Nancy. "Giminy, how those beasts can hop."

"Got one," said Roger. "Not very big."

"He was always picking out little ones the other day," said Titty. "They're the ones his birds like best."

They had half a dozen small grasshoppers in the paper box when they heard Miss Lee call "Nansee!"

"Coming," called Nancy and looked round at the others.

"We'll all come," said John.

"They can't exactly eat us," said Nancy, but they knew that she was glad she was not going up there alone.

"Better bring Polly," said Roger.

They stood in a row in front of the three Chinese. The Taicoon, Chang was scowling, though his eye softened a little as it fell on the parrot. The counsellor, looking far beyond them at the distant hills, was combing his wispy beard with finger-nails that, as Roger had said, were as long as his fingers. Miss Lee looked straight at Nancy. She spoke very slowly, word by word, so that, though she spoke in English, Chang should know what she was saying.

"I have asked the Taicoon, Chang, to let me have his plisoner. The Taicoon, Chang, says that he will keep him because unless he is a liar the people of San Flancisco will pay much money to save their Lord Mayor. . . ."

At this moment, Chang, who had been nodding as she spoke, held out a piece of paper towards Miss Lee and said something in Chinese.

Miss Lee took the paper and gave it to Nancy. "The Taicoon's plisoner has litten this," she said. "Lead it."

"All of us?" said Nancy.

"Yes," said Miss Lee.

The Taicoon and Miss Lee watched them while they read it. The old counsellor seemed interested only in the far-away hills.

The paper was a letter in Captain Flint's handwriting.

"To my faithful people of San Francisco: Greeting!

I, your Lord Mayor, lie in chains cheek by jowl with a vile ape. ['Gibber isn't a vile ape. He's got a tail,' Roger murmured as he read.] My only hope of freedom is in you. Do you value your Lord Mayor? If you think I am worthless, send nothing. But if you think that I, Captain James Flint, Lord Mayor of San Francisco, am worth half a million dollars, send that half million pronto by the trusted bearer of this. Say nothing to the police or the United States Navy or you will have to find a new Lord Mayor for this one will have lost his head.

(*Signed.*) JAMES FLINT, Lord Mayor."

They looked at each other uncomfortably. In his message to them he had spoken of writing a snorter. He had certainly spread himself.

Miss Lee spoke again. "The Taicoon Chang asks me if his plisoner is fooling him or not. Now, Nansee, you will tell the tluth. Is the Taicoon's plisoner Amelican or English? Is he Lord Mayor? Will the velly lich city of San Flancisco pay

BARGAINING FOR CAPTAIN FLINT

anything . . . for . . . him . . . at . . . all?"

Nancy swallowed, looked wildly round and, for a moment, said nothing. It was one thing to tell the truth to Miss Lee on Captain Flint's own orders. But ought she to tell the truth to Chang?

"Tell the tluth," said Miss Lee. "The Taicoon will find out, anyway."

Nancy made up her mind to trust Miss Lee. "He is English, not American. He is not a Lord Mayor. I don't think San Francisco would pay a penny for him." She said it slowly, and firmly, word by word.

"I chop him head," said the Taicoon leaping to his feet.

They gasped. In trying to save Captain Flint, they had made things worse instead of better.

"But you simply can't," said Titty.

Miss Lee was speaking again, very quietly. Her tiny hand touched the rim of an untasted bowl of tea. The Taicoon, Chang, towering above her, sat down again as if unwillingly. Miss Lee had not seemed to notice that he had stood up. She was not looking at him, but, like the counsellor, far away. She did not seem to know that her prisoners were waiting there before her. She was talking as if she were stating a number of facts in none of which was she particularly interested.

Chang listened till she had stopped, and then he too began talking in the same queer way, not as if he were arguing but as if he, too, had a set of facts to state.

"Nansee," said Miss Lee. "Is your Captain a lich man in England."

"No," said Nancy. "He spent all his money on buying the *Wild Cat* and fitting her out, and

Gibber set fire to her and now she is at the bottom of the sea."

Miss Lee spoke in Chinese, perhaps translating in case Chang had not understood. Chang grunted angrily.

For some time Titty had been making up her mind. Now she put the parrot's cage in front of Chang's chair. After all, she had told herself, she never would have had the parrot if it had not been for Captain Flint.

"If you will let him go," she said, "I will give you Polly."

For a moment the Taicoon seemed not to understand. Suddenly the scowl left his face. He smiled. "You numpa one good missee," he said. "Numpa one good bud belong stay with him missee. I no take him."

After that for a long time the talk was in Chinese and they had no idea what was being said. Miss Lee signed to her prisoners to go away."

"Would you really have given him the parrot?" said Roger.

"Don't you understand?" said Titty almost fiercely. "Polly was a present from Captain Flint."

They hung about wretchedly on the lower terraces, wondering if there was nothing they could do to help. At last they heard Miss Lee clap her hands. They looked up. They saw the old amah for a moment by Miss Lee's chair. Then they saw a signaller, with one of those queer bamboo flutes. Miss Lee was talking to him. A few moments later they heard shrill whistling on two notes, like a bar of very simple music repeated again and again. From far, far away, there came a whistling answer. The nearby whistling began again, a long uneven trilling. From far away, thin as a bat's song, came the echo. A man appeared with a small bag. He gave it to Miss Lee and went back under the orange-trees. They saw that Miss Lee was beckoning.

"I have bought him," she said as they ran up.

"Well done, Miss Lee," said Nancy.

"Everything'll be all right now," said John.

"You didn't pay too much?" said Roger.

"She couldn't," said Peggy indignantly.

Neither Susan nor Titty could say a word.

The Taicoon was pushing something away into one of his wide sleeves.

"Him tell lie," he said to the prisoners. "Him fool Taicoon. Moa betta I chop him head. But I sell him. I sell him velly cheap." Suddenly he tossed off his tea and, with a look of great cunning, got up to go. Miss Lee glanced silently at her own bowl. She had not touched it. Chang, with unwilling politeness, again sat down. Presently a new bowl of tea was brought and placed on the little table beside him.

Susan held out the paper box. The Taicoon looked at it. Susan shook the box close to her ear. The Taicoon took it and listened. He knew at once what was in it, gingerly opened the flaps that closed it, caught a grasshopper as it crawled out, twitched the cover from the cage beside him, and gave the insect to his lark. The bird gobbled up the grasshopper and broke into loud song. The Taicoon laughed with pleasure, forgot Captain Flint, and looked for applause to the counsellor, who nodded gravely, to Miss Lee, who smiled, and to the prisoners.

"Numpa one velly good bud," he said.

Time went on. Men brought out a tray with good things for the Taicoon to eat. He ate, while the counsellor and Miss Lee just nibbled a little to keep him company. Another tray was brought, with tea and sweetmeats for the prisoners. "I thought they'd forgotten us," whispered Roger. The Taicoon asked Titty to let the parrot out of its cage, and asked Miss Lee to see how when Titty called the parrot it would come to her. He fed grasshoppers to his lark. The prisoners went off for more, and brought him caterpillars, which the lark seemed to like even better. From time to time, the Taicoon glanced at the shadows to see how the day was passing. Again and again he made as if to go, but every time he saw that Miss Lee had not touched her tea.

At last there was a noise of shouting, and then, above the shouting, they heard Captain Flint in song:

"We'll rant and we'll roar, like true British sailors,
We'll range and we'll roam over all the salt seas.
Until we strike soundings in the channel of old England,
From Ushant to Scilly is thirty-five leagues."

Miss Lee looked up, smiled at Chang and drank her tea at last, stone cold now for several hours. Chang, scowling again, stood up to go. Miss Lee nodded to the prisoners and they ran through the house to the courtyard just in time to see the bearers come in with Captain Flint in his travelling hen-coop of a cage, singing lustily above their heads.

"Three million cheers," cried Nancy, and, as the cage was lowered to the ground, some frantic handshaking was done through the bars.

The Taicoon's bearers were waiting with his chair. He had said "Good-bye" to Miss Lee and, with the counsellor, came down the steps into the courtyard. He walked straight across to speak to Captain Flint.

"Numpa one liar," he said. "Numpa one bad man. Numpa one cheat. I sell you. I sell velly cheap. I think moa betta I chop head."

He stalked off to his chair. Captain Flint was let out of his hen-coop, but, under the eye of the old counsellor, was immediately shut up in one of the barred cages in the courtyard, next door but one to Gibber.

"Moa betta I chop head," the Taicoon called out again as his bearers lifted his chair. Ten solemn strokes of the gong sounded from the gateway tower. The Taicoon was carried out, followed by the empty travelling cage that had once held Captain Flint.

"That was why Miss Lee kept on not drinking her tea," said Titty.

"What's that?" said Captain Flint through the bars of his new home.

They told him what had happened. "Good for Miss Lee," he said. "Titty's quite right. The Taicoon could not go till his hostess scoffed her drink. Same all over China. The bird fancier would sooner have stood on his head than have cleared out before she gave him the signal. Lucky for me, I gather. If he'd got away and met me on his own island, he'd have sent her back her money and said, 'Solly. Plisoner him bloke. Come to pieces in me hands.' Bit awkward for me being bought all the same. However."

"But why have they shut you up again?" said Roger.

"Don't you worry about that, my lad. I can tell you I feel a lot more firmly stuck together than I was."

Nancy had run off after seeing Captain Flint being locked up once more. She came back.

"I asked if you couldn't be let out, and she said no, but you're coming to Cambridge breakfast with us tomorrow."

"She gave us a jolly good breakfast," said Roger. "Oxford marmalade. You know. Brown and really juicy."

"Glad it's not all Cambridge," said Captain Flint. "And don't you worry about my being locked up. If any of Chang's lads are hanging about, I expect I'm a good deal better off behind bars."

"Gibber's close to," said Roger.

"That's comforting," said Captain Flint. "Now, how on earth did you manage to persuade her to take a hand."

Between them they told him the story of the Latin lessons and the ultimatum.

"Latin?" said Captain Flint. "That's what she talked at me. This is the rummest go I ever struck. When's she going to let us go."

"She isn't," said Titty.

"We'll have to make her change her mind," said Captain Flint. "Hang it all, I wonder what she had to pay for me."

The amah came to call them in for supper, and a man brought a big bowl of rice for Captain Flint.

They left him, eating in his cage.

"Well, we've saved him," said Nancy. "For the moment."

CHAPTER XVI

CAPTAIN FLINT JOINS THE DUNCES

THEY were out in the courtyard talking to Captain Flint and Gibber through the bars of their cages when they heard the bell ring for Cambridge breakfast. They came to Miss Lee's room to find that an extra place had been laid at the foot of the table.

"We told him he was coming to breakfast," said Roger.

"He's rather bothered about shaving," said Susan.

Miss Lee gave a key to the amah who went out of the room. They were all sitting down to breakfast when the amah came back bringing Captain Flint, rubbing a hairy chin and looking a little sheepish.

"He's forgotten what it's like being lugged about by a nurse," said Roger.

"Good morning," said Miss Lee.

"Good morning, ma'am," said Captain Flint. "I hardly like to come in. Mr. Chang had a barber. . . ."

"No matter," said Miss Lee. "You shall be shaved after bleakfast." She pointed to his place. "I hope you slept well."

"As comfortable a prison as ever I slept in," said Captain Flint.

"You have been much in gaol?" said Miss Lee coldly.

"Only police court," said Captain Flint. "Boat-race night. High spirits. A fancy for policemen's helmets."

"Ah," said Miss Lee. "I know. Camblidge won and evellybody happy."

"Not that year, ma'am. We were the happy ones that year."

"Not often since, I think," said Miss Lee.

The others, eating their porridge, listened anxiously. This was not the sort of talk they had expected to hear. How soon would Captain Flint come to serious business. He had said, "We'll have to make her change her mind." How soon would he begin to try? But Captain Flint, enjoying his breakfast, sitting on a chair instead of on a perch in a cage, seemed to be in no hurry.

"You are interested in rowing, ma'am?" he asked politely.

"I coxed Newnham's second boat," said Miss Lee. "Did you low for Oxford?"

"I did not," said Captain Flint. "I chucked Oxford before Oxford made up its mind to chuck me. I went off to see the world instead."

"Pelhaps that is why you know no Latin," said Miss Lee.

"Um," said Captain Flint, and a moment or two later, "Beautiful ham and eggs, ma'am. I haven't tasted such a ham since I left England. And I see you have Oxford marmalade."

"Yes," said Miss Lee. "At Oxford the scholarship is poor, but the marmalade velly good."

"Oh come, ma'am," said Captain Flint.

"Oxford student and knows no Latin," said

Miss Lee severely.

"I have forgotten it," said Captain Flint.

Miss Lee was looking round the table. "Now Loger," she said, "is velly good, John not so good. Titty is tlying hard. Su-san, Peggee and Nansee know no Latin at all. They begin at the beginning."

"Poor kids," said Captain Flint.

"Not at all," said Miss Lee. "They will learn quick and catch up with Loger. We shall lead Virgil . . . Aeneid . . . Next year Georgics, pelhaps . . . . Later on Holace. . . ."

Captain Flint saw his chance.

"We can hardly stay so long, ma'am," he said. "I have to take my crew back to their families, and I was going to ask you. . . ."

Miss Lee's eyes had narrowed. Her mouth was a straight line.

"You will stay," she said quietly.

"But isn't it rather awkward for you, ma'am?" urged Captain Flint. "Nancy tells me something about a law of your father's, a law about not keeping English prisoners."

"Listen," said Miss Lee. "My father's law was to take no English plisoners. The Taicoon Chang bloke that law because he thought you were Amelican. Now he knows that you are English. We are here three Taicoons, Chang, Wu and I. And also there is my father's counsellor. All, except me, want to keep my father's law. . . . They want no English plisoners."

"Then why not let us go and make everybody happy?" urged Captain Flint.

"That would not make anybody happy," said

Miss Lee. "Not my counsellor, not Wu, not Chang. Not you. They want no English plisoners. They want to cut off heads to save tlouble. They are thlee. I am one. But I make my own judgement and I know my father is happy for me to have my class of students."

"But . . ." began Captain Flint.

"It is settled," said Miss Lee. "Hoc volo. Sic jubeo. Dixi."

Captain Flint was silent. The others stared at each other. Roger was grinning.

"Loger," said Miss Lee. "Tell him what it means."

"She means she's jolly well going to do what she wants," said Roger.

For some time no one said anything. Then Captain Flint tried again.

"But, ma'am," he said, "you will not want me hanging about eating my head off doing nothing. Now if I could be getting a telegram home to tell their mothers not to worry."

"You will stay here and learn Latin," said Miss Lee.

Captain Flint gasped.

"But . . . But . . ."

"I will teach you Latin," said Miss Lee. "But alithmetic, tligonometly, you will teach. . . . I will also have a class in histoly. . . ."

"I know all the dates of the kings and queens," said Roger.

"Loman histoly," said Miss Lee. "We lead Virgil. It is ploper to lead some Loman Histoly. Annus urbis conditae?" She looked round the table, and then at Captain Flint.

Roger looked at Captain Flint, his eyes sparkling.

"Um," said Captain Flint.

"Loger?" said Miss Lee.

"Date of the founding of Rome," said Roger. "Seven-fifty-three B.C."

"Velly good, Loger," said Miss Lee.

"Swot," said Nancy under her breath.

"What?" said Miss Lee. "I did not hear."

Nancy blushed. "I meant he's wasted. . . . I mean he's spent a lot of time on lessons."

"Velly good student," said Miss Lee.

This time Roger blushed. He knew very well what the others were thinking about him, wished he had forgotten the date of the founding of Rome, choked over a scrap of marmalade and did not say another word till breakfast was over.

Then, when they were walking through the garden to go to their own house, he spoke to Nancy. "Sorry," he said.

"That's all right," said Nancy.

"Beastly cheeky," said John.

Captain Flint, who had been told that he might go with them to see their lodgings, overheard them. "Rot," he said. "You speak up all you can, Roger. Save the rest of us. It's a good thing one of us knows something. And anyway, I'll get my own back out of Roger when it comes to arithmetic."

"You see what she's like," said Susan. "She'll never let us go."

"Used to having her own way," said Captain Flint. "There isn't much give and take about Miss Lee. But don't be in a hurry. Give me time. We'll find a way out yet. . . . Eh! What's that?"

The amah, Miss Lee's old nurse, was hurrying after them. She had a lot to say and seemed to want Captain Flint to come with her.

"All right. All right," said Captain Flint, when he understood. "Coming in a minute. . . ." He rubbed his chin tenderly. "Oh, well," he said, "he can't be a worse barber than Mr. Chang's."

*

Half an hour later, after they had watched Captain Flint in his cage being shaved by a bare-footed, straw-hatted Chinese, while Gibber in the cage next door pretended to put a lather on his own wrinkled face, they were all back in Miss Lee's Cambridge study. The breakfast things had been cleared away, and Miss Lee was ready for her class. She set Roger and John to go on preparing their Virgil, left the others to their struggles with the first pages of the Latin Grammar, and tackled Captain Flint with a short examination in which he came off very badly. She tried him first with a few adjectives. "Latin for big?" she asked.

"Magnus," said Captain Flint with a pleased smile. That, at least, he knew.

"Bigger?"

Captain Flint hesitated. "There's a catch here," he said. "I ought to know it . . . Mag . . . mag . . . magnior."

Miss Lee laughed. "Oxford scholarship," she said. "Biggest?"

"Well, it isn't magnissimus but it ought to be," stammered Captain Flint. . . . "Magnanimous?"

"Loger?" said Miss Lee.

Roger, who had not been able to help listening, though he was getting on at a great rate with the beginning of Father Aeneas's tale because he had been through it once at school, looked doubtfully at John and then at Nancy.

"Go on," said Captain Flint. "I've got to learn. Spit it out if you know it."

"You can always remember it because of the Great Bear," said Roger. "Ursa Major . . ."

"Of course," said Captain Flint. "Bigger is Major and Biggest is Maximus. I knew it all the time. It's just that being asked things unexpectedly puts everything out of my head."

He did not do any better when she tried him with irregular verbs. She went back to the nouns, but again his memory failed him. She tried him with "Artifex and opifex", and he stuck fast at the second line.

"Better begin at the beginning with the others," said Miss Lee, and Captain Flint had to join the dunces, Nancy, Peggy and Susan, who were clustered over the Latin Grammar and still at the first page; while Titty, with her eyes shut, was trying to remember what she could of the second.

They could all see that Miss Lee, who had started her class with great hopes, found their ignorance a little depressing. They could see that she cheered up a lot when Roger did a translation of the first ten lines of the Virgil. They saw her in gloom again when she had turned on John to construe the next ten. And then a worse thing happened.

"It isn't John's fault," broke in Titty from the other end of the table. "You see he doesn't really need Latin. You just try him in mathematics."

"Not need Latin?" said Miss Lee. "And why not?"

"I'm going into the Navy," said John. "Like Father."

Miss Lee started. "Your father? In the Navy?"

"He's a captain," said John. "He'll be an admiral when he retires."

"Captain?" said Miss Lee. "Blitish Navy?"

"Yes," said Roger. "A real captain, not like Captain Flint. I expect you've seen his ship. He was stationed at Hong Kong."

"Gunboats!" exclaimed Miss Lee.

There was a long minute of silence.

"Did you tell that to Taicoon Chang?" asked Miss Lee.

"No," said John.

"If he knew . . . If the counsellor knew . . . If Wu knew . . . If my father . . ." She stopped. "Better no one should know. You have told no one. . . . I, Miss Lee, keep you. You are safe, but if they knew . . ." Miss Lee made a slight movement with her right hand. Slight though it was, they knew what it meant. It was the same movement of chopping that they had seen made by the small boys in the courtyard of the Taicoon Chang.

"Daddy isn't there now," said Titty. "Or we'd have been sailing straight to Hong Kong."

"Better I do not know," said Miss Lee. "Better I fo'get. Better you never tell me. . . ." She flung out her hand as if she were throwing away what she had heard, took up the Virgil and began translating herself. But she could not keep her mind on it. She faltered, and put the book down. "All you four," she said, "Loger, John, Su-san, Tittee, children of a Navy captain. If he knew you were with Miss Lee he would come with gunboats and spoil my father's business. . . ."

Then, suddenly, looking round the table at her seven students, she said, "I shall not tell even my counsellor. You must not tell even my amah. There is no danger to the Thlee Islands so long as you stay here. My father knows I have given up Camblidge. He is velly pleased for me to have my Camblidge here."

"Oxford," murmured Captain Flint.

Miss Lee heard him. "In five, ten years pelhaps, no one will guess you only went to Oxford."

"But. . . ." Susan began.

Captain Flint reached out under the table with a foot and managed to give her a warning kick.

"Well, ma'am," he said. "I'm sure we'll all do our best."

"Velly good," said Miss Lee. "Let us begin." She left John and Roger to their Virgil and for the next ten minutes had Captain Flint desperately floundering among the declensions of the nouns, while Roger, unable not to listen, could not suppress a gleeful grin.

It was a long lesson and not an easy one. It was as if Miss Lee wanted to make herself forget what she had learnt about the father of four of her prisoners being a captain in the British Navy. No doubt, for her, that bit of news made even worse her breaking of her father's rule that the men of the Three Islands should never take English prisoners. But a Latin class, of seven English students, was a prize she was not going to give up if she could help it.

They all had their turns. Captain Flint made howler after howler. Under her questions he forgot all he had ever known. The others found it hard to think of Latin Grammar or of Aeneas when it had become clearer than ever that Miss Lee meant to keep them for years. Susan, John and Titty were in a stew about getting news home, which, they saw now, would be the very last thing to be allowed. Nancy and Peggy, while a little bothered about Mrs. Blackett at home, had their uncle with them and would rather have liked to stay with pirates, but not to spend their time in being taught what they did not want to know. And even Roger, though he enjoyed being head of a class, particularly when Nancy and Captain Flint were somewhere near the bottom of it, did not think it was quite right to be at a dame's school at his age, even if the dame was a Chinese pirate, with a revolver hanging behind her door.

They were all heartily glad when the lesson came at last to an end and Miss Lee told them to take the Latin Grammar and the Virgil and the dictionary and marked what she wanted them to prepare for tomorrow. Their gladness turned to joyful surprise with her last words.

"And now you are flee," she said. "Flee till man fan. Flee till evening lice. Flee till supper. Go anywhere you like. Dismiss!"

"Come on," said Roger to himself as they

went out into the garden. "Let's jump. Fleas always do."

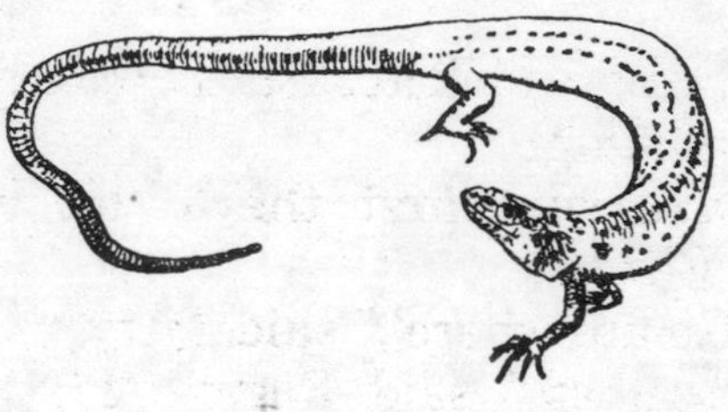

CHAPTER XVII

FREE BUT PRISONERS

"LET'S go and have a look at *Swallow* and *Amazon* first of all," said John.

"Got to make sure first they'll let us out," said Captain Flint.

"She said 'Go anywhere'," said Titty.

"Let's get started," said Roger. "I'll just get Gibber."

"If we take Gibber," said Captain Flint, "we'll have all the brats of the town following us. We don't want that. We've got a lot to find out. We'll leave Gibber to his bananas and Polly to her parrot food, and see what we can do by ourselves."

Even Roger saw the sense of that, and the expedition set out.

"Susan," said Nancy urgently. "Don't look as if you expected to be stopped." She led the way jauntily towards the gateway at the low end of the courtyard.

The guards at the gateway watched them coming, but stepped aside to let them pass. They walked straight out into the dusty town. No one shouted at them. No one ran after them.

"She's given her orders all right," said Captain Flint.

"Giminy," said Nancy. "We really are free. Come on. Which way now?"

"Let's go and see if they're still messing about with that dragon," said Roger.

"That's by the gate we came in at," said Titty. "We could go out there, to the ferry and get to *Swallow* by going along the bank."

"No, we couldn't," said Nancy. "You've forgotten that wall. It goes right down to the river. The creek's on this side of the wall. It's somewhere behind Miss Lee's garden."

"Make up your minds," said Captain Flint.

"Turn right," said John. "We'll go round outside Miss Lee's garden and we're bound to come to it."

They turned right from the gateway of the yamen, and followed a road that lay between the wall of the yamen and a row of low, earthbuilt, green-roofed houses. The road was just well-trodden earth and little clouds of dust rose about their feet. It presently turned sharply down hill, and though on their right was only a high smooth wall they knew that on the other side of it must be Miss Lee's terraced garden. They came to the door in the wall that they had found when exploring the garden. Roger tried it. It was still locked. "Oh, well," he said, "I expect she keeps the key to that herself."

"Everybody seems to know we're free," said Nancy.

Indeed, it seemed so. Men smoking their little bamboo pipes, squatting on their heels outside their houses, hardly turned their heads to look at them. Women, spinning silk with distaffs like large spinning tops, never stopped their work. It was as if, overnight, they had become old inhabitants of the pirate town. They helped an old woman catch a runaway pig. Only one small boy made as if to chop off his own head, and he got it smacked instead by a passer by.

"Free," said Nancy again. "It's almost as if we were pirates ourselves."

"Right again, I should think," said Captain Flint.

The houses were smaller here and there were more trees, palms and bamboos. Presently there were no more houses, and they caught a glint of water through the trees.

"That's the river," said Captain Flint. "Are you sure about that creek?"

"We must be coming to it," said John, and a few minutes later they saw the masts of the little painted junk they had noticed from the ferry-boat when they were being brought across from Tiger Island. They came out from the trees and saw the whole of her, and her reflection, bright red and blue and white in the still water among the brilliant greens reflected from the wooded bank on the further side.

"*Swallow* was on this side," said Titty. "And *Amazon*."

"There they are," cried John. "Just by those sampans. Somebody's pulled them right up. Come on."

There was no need for him to say "Come on." Nancy and the others were already running full tilt along the track.

Suddenly, as from nowhere, a man was standing in the path before them. He said nothing but, with a jerk, unhitched a short carbine from his shoulder.

ANYBODY COULD SEE WHAT HE MEANT

"We're only going to look at our boats," said Nancy.

The man put up a hand, wide open.

John pointed at the boats. The man did not turn round. Instead, with his hand open, palm towards them, he came nearer by a step or two. Anybody could see what he meant. That path was closed.

"There's only one of him," said Nancy hopefully, looking at Captain Flint.

"There'll be one less of us if we make him use his pop-gun," said Captain Flint calmly. "Right about turn. We'll have a look at the boats another day."

"Miss Lee can't have told him," said Titty. "Of course she didn't know we'd want to go here."

"Let's have that telescope," said John. "He won't stop us looking at them if we don't go any nearer."

"Is it all right letting him know we've got one?" said Titty.

"I don't think that matters now," said Captain Flint. "What we mustn't let them know is that I've got a pocket compass. What's happened to yours, John?"

"It's in Miss Lee's temple," said John, "with your sextant and everything else."

"We'll have to get hold of that," said Captain Flint.

Titty handed over the telescope. John had a careful look first at one boat and then at the other. The Chinese with the carbine dropped his hand and turned round to see where the telescope was pointing. Roger took a step forward, but the man swung round in a moment, lifting his carbine.

"You obey orders, Roger," said Captain Flint.

"They look all right," said John. "I say, Nancy, the oars are back in *Amazon*."

"Not much good if we can't use them. Let's have a look. . . ."

"Our sail's in a bit of a mess," said John. "I wish they'd just let us give it a proper stow. Somebody must have been having a squint at it."

"No good hanging about," said Captain Flint. "This chap wants to see the last of us. Let's make him happy."

They turned. Nancy scowled at the Chinese, but Captain Flint gave him a friendly wave. The man lowered his carbine, grinned and stood there watching till they were back among the trees.

"I don't call that being free," said Roger.

"It's just a mistake," said Titty.

Among the trees, after a look round to see that no one was watching them, Captain Flint pulled out his pocket compass, and made a note on a bit of paper.

"What we've got to do first," he said, "is to get the geography clear in our heads. I thought I saw some water over on the other side when they were carting me along in that rabbit-hutch."

"Hen-coop," said Roger.

"Mouse-trap," said Captain Flint.

"We saw water, too," said John.

Captain Flint glanced at his compass again. "Somewhere over there," he said. "Let's see if they've another landing place. If we keep on the low ground instead of going up into the town, we ought to be all right."

They followed the track back to the first of the houses and then bore to the right, through one lane after another. Nobody bothered them, and they were careful to saunter along as if they were going nowhere in particular. They came out on a well-beaten track, followed it through trees along the edge of a tiny stream and once more saw water ahead of them. Some distance away, to right and left, they saw high walls running to the water's edge.

"The whole town's got a wall round it," said Captain Flint. "Miss Lee's father must have known what he was about."

"They're building a junk," said John.

"Looks like another river," said Captain Flint.

"Shallow," said Nancy, looking at reed banks on the further side.

"There must be water to float a junk," said Captain Flint, "or they wouldn't be building. We'll go on and have a look."

"It's a little junk just like the other," said Titty, as they came nearer to the shore and could see what sort of a vessel it was at which a lot of men were busy working.

"Junks anchored lower down," said Captain Flint.

"Let's go and look at them building her," said John, but before they were near enough to have a proper look, a man with a carbine, who had been standing watching the boat-builders, turned, came towards them and waved them back.

"Botheration," said Roger.

"Naval dockyard," said Captain Flint. "Visitors not allowed."

He turned round and led them back towards the town.

"Jibbooms and bobstays," exclaimed Nancy. "She can't mean us just to stay in the streets."

"We'll soon see," said Captain Flint.

They began going up hill now among the houses, but presently came to a wide road, at the end of which they saw a gateway and a glimpse of open country outside.

"Let's try that," said Nancy.

They soon saw that the gateway led through the town wall. Half a dozen guards were squatting on the ground there, playing cards.

"Bet the beasts stop us," said Roger.

"Worth trying," said Nancy.

They came to the gateway and strolled through it, and the guards hardly looked up as they passed.

"That's all right," said Captain Flint.

"They know we're free," said Titty. "It's only that she never thought of our wanting to go down to the water."

"Well, we jolly well did," said Roger.

"What now?" said John.

"More geography," said Captain Flint, glancing privately at his compass, and looking at the long road crossing the paddy-fields and climbing the slopes beyond them. "Where does that road go? Left . . . Right . . . Left . . . Right. . . . Come on."

They were soon beyond the paddy-fields, where green rice was growing in shallow water, and small fish were rising at flies, splashing among the green stems. They were on open rising country. Away to their left they could see the great river, the junk anchorage, and the long hill of Tiger

Island. Looking back they could see Miss Lee's gateway tower, and the tall flagstaff, high above trees and houses inside the long brown wall of the town. They marched on at a good steady pace. The road climbed more and more steeply. It began to wind among rocks.

"Listen," said Nancy. "Rushing water."

"Rum," said Captain Flint.

Suddenly turning a corner between rocks, the road dipped, and they caught a glimpse of cliffs. A moment later they were looking down into a narrow gorge. Far, far below them they could see the white foam splashes of rapids.

"It's just a beck," said Peggy.

"Wolloping big beck," said Nancy. "I say, that's the sea over there."

"That chap said there were two islands," said John. "When we were on the donkeys. I thought there must be a way through."

"That'll be Turtle Island the other side," said Captain Flint.

"Our island with the temple's the other side of that," said John.

"They can't go down and cross those rapids in boats," said Captain Flint. "This road goes somewhere. There must be a bridge."

A few minutes later, at the next turn in the road, they saw it, and gasped. Seven or eight hundred feet above the water, the two cliffs leaned to meet each other. On either side was a small square tower, and between the two a narrow bridge, without rails of any kind, crossed the abyss.

"Look at those people," said Roger.

Half a dozen men, carrying loads slung from bamboos, were walking easily across the bridge as if they did not know that a single slip would send them diving to their deaths.

"Giminy," said Nancy.

"Bit of an engineer, old Lee, if he did that," said Captain Flint. "I've seen something like it in the Himalayas."

"Let's cross," said John.

"On all fours," said Roger. "It'll be easy that way."

But he did not have a chance of trying. Before they could get near the bridge, three or four guards came hurrying out of the guardhouse at the nearer end.

"Forty million chopsticks," said Nancy. "This is a bit too thick. I do believe they're going to stop us."

There was no doubt about it. Guns were lifted, and they heard the sharp click of bolts as the men made ready their carbines.

"No point in riling them," said Captain Flint calmly.

"But it's them riling us," said Nancy.

"Right about turn," said Captain Flint. After a last look down into the gorge and across at Turtle Island, they turned back along the road to the town.

"Free!" said Nancy.

"Free!" said Roger.

"It's a mistake," said Titty. "It was all right at the gateways."

"Not at the creek," said John.

"They wouldn't even let us look at their junk," said Roger.

"We'll never be able to get away from here," said Susan.

"We'll see what they say at the ferry," said Captain Flint.

"Shall we go through the town or along the wall outside?" said Nancy, as they were crossing the paddy-fields.

"Better keep outside now we're out," said John.

"If we once go in they may not let us out again," said Roger. "Pretty piggish."

"It looks to me as if she's got us on a string," said Captain Flint.

The guards at the gateway, who had watched them coming back, smiled at them and did not try to stop them when, instead of passing through, they turned along the wall to work round it to the road going down to the ferry. Their spirits rose again but dropped with a bump when they were not allowed even to go out on the landing-jetty to which the ferry boat was tied up.

"But why not?" asked Nancy angrily. "Miss Lee said we could go anywhere."

The guard at the ferry was one of those who knew a little English.

"No can do," he explained with the friendliest of smiles delighted at being able to answer and expecting them to be pleased at hearing him.

"Well, that's that," said Captain Flint. "We'll go and have a word with our Miss Lee. Better know the worst while we're about it."

There was no trouble about passing through the gateway into the town, the same gateway through which they had been led as prisoners on their way from Chang's yamen. But, though people were working on the dragon just inside, even Roger had no heart to look at it. Footsore, dusty and angry, they came back to Miss Lee's, and went to their own house, Captain Flint coming with them, because, as he said, there was no point in sitting in a cage if you didn't have to. Miss Lee's old amah had been on the verandah of the council room as they came into the courtyard and had gone in as soon as she saw them. They were scarcely back in their own house before Miss Lee herself appeared at the garden door.

"Did you have a good walk?" she asked. "Velly fine view flom the high glound."

They were too angry to make polite speeches.

"I don't call this being free," said Roger.

"But I tell you, you are flee," said Miss Lee. "Go anywhere. Do anything. Only not go away. All Dlagon Island for you. Now, when you have lested, pelhaps a little more glammar. . . . No. . . . Pelhaps better tomollow . . . after plepalation."

"They wouldn't let us go anywhere," said Nancy. "I told them you said we were free."

"Not to go away," said Miss Lee.

"We couldn't even get near our own boats," said Titty.

"I wanted to go out on that bridge," said Roger.

"They wouldn't even let us go and look at the ferry," said John.

"You closs to Tiger Island and Chang will cut off heads," said Miss Lee.

Nancy stamped her foot. "Then we're still prisoners," she said.

"Not prisoners," said Miss Lee. "Guests. Fliends.

Students. Can you not understand? My counsellor and the Taicoons, Wu and Chang, think you ought not to be here, not to be here alive. They lemember my father's law. I bleak it evelly day by keeping you here. They think gunboats will come and smash up evellything. I tell them it is safe. You do not know where you are. Gunboats do not know where you are. I, Miss Lee, must show evellybody they need not be aflaid. I must let them see you cannot get away."

"But we've got to some time," said Susan.

"How?" asked Miss Lee.

"You could let Chang's captain, the one who picked us up, take us out to sea till we meet an English ship," said Nancy.

"All light," said Miss Lee angrily. "Nan-see, you have no blains. Chang's captain take you out to sea. He will come back next day and say he stopped a British steamer and put you all aboard. I tell you, he will say that. But I tell you, Chang is aflaid. Wu is aflaid. My counsellor is aflaid. Chang's captain, any captain of Thlee Island junk, will take you out to sea. Yes. He will take you out to sea. But when night comes he will dlop you, one, two, thlee, four, five, six, seven and monkey and pallot. He will dlop you all to be chow for sharks. You think that is all light? Better stay here and be good students."

She turned her back on them and walked out.

"You've done it now," said Susan. "Making her mad."

"Miss Lee's just about right," said Captain Flint slowly. "She's our only hope."

"But if she won't let us go," said Susan.

"Irish pigs," murmured Captain Flint. "Irish pigs."

"We aren't," said Roger.

"Pig yourself," said Nancy. "You too, Susan. It wasn't my fault."

"When an Irishman drives a pig," said Captain Flint slowly, "he ties the string to its hind leg. Well, the pig thinks the Irishman wants it to hang back. So it goes forward. What we've got to do is to make these blessed pirates think we want to stay. That's the best way to make them want to boot us out. It's the only way with people like Miss Lee."

"Um," said Nancy. "I'd rather like to stay if only we were free."

"Good," said Captain Flint. "You try to show it. Now Miss Lee is the Irishman. We are the pigs. Miss Lee wants to give us lessons in Latin and what not. She thinks that even Roger doesn't really want them."

"I don't," said Roger.

"We've got to be so blooming keen on lessons that Miss Lee herself gets sick of giving them."

"Jibbooms and bobstays," said Nancy. "But she'd like to have twenty-four hours of lessons every day."

"Well," said Captain Flint, "we've got to let her see that we're glad of the chance and only wish we could cram thirty-six hours of lessons into the twenty-four."

"She'll just be pleased," said Titty.

"Well," said Captain Flint, "let's please her. We wouldn't stand much of a chance if she left us to the others. . . . Except you, perhaps, with the bird-fancier."

"It was Polly he liked," said Titty.

"Put Roger in a sweetshop," said Captain Flint, "and he'd soon get sick of chocolate. We'll try that with our Miss Lee."

"Chopsticks and congee," said Nancy, grinning. "If we've all got to sweat at lessons you must too. She thought you were awful this morning."

"I will," said Captain Flint. "Where's that Latin Grammar. If I don't know 'Artifex and Opifex' by tomorrow morning I'll eat my hat. Come on, the Lower School. And you, too, John and Roger. Get on with Aeneas where you left off."

"Come on," said John. "No skulking, Roger, even if you have read it already."

"I'm no good at languages," said Susan.

"We none of us are," said Captain Flint. "But we soon will be."

"Mensa, mensa, mensam," said Nancy ruefully.

They worked hard till supper-time. And after supper, when the amah and a guard came for Captain Flint to lock him up, he begged for a lantern, took the Latin Grammar with him into the sleeping-box at the back of his cage and late at night could be heard chanting verbs and things till the guards at the gateway came and told him to shut up.

[NOTE. "Susan says you ought to have put in somewhere how the Chinese took all our clothes one night and brought them back next morning washed and dried and ready to put on. I told her it wasn't important, but Susan says it made all the difference. N. Blackett, Capt."]

CHAPTER XVIII

MODEL STUDENTS

NEXT morning Miss Lee had a class of model students.

When Cambridge breakfast had been cleared away ready for the lesson, she had no need to send the amah for them. She came back into her study from the garden to find that they were already at their places round the table.

"Velly good," said Miss Lee.

"Salve, domina!" they said in return.

"Salvete, discipuli!" said Miss Lee.

Captain Flint stood up, put his hands behind his back and began to recite at high speed

"Common are to either sex
Artifex and opifex. . . ."

And so on, right through to the end of the rhyme.

Miss Lee listened in astonishment.

"But I thought that you . . ."

"I learnt it again last night," said Captain Flint simply, and sat down.

"Mensa, mensa, mensam, mensae, mensae, mensa," recited Nancy, and nudged Peggy who took up the tale . . . . "Mensae, mensae, mensas . . . ." She hesitated, got a glare from Nancy, who prompted her in a fierce whisper, and, in duet, hurried to the end . . . . "Mensarum, mensis, mensis."

"If you would hear me through the second

conjugation," said John. . . . "I got muddled with it yesterday."

"And Susan?" asked Miss Lee presently.

"She's been doing second declension with me," said Titty.

"We've done all that bit about the snakes coming over the sea and Laocoon and his two sons," said Roger.

"Velly, velly good," said Miss Lee.

*

The keynote had been struck, and they kept on sounding it day after day. In all the world Miss Lee could not have found a class of harder workers. There were groans in private, mostly from Nancy, but none in the presence of the happy lecturer. Even Roger, not very keen on lessons as a rule, finding his place at the head of the class challenged by John and Captain Flint, both of whom, brushing up their grammar, were soon hard on his heels, worked as never in his life and in the evenings was inclined to protest when other people wanted the use of the dictionary. It was not easy for them because there was only one Latin-English Dictionary, one English-Latin, one grammar and one Virgil. Also there was too wide a gap between the learned Roger and the unlucky ones who were learning Latin for the first time. But they did their best. Captain Flint used to copy out the bits he wanted to learn by heart and take them away with him when the time came for him to be locked into his cage. Nancy and Peggy used up two stumps of pencils when they found that copying bits was almost half-way to learning

CAPTAIN FLINT RECITES HIS PIECE

them. Writing with a brush in the Chinese way, though Titty enjoyed it, took too long to be really useful, but on one of their walks they came on an old woman plucking a goose. John begged a handful of the long feathers from her, and next time Miss Lee came into their house at preparation time, she found all seven of her eager pupils working away with good quill pens.

Each day, after their morning's work, they went for a walk, but they were careful now never to go to any of the places where they were likely to be stopped by a guard. They learnt a good deal of the geography of Dragon Island, but they never did anything that might look as if they wished to leave it. They never went near the ferry. They never tried to cross the bridge over the gorge. They kept well away from the place where the junk was being built on one side of the island, and on the other they never tried to go near the shore of the creek, but contented themselves with looking through the telescope to see that *Swallow* and *Amazon* were still lying there on the mud. Though they could not talk with them they became quite friendly with the people who were working on the dragon near the gateway to the ferry, who even let Roger splash some red paint on the dragon's gaping jaws.

"The great thing is," said Captain Flint, "to make everybody think we don't ever want to go away. What we've got to do is to make Miss Lee herself sick of lessons."

But it seemed an almost hopeless task. Far from tiring of her class, it seemed that she could never have enough of it. The idea had been that

Captain Flint was to teach mathematics, but Miss Lee sat by during his first lesson, more and more impatient. She never let him give a second. She announced that there was really no hurry about mathematics, that it was better to study one subject at a time, and that for the first year or so they would stick to Latin. Not content with the mornings, she was always ready to do a little extra coaching. Hopefully the prisoners used to choose a victim for the sacrifice, usually Roger, Captain Flint or Titty, to go round to Miss Lee's house, book in hand, and ask for learned help. Every time the victim was received with joy and Miss Lee would get going about irregular verbs or Latin quantities, or something like that, and would not stop until her amah came in to say that it was time for evening rice or that the guards were waiting to lock Captain Flint into his cage.

Miss Lee, far from getting tired of them, grew more and more pleased with her students and, in her own way, tried to show it. One day at breakfast Roger had been talking about the dragons they had seen at Chang's and here in Miss Lee's own town, and Miss Lee had been telling him about the Dragon Festival for which they were being made ready, and how the Three Islands kept the festival, dragons from the other islands coming to Dragon Town and prancing round the streets together. "Gosh, what fun!" Roger had said. That evening, when they were hard at work, Miss Lee paid them a surprise visit.

"Velly good students," she said as she came in from the garden. "Loger wants a dlagon, I think.

Each island has its dlagon. Why not my students? Come and see before it is too dark."

Wondering, they left their work, all but Captain Flint who, as Miss Lee turned to lead the way out, settled again to his copying of a page of grammar, the perfect, virtuous student.

"Better come too," said Miss Lee. "You will carry the head. John or Nan-see not stlong enough."

They went out into the garden just in time to see an enormous dragon's head dumped on the path by two men who were carrying it. Four others were carrying, on a sort of stretcher, something like a roll of carpet from the middle of which stuck out a stiff and scaly tail.

"Last year's dlagon," said Miss Lee. "You have seen they are making a new dlagon for this year. Fifty men will cally him. A hundled legs."

The dragon's body was being unrolled. It stretched the whole way along the path to the further end of the garden on the other side of Miss Lee's house and back again.

"Too long for you," said Miss Lee. "Seven. No. Six. Loger will dance in flont offeling a pearl to the dlagon." She pointed to a silver-painted gourd hanging from a golden rope and a small round lantern. "Day pearl and night pearl," she said. "But you will have only twelve legs. You must cut a big piece out of the body and then join up."

"Three cheers," said Roger. "Susan's jolly good at sewing."

"You shall have needles and thread."

Miss Lee, a tiny figure in her black silk coat and trousers, showed them, ten feet apart, the places for each pair of legs. Captain Flint, she explained, would carry the head and be the first pair of legs. With five others, and with the long stiff tail swinging behind it, the dragon would be small as dragons go, but still a dragon. Under her directions the long body was cut in two places. The part not wanted was rolled up to be carried away. The head, with one good length of body, and the tail with another, were stored in the large room of the students' house.

"Good students," said Miss Lee, "will have a good dlagon. And I think all my men will be velly pleased when they see. Good night, evellybody."

"Well," said Captain Flint when she had gone. "Roger, you young scoundrel, you seem to have wished a bit more work on some of us."

"I'll do the sewing myself," said Roger.

Susan laughed. "That means Peggy and me," she said. "And it'll take ages. I don't know how we'll manage to learn our grammar at the same time."

"Never mind," said Captain Flint. "We'll lend a hand. It may be well worth while. The more of these people we can please, the better."

The amah, looking very sour, was standing in the doorway. "Belong walkee plison," she said.

"Coming, coming," said Captain Flint. He hurriedly scribbled a sentence from the Latin grammar, and meekly followed her out to the waiting guards.

*

Miss Lee was growing more and more pleased with her model students, but it was very different with the amah and the old counsellor. The old counsellor, they knew, had been against them from the first. They were on good grinning terms with the guards and with the people they met about the town, but from the old counsellor they had never won a smile. At first, when they passed him in the garden, sitting on a chair combing his thin beard, he had looked through them as if they were not there. Now they sometimes caught him looking at them, as Roger put it, "as if we were snakes instead of human beings". As for the amah, it had seemed at first that she was pleased to have them about the place. She had been Miss Lee's nurse, and it had almost seemed she was pleased to have children to look after once more. She had fussed after them, chattered to them proudly in her "velly good English", and been rather like a hen with chickens, treating even Captain Flint like a large duckling who had somehow got in among the rest. Now, day by day, as Miss Lee spent more and more time over her class, the amah had turned silent. She never spoke a word to them unless she had to. And her face grew more and more grim.

"Have we done anything to offend the amah?" Susan asked one day when the old nurse had called them to breakfast as if she thought they did not deserve any.

"No," said Miss Lee. "You are velly good students. It is me she is not pleased with. She thinks I take more tlouble with my class than with my father's business. She is like Cassandla plophesying doom. She is as bad as the counsellor. He visits Chang. He visits Wu. And then he tells me I shall lose the Thlee Islands. It is all lubbish.

My father told me to make my own judgements and I do."

"Hoc volo, sic jubeo," said Roger, and she laughed.

That day, when the whole class were at work, and Miss Lee, for a change, was showing them how translation should be done, reading the story of the fight in burning Troy into a lively English of her own, English with a slight tang of Chinese as, for example, when she spoke of Priam's palace as his yamen, and of Hector as a Greek Taicoon, the amah came to the door and said something in Chinese. Miss Lee waved her impatiently away. She came back again later and, once more, Miss Lee frowned, pointed to the door and went on with her reading. Then, at last, the counsellor himself came, and Miss Lee slammed the book shut and broke up the class.

The students, hearing a noise in the courtyard, went out to find a crowd listening to a man who was talking angrily, with his eyes all the time turning to the verandah. The counsellor came out and spoke to him. He ran off shouting. There was a rush of men out of the gateway and down to the ferry. The students followed the crowd, and saw four of the great junks making ready for sea. Men were rowing off to them in sampans. Sails were going up. Capstans were creaking. One after another the big junks hauled up their anchors and were away, beating down the river against an easterly wind. Later that day, Miss Lee took up her interrupted reading, but anybody could see she was uneasy. Next day there was a lesson as usual, but in the afternoon when the students were taking their walk, they saw the junks driving slowly up the river over the current.

"There'll be fireworks," said Roger.

But there was only a meagre crackle let off by small boys at the landing-place and it stopped almost at once. On their way home the students saw the men from the junks pouring angrily back into the town.

Primed by Captain Flint, Roger was sent in to Miss Lee on the excuse that he wanted to know something about Virgil, himself, the poet who had written the book. The others waited, unable to think about Latin, while Susan and Peggy went on with the slow business of stitching together the two halves of their dragon. Roger was not gone as long as usual.

"I say," he said when he came back, "I asked her why everybody looked so cross. I thought she wasn't going to tell me but she did. You know what happened yesterday? A junk came in with news of a lot of traders sailing past who hadn't paid their dues. . . ."

"I thought it was that," said Titty. "A pinnace like a fluttered bird came flying from far away. . . ."

"That was just it," said Roger. "Only Sir Richard Grenville wasn't giving Latin lessons like Miss Lee. You remember how she wouldn't listen to the amah. Well, by the time the counsellor came in and told her and she gave the orders it was too late. They'd got past and the junks couldn't catch them. That's why everybody looked so mad when they came back."

"I don't wonder," said Nancy.

"Um," said Captain Flint. "One way or another . . ."

"You didn't stay with her very long," said John.

"The old beast of a counsellor came in," said Roger. "I think he was scolding like anything. Miss Lee stamped her foot but he went on, and then she told me to clear out."

"It's working," said Captain Flint.

"It's not working our way," said Nancy. "The more we sweat the more she wants us to."

"It doesn't matter which way," said Captain Flint. "Come on, we must stick to it. Where's that grammar?"

"Under the dragon somewhere," said Roger, looking round.

But it was not. Grammar, Virgil and both dictionaries had disappeared.

"Three cheers," said Roger. "She's giving us a holiday. No prep tonight."

"We've jolly well earned it," said Nancy.

"Not a bit of it," said Captain Flint. "If she's getting tired of lessons, now is our time to show we're greedy for more. Back you go, Roger, and tell her we're only waiting for the books."

Three minutes later Miss Lee was in the room.

"Nan-see," she said. "Did you hide the books?"

"I didn't," said Nancy, all the more indignantly because she would have liked to.

Miss Lee looked suspiciously at her largest student.

"Not me," said Captain Flint.

"We none of us did," said Titty. "They were here when we went out."

"We came back just bursting to get at them," said Captain Flint. "Irregular verbs?" he added, as if he were Roger talking of his favourite kind of chocolate.

"We thought you were tired of lessons and wanted a holiday," said John.

"We do have holidays at school in England," said Roger, but caught a look from Captain Flint and shut up.

Miss Lee clapped her hands, and they heard the padding footsteps of the old amah. She shook her head. Miss Lee's eyes closed to narrow slits and she spoke through hardly opened lips. The amah broke into a flood of talk. They could not understand a single word of it but they could see that the amah had thrown off twenty years or so and was lecturing Miss Lee as if she were still a nurse and Miss Lee her naughty baby. Miss Lee waited till the amah had finished. Then she said one short sentence. The amah ran out of the room.

"She took the books," said Miss Lee. "She and the counsellor say the same thing. They say my lessons bad for Thlee Islands, bad for me. They say my father would not be pleased. I say, my father is velly pleased."

The amah came back into the room, slammed the books on the table and went off angrily weeping.

"She meant well," said Miss Lee. "Good amah, but an uncultured woman. And now you can go on with studies leady for tomollow."

"Botheration!" said Nancy, when Miss Lee had gone.

"All for the best," said Captain Flint. "Come

on. Let's have a bit of paper. Domina Lee amet nos. Let Miss Lee love us. You, too, Roger. Get down to the Virgil. You're our trump card. Now then, Susan, chuck that dragon for the night. . . ."

And they settled dismally to work.

*

Next morning they had an unexpected reward.

Miss Lee had not shown at the time that she had heard what Roger had said about having holidays at school in England. But she had clearly been thinking about it, remembering, perhaps, what had happened when she was at school herself. Breakfast was over. They had come back to the study ready for the lesson to begin. Roger and John were going hurriedly through the Virgil they had prepared. The others were hearing each other reciting bits of grammar. Miss Lee came smiling into the room. "You are velly good students," she said. "Today we take a holiday. Today I visit the Taicoon Wu. I will take my students with me. But first I go to visit my father's glave. You will come with me to my island."

"Three million cheers," said Nancy. "I and Peggy have never seen it."

"And we can get our things," said Susan. "And tidy up."

"We will go to my father's glave," said Miss Lee, "where he made the Thlee Islands men stop fighting, and then we will go to my father's chair where he watched the ships and the sea."

"How shall we get there?" said Roger. "Over that bridge?"

"We shall sail there," said Miss Lee.

"Jibbooms and bobstays!" exclaimed Nancy.

"And then we will come back over Turtle Island and see Taicoon Wu. We will come back over the blidge. My father built it. A velly fine blidge."

"We've seen it," said Roger, and just in time remembered not to say anything about being stopped when they tried to cross it.

"How soon can you be leady?" said Miss Lee.

"Now," said John and Nancy at the same moment.

"Velly well," said Miss Lee. "Dismiss. I will send my amah for you in ten minutes."

*

"Sailing," said Titty.

"I wonder what in," said Nancy. "One of the big junks I bet you anything."

"I say, John," said Captain Flint. "You did say you had my sextant there all right."

"It was there when we went across and got grabbed," said John.

"She says nobody ever goes there without her orders," said Susan.

"You never know," said Captain Flint, "but we want that sextant if we're going to get away."

"She'll never let us go," said Susan.

"A chance'll come," said Captain Flint, "if we're ready to take it."

"But it's to come quick," said Susan. "Mother'll be worrying already."

"Not yet," said Captain Flint. "There are all those Dutch islands we might have gone to.

There's Formosa. They know we're not a liner and don't work to a time-table."

"We've been here a long time," said Susan.

They heard the footsteps of the amah.

"Model students on holiday," said Captain Flint. "On holiday, but bursting to get back to work. That's what we are."

The amah, grim and unsmiling, was beckoning at the door.

"She doesn't think Miss Lee ought to take us," said Titty.

"Who cares?" said Nancy. "We're going."

CHAPTER XIX

HOLIDAY VOYAGE

THERE was no sounding of gongs when Miss Lee, with her amah and her students, left the yamen, perhaps because she did not go through the courtyard and the great gateway but down the garden and out through the door in the wall.

In the lane outside a chair and bearers were waiting for her and half a dozen tough-looking guards with rifles slung across their backs. Miss Lee sat herself in the chair, the bearers lifted the carrying poles, and the holiday party was on its way, the amah and the students following Miss Lee, with the guards close behind them.

"We're not going to the ferry," said Roger, as the little procession turned right along the garden wall.

"We're going to the creek," said Titty.

"We'll see our boats," said John.

They left the houses and went on by the now well-known path that led through the trees to the creek. Today there was no need to stop at the edge of the trees and look at the boats through the telescope. Miss Lee, in her chair, was going straight on. Out in the creek, the little brightly painted junk was riding to a single anchor. Men were busy with her ropes. Sails were ready for hoisting. Sampans, each with a couple of men, were waiting to take the passengers aboard.

"Gosh!" said Roger, "we're sailing in the little

junk."

"I thought we must be," said Titty.

John and Nancy, as soon as they saw that they were free to do it, made a dash for their own boats. No one stopped them. They fingered the badly stowed sails, looked over the ropes and anchors, and searched anxiously for damage to the planking.

"She's all right," said Nancy. "I was bothered about the centreboard."

"*Swallow's* all right too," said John.

They looked round to see that Miss Lee had left her chair and was standing beside them.

"Sail well?" she asked, looking at *Amazon*.

"I should think she does," said Nancy, and then, suddenly daring, stopped being a model student and became a captain once more. "Lend a hand here, Peggy. Stir your stumps. You heave at the bows, John. Miss Lee, we'll have her afloat in a minute and we'll show you."

Miss Lee shook her head, glanced at the amah and the waiting sampans and said, "No".

"Another time," said Nancy.

"They're in a hurry to start," said John.

"Oh well," said Nancy, "we'd have got pretty muddy getting her off."

"There's more water in the creek than there was the other day," said John. "*Swallow's* stern wasn't in the water when we looked at her last."

They ran after Miss Lee.

"Is it a tide?" John asked. "There's more water than there was."

"Ah, you see that," said Miss Lee. "No. Not tide. It is lain."

"But there hasn't been any," said Nancy.

"Lain in the hills," said Miss Lee. "Lain a thousand miles away."

Already the others were crowding into the waiting sampans, reaching them one by one by walking over the mud on a narrow bamboo landing-stage. They were ferried out to the little gaily painted junk. A long black pennant with a golden dragon on it was fluttering to the masthead.

Miss Lee gave an order the moment she was aboard and ran up the steps to the high poop.

"Hi . . . ya . . . hee . . . yo!" chanted the Chinese sailors as naked to the waist they worked the windlass, got the anchor up and hoisted the big mainsail with its bamboo battens creaking up the mast.

"Let's help," said Roger.

"Better keep out of their way," said Captain Flint, looking round him like a schoolboy on holiday.

"She's moving," said Roger, looking over the side.

"Giminy," said Nancy. "Miss Lee's got the tiller herself."

"She'll never get her round in this creek," murmured Captain Flint.

But Miss Lee, up there on the high poop, knew her ship. The little junk reached over to the further shore so near that they were waiting to feel the scrunch of her keel on the ground, or to see her foremast caught among the trees. She swung right round into the wind, came about without a hitch and, with gathering speed, was heading for the open river.

"What about that?" said Nancy.

"She's a sailor all right, our Miss Lee," said Captain Flint.

The mizen had been hoisted. Up went another little lugsail on the foremast, and the sailors squatted on the decks, smiling, their eyes on Miss Lee, ready at any moment to ease the sheets or haul them in. The guards, in the waist of the ship with the prisoners, were sitting with their backs against the bulwarks, their rifles across their knees. The amah had disappeared into a cabin under the poop, and Roger, peeping in, reported that she was looking into a couple of big bamboo baskets, no doubt with the provisions. The others, with the eyes of experienced seamen, were looking at everything they could see, the way the Chinese belayed their halyards, the queer arrangement of the sheets, the shifting stays. Nancy, because of having sailed in a pirate junk already, pointed out one thing after another. "She's small, of course," she said, "and the one we were in had guns." Titty was lifting on her toes the better to feel that she had a moving deck under her feet once more.

A Chinese sailor touched Captain Flint's arm. "Missee Lee," he whispered and pointed towards the poop. Miss Lee was beckoning. They hurried up the steps to join her.

It was hard to believe that this Miss Lee, her little gold shoes set wide apart, her face upturned to the wind, balancing easily with her hand on the tiller of her ship, was the same Miss Lee who day by day had been pumping Latin grammar into them. She looked as if she had never heard of Cambridge or Latin verbs in all her life.

"Good ship?" she said.

"She's a beauty," said John.

"What's her name?" asked Titty.

Miss Lee said a name in Chinese and put it into English for her. "*Shining Moon.*"

"She's pretty good to windward," said Captain Flint, watching the shore as the little junk worked close-hauled across the river against the wind coming in from the sea.

"Stlong cullent helping her," said Miss Lee.

"She'd be pretty good if there was no current at all," said Captain Flint. "Where was she built?"

"My men build her for me," said Miss Lee. "They are building another now."

"We saw her," said John.

"Only they wouldn't let us come near," said Roger, though the last words faded into silence as he remembered that they were to say nothing more about being prisoners.

"There's the cormorant man," said Titty.

Close under the shore was the long narrow punt of the fisherman with the row of black cormorants perched along the gunwale. The *Shining Moon* swept nearer and nearer to him. Suddenly, just as she went about, he caught sight of Miss Lee on the poop. He stood up, put his hands together and made a low bow.

"Gosh, he was frightened when he saw us on your island," said Roger.

"He knew nobody had a light to be there," said Miss Lee. "He told Wu, and Wu sent men to kill you."

"Lucky we'd cleared out in time," said John.

"And then," said Miss Lee, smiling, "I saw what Loger had litten in my book."

Roger said nothing but looked at Susan to make sure that she had heard.

To and fro went the little junk between the rising cliffs of Dragon Island and the low bank on the further side where, they could see, there was a sort of towpath. They asked Miss Lee about that, and she told them when there was no sea breeze to help them the junks were hauled up against the current by teams of men walking along on land. To and fro went the little junk, sometimes going close inshore before turning, sometimes turning long before they expected because of rocks off shore they could not see.

"She steers much easier than the *Wild Cat*," said Roger, watching Miss Lee's gentle use of the tiller, and then, feeling disloyal to the old schooner, he added, "Not *Wild Cat's* fault. Only she steered with a wheel. A tiller's more fun."

"*Shining Moon* pulls too hard in a stlong wind," said Miss Lee.

"Giminy," said Nancy, nudging Captain Flint. "She hasn't got a binnacle."

Miss Lee heard her. "No need," she said. And then she told them about the south-pointing compass invented by the Chinese, and of how, in the past, Chinese junks had made long voyages. "India often," she said. "Aflica. . . . Alabia. . . . But *Shining Moon* never goes far flom home."

"I remember," said Captain Flint, "there was a junk sailed from Shanghai to England a year or so ago."

Miss Lee stopped smiling and eyed him narrowly.

Captain Flint tried to put things right. He laughed. "You're not afraid we'd try to seize the ship?" he said. "Is that why you have the guards?" He pointed into the waist.

"No," said Miss Lee.

"You are safe enough with us, ma'am," said Captain Flint.

"Safe with evellybody," said Miss Lee, quietly, her fingers tapping lightly on her pistol-holster.

The *Shining Moon* was heading across towards the steep cliffs.

"Look, look," cried Titty. "There's that gorge."

"Gosh, what a height," said Roger.

They were looking now from the level of the water into the narrow gorge they had seen from the cliff top. It was as if a giant had cut the great mass of rock in two with an enormous hatchet to make the two islands, Dragon and Turtle. Until they had come almost opposite the gap it had looked as if the two were one.

"Must not go too near," said Miss Lee. She pointed to a black rock sticking up out of the water as if it had fallen from the cliff. "If we go past that lock the cullent take us thlough . . . many locks . . . not deep water. . . ."

"I say, couldn't we sail through?" asked Nancy.

"Only when the water is velly high," said Miss Lee. "Many locks, a whirlpool. . . . Velly dangelous. You will see when we closs the blidge."

"What's it called?" asked Titty.

"Loaring Gorge," said Miss Lee.

"Why roaring?"

"Because the noise of the water there echoes between the cliffs."

"And what's the river called?"

Miss Lee said a Chinese name and translated it. "Silver Liver."

"And the one on the other side?"

"Dead Water."

"Why dead?" asked Roger.

"Because it is not a liver any longer. Old liver ran there. Closed at the top. No cullent thlough it. That is why when this liver rises the water pours thlough into the old liver and makes the noise in the gorge."

"Has anybody ever sailed through?" asked Nancy.

"When water velly high, yes," said Miss Lee.

"Have you?" asked Roger.

"Long ago," said Miss Lee. "And my father was velly angly. He said that one junk captain more or less was no matter but for me it was lisking too much." Miss Lee laughed, and, close to the black rock, sang out a single word in Chinese and put the tiller over. The *Shining Moon* swung round, the Chinese sailors trimmed the sheets, and a few moments later, looking back, they could see the mouth of the gorge no longer.

With a few more tacks they were nearing the mouth of the river and looking at the two small forts, one on either side. Close along the bank above each fort was what looked like a long raft moored to the shore, or perhaps a lot of logs floated down from some forest further up.

"Do you send timber out from here?" asked

Captain Flint, quite forgetting Miss Lee's proper business.

"No," said Miss Lee with a laugh when she saw what he was looking at. "When an enemy tlies to come in we can pull logs light acloss the liver."

"Has anybody ever tried?" asked Nancy.

"Long time ago," said Miss Lee. "But the boom is always leady."

"What happened?" asked Roger.

"The enemy junks did not see the boom in the dark," said Miss Lee, quietly putting the ship about as she spoke. "Two junks lammed the boom and sank. Thlee junks were sunk with guns. One junk went aglound. Not one junk went home. They left Thlee Island men alone after that."

"And were you there?" asked Nancy eagerly.

"Velly little girl," said Miss Lee, showing with her hand that at that time she stood only about two feet high.

She sailed close up to one fort and then to the other. From each fort half a dozen men ran out and cheered. Another tack and they were at the mouth of the river. "Here's where our junk anchored," Nancy was saying. "There's our island. . . . I mean Miss Lee's," Roger was saying a moment later. "There's where Wu's men were coming down the cliff," said John, pointing up to the long scratches that marked the road slanting to and fro across the face of the rock. The voyage was all but over.

There was no more tacking now. The *Shining Moon* was reaching easily along under the cliff, nearer and nearer to the little island where the

Swallows had landed after that night of wind. She was sailing into the narrow passage between the island and the cliff. Already the Chinese sailors were making ready warps on poop and foredeck.

"There's the landing-place," said Roger, "and the one on the other side."

"There's the green roof of the temple," said Titty.

Miss Lee called an order and gently, gently, moved the tiller. The *Shining Moon* was turning in towards the island landing-place. The Chinese sailors were slackening the sheets. The little junk turned more and more slowly, and came to rest alongside the jetty so gently that if she had had eggshells hanging out for fenders instead of bamboo bundles, she would not have cracked a single shell.

"Lovely work," said Nancy. "Well done, Miss Lee."

Miss Lee, smiling happily, led the way ashore.

CHAPTER XX

CAPTAIN FLINT GETS BACK HIS SEXTANT

THE amah and the model students followed Miss Lee up from the jetty to the little temple with the carved scarlet dragons at every corner of its green roof. Nancy, Peggy and Captain Flint were seeing it for the first time. Roger was pointing out the trickle of fresh water among the rocks, and telling about the way they had startled the cormorant fisher.

"I do hope we didn't leave things in an awful mess," said Susan.

"We wouldn't have gone in if we'd known it was a temple," said Titty.

"It's that sextant I'm thinking about," murmured Captain Flint.

"It's sure to be there," said John.

*

On the threshold, Miss Lee stopped for a moment, frowned, and then, remembering the goodness of her students, went on into the inner room. There certainly was rather a mess. When John and Susan had been called across the island to row after the Amazons, they had had to leave things just as they were. Seed husks from the parrot's breakfast still lay on the floor. There were the sleeping-bags, spread out like beds. There was the tin box of the iron rations. The green-headed pin was still lying on the table where they had found Miss Lee's books. The amah saw it at once.

"I picked it up on the jetty," said Roger.

The amah said nothing but, unsmiling, took the pin and stuck it in her hair.

"The sextant?" said Captain Flint and the next moment had seen it, a square, mahogany box, with a lock and a brass handle and two small brass hooks that held the lid down.

"I do hope it's all right," said John.

Captain Flint put the box on the table, flicked back both hooks and lifted the lid. He took out the little bit of chamois leather kept there for cleaning. He took out the sextant itself. He fingered one by one the little telescopes and eyepieces.

"Nothing wrong there," he said. "John, if ever we get back to England, you shall have a sextant for yourself."

"I've got the almanac too," said John, taking it out of the box in which he kept his barometer and compass.

Captain Flint closed the sextant in its case, went quickly out on the verandah and glanced at the sun. He came back, stepping over the legs of Titty and Susan, who were hurriedly picking up the parrot's husks.

"Let's have a look at that almanac," he said. "It's not noon yet. We've time to do it, if we can only get a sea horizon. I can make a good guess at the longitude. Wish I was surer of the day. One night in that junk, one in the fort, three in Chang's zoo. How many days have I been cramming Latin?" He turned the pages of the almanac, tore out the table of corrections, folded it carefully and put it in his pocket, and then tore out an advertisement page and scribbled some figures in the margin.

"What are you going to do?" asked John.

"Take an observation if we get a chance," said Captain Flint.

In the shadows of the inner room they saw Miss Lee with a lit match. A thin stream of bluish smoke curled upwards from a stick of incense on the oblong chest that they knew now was not an altar but a grave. Miss Lee, with her back to them, was bowing again and again.

She came out and, seeing her students busy rolling up sleeping-bags, became again the happy smiling schoolmistress on holiday. "That is light," she said. "You can leave your things on the velandah. My amah will see them safe aboard and you will find them this evening when we come home."

"But is the *Shining Moon* going back without us?" said Nancy.

"We go to visit the Taicoon Wu," said Miss Lee. "The *Shining Moon* must go back now, before wind dlop. She needs the wind to take her up the liver."

"Bother the Taicoon Wu," said Nancy, but not so that Miss Lee could hear her.

"And now," said Miss Lee, "we will go acloss the island to my father's chair."

Miss Lee and her students set out along the path through the trees.

"You're not going to carry that all the time, Uncle Jim?" said Peggy.

"I'm not going to risk losing it twice," said Captain Flint, who was walking in front of her, holding the mahogany box by its brass handle.

"But she said we could leave everything on the verandah," said Peggy.

"Peggy, my dear," said Captain Flint. "Shut up. When Nancy calls you a galoot she's often wrong but sometimes very right."

When they came out on the rocky point at the other side of the island, Miss Lee bowed in memory of her father, and sat herself in the great stone chair overlooking the open sea.

"Here," she said, "my father loved to sit. Here he watched his ships go out and come in. No one has sat here, only my father and now I, his daughter."

Roger and Titty, both of whom had used the chair as a lookout post, glanced at each other but said nothing. Miss Lee, her mind full of old memories, began talking of fights between one junk and another, of battles between whole fleets of junks, grappling, setting fire to each other, filling the quiet bay with the thunder of their guns. Her students, lying on the ground about the chair, listened, and as one story ended, Nancy begged for another.

John saw Captain Flint beckon from behind the chair. They slipped quietly away.

"Just about time," said Captain Flint, glancing at the sun, taking the sextant lovingly from its case, as they came down on the shore at a place where the others could not see them. Ten minutes later they came back with triumphant smiles. The navigators, even if without a ship, had been at work once more.

"What are you grinning about?" asked Nancy.

"Oh just this," said Captain Flint, waving towards the sea.

"It is a velly fine view," said Miss Lee.

"Sorry I interrupted," said Nancy. "Miss Lee, do go on, about that time when your father was taken prisoner and captured the junk that had captured him. How did he get her away when she was in the middle of an enemy fleet?"

Miss Lee went on, told that story and another after that, and at last, with a glance at Roger, said that they would go back to the temple to picnic Cambridge fashion. By now, she thought, the amah would have the picnic ready.

"I knew there was something in those baskets," said Roger.

They came back to find that the *Shining Moon* was already gone, though the guards were still waiting on the jetty. All their things were gone too, and a picnic meal was waiting on the verandah. It was a queer mixture of China and Cambridge. For China there were persimmons, queer fruits with squashy red insides, and bowls of rice and chopped chicken. For Cambridge there were fat ham sandwiches which tasted unlike any sandwiches that Cambridge ever knew, made with spiced bread that might have been a sort of cake. A kettle for tea was boiling on the Primus stove which, as Susan tried to explain to the silent and hostile amah, she had meant to clean after their last breakfast.

"Have they left that behind?" asked Miss Lee suddenly, seeing the mahogany box on the ground beside Captain Flint.

"That's all right, ma'am," said Captain Flint

hurriedly. "It weighs almost nothing. I'll carry it."

They had finished their picnic meal when they saw three sampans coming across to the jetty, and a lot of people at the landing place at the foot of the cliff.

"And now," said Miss Lee, "we go to see the Taicoon Wu. I hope you have had a happy picnic."

"First rate," said Nancy. "Specially the sailing, and those stories."

"It's not over yet," said Roger. "We're going to cross that bridge."

"It has been very pleasant," said Captain Flint, "but, of course, it's not like lessons."

"Ah," said Miss Lee, "there is no pleasure like learning. Labor ipse voluptas. Work is a pleasure itself." It was the only time she had used a Latin word that day.

The sampans were coming into the jetty. The amah was bundling the empty bowls into their baskets. Her students waited while Miss Lee went once more into the inner room to bow before her father's grave. A few minutes later the whole holiday party and the guards, with Captain Flint still clinging to his sextant, were being ferried across to the landing-place under the black cliff of Turtle Island.

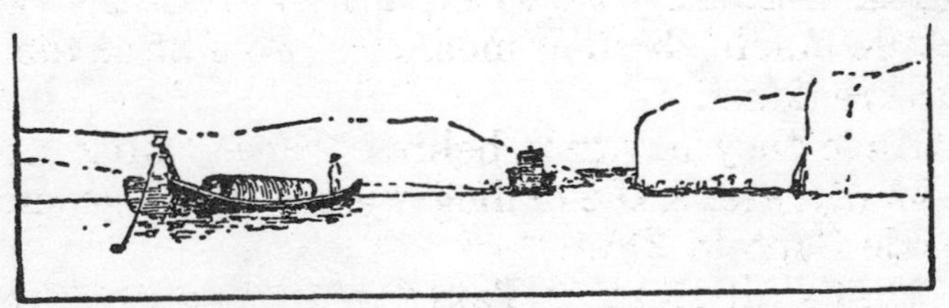

CHAPTER XXI

OLD SEAMAN WU SEES IT

Miss Lee, going for a picnic, had slipped away from Dragon Town without formality. It was different now that she was going to pay a visit to the Taicoon Wu. A crowd of people were waiting at the landing-place under the cliff. There were more men with rifles, some who had come over from Dragon Island and some sent by Wu himself as a guard of honour. There was Miss Lee's travelling chair, and eight others, each with its bearers. As Miss Lee stepped ashore, a man unfurled a black banner with a golden dragon, like the tiger banner that had been carried in front of the Taicoon, Chang, on the march home after giving an airing to his birds.

"Gosh," said Roger, "we're all going to be Taicoons. . . . I say, I'm sorry for the ones who have to carry Captain Flint."

"Don't you think, ma'am, I'd better walk?" said Captain Flint himself.

"Evellything allanged," said Miss Lee, who was already sitting among the golden cushions of her chair. "We visit the Taicoon, Wu. Please . . ."

"It's all right," called Roger. "There's one with four men to carry it, specially for you. All ours have only two."

A moment or two later they had started. The man with the dragon banner walked in front. Then came half a dozen guards. Then Miss Lee, in her gold-cushioned chair. Then the old amah in a rather plainer chair lined with blue silk. Then one after another in chairs like the amah's came six of the model students. Then, in a larger chair Captain Flint, still firmly clutching his sextant. Then the rest of the guards.

Some of the guards in front set up a chant, taken up by those at the rear, tossed to and fro as it were, from one end of the procession to the other and back again. There could be no talking. Swinging in their chairs, slung from bamboos on the shoulders of the coolies, the students had enough to do to pretend they did not mind as the procession began to climb the narrow track cut in the face of the cliff. Up and up they went, the wall of the cliff above them on one side, a precipice below them on the other. Up and up, till they could see the blue water over the topmost trees of the little island they had left. Up and up, till the island looked no more than a small green blot on the water beneath them, and the green roof of the temple no more than a pinpoint different in colour from the trees. Again and yet again the track twisted back upon itself climbing always till it reached the top of the cliff.

Here the men rested, but only for a moment, and then went swinging on along a wider road now dropping gently into a wide valley. On the further side of the valley they could see the road again climbing over bare rock. But in the middle of the valley they could see paddy-fields, with women working among the rice, trees, and a walled village. The procession, with the dragon banner waving before it, hurried down the road towards the fields.

At the gate in the wall of the village a gong sounded, twenty-two times. The procession was growing like a snowball. The women in the rice-fields left their work and ran to join it. Men and women poured out of the one-storied houses, to bow, to shout "Missee Lee" and to run beside the chair-carriers, staring at the students. Men and women, getting their dragon ready for the feast, left their work to join the crowd.

Suddenly, a little way ahead, the students saw another banner, grey and scarlet, coming out of a gateway, and knew it for the turtle banner of the Taicoon Wu that they had seen once before in the courtyard at Miss Lee's. The Taicoon Wu was coming out to meet his chief. They saw him, the same little stout man with the wrinkled face, in his blue and purple robe, whom they had last seen sitting beside Miss Lee in the council hall. The crowd came no further but waited. The banner-bearers met. The Taicoon Wu was bowing to Miss Lee, and pointing towards the gateway. He bowed to the old amah but took no notice of the students. Miss Lee, in her chair, was carried in, the stout little man walking, bandy-legged, beside her. "Boom, boom . . ." Twenty-two times a gong was sounded. Miss Lee and Wu disappeared under the gateway. The amah was carried in after them, and the chairbearers lowered the chairs of the students, stretched their arms and squatted on their heels.

"Great chopsticks," exclaimed Nancy, getting out of her chair. "Call that manners! I do think he might have invited us in too."

"How did you like being a Taicoon?" said Roger, running up to join Titty.

"I wish they weren't humans," said Titty, thinking of the coolies.

"They're much better than donks," said Roger.

Peggy, still a little shaky, joined them. "Again and again I thought we'd be over the edge," she said.

"So did I," said Nancy. "till I saw they were as good as goats."

"There's still that bridge to cross," said Roger. "I say, they're bringing out something to drink."

They were, but it was not for the students. A huge bowl was brought out from the gateway, and a great pile of small ones; guards and coolies crowded round, dipped, drank and smacked their lips.

"Mr. Wu didn't look too pleased to see us," said Captain Flint, strolling up with John and Susan.

"I wonder how long she's going to stay in there talking to him," said Susan. "There won't be light enough to do much at the dragon by the time we get home. I simply can't sew with those lanterns."

"Did you spot the dragon they've got here?" said Roger. "It looks about ready."

"Well, they've got about a dozen people working at it," said Susan. "Not only Peggy and me."

"I put in at least a hundred stitches yesterday," said Nancy.

"I wonder what they're talking about," said John.

"I had a sort of idea she was going to talk to

him about us," said Captain Flint. "I think it was in her mind to get him on her side against the old counsellor. Hullo. Cheer up, Roger. This looks as if he's relented."

A man was coming out of the gateway carrying a tray with a row of little bowls on it.

"It isn't as if we were really thirsty," said Roger. "And anyway, it won't have sugar in it."

All the same they felt a little less like unwanted guests when the man came up to them and they were sipping pale tea out of the little bowls.

Ten minutes later it seemed that the Taicoon had relented a little further, for a man came out to them with a tray heaped with sweet and sticky lumps, each pierced with a thin bamboo with which to lift it to the mouth.

Perhaps twenty minutes after that there was a stir among the guards. The old amah in her chair was coming out of the gateway. As soon as they saw who it was the guards settled again in their places. The amah was set down close to the little group of waiting students. Her face was grimmer than ever. They all wanted to ask questions, but even Roger thought it better not. "No relenting there," said Captain Flint.

Suddenly coolies and guards sprang to their feet. Miss Lee and the Taicoon Wu were walking towards them together, followed by the bearers with Miss Lee's empty chair.

"She's talked him round," said Captain Flint.

"She doesn't need to," said Nancy. "She's a twenty-two gonger and he's only a measly ten."

Miss Lee was talking happily, and the Taicoon, Wu, was smiling all over his wrinkled walnut of a face. They came up to the group of waiting students.

"I am telling the Taicoon, Wu, how happy I am with my students," said Miss Lee. "My velly good students. I am telling how you love your work, how quick you learn. . . ."

The students shifted uncomfortably on their feet. This was a little too much like prize-giving day at school when people who had spent most of the term in trouble were being given prizes for good conduct before a lot of admiring visitors. Then Miss Lee began introducing them one by one.

"Loger," she said and, after naming him, turned to the Taicoon with a lot of talk in Chinese. The Taicoon listened, and smiled at Roger. Roger, hardly knowing what he ought to do, put out his hand. The Taicoon laughed and shook it heartily.

"John," said Miss Lee and went on in Chinese, perhaps telling how fast John was picking up the Latin he had forgotten. John too shook hands with the Taicoon.

"Tittee" was the next name. Miss Lee was evidently going through the list of her pupils in order of merit. There followed "Su-san", "Peggee" and "Nansee". Each in turn shook hands with the little smiling brown-faced man.

Miss Lee turned to Captain Flint, and Captain Flint, ready for the handshaking, shifted the mahogany box from his right hand to his left.

"Captain Flint," she began and stopped.

The smile had left the Taicoon's face. Much shorter than Captain Flint, though no less stout, he was pointing at the polished wooden box. His brown, wrinkled face looked almost black. He spoke to Miss Lee and pointed angrily at the box. Miss Lee answered him, and said in English, "The Taicoon, Wu, asks what you are carrying. I tell him it is part of the luggage John and Su-san left in my father's temple."

The Taicoon, scowling furiously at Captain Flint, spoke to Miss Lee.

"He asks to see what is in it," said Miss Lee. "Please show him."

There was nothing to be done. Captain Flint put the box on the ground, flicked back the catches and opened it. Wu stopped, snatched away the bit of chamois leather, took hold of the sextant and tried to lift it out. It stuck.

"Let me," said Captain Flint, and tenderly lifted his precious instrument from its case. Wu put out his hand and Captain Flint unwillingly let him have it, waiting to save it if the Taicoon should let it drop.

The Taicoon stamped his foot.

"Six-tant," he said and began talking something like English. "Six-tant," he said. "Missee Lee tell my she keep you . . . you stay here. . . . Safe. . . . You no can find Thlee Islands. . . . You no can tell gunboats where to find Thlee Islands. . . . This is six-tant. You take melidian altitude. . . . You put finger on map . . . so. . . ."

Captain Flint started, and John, remembering what they had done only a few hours earlier, turned a deep red.

"Here, I say," said Captain Flint, "what do you know about meridian altitudes?"

"Olo seaman," said the Taicoon Wu, setting his bandy legs wide apart and looking through the sextant at the sun, which was now well down in the west. "Olo seaman. . . . Blitish ships. China Merchants. . . . Boy . . . Deckhand . . . Bo'sun. Take time for my captain when him take melidian altitude. I olo seaman. Know sixtant velly well. You fool Taicoon Chang. . . . You fool Missee Lee. You no fool Taicoon Wu. . . . I tell Missee Lee. . . . I tell Taicoon Chang. . . . Not safe keep you here. Moa betta chop you head. . . ."

He showed the sextant to Miss Lee, talking angrily in Chinese. His voice grew louder as he talked. The guards and bearers were listening. The amah, in her chair, leaned forward, listening too. The Taicoon made as if to throw the sextant on the ground. Miss Lee put out her hand for it. He gave it to her.

"The box, please," said Miss Lee coldly.

"I'll put it in," said Captain Flint. She let him have it and he lowered it carefully into the felt-lined box, found the chamois leather on the ground, laid it over the sextant and closed the catches.

Wu put out his hand for it. Miss Lee shook her head without a smile and herself took the box from Captain Flint, and put it on the footboard of her chair. Polite farewells were being said. Wu and Miss Lee were bowing to each other. There were no farewells for the model students, who seated themselves silently and nervously in their chairs. The banner-bearer waited for the signal. It came. One after another the twenty-two gong strokes sounded from Wu's gateway. The banner-bearer

BO'SUN WU DOES NOT SHAKE HANDS

marched ahead, followed by Miss Lee in her chair, using the sextant for a footstool. The procession was on the move again. The Taicoon Wu, standing with his men, watched Captain Flint being carried away and made that same quick gesture that they had seen for the first time in Chang's yamen, a sharp cutting motion with his hand at the back of his neck.

Gone now was the holiday feeling of the day. Each one of them was feeling more prisoner than student. Each one of them knew that something serious had happened. It was worse because, each in a chair, carried in single file along the narrow road up out of Wu's valley, they could not talk. They had no eyes for the road, no eyes for the sun sinking in the west. In gloomy silence, swinging in their chairs, they came to the gorge and were carried across that narrow bridge, hundreds of feet above the rocks below.

They had hardly crossed the bridge before they heard shrill whistling from behind them. It was answered not from Dragon Town but from Tiger Island, on the other side of the river. They saw Miss Lee, riding in her chair ahead of them, put up her hand. Instantly the procession stopped and the chairs were put down. Roger, less easily dismayed than any of the others, and anyhow delighted to have passed the bridge, skipped out of his chair and ran forward to ask Miss Lee what the whistling was about.

He found her sitting still and listening with a dead face.

"What is it, Miss Lee?" he asked. "Do tell me what it is."

The whistling ended.

"The Taicoon, Wu," said Miss Lee dully, "is asking the Taicoon Chang to come acloss the liver and have a talk with him." She gave the word for the procession to go on.

Roger, dodging back to get to his own chair, shouted the news to the others. It did not cheer them.

Outside Dragon Town the people were coming in after the day's work tending the growing rice. At the sight of the dragon banner they came running and splashing to the roadside to cheer as Miss Lee went by. A crowd was waiting at the town wall to cheer as the twenty-two gong strokes sounded. All through the streets the people poured out of their houses to cheer and cheer again. People lifted their children to see her as she passed. Crowds, running together from other parts of the town were waiting to cheer her at her own gateway. Once more the gongs sounded for her. The chairs one after another were carried through into the courtyard. The holiday picnic was over and Missee Lee was home again.

"Well, there's one comfort," said Captain Flint as he left his chair and joined the others, "she may be at outs with Mr. Wu and Mr. Chang, but she reigns in the hearts of her people."

"We ought to thank her for the picnic," said Susan.

It was too late. Miss Lee had left her chair and, carrying Captain Flint's sextant, was already going up the steps and in through the verandah of the council room.

The prisoners went into their own house. There,

neatly piled on the floor, were all the things they had left in the temple, everything except Captain Flint's sextant.

"If you'd only left it with the rest," said Nancy, "it would have been here and you wouldn't have lost it."

"I've mucked it," said Captain Flint. "And now we've got another enemy."

"I saw him do that beastly thing with his hand," said Roger.

"So did I," said Captain Flint, tenderly rubbing the back of his neck.

CHAPTER XXII

MONEY RETURNED

SUSAN was waked early by the shrilling of whistle signals. She got up at once. With only one more day before the Dragon Feast it was not going to be easy getting that dragon done. What with Latin and then being out all yesterday and not getting home till lantern-time, what should have been an easy job was going to be a hard one. Miss Lee had said the students' dragon would please her men. Captain Flint had said that it was a good thing to please them. Susan was near the bottom of the class in Latin, but when it came to sewing she knew that she could pull her weight and more. Somehow or other that dragon should get done. The others woke to find her busily stitching, and ready for help as soon as she could get it. It was a dreadful piece of work. The dragon's skin was made of stout red cloth with an outer skin of golden scales. A solid join had to be made between the two parts of the skin, and then a lot of scales had to be fitted in and sewn on so as to hide the join. The enormous head of the dragon was made of a sort of papier mâché, to be light for carrying. A lot of the gold paint had worn off, as well as much of the red from the gaping jaws.

"He looks a bit shabby," said Titty.

"It'll do," said John. "Miss Lee said it was an old one they weren't going to use again."

"If we could get some paint," said Titty.

"Ask Miss Lee," said Susan, sucking the end of a bit of thread. "Oh, look here, Nancy, if you get it crooked that side we'll have to unpick and start again."

"Bother your dragon, Roger," said Nancy, as Roger came in from the courtyard, where he had been paying a visit to Gibber.

"I say," said Roger, "Gibber and I watched Captain Flint being shaved in his cage, and we saw old three-hair beard being carried out in a chair, and Captain Flint got himself cut turning round to look at him."

The bell rang, and they left the dragon to hurry through the garden to breakfast.

"Salvete discipuli!" said Miss Lee as they greeted her, but they knew she was thinking of something else.

The amah brought in Captain Flint, with a thin line of red on his chin, where the Chinese barber had cut him. He was looking worried and mumbled a "Good morning" which Miss Lee hardly seemed to hear.

Breakfast began in silence. They were half way through it before John dared to say, "Miss Lee, we never thanked you yesterday for taking us to the island."

Miss Lee looked at him. "I had hoped," she said, "to show the Taicoon Wu that he could aglee with me against my counsellor and Chang."

"I fear I spoilt that, ma'am," said Captain Flint.

"It is now worse. Velly much worse," said Miss Lee. "Wu and Chang have asked to see my counsellor. Why not me?" Miss Lee seemed to ask that question of herself. "Well, I have sent them my counsellor. . . ."

"We saw him going out," said Roger. "That's how Captain Flint got his chin cut."

"Only his chin," said Miss Lee.

It was not until breakfast was over that Titty dared to ask about the paint. "It doesn't want a lot," she said. "It's just for places on his head, and bits of his jaws are white instead of bloody."

For the first time Miss Lee smiled. "Loger's dlagon?" she said. "All light. You shall have some."

Then Roger, the favourite pupil, dared to remind Miss Lee that yesterday's holiday had given them no time for preparation. "No matter," said Miss Lee. "We will see how much you have forgotten and we can tlanslate without plepalation."

*

It was a queer lesson. They were surprised themselves to find how much they had remembered. If they had been model students, Miss Lee had certainly been a most successful teacher. Or else, as sometimes happens, she asked each one the question to which he knew the answer. Even Nancy satisfied the examiner. But, though Miss Lee was pleased, they knew her mind was somewhere else. Sometimes there was a long wait between one question and the next, while Miss Lee turned the pages of the grammar book as if she did not see them. Sometimes even, though it was answered promptly, she seemed to have forgotten what question she had asked.

Towards the end of the morning they heard a noise in the courtyard outside. The amah came in and spoke to Miss Lee.

"The counsellor is come back," she said, and went out after the amah.

"We'll know the worst now," said Captain Flint.

"If we're in disgrace," asked Roger, "what do you think she'll do? Not let us go to the Dragon Feast?"

"Much worse than that," said Captain Flint.

She was a long time gone. When she came back, she was no longer the kindly schoolmistress, but much more like the Missee Lee they had seen for the first time, sitting formidable in the council room among her captains. She sat down, her lips tightly closed, her eyes narrowed, her fingers drumming on the table.

"The Taicoons thleaten mutiny," she said at last. "Wu has told Chang it is not safe to keep you here one minute. They say my father was light. No English plisoners. They ask me to cut the heads of my students. . . ."

There was a long silence.

"What cheek," said Nancy at last.

"Yes," said Miss Lee. "They ask for an answer, now. They ask me to aglee, Yes or No."

They heard the shrill whistling of the signaller, a very short message. Roger looked up.

"I send them the answer," said Miss Lee. "I send them the answer, No."

"Good for you," said Nancy.

"That's all right," said Roger.

"Thank you, ma'am," said Captain Flint.

"What will they do now?" said Titty.

"Nothing," said Miss Lee. "Wu will do nothing without Chang. Chang will do nothing because you are not his plisoners. Chang is gleedy, velly gleedy. I paid him money. Much money. I let Chang keep his San Flancisco in exchange for my students. And then I bought him because you wanted him. Chang will take big lisk lather than give up money. Chang will do nothing at all."

"I don't much like your having bought me," said Captain Flint and stammered into silence under Miss Lee's eyes.

"You should be happy I did," said Miss Lee.

And then, as if nothing had been the matter, she set them their work. "No lesson tomollow," she said, "because of Dlagon Feast. But you must do some plepalation for the next day."

"Miss Lee," said Roger, "we'll go to the Dragon Feast just the same?"

"I plomised you should," said Miss Lee, "and you shall."

*

Work on the dragon was in full swing. A man had brought in two bowls, one of red paint and one of gold, and had showed by hard stirring how it was to be used. Titty, with splodges of gold on her face and hands, was making the dragon's head look like new. Roger was painting its fiery tongue. The tail end of the dragon was flopped along one side of the room, with a bit of it hanging over the table to meet the other end draped over a couple of chairs. John, Captain Flint and Peggy were holding the join so that Susan and Nancy could pass from one to the other the needle to and fro, doing the long lines of stitching that were to hold the ends together. Miss Lee came through the garden.

AT WORK ON THE DRAGON

"Vide, nostra domina, nostrum draconem," said Roger.

"Domina nostla would be better, Loger," said Miss Lee. "But velly plomising."

She stayed, watching her pupils for some minutes, and went away again.

"Funny," said Captain Flint. "I wonder why she came."

"She's bothered about something," said Titty.

"Wondering what those bloodthirsty Taicoons'll be up to next," said Captain Flint.

"They can't do a thing," said Nancy. "You heard her say so. She swopped us for you, letting Chang keep you, and then she bought you. We're her property, not theirs."

*

The dragon needed no more red paint and Roger had more than once asked if they were not going for a walk at all, and Susan had said that he and John too were more of a hindrance than a help in difficult sewing, when Captain Flint said "Come on, Skipper, and you, too, Roger, we'll clear out and leave the experts to it."

"Now we'll really get ahead," said Susan as soon as they had gone, and as soon as Titty had covered the last bare patch on the head with gold and left it to dry, she and Susan worked at one seam, while Nancy and Peggy worked at another. "Four rows of stitching at the very least," Susan had said when they began. "It'll only pull apart if we have less."

John, Roger and Captain Flint had been gone about an hour and a half when the dragon-menders heard a noise in the courtyard.

"Who is it this time?" said Titty. "Shall I go and see?"

"What does it matter?" said Susan. "If we don't hurry we'll never get done."

And then Miss Lee came in again. She looked all round at once.

"Where is Loger?" she asked.

"Gone for a walk with John and Captain Flint," said Susan.

"Do you want him?" said Titty. "Shall I go and look for him?"

"Which way did they go?" asked Miss Lee.

"They didn't say," said Nancy.

"John was saying something about looking at the river," said Peggy, "just as they went out."

Miss Lee made as if to go through the house to the courtyard but changed her mind. She went out to the garden but only for a moment. She came back and sat down. The others went on with the mending of the dragon.

Miss Lee stood up again, and began walking to and fro. Titty, underneath a fold of the dragon, passing the needle through to Susan above, watched the flickering of her little gold shoes.

"Velly clever painter," said Miss Lee, looking at the dragon's head, and then, "Pelhaps I had better send . . . Susan, were they going for a long walk?"

They all felt the worry in her voice. Susan lost the thread out of her needle.

"What is it?" said Titty. "Has something happened?"

"I will tell you," said Miss Lee, after listening

for a moment. "I will tell you. Chang has sent back the money that I paid him."

"Oh good," said Titty. "Captain Flint was awfully bothered about it."

"It is not good," said Miss Lee. "You do not understand. It means that Chang will now count that you are still his plisoners, not mine. He has got nothing for you, not even Captain Flint. . . . He is flee to do what he likes. It means that . . ."

The door from the courtyard burst open and Roger came racing in holding his hat at arm's length before him.

"Look, look, Nancy," he shouted. "We were looking at the river all in flood. . . . No, no, Miss Lee, we hadn't gone to the ferry or anywhere we mustn't. . . . We were looking at the river and there was a bang . . . and I heard something whizz . . . and my hat flew off, and look at it!" And he pointed to a clean hole through the brim.

"Roger," cried Susan.

"Roger," cried Nancy. "You lucky, lucky beast!"

"Some careless fellow shooting at birds," said Captain Flint as he came in with John.

"No," said Miss Lee. "Shooting at you. That is what it means. . . . Tell him what has happened. . . . Listen! You are none of you to go outside the yamen. No. Not one. Not even in the garden. I must see my counsellor at once. . . ."

And Miss Lee was gone.

CHAPTER XXIII

MISS LEE AGREES WITH HER COUNSELLOR

ROGER with a bullet through his hat was enough to slow up any sewing party. Nancy was full of envy. Titty wanted to know exactly what had happened. Susan turned away from the hat and would not look at it, thinking how near the bullet had passed by Roger's head. Captain Flint sat gloomily down on a bit of dragon where it spread over a chair.

"It's all my fault," he said.

"Well, you were a bit of a gummock, Uncle Jim," said Nancy. "Going and letting Wu see the sextant."

"How was I to know the little beast had been a bo'sun?" said Captain Flint. "I'd never heard him open his mouth. And most of these chaps get along all right with coastal sailing but wouldn't know what a sextant was if you shoved it at their noses."

"One thing," said Nancy, "if we're not allowed out any more, there's no need to go on pricking our fingers. My thumb's nearly raw pushing that needle through or having the needle jabbed into it by Peggy pushing it back."

"Gosh!" said Roger. "We won't even be allowed to see the other dragons."

"They cut it up for us," said Susan, "and we've nearly done now. We may as well finish it."

"I suppose we'd better go at that Latin," said John.

It was nearly dusk. Susan was finding it too dark to see, and the others, stirred to it by Captain Flint, were asking each other grammar questions, expecting every minute to see their evening rice brought in, when there was a sudden shadow in the doorway. Miss Lee had come back.

"Salve, domina," said Roger.

"Salve, Loger," said Miss Lee, but not as if she really meant it. She looked back into the garden and beckoned. The amah came in and Miss Lee spoke to her in Chinese, setting her to keep watch through a window looking on the courtyard. She herself glanced back again into the garden and said, "Loger, please sit in the doorway, so you will see if anyone is coming."

Captain Flint offered her a chair and she sat down, but only for a moment. She stood up again, looked at the Latin Grammar and at the page Captain Flint had copied out to study in his cage, picked up the dictionary, opened it, closed it again and put it down. Suddenly she swept books and papers together.

"No more lessons," she said.

"But we like them," said Captain Flint. "And we're getting on."

"No more lessons," said Miss Lee. "No good. I was velly happy. I thought Camblidge had come to me. Velly good students. All finished now. My father made a good law when he said 'No English plisoners in the Thlee Islands'!"

Her students listened with puzzled and rather frightened faces. This was a new Miss Lee. They had seen Missee Lee, chief of the three islands, sitting in the council room of her yamen, sitting in her father's chair, with the Taicoons and captains listening to her every word. They had seen Miss Lee, the happy lecturer, helping lame dogs over the stiles of Latin grammar. They had seen Miss Lee, the skilful steersman, master in her own ship. They had never seen a Miss Lee who looked as if she had failed in getting her own way.

"Thlee Islands," said Miss Lee, talking as if to herself and not to her listeners. "Thlee Islands, my father made them one. He tlusted me to keep them one. And now I make them thlee again. The counsellor is light. Better to have no English students, no English plisoners, no Camblidge, but keep Thlee Islands one, and my father happy in his glave."

"Are you going to let us go?" said Roger from his seat in the doorway, keeping watch on the garden path.

Everybody stirred uncomfortably. Roger had said what was in all their minds.

Miss Lee flashed for a moment into anger. "You all velly pleased. Even Loger."

"We've loved being here," said Nancy. "We'll remember it all our lives."

"Short lives," said Miss Lee. "Plobably velly short lives."

Suddenly they heard the shrill piercing whistling of the signaller. Miss Lee's mood changed again.

"You hear that?" she said. "I have agleed with my counsellor. I have told him he may tell the Taicoons I have agleed with them. He has sent the message now. I have plomised to make an end and have no more English plisoners after the Dlagon Feast."

"But that's tomorrow," said Susan.

"But you're not going to let them do any chopping?" exclaimed Roger from the garden door. "We wouldn't really like it."

"They say they will be quite content if I chop heads for them."

"Miss Lee!" said Titty.

"Jibbooms and bobstays," said Nancy. "But it isn't fair."

"Vale, domina," said Roger sadly.

Miss Lee laughed in spite of herself.

"Loger's Latin leally velly plomising," she said. "And all have been good students. . . . Tlied hard . . . . Even Nansee is not so velly bad." (Nancy opened her mouth to speak but changed her mind.) "No. Miss Lee will not chop the heads of her students."

"How are you going to get rid of us, ma'am?" asked Captain Flint. "Send us off to Hong Kong . . . or Singapore . . . or any treaty port? We'd be all right anywhere if we can get in touch with a consul."

Miss Lee flared up at him. "Yes," she said. "That is what the counsellor told me. You will talk to a consul. The consul will send teleglams to the admilal. The admilal will send orders to gunboats and gunboats will come and smash up all Thlee Islands business."

"But we wouldn't let them," said Titty.

"Not Chang, not Wu, not one of our captains would let you have a chance of talking to one of your consuls," said Miss Lee. "They would take no lisk. Chop heads. Dlown and be safe."

"But if you tell them they've jolly well got to," said Nancy.

"What happened today?" said Miss Lee. "An accident. A sampan will upset taking plisoners ashore. Plisoners all dlowned. Velly solly. All a lie. But what can I do? I chop off the head of the captain. Velly good. But plisoners will still be dlowned. The same thing will happen if you stay here. A stone will fall down a cliff. Poison in food. A man shoots a pigeon and hits Loger by mistake. No. Better no more Camblidge, no more lessons, and my velly good students must tly to go away."

"But how?" asked Nancy.

"If we could have *Swallow* and *Amazon*," said John. "Our two boats."

"Too small," said Miss Lee. "Too slow." She looked narrowly at Captain Flint.

"If Miss Lee tlusts you," she said. "If I give you a junk, can you plomise to sail light away, not to go to Hong Kong, not to go to Macao, not to go to Hainan, not to go to any harbour till you leave all China seas?"

"We all promise," said Captain Flint. "We'll touch nowhere before Singapore."

"Singapore harbourmaster will say 'Hullo, you China junk, where are you flom?' What will you say?"

Captain Flint thought for a moment. "Awkward without papers," he said. "Best tell them as much truth as we can. Tell them we lost our schooner at sea, got ashore somewhere, bought the junk from fishermen, put out again, lost our reckonings and glad to find out where we are."

"And not send gunboats?"

"Of course we won't," said Nancy.

"You plomise?" Again Miss Lee looked at Captain Flint.

"They'll chop us to pieces before we give you away, ma'am. But what about sending the junk back? Port officials might follow her."

"Who blings her back?" said Miss Lee scornfully. "If I send Thlee Island men with you, you will never get to Singapore. Door-nail dead before you are gone two days. They will not tlust you. Only I, Miss Lee, tlust you." Another thought struck her. "Could you sail one of our junks without Chinese sailors?"

"Seven of us," said Captain Flint. "And we took a schooner half round the world before we burnt her. . . . I don't know about a big junk, but we could manage a little one."

"I will give you *Shining Moon*," said Miss Lee.

"Miss Lee!" exclaimed Nancy.

"Gosh!" said Roger.

"I'd take that little ship anywhere," said Captain Flint.

"We'll take awful care of her," said John.

"But what will you do without her?" said Titty.

"Building another . . . better," said Miss Lee. "But *Shining Moon* is a good boat. She will take you to England. She will show what a Chinese junk can do. And I will stay here on Dlagon Island and fo'get Camblidge altogether."

"Come with us," said Titty.

"Chuck this piracy business," said Captain Flint.

"You come back to England with us, go back to Cambridge, take one degree after another and end up head of a college."

Miss Lee's eyes sparkled for a moment. Then the light in them went out. "I must stay in the Thlee Islands," she said.

"Will the others ever let us get away?" asked Susan.

"No," said Miss Lee.

"Then it's all no good," said Roger.

"Sail at night," said Miss Lee, "and they will not see you go. In the morning, if there are no plisoners, there will be no heads to be chopped."

"Those big junks are pretty fast," said Nancy.

"Our captains do not make long voyages. If you are gone clear out of sight they will not catch you."

"When can we start?" said Susan.

"Tomollow," said Miss Lee. "Dlagon Day. The Taicoons come here to feast in my yamen. The Tiger Island men will bling their dlagon. The Turtle men will bling their dlagon. They will see you all day. They will see your dlagon dance at night. They know I have agleed to have no English plisoners. They will think, 'All light. Chop off heads in morning'. No shooting, no chopping on Dlagon Feast Day. Sunlise to sunlise evellybody fliends. That night you go. Evellybody feast and sleep. When they wake you will be gone."

"How do we get out of here without being seen?" said John.

Miss Lee looked from face to face in the dusk. "Better I talk with your captain alone. Better you should not know. You can go out. Too dark for shooting now."

"Out," said Captain Flint.

There was no waiting. The six of them went out into the garden, leaving Captain Flint and Miss Lee to talk secrets alone in the swiftly darkening room.

In the dusk outside, Susan looked up at the tops of the trees that showed here and there shadowy against the sky above the garden wall. "Roger, you come here," she said. "Don't go out on the terraces. We'll keep under the orange-trees where we can't be seen."

"Giminy," said Nancy. "I wish we hadn't really got to go."

"You don't want to stay and have your head cut off?" said John. "We're jolly lucky it hasn't happened already."

"How long will it take us to get to Singapore?" said Susan. "We shan't be able to let Mother know we're all right until we get there."

"Depends on the wind," said John. "But she's a grand little ship."

"I say," said Titty. "We shan't be going home in a liner after all. We'll be sailing in our own ship."

"Chinese junk," said Roger. "Gosh, it's really almost a good thing Gibber set fire to the *Wild Cat.*"

"It isn't," said Titty.

"Well, of course *Wild Cat* did have an engine," said Roger. "There'll be nothing for me to do."

"Won't there?" said Nancy.

"We'll have to get a tow through the Red Sea," said John, thinking far ahead. "North wind there all the time. Captain Flint was counting on the engine to push *Wild Cat* through to the Mediterranean."

"It's the getting away that's going to be difficult," said Susan. "Sentinels everywhere. And it'll be worse if we try and they catch us."

"Galoot!" said Nancy. "Even you, Susan. We get our heads chopped off if we stay. They can't chop them off more than once even if they catch us trying to bolt. And of course we'll get away. No more beastly Latin. That's one thing. No more listening to a ship's boy cockily spouting Latin. . . ."

"Able seaman," said Roger.

"Jibbooms and bobstays! Won't we mates and captains make you work," said Nancy, who, even if she was sorry to be leaving a pirate island, had not much enjoyed being bottom of a class in which Roger was top. "Latin!" she added scornfully. "Polishing brass work'll do you good."

"There isn't much brass to polish on *Shining Moon*," said Roger.

"Plenty of teak to keep holystoned," said Nancy.

"Probably no holystone," said Roger. "Anyway, who cares?"

"We'll be at sea again," said Titty.

"I wonder how they reef those sails," said John.

"Easy with all those battens, I should think," said Nancy, and the two captains went off into a debate as to how best to do it.

They walked up and down among the orange-trees, sailors ashore only in passing, happy in the thought that very soon they would have a swaying deck under their feet once more. In the noise of the cicadas among the leaves they were hearing the creaking of the blocks. Up and down they walked in the dusk, keeping an eye on the door from the garden into their house, watching for Miss Lee or Captain Flint to call them in.

At last, when it was almost dark they saw a shadow flit to and fro carrying bundles from their house to Miss Lee's. Then they saw Miss Lee herself going home. They waited a little longer and saw a flicker of light in their rooms. The amah had lit the lanterns. They saw her flit away for the last time.

They went back to the house and found it empty. Captain Flint had gone.

"Locked up for the night," said Nancy.

"Better make sure," said John.

"I say," said Susan. "All our things from *Swallow* have disappeared."

"That's what the old amah was carrying," said Roger.

They went out in the courtyard to the bars of Captain Flint's cage, all but Roger, who went to have a word with Gibber through the bars of the next cage but one. They could see a glimmer of light through the door of Captain Flint's sleeping-box.

"Hey!" called Titty quietly. "Captain Flint!"

The prisoner, with a bowl of rice in his hand, came out to the front of his cage.

"Go home," he said. "What are you doing here?"

"We wanted to be sure everything was all right."

Captain Flint spoke low. "I've got our sailing directions, if that's what you mean."

"All our things have gone," said Susan.

"I know," said Captain Flint.

"What about the dragon?" said Susan. "We shan't want it after all."

"More than ever," said Captain Flint. "Go home and make the best job of it that ever you did in your life. And get it done before you go to sleep. Good night!" He turned round, went back into his sleeping-box and closed the door behind him.

They went home and found their supper just coming in. They hurried through it. It was hard working by lantern-light, but when they went to bed the little dragon was all but ready for his twelve legs.

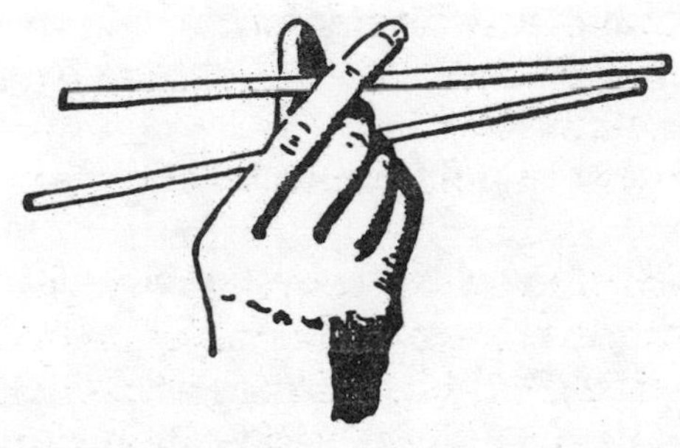

CHAPTER XXIV

THE DRAGON FEAST

THERE was no Cambridge breakfast on the day of the Dragon Feast. Captain Flint was let out of his cage earlier than usual and was brought in to share a chopstick breakfast of rice and chicken with the rest of the students. Even in their house at the high end of the courtyard they could hear the buzz of holidaymakers in the pirate town. Their own dragon lay in shining folds on the floor. After hurrying through her breakfast, Susan was stitching on the last of the extra scales to cover the join in the body when Miss Lee came in through the door from the garden.

She looked round. "You are velly happy," she said sadly. "No more lessons. No more Latin. You are all glad to leave Miss Lee."

"It's not that," said Titty.

"You've been very good to us, ma'am," said Captain Flint. "But, you know, people do like to be sure of keeping their heads on their shoulders."

"And we've got to get home some time," said Susan.

"Schools," said Miss Lee.

"Mother and Daddy," said John. "And schools too, of course."

"Camblidge," said Miss Lee. It was as if Cambridge and the lessons that had come to an end were all one in her mind.

"We'd love you to come with us," said Titty.

Miss Lee shook her head.

"Good-bye," she said. "And happy voyage. I shall not be able to talk to you again. Captain Flint knows what to do. . . ."

Just then the great gong began to sound.

"What's that for?" asked Roger.

"Taicoon Chang," said Miss Lee. "Or Taicoon Wu. I must go to meet them."

"Just half a minute, ma'am," said Captain Flint. "Let me be sure I've got my sailing directions right. . . ."

Roger slipped out into the courtyard. He was back again before Captain Flint and Miss Lee had finished talking.

"It's Chang," he said, "but he hasn't brought a dragon. Miss Lee, why hasn't Chang brought a dragon?"

"The dlagon dance does not begin till later," said Miss Lee. "Tiger Island dlagon on the way plobably. . . . You had better go out to see them coming. No more lessons. . . ."

"Is it safe for them to go out?" said Captain Flint.

"Quite safe," said Miss Lee. "Dlagon Feast. Nobody will shoot today. Evellybody fliends with evellybody till sun lise tomollow. Better go out so evellybody see you are not aflaid." The gong had begun to sound again, another ten strokes.

"Wu," said Miss Lee and hurried out into the garden to be ready to receive the two Taicoons.

"We've never said good-bye to her properly," said Susan.

"We'll never see her again," said Titty.

"We'll see her all right," said Nancy. "We'll see her, but she can't very well talk to us with the other Taicoons scowling round. Jibbooms and bobstays, I suppose we've got to go, but it won't be much fun at school after living with Chinese pirates."

"You won't have to work so hard at school," said Captain Flint. "And anyway, we aren't out of this yet. I wish we were."

"Come on," said Roger, twiddling his hat with a finger through the bullet-hole. "Let's go out and meet the other dragons."

*

They went out into the courtyard where they saw the tiger and the turtle banners propped against a wall, and knew that two of their enemies were talking with Miss Lee. They went out through the gateway. In spite of what Miss Lee had said about the feast they half expected, after what had happened yesterday, to meet hostile faces and to see people making signs of chopping heads. But everybody had a cheerful smile. In all the town nobody was doing any work unless it was cooking, for from house after house came good kitchen smells, mostly that of roasting pork. People were just hanging about in the streets, smoking, talking, laughing, like people waiting to see a circus march through. They took the road towards the southern gateway in the town wall, thinking to meet Wu's dragon coming from Turtle Island and, from the high ground, to be able to see Chang's dragon as well on the road to the ferry on the other side of the river. They saw the Dragon Island's dragon almost at once, but not in a very lively state. It lay, flopped and empty, along one of the streets, a trailing carpet of shining scales and bright red silk, with here and there one of the bamboo poles sticking out from under it by which, when it was time for it to wake, one of its many pairs of legs would hold it up. The legs were squatting on the ground beside it, drinking stuff out of little bowls. Some of the legs called a greeting to them as they passed.

"What are they saying?" asked Roger.

"I don't know," said Captain Flint. "Happy Dragon, I suppose, or something like that."

"They're all jolly friendly," said Nancy.

"Yes," said Captain Flint. "'Happy Dragon!' today and 'Off with your head!' tomorrow. Well, by this time tomorrow, if all goes well, we'll be hull down and out of reach of them."

"Everything will go well, won't it?" said Roger.

"If Miss Lee plays the game," said Captain Flint.

"She will," said Titty.

"And if our dragon's up to his job."

"What's he got to do with it?" asked Roger, but got no answer out of Captain Flint.

Again at the gate in the outer wall, nobody stopped them. Everybody was looking out over the rice-fields towards the high ground as if at any moment something for which they were waiting might come in sight.

"We'd better not go too far," said Susan.

"We've got to see those dragons," said Roger.

"Of course we have," said Nancy. "We've got to see just what they do so that we can do it better. Jibbooms and bobstays! Swallows and Amazons for ever! Our dragon's got to beat the lot of them."

THE GORGE

"River's still rising," said Captain Flint, looking back towards the ferry as they were crossing the rice-fields outside the wall. "That ferry-boat's nearly level with the jetty on the other side."

"Look at the people coming ashore from the junks," said Roger.

"We'll have to get past those junks," said John, who was trying to get the whole shape of the river in his mind. Somehow or other, they would have to sail that river in the dark. "Which way do you think the wind'll be?"

"Land breeze at night with luck," said Captain Flint. "We won't stand much of a chance if we have to tack. Take us too long getting out." And then, as John and Nancy began talking about the ropes of the junk and wishing they had had a chance of feeling for themselves how she steered, he swept the subject away. "We're not aboard yet," he said. "One thing at a time. What we've got to think about now is dragons."

They hurried on up the slopes beyond the rice-fields till they came to the place from which they could look down into the gorge and see that narrow bridge, without even a handrail, crossing from cliff to cliff.

"Nancy," said Roger, "did you look down when they carried us across? I did."

"Think of Miss Lee taking a boat through that," said Nancy.

"Telescope, Titty," said Captain Flint. "It's a dragon all right," he said a moment later.

"Let's look," said Roger.

The telescope was passed from hand to hand. High on the cliff at the other side of the gorge a dragon was winding its way out from among the rocks on the road to the bridge.

"Listen! Listen!" said Titty.

They heard a steady drumming noise, and now and then snatches of queer tuneless shrilling on a flute.

"Look at the one dancing in front," said Roger.

"Your job," said Captain Flint. "Have a good look and take a lesson from him."

"Look at him jumping," said Roger. "Spinning . . . . He's whirling something round his head."

"A gourd like yours," said Captain Flint.

"Snakes and centipedes," said Nancy, "the dragon's got a thousand legs."

Far away on the other side of the gorge a man in bright red clothes and a pointed red hat was leaping, somersaulting, high-kicking, jumping up and spinning in the air, and whirling some sort of ball at the end of a string in front of the dragon's monstrous head. The head swung from side to side, and behind it the whole shining length of the dragon twisted this way and that. Through the telescope they could see the legs of the men who were carrying the dragon flickering beneath it. This way and that the legs ran. This way and that the long body of the dragon snaked its way after the dancing man.

"I haven't got a hat like that," said Roger. "And I haven't got the proper clothes."

"What does he do it for?" asked Titty.

"A pearl," said Captain Flint. "That's what it's meant for. A pearl to tempt the dragon."

"Carrot for a donkey," said Nancy. "All right, Roger. You've got a beauty."

"We could make him a hat," said Susan.

Roger, watching carefully, tried a kick or two.

"I say," he said, "they'll have to stop snaking when they come to the bridge."

As the dragon came near the bridge, the dancing man ran on ahead and the dragon straightened out like a rope to follow him.

"Look at him showing off," said Roger, as the dancing man stopped in the middle of the narrow bridge, turned round and did a jump and spin. "I say, hadn't we better go home and practise."

"Let's just see it cross," said Nancy.

The dragon crossed the bridge soberly and safely and they saw that its legs had decided that they had earned a rest. They lifted the long body of the dragon on their bamboo poles and laid it on the ground, limp and dead like the one in Dragon Town. The legs gathered in groups to smoke their pipes, and through the telescope Nancy saw that they were mopping the sweat from their faces.

"Come on," said John, "we'd better get back to our own dragon. We know what to do now, but we'll never be able to do it as well as that."

"Of course we will," said Nancy.

They almost ran back to the town. People at the side of the road across the rice-fields shouted questions to them. They guessed that they were being asked if the Turtle dragon was in sight and pointed back over their shoulders. Then they passed people who were looking across the river. In the distance, on the road leading down from the long hill of Tiger Island, another dragon was snaking on its way towards the ferry.

"Chang's lot," said Captain Flint.

"Come on," said Nancy. "Go it, Titty."

At the gateway in the town wall a crowd was waiting. News had somehow reached them that the other dragons had been sighted. Inside the town people were hurrying, some towards the ferry, others towards the southern gate. In the main street the legs of the Dragon Island dragon were getting ready to swing it into action. They raced past, into the courtyard to Miss Lee's yamen, and so to their own rooms, where the little dragon, cut down to fit, was in a heap on the floor, with its great head gaping towards the door into the garden.

Roger grabbed the gilded gourd on the end of its rope and began swinging it round and round his head.

"Look out, you little idiot," cried Captain Flint, as the gourd missed him by an inch. "My head's tough enough, but if you smash that pearl we shan't be able to get another. Go out into the garden."

"There's someone there," said Titty. "Miss Lee and a lot of the others."

"Give Roger a room to himself," said Nancy. "Go on in there. And for goodness' sake keep in the middle when you swing that thing. That's all right. Higher than that. Higher. Now, right off the ground with both legs and do a spin."

"Keep that up and you'll do all right," said Captain Flint, watching in safety from the doorway.

"Come here, Roger," said Susan, needle and thread in one hand and a bit of scarlet stuff from the dragon's underskin in the other. "Let me get the size of your head."

Nancy and Peggy were cutting narrow strips of red and yellow and threading them on a piece of string.

The hubbub from the town grew louder. Suddenly there was a rattle of firecrackers near at hand.

"Starting early with the ammunition," said Captain Flint.

"They're here," said Nancy, as the noise of drums, bamboo flutes and firecrackers was drowned in a great outburst of shouting at the yamen gates. "Don't be a donk, Roger. Stand still."

"I only hope it'll stick on," said Susan. "Anyhow, it's the best I can do."

"Now for it," said Captain Flint. "We do a round of the town before the feast. The main thing to remember is to watch the feet of the man in front of you."

"And step just where they step," said Nancy, "so that we get a proper wavy waggle. Great chopsticks, I wish there were fifty more of us. Twelve legs to a dragon is pretty measly compared with those centipedes."

"Never mind," said Captain Flint. "Each leg must do its duty. We've just got to be a popular turn. If we get booed the whole plan goes to blazes."

"What?" said Roger. "What plan?"

"Wait and see," said Captain Flint.

The amah was beckoning at the garden door. "Missee Lee say walkee," she said, and suddenly laughed as she saw Roger jumping for practice with his scarlet hat on his head and the string round his middle from which dozens of red and yellow streamers flapped like flames. "Walkee this way," she said and was gone.

"If we can get a grin out of that old enemy, we're all right," said Captain Flint. "Slowly at first, till we get the hang of it."

Roger, swinging his silvered gourd at the end of its rope went out first. He looked this way and that. The amah was standing outside Miss Lee's and pointed the way they were to go. There was no one else in sight. He did a skip or two, and looked back to see the students' dragon coming out. Its huge head ducked under the doorway, ducked again as Captain Flint stumbled on the steps, and then reared itself high in the air. Through a hole in the chest of the dragon, Captain Flint laughed at Roger, while he did a little prancing with his legs. More and more of the dragon came out, and Roger backed along the path before it. There were Nancy's legs, John's, Susan's, Peggy's and, last of all, Titty's. The stiffened tail of the dragon, swinging behind her, scraped a doorpost, and Titty looked anxiously out from under her part of the body to see if any damage had been done.

"All clear now," said Roger.

"Remember never to go in a straight line," came the voice of Nancy.

"Let's get my teeth into that pearl," growled the dragon in the voice of Captain Flint, and Roger swung the pearl towards the dragon's nose, flicked it away and began his dance.

He led the way along the path under the orange-trees behind the council hall and Miss Lee's house. The door into the courtyard was open. He went through it and, for a moment, hesitated.

"Get on," said Captain Flint, and Roger, throwing out first one leg and then the other, spinning round, sometimes hopping backwards, sometimes forwards, swinging the gourd round his head, offering it to the dragon and snatching it away, set out through the courtyard to the gateway. He had expected to see Miss Lee and the other Taicoons, but there was no one on the wide verandah except men busy with chairs and a long table. The men laughed and cheered, and every leg of the dragon felt more confident. No booing yet.

Everybody at the gateway was looking out into the town.

"Hey! Hey!" shouted Roger. The guards and their friends turned round. There was a shout of surprised laughter and room was made for the dragon to pass. The swinging tail tapped a guard on the head, but the other guards only pushed the man out of the dragon's way.

They were out in the street. The town's enormous dragon was already on its hundred legs, and its huge head, nodding up and down, seemed to greet the little dragon as a friend. There was a roar of laughter when, as the big dragon twisted round on itself, the little dragon joined in behind it and followed where it went. The noise was tremendous and from elsewhere in the town could be heard the drums, flutes and shouting of other crowds bringing in or welcoming the dragons from Tiger and Turtle.

THE LITTLE DRAGON LEAVES THE YAMEN

"You all right?" shouted Captain Flint to the rest of his body. "You all right?" the word was passed from one pair of legs to the next. "Aye-aye, sir," the word came back from tail to head along the dancing dragon.

The three crowds met, each with its dragon and there were fresh shouts of laughter from the folk of Tiger and Turtle when they saw that the Dragon Island dragon had a young one copying its every movement. The dragons met and parted, dancing their way among the houses, waiting for the signal. It came at last with the deep booming of the gong, twenty-two times.

"Missee Lee!"

There was a sudden swirl among the crowds. Wherever they were in the town, the dragons turned and made for the yamen. They came, one after another, to the gateway of the courtyard. Chang's dragon was there first and was the first to go in. Wu's dragon beat the Dragon Island dragon by a short head. The little dragon went in last. Tables of food were waiting in the places where on the day of the council the accountants had been busy. On the verandah before the great hall sat Miss Lee, with the old counsellor and Chang and Wu beside her, and a row of smiling captains from the pirate junks. The dragons danced up the courtyard to the steps and, while their leaders capered, bowed their monstrous heads. After the three big dragons had made their bows, the fourth dragon, the little one, pushed its way in beside them. Captain Flint knelt on the ground and brought the dragon's head down so that its chin rested humbly on the lowest step. Roger, doing a prodigious leap, slipped and fell, but hopped up again in a moment to see the Taicoon Chang, helpless with laughter, rolling in his chair. Miss Lee was smiling. Wu and the captains were laughing too.

The old counsellor lifted his claw-like hand. There was sudden, absolute silence. Then Miss Lee was making a speech of welcome to the dragons. She stopped. Each dragon's leader leapt in the air. Each dragon raised its monstrous head. There was a roar of cheering, taken up at the gateway and all through the town. The next moment, tired legs were coming out from under dragons' bodies. The bodies were left lying in the courtyard and the legs were making a rush for the food that had been made ready for them.

"What do we do?" asked Roger quickly.

"Drop our dragon in its own lair," said Captain Flint. "Prance away." And Roger, prancing till he was out of sight round the corner of Miss Lee's house, led the little dragon back through the garden.

"Gosh," said Captain Flint, dumping the head on the ground. "Talk about hard work!"

"I say, I'm awfully sorry I went and tumbled," said Roger.

"It was the star turn of the show," said Captain Flint. "It was that that settled the rascal Chang. He must have got a stitch with laughing."

"Hiccups at least," said Roger hopefully. "I say, are we to go and grub with the others?"

"We are," said Captain Flint. "Pirates with the best of them. Don't want to start anybody asking what's become of us. Just let me have a dip from your water kong to splash over my bald head."

"Good idea," said Nancy.

"The way to get cool quick," said Susan, "is to wet the back of your wrists."

"I know," said Titty, "like hanging your hands out of the window of a railway carriage."

*

They cooled off as quickly as they could and went out into the courtyard. Miss Lee, sitting with the Taicoons and captains on the verandah, gave no sign that she had noticed them, but there were shouts at once from the tables where the legs of the other dragons were settling to the feast. Pirates squeezed up to make room for them, and in a minute they were sitting with the others, being chattered at in Chinese which they could not understand and hearing the ex-cook, who had carried the head of the Tiger Island dragon, shout to them in his pidgin-English, "Numpa one first chop dlagon!" by way of applause for their performance.

They had fed pretty well during their stay with Miss Lee but had never sat down to such a feast as this. Even Chang's supper to his captains on the evening when they had been taken prisoners was a mere snack beside it. Congee, birds' nest soup with floating lumps of jelly in it . . . "like frog spawn," Roger whispered . . . shark's fin, curries, bowls heaped with rice and bits of roast pork, steaming bowls with rice and bits of chicken, more bowls with rice and bits of fish . . . "sicked up by the cormorants," said Roger . . . bowls of tea, and bowls of a queer drink that they did not like, though the pirates were sucking it in, swallowing with hearty gollops and loudly smacking their lips while their bowls were being refilled. The noise of eating was such that even if they had been able to understand it, they could not have heard what anybody said. And there seemed to be no end to the feast. Again and again they thought they had come to the last dish, but always new bowls, piled high, were set before them. Even Roger wilted, and long before the pirates had had enough the prisoners were leaving things untasted and praying that there would be no more.

At last Titty, who was sitting with her back to the courtyard, looked over her shoulder and saw that Miss Lee was no longer there. The Taicoons, the counsellor, the captains, were still on the verandah, drinking and smoking their little pipes, but the grand chorus of loud and cheerful eating was weakening like bird-song at dusk. Man after man, with glazed, smiling face, left the table, found a place for himself in the shade, lay on the ground and slept. The man who had been sitting between Titty and Captain Flint had fallen forward where he sat and was snoring with his head among the bowls of food. Titty reached across his back and touched Captain Flint. He nodded and stood up.

"Sleeping it off, ready for the night," he said to the others.

"Our lot had better do the same."

"Not here," said Susan.

"No," said Captain Flint. "Back to our dragon."

Picking their way among the torpid pirates they left the courtyard and went home to their own house.

"Barbecued billygoats," said Nancy. "I feel as if I'd eaten an elephant."

"Sleep it off," said Captain Flint. "Sleep it off. We've done all right so far, but tonight our dragon's got to dance the others off their feet. What about you, Roger? Feel like prancing?"

"Not just now," said Roger gravely.

"Well, go to sleep the lot of you," said Captain Flint. "In Dragon Town do as the dragons do. And afterwards we'll do the dragons. I'm going out to sleep in the courtyard, where anyone can see me if there's anyone awake. I'll come and fetch you when it's time to start again. Hullo. Peggy's off. Sensible girl. . . ."

Peggy was as torpid as a Chinese pirate and was asleep already. In two minutes the others were either asleep or only awake enough to wish they were not quite so full. The whole yamen was silent except for the grunts and snores of the men sleeping in the courtyard.

*

It was late at night when they woke to find Captain Flint busy doing something to the inside of the dragon's neck. Someone had been in and lit lanterns in their house while they were still asleep. Lanterns were swinging from the trees outside.

"Time," said Captain Flint, clumsily stitching away. "One dragon's off already and the other two are getting on their legs. How do you feel? It's a rum thing. I suppose I over-ate as much as anyone, but I'm all right now." As in the morning the whole town seemed to be chattering at once.

"Come on," said Roger, "let's get started."

"Lantern this time, Roger," said Captain Flint. "Take that gourd off it's rope and put the lantern on instead."

"What are you doing?" said Susan. "You'd much better let me."

"Giminy," said Nancy. "How did you get it back?"

"Lying in the middle of the floor when I came in," said Captain Flint. "It really does look as if she means to let us go."

He had cut a bit of stuff from the side of the body and was sewing the sextant into the dragon's neck. Susan took needle and thread from him and finished up the job while Captain Flint for the first time told them exactly what it had been planned for them to do.

"If we aren't coming back," said Titty, "hadn't we better say 'Good-bye' to Miss Lee?"

"She said 'Good-bye' this morning," said Captain Flint.

"But we didn't," said Titty.

"We can't be sure it's coming off now," said Captain Flint. "She said we were free before, you know, and we found sentinels all over the place."

"I'll just see if I can find her," said Titty.

"No harm in that," said Captain Flint, "but don't go anywhere near her if she's with the counsellor or Chang or that walnut-headed little bo'sun."

Titty ran through the doorway to Miss Lee's house. She was stopped in the doorway by the amah.

"But I want to see Miss Lee," said Titty.

"Missee Lee tired," said the amah. "Missee Lee see no one. . . . What for you make Missee Lee cly?"

She went back to the others, and found Roger holding Gibber by his lead while with the other hand he dangled the round lantern, lit, at the one end of its rope. John and Nancy were holding up the dragon's head while Captain Flint was wedging the parrot's cage inside it.

"Did you see her?" said Susan.

"No," said Titty, "and the amah said she's been crying."

"All very well," said Captain Flint. "We can't help that. She's a good girl, though a rum one, but I don't see the good of our getting our heads cut off, and, if anything goes wrong, Chang or the bo'sun'll have them off in two ticks."

"And anyhow we've got to get home," said Susan.

Two minutes later they were ready, and Susan was looking round to see if they had left anything behind. She found Roger's white hat with the bullet-hole through it on his bed where he had flung it when he put on his pointed scarlet one.

"I'm not going to leave that," said Roger, taking it and stuffing it into the front of his shirt.

The little dragon was on its feet again. They were off along the garden walk and into the courtyard, now a blaze of lanterns. Captain Flint had Gibber by his lead. Roger, swinging his lantern, danced ahead, out of the gateway into the town.

"Don't overdo it, Roger," called Captain Flint. "We've got to keep it up now to the end. And swing that lantern steady or you'll have it out."

"All right," said Roger, dancing backwards. "I mean, Aye-aye, Dragon."

Lanterns were hanging from the roof corners of every house, from bamboos stuck out of the windows, from the trees. The noise was like the noise of a battle with the sharp bangs of the firecrackers which boys and men alike were letting off in all directions. They soon found the other dragons. All three were dancing and snaking through the streets in and out among the houses, with people running beside them with firecrackers, long strings of them wound round bamboos, banging, banging all the time. The little dragon did the same, with Roger prancing and swinging before it and Gibber, bothered by the firecrackers, hopping and running beside it. They were in the main street when Gibber, tired of trotting on his own feet, leapt at the dragon's fiery mane, grabbed it and swung himself up, while the people laughed and cheered.

"Where's that monkey?" shouted Captain Flint.

"Sitting on your neck," shouted Roger: "I mean, the dragon's."

"Good," said Captain Flint.

On and on they snaked their dragon through the streets, round this house, down that lane, round again between two houses, back through the main street, into the courtyard where the Taicoons and captains sat laughing on the verandah of the council room, back again into the streets, now chasing one of the big dragons, now running away from it, now meeting it when both dragons nodded their huge heads and there were shouts of delighted laughter.

"Gosh!" panted Titty. "Tell him not to go so fast."

The word was passed along from tail to head and they took a short rest in a side street. After all the other dragons were doing the same from time to time.

"How much longer?" asked Roger after another rest much later.

"We'll pick our moment," said Captain Flint. "But we've got to keep going."

"Bother that feast," said Roger, and then "I can manage another go now."

With wearying feet, the little dragon danced on and on.

CHAPTER XXV

LITTLE DRAGON ALONE

It was long after midnight. Here and there the lanterns hung from the houses were guttering out. The legs of the little dragon felt as if they were made of lead.

"Keep it up," said Captain Flint, as the little dragon, wearily snaking this way and that, passed down a street where one of the longest of the dragons had come to a standstill while its legs were being given drinks by its admirers.

"Keep it up. Go it, Roger. Throw in a high kick or two if you can manage it. Let them see our dragon's still full of beans. We've got to slip off soon before the others go back to the yamen for a last blow out."

"Bang! . . . Bang! . . . Bang! . . . " A Chinese boy with a long string of firecrackers wound round a bamboo pole was dancing along beside them.

"All right," said Captain Flint. "We must go on till he drops out. His firecrackers won't last for ever. Sidestreets now, Roger. Work round to the back of the yamen."

"Bang! . . . Bang! . . . Bang! . . ." The Chinese boy danced along, sometimes at the head of the dragon, as if to encourage Roger, sometimes dropping back to urge on the dragon's swinging tail and succeeding, because Titty, following as well as she could the feet of Peggy, next ahead of her, could not help giving an extra jerk when the crackers were banging just behind her.

They sputtered to an end.

"He's gone," said Roger.

"Our time's coming," said Captain Flint. "Pass the word along. We'll have a shot now."

Nancy, under the dragon's shoulders, passed the message to John. . . . John, swaying this way and that as he kept his eyes on Nancy's feet, passed it to Susan. . . . Susan to Peggy. . . . Peggy to Titty.

"Aye-aye, sir," panted Titty and wondered how much longer she could keep going.

But just then there was a burst of fireworks near at hand, and one of the larger dragons and a crowd with it came round a corner close behind them.

"Better twirl round and go and meet them," Captain Flint called to Roger. "Make it look as if we didn't want to be done out of any of the fun. Now then, Roger. . . . Give them a star performance. Hold tight, Gibber!"

Roger, leaping, throwing out first one leg and then the other, whirling the lighted lantern round his head, danced back towards the dragon's tail. Captain Flint, Nancy, John, Susan, Peggy, Titty, danced after him and there was the little dragon turned and snaking back again. The parrot screamed inside the dragon's head. Gibber chattered, seated on its neck, and there were more shouts of laughter as people saw that Roger, leaping in front, was doing his best to copy every antic of the leaping man who led the hundred-footed dragon.

They met and passed it. The crowd went on

STARTLING THE DRAGON'S TAIL

with the larger dragon. At a word from Captain Flint, Roger turned again down a side street. It was suddenly much darker. There were fewer lanterns here. It was quiet. The hundred-footed dragons were keeping near the middle of the town. The little dragon, with its twelve tired feet, was twisting away between empty houses, from which everybody had gone to see the fun.

"Bang!"

The tail of the little dragon swung sideways as Titty shied.

"It's that same boy again." said Roger. "Someone's given him another lot of crackers."

"Tell Titty to fetch him one with the tail if she can," said Captain Flint, and the order was passed along the dragon, and Titty did her best, but only pleased the boy who dodged the tail and danced along beside her while his crackers went off almost in her ears.

There was nothing for it but to turn again, and the little dragon turned and snaked wearily along this way and that until the boy, after using his last cracker, ran off towards the noise of other fireworks.

"Now," said Captain Flint. "We'll have another shot at it. Keep it up. . . . Just in case there's someone watching us. . . . Bear to the right, Roger, and right again. That's the yamen wall."

The little dragon, still earnestly twisting as it went, was working once more towards the outskirts of the town, beyond Miss Lee's garden. The noise of the festival was fading behind it. . . . There were hardly any lanterns. . . . There were none. . . . It was dark, except for the starry sky which the legs of the dragon could not see.

"Done it," said Captain Flint. "Now Roger. . . . Blow out that lantern. . . . Straight ahead. . . . Follow the path to the creek. . . . As fast as you can go."

"What about chucking the dragon?" said Nancy.

"Not yet. She said there'd be no sentinel at the creek, but we don't know for certain."

"What if there is?"

"We'll have to do a bit of a dragon dance and go back."

So the little dragon, no longer corkscrewing but straight as a rope, hurried on all its twelve feet away from the houses along the trodden earthen path through the bamboos.

"Easy!" Captain Flint spoke quietly as they came out of the trees. The word was passed back. "That's that. Put the beast down."

The legs of the dragon, very hot and tired, came out from under it, and the body of the dragon lay crumpled and lifeless on the ground.

"It's all right," said Nancy, slipping forward. "No sentinel. What shall we do with the dragon?"

Captain Flint had taken the parrot's cage out of the head, and had given it to Titty. He was ripping the sextant out of the dragon's neck. Roger was telling Gibber what a good monkey he had been.

"Better take it with us," said Captain Flint.

John's voice came, low, out of the darkness.

"I can only find *Swallow*," he said. "*Amazon's* gone . . . and the creek's bank is high. The river's risen a most awful lot."

"More current to take us out," said Captain Flint. "There isn't much wind."

"We can't leave *Amazon* behind," said Nancy.

"Can't be helped," said Captain Flint. "We'll have to cram into *Swallow*."

"Dragon and all?" asked Roger.

"We'll shove the dragon into the wood," said Captain Flint.

With Peggy, Susan and Titty to help him, Captain Flint rolled up the dragon and pushed it in among the bamboos. Nancy was hunting along the bank for *Amazon*.

"She's gone," she said. "And the sampans too. And the landing-stage is under water."

"We've got to get afloat," said Captain Flint. "Any minute some meddlesome fellow may spot we're not on view."

Firecrackers were still going off in the middle of the town and there was a cheerful glow of light above the trees.

"But look here," said Nancy. "We can't . . ."

"If we get out of this, I'll get you another *Amazon*. We're lucky to have *Swallow*. With a flood like this she might easily have gone with the rest. I thought this morning the river looked pretty high."

"I've got the oars out," whispered John.

"Pieces of eight!"

"Keep that parrot quiet. Cover him up with something."

"Gibber's aboard," said Roger, "and so am I."

"I'll take the oars," said Captain Flint. "No. . . . You stick to them, John. Paddle as quietly as you can. Can you see the junk?"

"I know just where she is."

There was no room to spare. John was on the

rowing thwart in the middle. Titty and the parrot-cage were in the bottom of the boat behind him. Roger, protesting that he was not allowed in the bows, had taken Gibber to join Nancy, Susan and Peggy in the stern.

"Ready?"

Captain Flint shoved quietly off and came aboard over the bows. John turned her round and began rowing out into the creek.

"Can't see her yet," said Captain Flint in a low voice. "Pull right. . . . Pull right. . . ."

"I can see something," said Roger. "Over there . . . . We're passing her."

"Good man. . . . Pull left. . . . Pull left. . . . Easy. . . ."

The dark wall of the junk's side loomed up close ahead.

"Look out for your port oar."

"Aye-aye, sir."

There was a slight jerk as Captain Flint reached out, felt along the side of the junk and held on.

"Get your oars in. . . . Ease her along. We're too far forward. . . . Less freeboard amidships. . . . Hullo. . . . They've left a ladder over. . . ."

"Oh, good," breathed Titty.

"Up you go, John. Here's the painter. . . . Who's next? . . . Quiet, for your very life. . . ."

One after another they climbed up in the darkness and down over the rail into the waist of the little junk. Gibber followed Roger aboard and, freed at last from his lead, went off exploring his new ship. The parrot's cage was passed up, and the parrot, as if he knew the danger, said never a word.

"Let her go astern now, John. We'll never get her aboard in the dark without making a noise."

John went aft with *Swallow's* painter, climbed to the poop and made the painter fast to a cleat at the stern rail.

Nancy tiptoed back from the bows. "One anchor down," she whispered, "and a rope to the shore."

"Wonder if there's enough current to swing her."

"There was quite a lot the other day," said Roger.

"Don't want to tow if we can help it. More noise. But we'll want the mainsail. . . . Precious little wind, anyway. . . . Can you find the main halyard in the dark?"

"I've got it," said John, after a fumbling search, "and the tack-rope's by my other hand."

"Those bamboo battens'll sing a song as they go up," said Captain Flint. . . . "But once we're off. . . . Ought to have got away before. Those dragons'll be going back to the yamen before we're out. Now look here. I'm going to cut the shore rope and take the anchor rope to the stern. Then, as soon as she's heading down the creek, I'll cast loose. . . . Can't help losing the anchor. . . . She's got another. . . . And you'll get the mainsail up or some of it just as quick as you can."

"Aye-aye, sir."

"Who steers?" said Roger.

"I'll be handy to the tiller when I cast loose the anchor rope. But look here, one of you must cut it at the windlass as soon as she begins to swing. We don't want to find ourselves anchored by the bows again and as we were before."

"I can do that," said Peggy.

"You've got the sharpest knife," said Nancy. "I sharpened it."

"Susan tallies on with John and Nancy at the main halyard," said Captain Flint. "My word, lucky the stars show the water up a bit. Now then. . . ."

Slowly, fumblingly in the dark, each went to his job.

Away in the town, beyond the bamboo wood, there were still bangs from fireworks, but not so often. The stock was running out and the dragon festival was coming to an end.

Aboard the *Shining Moon* there was dead silence. Suddenly there was the faint noise of a knife cutting rope somewhere in the bows. Captain Flint, with all his weight on the anchor rope was working slowly aft. Again there was the noise of cutting, Peggy at her work.

"She's turning," whispered Titty, watching the dim path of starlit water that led to the main river.

"Hullo!" said Captain Flint. "What's this? Someone's left a boat amidships on this side. . . ."

"Sampan?" whispered Nancy eagerly.

"Can't see. . . . No. . . . I believe it's old *Amazon*."

"Oh good," cried Nancy, darting from her place at the foot of the mainmast.

"You go back to your post," whispered Captain Flint. "Right-o, Roger, I felt the painter somewhere here. *Swallow's* made fast on the port quarter. Make *Amazon* fast to starboard as soon as the anchor rope's gone."

"Gosh! Gosh! Gosh!" whispered Nancy. "And

I thought we'd lost her for ever. Good for Miss Lee. I bet she thought we wouldn't want to have to use two boats in the dark."

"She's swinging fast now," whispered Titty.

High up on the poop, Captain Flint spoke . . . two words only. . . . "Hoist away!"

John, Susan and Nancy hung their weights on the halyard. With a dreadful creaking, the sail began to lift. They stopped, because of that noise and heard the faint splash of a rope in the water. The *Shining Moon* was adrift.

"Hoist away," said Captain Flint out of the darkness astern. "Can't help that noise now. . . . Come up here, somebody. . . . Oh, Roger, you'll do. There's no pull on the tiller. Can you see the mouth of the creek? Keep her so, straight for the middle. . . ."

He leapt from the poop, gripped the halyard higher than the others could reach and had the sail going up, hand over hand, every batten creaking in protest.

"There you are. . . . Make it fast now. . . . She's sailing. Gosh! I ought to have eased that main sheet."

"Help," cried Roger, "it's pulling like anything now."

John scrambled up on the poop and forced the tiller over. The *Shining Moon* was gathering way and slipped down the creek.

"We'll want that foresail," said Captain Flint. "Where's Nancy?"

"Ready to hoist." Nancy's voice came from the high foredeck.

"Let her have it." And with more creaking,

though not so loud, the little foresail climbed its mast.

The *Shining Moon*, moving faster and faster, ghosted out of the creek into the river.

"We've done them," said Captain Flint, who, after dealing with the network of sheets and hoisting the little lugsail on the mizen, had joined John and Roger at the tiller. "We've done them. . . ."

And at that moment a bell that they had never heard before sounded, loud and jangling, from the middle of the town.

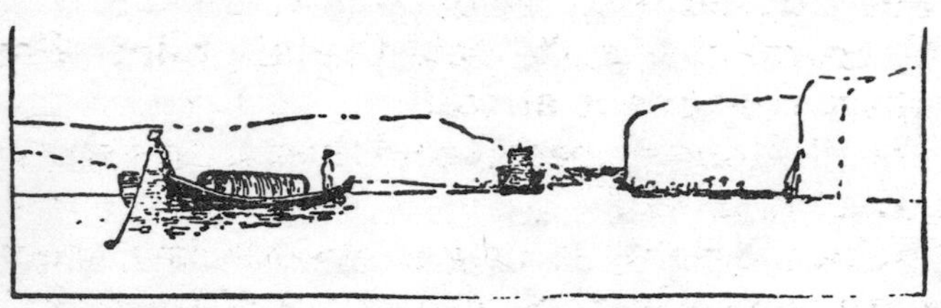

CHAPTER XXVI

ONLY ONE WAY OUT

A SHIVER ran through the little group clustered in the dark on the high poop of the junk.

"Alarm bell," said John.

"They've spotted there's a dragon missing," said Roger.

"They've guessed we've bolted," said Nancy.

"Miss Lee'll fend them off somehow," said Titty.

"She can't stop them looking for us," said John.

"She'll do her best," said Titty.

"Of course she won't," said Captain Flint. "She thinks we're already at sea."

"They'll bring us back," said Susan. "We shan't get away after all."

"We're all right, so long as no one saw which way we went when we dodged out of the town," said Captain Flint. "And I don't think anyone did . . . unless that firecracker brat was still tailing after us."

"He'd used up his last cracker," said Roger. "Why should he?"

"No," said Captain Flint. "He'd go where there was most noise."

"Look out!" said Nancy, "we're going to be into that junk!"

"Teach your grandmother," said Captain Flint, as the huge black shape of a junk loomed up above them. They were well out now on the flooded river, caught already in the main stream sweeping down towards the sea. Another big junk towered above them. There was another ahead. And then another.

"Why haven't they put up their riding lights?" said John.

"Lucky for us they haven't," said Captain Flint, "or they'd see us from the shore going past."

"It's a wee bit lighter over there," said Roger.

"East," said Captain Flint. "There'll be a sunrise some time."

"How soon?"

"Not till we're out, I hope. But it was so jolly late before we had a chance to slip away."

"They're fairly buzzing in the town," said Nancy.

It was hard, looking that way, to see where water ended and land began, but the pirate town began to look like an exploding firework. At first there had been the single glow of the festival, but now lights were moving out from it, threading the darkness. Sound carries well over water and the little worried group on the high poop of the *Shining Moon* could hear orders being shouted and the monkey-house chatter of the crowd.

"Let them jabber," said Captain Flint. . . . "So long as they don't think of the creek."

"There are lights going that way," said Titty. "Through the trees . . . like fireflies. . . . Look . . . . You can see them and then they're gone again."

"They can't see us, can they?" asked Peggy.

"Gummock," said Nancy. "We haven't even flashed a torch."

"Too far off," said Captain Flint. "We've got the background of Tiger Island. . . . Black shadow on black shadow. . . . No. . . . They won't see us. . . . Not yet."

"They'll know we wouldn't go upstream," said John.

"If they find the boats are gone, they'll only think it's the flood," said Nancy.

"They won't think of our grabbing the junk," said Captain Flint. "They won't know she's gone, unless they can see in the dark."

"Some of them can," said Nancy. "Miss Lee's father could and so can she. She said so when she was telling stories on the little island."

"Most of them can't see any better than we can," said Captain Flint, but he had hardly said the words before they heard a sudden burst of shouting away in the darkness astern of them.

"That sounds most awfully as if it came from the creek," said Roger.

"She's a fast little junk," said Captain Flint. "They won't catch us in a sampan . . . and it'll take them a long time to get their blessed warships under weigh. Some of their chaps'll be pretty drunk and if any of them have been legs for dragons and are half as stiff as I am they'll be a bit slow on their pins. . . ."

The wind was not strong but it was driving the *Shining Moon* through the water and the river, sweeping to the sea, was carrying her with it. Before them they could dimly see a watery path, with the reflections of the stars. They could see each other only as black shadows. They felt for each other as they talked. Away to starboard they could see the cliffs at the higher end of Dragon Island cut out as if in black cardboard against the starry sky. Away to port was the long rising mass of Tiger Island.

"Whereabouts are we?" said Roger, plucking at Titty.

"About opposite where the cliffs begin," said Titty. "You can see how high the black goes before it gets to the stars."

"I've lost Gibber," said Roger. "Hi! Gibber!"

"Keep quiet," said John. "If we can hear them they can hear us."

"He'll come back again," whispered Titty.

"Up the masthead probably," said Nancy.

"Oh well," said Roger, "if he's keeping a look-out . . ."

Lights were still moving out of the town towards the rising ground. Lights were still moving through the woods.

"No shouting for a bit," said Nancy. "Perhaps it didn't mean they'd seen the *Shining Moon* was gone."

"If they found the boats were missing and hunted along the bank they'd find the junk's mooring rope slack," said Captain Flint. "They'd pretty soon guess we'd got away with her. Well, we've a good start now. Steers like a daisy, the little ship."

"Great-aunts and Grandmothers!" exclaimed Nancy. "What on earth's that?"

A curious, billowing roar, it might almost have been the big foghorn they had had on the *Wild Cat*. But this noise was rounder and even louder and longer than the old foghorn's longest blast.

"I bet that means something," said Roger.

"That's a horn conch," said Captain Flint.

Three or four minutes later it was answered by a noise of the same kind, a long, echoing hoot from somewhere down the river, and then by another.

A light flashed out far ahead of them.

"That's one of the forts," said John. . . . "And there's the one on Turtle on the other side." A second light had flashed out opposite the first.

"Um," said Captain Flint, "they won't be able to do much shooting in this light."

"Shooting?" said Peggy.

"I don't suppose they'd even try it," said Captain Flint. "But we might have to fend off enquiring sampans. They've got no junks down there."

More lights showed, a little cluster beside each of the two first, and presently these lights seemed to spread out into a sort of chain, two chains, moving towards each other.

"Sampans?" said John.

"I never thought of that," said Captain Flint, and there was a new grim note in his voice. They all felt that there had been a sudden pull at the tiller, as the junk swerved and then straightened again on her course towards the lights.

"You've put a waggle in your wake," said Roger.

"What is it?" asked Nancy.

"They're rigging the boom," said Captain Flint. "Pulling it across the river. We're trapped."

For a moment or two there was silence, as the *Shining Moon* sailed on.

"I didn't think she'd have done it," said Captain Flint.

"Playing cat and mouse. Letting us go like that and then pulling us in at the end of a string. . . ."

"She never would," said Titty, indignantly. "It's the others. It's Chang, and he gave the signal before she could think of a way of stopping him."

"She set us free before," muttered Captain Flint. "Free . . . only with a sentinel on every bridge and boat. . . ."

"But she had to do that," said John.

"What's the difference now," said Captain Flint.

There was another silence. Away down the river the lights were moving this way and that between the dark islands. It was as if a necklace had been strung across from side to side. Then, one by one, the lights began to gather into two clusters, one by either shore.

"We're trapped all right now," said Captain Flint. "They've put the boom across. If it was good enough to stop big junks coming in, it'll be more than enough to stop us getting out."

"Let's go right on and ram it," said Nancy.

"We might as well ram the cliff," said Captain Flint. "That boom's made of teak logs. The little junk would break up like a matchbox."

He was still steering down the middle of the river.

"Hadn't we better go back?" said Susan.

"Can't against the current," said John.

"We'd better anchor," said Susan, "If we can't get away we just can't."

"It's no good landing anywhere," said Captain Flint, talking more to himself than to them.

"There is one other way," said Titty. . . . "If we could get through the gorge. . . ."

Again they felt that Captain Flint was not

steering quite as usual. Titty flung out a hand to steady herself.

"I say, look out," said Roger.

"You can get through if there's enough water," said Titty. "Miss Lee said she'd done it."

"It was bank high in the creek," said John.

"Stiff with rocks," said Captain Flint. "And with all this water in the river it'll be going through there like a mill race."

"Come on," said Nancy. "We'll never get away if we don't do it now."

Again there was a silence, broken, suddenly, by two more long groaning hoots from the forts down the river.

"Everything ready for the mouse," said Captain Flint.

"We must be pretty near that gap," said John.

"Look here, Susan," said Captain Flint. "It's like this. You know what Chang and the others feel about us. If we get caught anything may happen. Accident or on purpose, what does it matter? We've just a chance of getting through that gorge. I don't believe we've any chance at all if we let them catch us. What about it?"

For a moment or two no one spoke. The junk sailed on in darkness. Not even Nancy said a word. Like Captain Flint, they waited for Susan.

"All right," said Susan at last in a low voice.

Nancy let loose a great sigh of relief.

"Gosh!" she said. "I was afraid you wouldn't see it. It's the only possible thing to do."

"Daddy'd say just the same," said John. "I've heard him. 'If you can't do anything, grin and bear it. But if there's one chance, grab it with both hands.'"

"And we will," said Captain Flint. "And it's not such a bad chance. . . . If only I could see in the dark . . . or if it was a bit lighter. But if it was light they'd see what we were doing and be cutting us off at the other end. It all depends on how much water there is and what we draw. You know a boat can go down a stream full of rocks and not touch a single one. The water cushions up against the rocks and fends her off."

"She must draw a good bit," said John. "Look at the way she went to windward the day we went to our island. But there's a channel right through when the river's high, and it's jolly high now. Miss Lee's done it. Why shouldn't we?"

"We'll try it," said Captain Flint.

"What about *Swallow*?" said Titty.

"And *Amazon*?" said Nancy.

"They've got to take their chance," said Captain Flint. "We can't get them aboard in the dark without hanging about while we do it. And we must be pretty near the gorge now. . . . Hullo. . . . Somebody's afloat upstream."

Lights were moving on the water far astern.

"Going aboard the junks," said John.

"Good," said Nancy. "They'll be bottled up by their own boom. They won't open it till it's light enough to see we're not in the river, and by that time. . . ."

"Better not look at those lights," said Captain Flint. "Don't look at the forts either. We'll want cat's eyes in the next half hour, and if we start staring at lights we'll be as blind as moles. Let's see. There's a big rock off shore at the end of Dragon Island just above the mouth of the gorge. We went about there the other day. . . ."

"Yes," said John.

"Care to go forrard and watch out for it?"

"Aye-aye, sir."

"I'm going too," said Nancy.

"Go careful," said Captain Flint. "And when you're there, hang on to something all the time. When you see a rock sing out 'Starboard' if it's on the starboard bow. . . . Understand? . . . Don't tell me where to steer. You just sing out where the rock is."

John and Nancy were gone, down from the poop, feeling their way forward, climbing the fo'c'sle.

"If they shout, won't the pirates hear them?" said Peggy.

"Hardly," said Captain Flint, "and it won't matter now. Look-outs standing forrard?" he called softly.

"Aye-aye, sir. Aye-aye," a murmured answer came back.

"Look! look!" said Titty. "There's the gap. . . . Stars low down. . . ."

It was as if a thin wedge of starry sky cut down into the black mass of the cliffs towards which the *Shining Moon* was moving crabwise across the river.

"Don't want to get carried past," muttered Captain Flint and brought that wedge of starry sky on the port bow.

"Starboard!" a hurried call came from the bows. "The big rock."

Captain Flint changed course again.

"Gosh, she's steering funny," he grumbled to himself, and then aloud, "Current's got us. . . . Taking us in. . . . No going back now. . . ."

It was as if they were sailing straight into the cliff. The starry sky was narrowing overhead. On either side of them was a towering wall of solid black.

The little junk made a sudden swerve. Titty, Roger and Peggy staggered but recovered their balance without falling.

"Lie down, everybody," said Captain Flint. "Lie down and hang on to anything you can get hold of. If we touch, we don't want anybody catapulted overboard. . . . Lie down. . . . The wind'll be stronger in the narrows. . . . Lucky for us it's blowing through from this side. . . . If she gybes, she gybes. . . . Can't help that. . . . But don't let anybody get mucked up with the sheets. . . . Gosh, if only I could *see*. . . ."

A door slammed below the poop.

"What's that?" said Peggy with a gasp. "There's someone in the cabin . . ."

"Gibber exploring," said Roger. "May I go and get him?"

"Lie still," said Captain Flint almost angrily.

"Gibber!" called Roger.

"Shut up," said Captain Flint.

"But he'll come if I call him. . . ."

"Damn that monkey!" said Captain Flint.

Titty felt about her, found Roger's wrist and held it firmly. She knew. They all knew. For the first time since they had known him, Captain Flint was afraid.

The night was no longer silent. There was

a noise of rushing, splashing water, growing louder every minute, echoing to and fro between the high cliffs of the gorge. The little junk leapt and swerved, so that even lying down they had to hang on to something so as not to slide across the deck. On the open river they had seen the first faint promise of dawn. Here, between the cliffs, they were back at midnight. They could see nothing. Water that must have been tossed up a wall of rock came down in spray, like fine rain, wetting them where they lay. The mainsail with a frantic creaking of the bamboo battens flung violently across, and was brought up with a jerk and twang of the sheets.

"Gybed," grunted Captain Flint.

Hardly a moment later, with a huge flap the sail gybed back again.

"Can't see," muttered Captain Flint. "I can't see. . . ." And then, "She'll break right up if we touch. . . . Hang on to anything you can and trust to being carried through. . . . Sorry, Susan. . . . I was wrong. . . . Thought there'd be more light than this. . . . I can't do anything with her. . . ."

Roger jerked suddenly. Titty felt somebody stepping over her. . . . soft, silent feet against her body. . . .

"Who's standing?" shouted Captain Flint. "Lie down, I say. Lie down!"

"Solly. Better let me have tiller, I think," said the voice of Miss Lee.

CHAPTER XXVII

THE PATH OF DUTY

IN the pitch darkness under the cliffs something had changed. Titty, Roger, Peggy and Susan, lying there, flat on the poop-deck, knew that the *Shining Moon* no longer had a blind steersman. Miss Lee could see. That awful feeling of helplessness had left them all. They did not ask why Miss Lee was there. It was enough for them to hear her asking quietly for Captain Flint's weight on the tiller when she needed it. "Pull, please," she would say, or "Please, push". The swerves of the *Shining Moon* were not so sudden or so soon one after another. Moving faster and faster towards the narrowest part of the passage, she seemed to be picking her way for herself and no longer to be swirling downstream like a bit of wreckage.

Roger turned over on his back. "Have we passed the bridge yet?" he whispered. "There it is . . . against the stars . . . look! right overhead. . . . We've passed the bridge," he shouted aloud.

"That's the narrowest bit, isn't it?" they heard Captain Flint say and could hear the relief in his voice. "Sorry," they heard him add. "Mustn't talk to the man at the wheel."

On and on swept the little junk. Splashes of water leapt and dropped into the waist of her. Cool spray flung from the cliffs fell on the high poop.

Suddenly they heard Miss Lee talking.

"Better tell John and Nansee to lie down," she was saying. "We are coming to the whirlpool. . . . Will you please shout?"

And Captain Flint roared above the noise of the water that was echoed to and fro between the cliffs overhead, "Nancy. John. Lie down and hold fast. Do you hear?"

Two shouts from forrard, "Aye-aye, sir," sounded like the twittering of mice.

"I keep on the edge of the whirlpool . . . if I can," said Miss Lee. "You will pull hard when I say . . ."

"Aye-aye, sir," said Captain Flint.

"Whirlpool!" said Roger.

"It'll be all right," said Susan.

"I wish Nancy was here," said Peggy.

The next moment they were in it. They could see nothing, but could hear the enormous swirling of the water. They heard Miss Lee, "Pull . . . Pull now . . . Pull . . ." There was a crash that shook the ship as the mainsail flung across. . . . A gybe . . . Another crash as the mainsail flung back again. . . . Tremendous flapping. For the first time the feel of wind in their faces . . . The *Shining Moon* had been turned right round and was heading upstream. . . . There was a thunderous flap as the sail filled again. . . . Another gybe . . . Another . . . And then, with the wind aft, the *Shining Moon* was picking her way downstream below the whirlpool.

"Thumping good mast," they heard Captain Flint mutter to himself.

And then, quite suddenly, they knew that the darkness was not what it had been. The cliffs on either side were further away and not so high. They could see the mainsail no longer as a curtain of solid black against the stars but dark and ribbed. Looking past it and under it they could see the door into the fo'c'sle, square windows, the high foredeck and up in the bows the two look-outs on their feet again now and peering forward. The water was smoother. The *Shining Moon* was moving more and more slowly down the widening channel, the wind behind her no longer gathered together by the funnel of the gorge. It was growing lighter every minute. A cock crowed somewhere on land. And now that they were clear of the echoing cliffs they could hear quite a lot of other noises, the beating of the alarm bell and the piercing shrill notes of a signaller far away in Dragon Town.

"Open water now," said Miss Lee and gave up the tiller to Captain Flint.

The look-outs on the foredeck turned round.

"We've done it," shouted Nancy cheerfully. "Good for you, Uncle Jim!" and then, in an altogether different tone, "Miss Lee!"

And with that call of Nancy's the hearts of Titty, Roger, Susan and Peggy turned suddenly to lead. They were prisoners still. They had never thought of that. They had thought of Miss Lee only as being there in the very nick of time to save their lives and to save the ship. They scrambled unhappily to their feet. John and Nancy climbed up to the poop and joined them.

"Well," said Nancy. "I don't care what you say, I think it's pretty beastly."

Captain Flint spoke. "If Miss Lee hadn't taken

the tiller in time we'd never have got through at all. We're lucky to be alive and we're a lot better off as her prisoners than if we'd been caught by Bo'sun Wu or Mr. Chang."

Nancy turned her back on him. Suddenly she flung round again.

"Rot," she said. "No guards now. We're not her prisoners. She's ours. Shut her up in the cabin."

In the dim light of early morning a little smile showed on Miss Lee's face. "Nansee," she said. "You are a blave but foolish child. I am coming with you. Going back to Camblidge."

"Three thousand million cheers!" exclaimed Nancy, not even minding being called a foolish child. "Barbecued billygoats, I thought Captain Flint was right. Cat and mouse, you know."

Miss Lee looked at Captain Flint, who looked away and attended to his steering.

"Giminy," said Nancy. "Miss Lee, I'm jolly glad you're coming. And you'll come to Beckfoot for the holidays. . . ."

"Long vacation," said Miss Lee. "We will have a reading party. . . ."

"Oh, Gosh!" murmured Roger. "Not lessons in the summer holidays! I say, Gibber isn't up the mast. Gibber . . . Gibber!"

"In the cabin, your monkey," said Miss Lee, who, though thinking of other things and listening for other noises, had heard the fear in Roger's voice. "He came in long ago."

"And you let him stay," said Roger, remembering how Miss Lee had forbidden the monkey in the house. "Thank you very much."

"I thought it better," said Miss Lee.

Roger slipped down from the poop to open the cabin door and set Gibber free. Titty went down to fetch the parrot from the safe corner between poop and bulwarks where she had wedged his cage to be out of the way when first they came aboard.

"He's pretty wet," she said, "but he's all right."

"I say," said Roger, "it was a good thing she was here when we were coming through that gorge. Even Captain Flint . . ."

"I know," said Titty.

Titty passed the parrot-cage up to John on the poop and climbed up herself. Roger followed her.

"That is a new signal," Miss Lee was saying. "You heard the first signals?"

"We heard them all right," said Captain Flint, "but we did not know what they meant, except that after that bull-roaring horn we saw that they were closing the boom."

"The first signals said that you were in *Shining Moon* and that Miss Lee wanted you blought back alive or door-nail dead. Dead or alive. Miss Lee wanted the pallot and the monkey alive and the foleign devils alive or door-nail dead."

"That must be Chang," said Titty. "He always rather liked old Polly."

"Sounds like the bird-fancier," said Captain Flint.

"The new signal is diffelent," said Miss Lee. "It tells the junks to take no plisoners and to sink the *Shining Moon*."

"But why?"

"Whoever sent that signal," said Miss Lee,

"knew that I was aboard and did not want me back."

"Who knew you were coming with us?" asked Captain Flint.

"Nobody. Not even my amah. I did not know myself. Only, when I thought of my students gone. . . ." Miss Lee was silent for a moment. "I did not mean you to know till we were out at sea. But when they closed the boom and you turned into the gorge . . ."

"We heard the cabin-door," said Peggy.

"Who knew we were taking *Shining Moon*?"

"My amah . . . And my signaller, perhaps. He helped to take your things aboard."

"They were awfully quick in spotting we'd gone," said Nancy.

"Chang is a clever man," said Miss Lee.

"Well, we've done them, anyway," said Nancy. "With their junks bottled up inside the river, looking for us when we're not there. They'll never guess we got through the gorge. We're out now, and they'll never catch us."

"Light for us is light for them," said Miss Lee. "There was a signal from the junks just now to say you were not in the river."

"It'll take them some time to get out. And longer to get the junks under weigh on this side," said Captain Flint, glancing towards the little green pagoda on the southern point of Dragon Island and at the mouth of the Dead Water beyond it.

There was the billowing roar of a horn from close at hand.

"Ah," said Miss Lee. "They have seen us from

the pagoda. I was wondering if they were all asleep."

"Watchtower?" asked Nancy.

"Yes," said Miss Lee. "Evellybody knows where we are now."

"No matter," said Captain Flint. "We're out now and we've got a good start."

"This wind will dlop at dawn," said Miss Lee.

*

Dawn was coming fast, as the *Shining Moon* sailed out past the green pagoda on the point and into the open sea. Watching Miss Lee, they saw her start as her eye fell on the ropes about the mizen-mast. They saw her glance forward.

"All the halyards are in an awful mess," said Nancy.

"We did it in the dark, you know," said John.

"Come on," said Captain Flint. "We want to get the most out of those sails. Here you are, Titty. Easy steering. We've got to tidy up." And with John, Susan, Nancy and Peggy, he set out to put things right. That night, in hoisting sail aboard a strange ship, they had had to feel for ropes and feel for cleats. Halyards had been twisted and belayed across each other. Yards had not been hoisted as far as they would go. Now, in the half light before dawn, working like ants, they went from mast to mast, from rope to rope, Miss Lee going with them and showing them how things should be. Then the two dinghies that had been towing astern were hauled alongside, emptied of gear and baled by happy captains who had thought that the little boats must have been smashed to pieces in the gorge. "Hurry up," called Captain Flint. "We'll have them aboard and she may move a little faster." There was no need now to heave to while the *Swallow* and the *Amazon* were hoisted in. The wind was dropping already.

Minute by minute the sky was growing lighter.

"Hullo," shouted Roger. "Sampans coming down to those junks at anchor."

Looking back up the Dead Water they could see black dots moving towards the junks.

"Lucky they didn't think of that at first," said Captain Flint.

"They never thought of our coming out this way," said Titty.

"We'll do them yet," said Captain Flint. "It'll take them some time to get going. We'll do them yet, if only the wind would buck up."

*

But the wind was slackening more and more as the glow in the sky grew brighter. The *Shining Moon* was hardly more than clear of the islands, when, in the East, the rising sun split the horizon like an explosion. A path of fire ran from it towards them over the sea. The bulwarks cast a shadow. Sunlight lit all faces, and the crew of the *Shining Moon* looked at each other as if meeting for the first time. Far away to port, under the black cliff, the sunlight lit the trees of Temple Island like an emerald. The parrot, in his cage on the poop, began to preen his feathers. The monkey perched to sun himself on the anchor burton in the bows, high over shimmering water.

"Sun lise," said Miss Lee. "The Dlagon Feast is over."

Suddenly the great mainsail of the *Shining Moon* flapped, flapped again and hung limp. Titty's eyes grew bothered. She moved the tiller this way and that. "I can't steer," she said suddenly. "She isn't moving . . . She hasn't got steerage way . . . She's stopped."

"Never mind, Titty," said Captain Flint. "Nothing to be done. I'll lash the tiller. Fine weather. Land breeze by night, sea breeze by day. Calm at sunset and sunrise. We'll be getting wind again as soon as the sun's a bit higher."

"There's a sail going up on one of the junks in Dead Water," said Roger.

"We'll get the wind before they do," said Captain Flint.

"Telescope, Titty," said Roger. "Quick . . . One of the sampans hasn't stopped by the junks. It's coming after us."

"We can deal with sampans all right," said Captain Flint, "and all the better if they come one at a time. It's the junks in the other river I'm worried about. Miss Lee, ma'am, how long does it take them to open that boom once they've closed it?"

Miss Lee, who had been standing on the poop, looking at the bright green of the trees on the little island that held her father's grave, turned. "Longer to open. Velly easy to close. Because of the cullent," she said.

"Well, they've done it," said John.

One after another, four war junks, with their big brown sails, came into sight beyond the cliff, slipping slowly out along the shores of Tiger Island.

"How are they moving with no wind?" exclaimed Titty.

"Current out of the river," said Captain Flint. "When the wind does come, we shan't have much of a start."

"We haven't escaped after all," said Susan.

It was as if the flying hare had been frozen stiff, in full view of the pursuing hounds.

"When you can do nothing," said Miss Lee, "it is better to be calm. Loger, you will please go to the cabin and bling me up my Holace. You will find it with the other books. . . . And I have there a chart for Captain Flint."

Roger came up from below with the chart and Horace. Miss Lee took the Horace, but, for a moment or two watched John and Captain Flint, as they unrolled the chart and spread it on the deck. It was an old chart, of 1879. "My father's," said Miss Lee. Captain Flint took a scrap of paper from his pocket, a bit of a page from the Nautical Almanac on which was a pencilled latitude. A moment later he marked a cross on the chart.

"Let me see," said Miss Lee . . . "Yes . . . Velly nearly light. How did you know?"

"I took an observation that day we were with you on Temple Island," confessed Captain Flint.

Miss Lee's eyes narrowed. Then she took his pencil and made a mark herself. "We are here," she said.

"Thank you, ma'am," said Captain Flint humbly, and looked in the left-hand bottom corner of the chart for the entrance to Singapore.

"It's not much good now, if they're going to get us," said John.

"She's a nippy little boat," said Captain Flint.

"All our things are in the cabin," said Roger. "But no food."

Miss Lee looked up from her Horace with a smile. "Plenty of stores fo'ward," she said. "And plenty of water."

"Susan," said Captain Flint. "Could you do something about it? If we're going to be sunk, we may as well not sink hungry."

"Come on, Peggy," said Susan, and the two mates went forward and into a door under the foredeck.

"Those junks are towing," said John a little later. "They've each got sampans towing ahead."

"Look here," said Nancy, "I can't stand this. Simply sitting here and waiting for them. Let's tow too."

"No good," said Captain Flint. "And we'll need all hands presently if that chap in the sampan think's he's going to board us."

Miss Lee glanced at the small boat with a round matting roof over a little cabin that was coming fast towards the *Shining Moon*, swaying to one side and to the other as a man standing in the stern worked his long sweep.

"Dlagon town sampan," she said. "Fisherman pelhaps . . . Thinking I shall pay him much money for catching you dead or alive . . ."

She closed her book suddenly and stood up listening. A pink spot showed on the gold of her cheeks. She tapped with one finger on the rail listening again to a shrill whistling far away.

"It really is just like Morse," said Roger.

"I wish we knew what it meant," said Titty.

"So do I," said Miss Lee. "That was an order . . . *my* order . . . for a Taicoon Council in the yamen . . . *my* yamen . . ."

"Never mind that," said Captain Flint. "If you're going back with us to Cambridge, to be a don and a doctor and what not, you can't be worrying all the time about what tunes are whistled at the other side of the world. Just forget about it. Somebody'll be whistling when we're all dead, and the tune won't matter to us a twopenny . . . not twopence if you know what I mean . . . What we've got to do is to whistle for a wind and to hope the *Shining Moon* can show a clean pair of heels to all those junks. Hi! Nancy, John. Get those capstan bars off the fo'c'sle head. All hands on deck. This fellow'll be aboard us in a minute." The sampan was hardly thirty yards away.

Peggy came running out of the fore-cabin. Susan followed with a steaming saucepan. Nancy and John were tossing capstan bars down into the waist. Susan wedged her saucepan in a coil of rope and took a bar. Peggy doubtfully picked up another. John and Nancy jumped down into the waist as the sampan came ranging up alongside.

"A capstan bar for everybody," cried Captain Flint, picking a bar and whirling it round like an Indian club, suppling his wrist. "Bring it down hard on any paw that touches our rail. Hold off there. What do you want?"

"It is my signaller," said Miss Lee quietly from the poop above their heads. "Let him come alongside."

They knew the signaller now and saw that he had his signalling flute slung on his back. The next moment his hands were on the rail. No capstan bar came down upon his knuckles. John gave him a rope and he made fast. Nancy hung a couple of bamboo fenders over the side. From under the matting shelter in the middle of the sampan came the old amah in her blue coat and trousers. Sitting just inside the shelter, combing his beard, they saw the aged counsellor.

"Let them come aboard," said Miss Lee.

With the help of Captain Flint and the signaller, the amah was hoisted over the rail, followed by the counsellor. The old woman clambered up to the poop, knelt on the deck and threw her arms round Miss Lee's feet, weeping and talking as if she would never stop. The old man went up to the poop, bowed to Miss Lee, sat himself down on a coil of rope and waited in silence, running his long nails slowly through the sparse hairs on his beard.

Miss Lee lifted her hand and the amah stopped talking. Miss Lee signed to the old man and he began. The crew of the *Shining Moon* waited and listened, while the signaller lay panting in the bottom of his sampan, and the big junks were coming slowly nearer.

At last the Chinese talk came to an end, and Miss Lee spoke in English. "They lan away," she said, and went on to tell what little she now knew of what had happened. Chang had asked for the little dragon the moment the big ones had come back to the yamen without it. He had asked for Miss Lee, and the amah had told him he could not see her. He had asked again, after the counsellor had given orders for sounding the alarm, and the amah, going into Miss Lee's room had found her gone. She had seen gaps in the bookshelves and had guessed at once that Miss Lee had gone with her prisoners. She had told the counsellor. At that moment they had heard the great horn giving the signal for the closing of the boom, and knew that the *Shining Moon* was trapped in the river. It had been the old counsellor who had remembered the gorge and how Miss Lee had sailed through it long before. They had taken the signaller with them, slipped out through the garden, and taken a sampan from below the place where the new junk was being built, and had got away long before anyone in the town had thought of that way out for the *Shining Moon*.

"And now?" said Nancy. "They'll have to come too . . . if we don't get grabbed."

"They want me to go back," said Miss Lee, and, for the first time, looked doubtful.

"They heard the signal to sink the *Shining Moon*," said Miss Lee. "The signaller told them what it meant. The counsellor says that Chang must have found I was gone. He wants to sink me with the *Shining Moon*. He will take the Thlee Islands for himself."

"But they'll never let him," said Titty.

"And if they fight," said Miss Lee.

"Those junks are getting pretty near," said Roger. "Hullo. What's that?"

"Wind coming," said John.

"Not that," said Roger. "Listen! There it goes again. That's the second."

"Boom." The sound of a gong came from far away. "Boom . . . Boom . . ."

"The Taicoon Council," said Miss Lee. "Chang is taking my place . . . No Miss Lee . . . No counsellor . . . Chang . . . a ten gong Taicoon."

"Your men won't like that, will they?" said Nancy. "It was always twenty-two for you. . . ."

"Boom . . . Boom . . . Boom . . ." The gong strokes sounded far away in Dragon Town where until that morning Miss Lee had ruled like her father before her.

"Boom . . . Boom . . . Boom . . ."

"Ten gong Taicoon," said Miss Lee scornfully.

And then there was another "Boom" and then another, and another.

"Thirteen," said Roger, "Fourteen . . . fifteen . . . sixteen . . ."

The old amah burst into tears again. Miss Lee listened as if she could not believe her own ears. The old counsellor watched her and combed his beard. Miss Lee stared far away inland, up the Dead Water, past the anchorage, over the low swamps to the place where the flagstaff showed above the trees. There, when the salute was ended, Miss Lee's black flag with its golden dragon would climb into the sky.

Roger was still counting the booming of the gong. "Nineteen . . . twenty . . . twenty-one . . . twenty-two . . ."

Miss Lee gasped. As the gong sounded for the last time, Titty, watching through the telescope, saw a flag climbing up above the trees. It was not black and gold. There was green on it and orange. It was the tiger flag of the Taicoon Chang.

THE *SHINING MOON*

"He has told them I am dead," said Miss Lee quietly.

There was a sudden distant sputter of rifle-shots. The old counsellor did not change the expression of his face, but his eyes looked for Miss Lee's.

"Fighting in Dlagon Town," she murmured. She gripped her Horace as if the book were a pistol holster and she were about to pull a pistol from it.

The old counsellor began talking, very quietly, looking far away, up the Dead Water, where, far away, they could see the tower over the gateway of the yamen, and, through the telescope, the tiger flag above the trees.

Miss Lee spoke, as quietly as the counsellor. "He thinks that is Wu and Chang fighting over who shall be chief . . . or Dragon men fighting both of them. . . . He says that means the end of Thlee Islands . . . fighting with each other . . . evellything my father stopped. . . . He says my father turns in his glave. He says that Chang and Wu cannot hold the islands together . . . only I, Miss Lee, my father's daughter . . ."

The wind had reached the junks astern before it swelled the sails of the *Shining Moon*. They were coming up fast before the little junk had begun to leave a wake astern of her.

"Bang!"

A puff of smoke covered the nearest junk and something crashed into the water near enough to shower a spray over the poop of the *Shining Moon*.

"They'll get us next time," said John. "We'll have to take to the boats again."

Miss Lee, moving like quicksilver, had left the poop. She came out of the cabin with a black bundle.

"Let them fire on that," she said.

Nancy was at the flag halyards in a moment, and just as a second cannon ball lobbed overhead, Miss Lee's dragon flag of black and gold blew out from the *Shining Moon's* masthead.

"Gosh, look at their steering!" said Roger.

Two of the big junks, one gybing, the other turning into the wind, very nearly rammed each other. The steersman of the other two had left their tillers. On all four people seemed to be running in all directions. Suddenly, on one of the junks, a man began beating a bell, then on another. Then on all four junks the bells were going. It was impossible to count the bellstrokes because they had not all begun at the same moment, but Nancy guessed what it was.

"Twenty-two gong Taicoon," she said, turning to Miss Lee. "That's for you." But Miss Lee had gone again. She came out of the cabin with her pistol belt. She had a little difficulty with the buckle as she fastened on a bandolier of cartridges.

"I am going back," she said. "He has told them I am dead. We will see . . ."

"Oh, look here," said Captain Flint. "Are you going to be all right?"

"Quite all light," said Miss Lee. "And Chang all long. Chang, a ten-gong Taicoon, sitting in my father's chair."

"But what about Cambridge?" said Titty.

"No more Camblidge," said Miss Lee.

"Your books?" said Captain Flint.

"I shall not want them again," said Miss Lee. "You will go on with your Latin on the voyage home."

The old amah was laughing and crying at the same time. The counsellor had come slowly down from the poop. Running his fingers through his beard, he was saying something that sounded like a charm.

"What's he saying?" asked Roger.

Miss Lee hesitated a moment. "Vir pietate glavis," she said. "He quotes Confucius. He speaks of duty to a father. He is light. My place is here."

The amah and the counsellor clambered down into the sampan.

"Good-bye, Loger. Good-bye, Tittee. Good-bye, Su-san. Good-bye, Peggee. Good-bye, Captain John. Good-bye, Nansee." They all said "Good-bye" and Miss Lee went down into the sampan.

"Will you kill Chang?" asked Roger.

"No," said Miss Lee. "Chang is a useful man. Good ten-gong Taicoon. But twenty-two gong Taicoon? No."

"Put him in a cage like Captain Flint," said Nancy.

"But let him have his canaries," said Titty.

"All light," said Miss Lee. "Put him in a cage with cana'ies. Let him out by and by. Good-bye, my velly good students."

The sampan was moving off towards the biggest of the junks. The *Shining Moon's* mainsail flopped overhead as she swung slowly round into the wind.

"Gosh!" said Captain Flint leaping for the poop. "Who's at the tiller? We're as bad as those chaps aboard the junks. Haul the foresail aback, John, and you Nancy, come and lend a hand in getting the main in. We'll heave to and see what comes."

"What are we going to do now?" asked Roger.

"There's a good wind," said Susan.

"Stick where we are," said Captain Flint. "We can't do much, but I don't quite like going on till we see she's all right. That Chang might put up a scrap, though I don't think he will. His own folk won't let him. You saw what his junks did when she showed her flag . . . Tell you what. We'll just hang about till she gets home. We'll keep within sight of that flagstaff . . ."

Up on the poop of the *Shining Moon*, hove to, rising and falling in the gentle swell, they watched Miss Lee, with the counsellor, the amah and the signaller, go aboard the largest of the junks. They saw the sails trimmed, heard orders shouted, and watched the junks turn all together and sail off towards the entrance to the Dead Water where more junks, now the wind had come, were beating out to the attack.

"Why that way?" said John.

"No current once they get inside. Quickest way to put Miss Lee ashore. And she wants to stop the other fellows coming out."

"Poor Miss Lee," said Titty.

"Don't know about that," said Captain Flint. "She's got a rum job, but she knows how to do it, and to have a job and know how to do it is one of the best things in this life. And if only she stops hankering after Cambridge . . ."

"I say," said Roger. "Did you see Gibber? I knew he'd do it if he had a chance. Jolly lucky the counsellor didn't see him. Look at him now." And they all laughed as they saw the monkey, sitting on a coil of rope, solemnly combing with his long fingers the beard he had not got.

They watched the junks sail in and drive slowly up between the swamps. They saw the junks that were coming out turn and go in with them. They saw the sails nearer and nearer to the town. Suddenly there was a sound of guns.

"Fighting?" said Nancy. "Gosh, I hope she wins."

"Doesn't sound like fighting," said Captain Flint. "Too regular."

"It's twenty-two guns they're firing," said Roger.

"Clever girl," said Captain Flint. "Chang won't have a man to help him by the time she steps ashore. That's it, Titty. You keep an eye on that flagstaff."

Half an hour later Titty, holding the telescope in one hand, waved the other. The tiger flag was tumbling down into the trees. The black and gold dragon climbed in its place. And then, "Boom . . . Boom . . . Boom . . ." They heard the faraway gong sounding in the yamen.

"She's done it," said Captain Flint. "Miss Lee, twenty-two gong Taicoon, is back in her own place. I wouldn't much like to be Chang at this minute. That cage is none too comfortable. It's that miserable perch instead of a seat . . . Well, well. Bring the foresail across, Captain Nancy. Ease out the main, Captain John, and let draw. We'll be getting on our way . . ."

THE END

Well, not quite the end. With the ancient chart that had belonged to Miss Lee's father, two pocket compasses, the sextant and the nautical almanac, they found their way to Singapore. Here they sent off a telegram, carefully worded so as not to stir up their mothers, just to say they were all well and had changed their ship for a new one. "We'll tell them the rest when we see them," said Nancy with a glint in her eye. They fitted out with charts, navigation lights and a proper compass in a binnacle, and went on with their voyage. And you may, yourselves, have read in the newspapers how the people of St. Mawes, in Cornwall, woke one morning to find a little Chinese junk, with a monkey at the masthead, anchored off their harbour mouth.

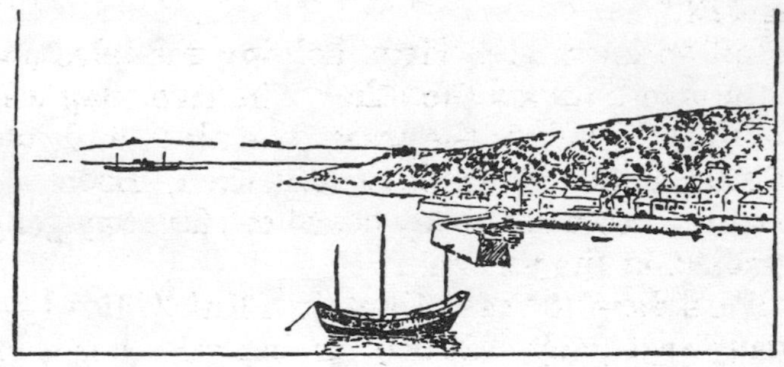

THE ARTHUR RANSOME SOCIETY

The Arthur Ransome Society was formed in June 1990 with the aim of celebrating his life and his books, and to encourage both children and adults to take part in adventurous pursuits – especially climbing, sailing and fishing. It also seeks to sponsor research, to spread his ideas in the wider community and to bring together all those who share the values and the spirit that he fostered in all his storytelling.

The Society is based at the Abbot Hall Museum of Lakeland Life and Industry in Kendal, where there is a special room set aside for Ransome: his desk, his favourite books and some of his personal possessions. There are also close links with the Windermere Steamboat Museum at Bowness, where the original *Amazon* has been restored and kept, together with the *Esperance*, thought to be the vessel on which Ransome based Captain Flint's houseboat. The Society keeps in touch with its members through a journal called *Mixed Moss*.

Regional branches of the Society have been formed by members in various parts of the country – Scotland, the Lake District, East Anglia, the Midlands, the South Coast among them – and contacts are maintained with overseas groups such as the Arthur Ransome Club of Japan. Membership fees are modest, and fall into three groups – for those under 18, for single adults, and for whole families. If you are interested in knowing more about the Society, or would like to join it, please write for a membership leaflet to The Secretary, The Arthur Ransome Society, The Abbot Hall Gallery, Kendal, Cumbria LA9 5AL.

SWALLOWS AND AMAZONS FOR EVER!

Swallows and Amazons

Titty drew a long breath that nearly choked her. "It is . . ." she said.

The flag blowing out in the wind at the masthead of the little boat was black and on it in white were a skull and two crossed bones.

To John, Susan, Titty and Roger, simply being allowed to use the boat *Swallow* to go camping on the island is adventure enough. But they soon find themselves under attack from the fierce Amazon Pirates, Nancy and Peggy. And so begins a summer of battles, alliances, exploration and discovery.

By the winning author of the first Carnegie medal.

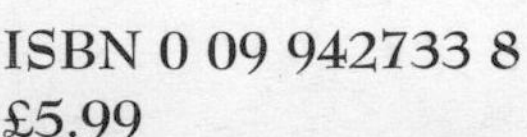

ISBN 0 09 942733 8
£5.99

ARTHUR RANSOME

The Big Six

'But who are the Big Six?' asked Pete.
'It's the Big Five really,' said Dorothea. 'They are the greatest detectives in the world. They sit in cubby holes at Scotland Yard and solve one mystery after another.'

It's great detective work that's needed now. Bill, Peter and Joe are falsely accused of setting boats adrift and the whole river is against them. Only Dick, Dorothea and Tom Dudgeon are there to stand by their friends and they soon set to work to investigate the crimes and trap the real criminals.

By the winning author of the first Carnegie medal.

ISBN 0 09 942724 9
£5.99